Questions of Iron and Blood

Finn Koenen Book 1

About the Author

Over the past 20+ years, Chip Brewer has balanced his career in international business development with a deep and abiding passion for storytelling.

Alongside his day job, Chip performed Improv professionally in Europe and the US until kids came along, at which point he shifted to teaching it. He has since worked with Fortune 100 corporations, Maine's Department of Education, at-risk youth, and hundreds of individuals to help them utilize Improv's powerful principles to increase self-confidence, foster genuine teamwork and tell amazing stories.

Chip's debut novel, *Questions of Iron and Blood*, is the first in the Finn Koenen series of thrillers that will have you turning pages well into the wee hours. Its existence is a direct result of everything Chip has learned from others, both on and off the stage, over the past two decades.

He currently lives on the coast of Maine with his family and – when his knees allow – plays hockey and surfs

Human beings were made to tell stories. Chip hopes you enjoy his.

QUESTIONS OF IRON AND BLOOD

| Finn Koenen Book 1 |

Chip Brewer

This is a work of fiction. All of the characters, organizations, locations and events portrayed in this book are either products of the author's imagination or are used fictitiously.

Cover design by Megan McConagha

ISBN: 978 1 7366 7941 8
EBook ISBN: 978 1 7366 7940 1

For Biz, Meg & Tim

PART ONE

The West won the world not by the superiority of its ideas or values or religion (to which few members of other civilizations were converted) but rather by its superiority in applying organized violence.

Westerners often forget this fact; non-Westerners never do.

— Samuel P. Huntington[1]

CHAPTER 1

APRIL 15TH, 2013, 2:41PM
BOSTON, MA
PATRIOTS' DAY — THE 117TH RUNNING OF THE BOSTON MARATHON

Amanda Kraft was killing it.

She was exactly on time, on Pace (always with a capital "P"), and in control.

The crowds, unbroken along both sides of the route for the past almost four hours, were ten or twelve deep now. She had expected to experience her first marathon in a kind of never-ending personal hell, focused completely inward in order to will her body through the long, grueling course. Instead, she had been delighted to realize that she was anything but alone as the miles slowly rolled by. She must have run past literally hundreds of thousands of people today, every single one of them urging her on with applause, shouted words of encouragement, cups of water, and unflagging positive energy. She was high on it.

High on that, and the fact that she had been running nine-and-a-half minute miles every mile for the last... a few more strides and she passed another marker... twenty-five miles. One point two to go. As long as she stayed on her feet, and didn't trip or pass out or anything, she was going to make it! And not just make it, but beat her stretch goal time of four hours and ten minutes. Running nine minute, thirty second miles straight through would get her across the finish line halfway between Exeter and Dartmouth streets in 4 hours and 9 minutes. Even the weather was cooperating, with the temperature a runner-friendly 48F at the starting line in Hopkinton a very pleasant departure from the almost 90F endured by last year's runners, the heat sapping their strength and materially slowing the pace.

She had a sudden image of herself six years ago as an eager, awkward freshman at Boston College. Arriving on campus as a young seventeen-year-old, she hadn't been able to walk a mile without taking a break. Smart enough to skip a year in elementary school, she had always been perennially insecure (sometimes a lot) about always being the youngest in her grade. It had made her shy, which, when combined with a natural disinterest in spending time at immature, boozy high-school parties, left her home alone many nights, eating more than she should as she watched TV and wrote long, florid entries in her diary.

So she arrived at BC not just out of shape, but legitimately overweight. The idea that she might someday run the Boston Marathon had been even more ridiculous than her unexpressed fantasy that Chad Martin, the captain of the football team at Lincoln-Sudbury High School, would show up at her house unannounced and sweep her off to prom.

Amanda snatched a cup from a forest of Middle School arms proffering them to the runners. A girl squealed with delight to have hers selected, making Amanda smile as she carried on, steady as a metronome, though finding it harder and harder to stay on Pace. The closer she came to the finish line, the hotter the fire burned in her chest and the faster her legs wanted to pump but she tamped the flames down and forced her legs to comply. Pace was everything. If you stuck by your Pace, fed it with patience and persistence, believed in it, then Pace always paid you back with success.

As her legs ate up the pavement in regular, efficient strides, her mind wandered back to that first time she had screwed up the courage to go to the gym. Nervous, embarrassed, excited and afraid all at the same time, she wasn't even sure she had purchased the right kind of outfit to wear. Too ashamed to ask for help at Dick's Sporting Goods, she just grabbed stuff she thought looked sporty but comfortable. None of the other gym patrons gave her a second look, however, thus raising the faint hope that perhaps she could get through this first workout invisible and anonymous. She walked with false confidence up to a row of large contraptions that were something like a weird cross between a treadmill and a StairMaster. She stopped short, suddenly unsure how they worked, what they were actually for, or even how to get on one. She cursed herself for letting her bravado outpace her caution.

"It's called an elliptical," said a gravely, older male voice over her right shoulder. Horrified, Amanda realized she must have been standing frozen long enough to be noticed. "They're a little tricky to use at first, but they're great if you've got dodgy old knees like mine."

Face flushed with embarrassment, Amanda turned to see a short man in perhaps his mid-60s with a handsome, friendly face, new to wrinkles and with soft brown eyes. For some reason his deep, weathered voice had suggested a burlier frame.

The stranger raised his left knee a few inches and patted it ruefully. "No more meniscus means no more pounding the streets."

"You don't look old enough to have bad knees," came tumbling out of her mouth as she tried to regain her composure.

"It's not the years, it's the miles," he said with mock gravity. Then, politely ignoring her continuing embarrassment, stepped carefully around her to stand next to the machine (the *elliptical*) in front of her. He tapped the screen and it came to life with numbers and pictures and words. He inclined his head to indicate she should climb on. She gingerly put first her right foot — then her left — onto the wide flat peddle / step things, standing awkwardly as they marginally swayed forwards and backwards.

"These screens are overly complicated," he said, "so if I were a beginner, I would just select, 'Manual'," and here he pressed a button at the bottom of the screen, "and then you get to choose how long and how hard you want the workout to be, here and... here. Bigger numbers mean more resistance from the machine which means more work for you." He looked her in the eyes. "Make sense?"

Amanda nodded. He nodded back, picked his gym bag up from behind her elliptical – it *was* her *elliptical now* – and said, "You can make your legs move the steps forwards or backwards, it works either way. Most people spend most of their time going forwards, but you do whatever you want. It's your workout." And with a small salute, he was off, striding deeper into the gym.

Looking back, especially from the vantage point of 25.5 miles into the Boston Marathon, still on Pace if not slightly ahead, she once again sent silent gratitude to that helpful stranger for recognizing her need for support — but not for pity — and for treating her like an equal and not some clueless gym newbie which is exactly what she had been. Thanks to his small, random act of kindness, her fear of going to the gym vanished and was replaced by the first tightly burning spark of self confidence.

She came back later that first week and twice more the week after that. Then soon, three and sometimes four times a week. And now here she was turning left from Hereford onto Boylston Street and the Finish Line(!) was a mere three and a half blocks ahead. She could easily make out the iconic finish line arch and she imagined that her friendly but nameless gym-elf would be standing up there, watching her finish and rubbing his knee with a rueful grin, a little jealous he couldn't run the race himself anymore but happy she had. She couldn't help scanning the crowds for his face, which of course wasn't there. Nonetheless, she was blown away by how many people — *really, so many people!* — were here to cheer the amateur runners across the line, almost two hours after the winners had coasted home.

Despite having inherited her father's natural skepticism, Amanda now found herself moved to actual tears that started to spill from the corners of her eyes by this incredibly generous outpouring of love and support and encouragement from all these people she didn't know and would never meet, and who seemed to want nothing more than for her to finish this race, this crazy-difficult, painful, entirely unnecessary 26.2 mile test of character. She told herself it was stupid, that it was probably just her total and utter exhaustion making her cry, but her heart said otherwise. These were tears of happy, humble gratitude for the kindness of others, especially strangers who were nice to you in the gym, not because they felt sorry for you or wanted to get in your pants. Some people simply wanted to help you be a better you, which may be how they became better them.

She was just two blocks away now.

Mom and Dad are going to be so proud, she thought with a joy so intense she almost stumbled.

Then came the loudest noise Amanda had ever heard, a crazy sensation of flying, and pain sharp enough to cut time, which it mercifully did.

She was unconscious before she hit the pavement.

PART TWO

I used to attack because it was the only thing I knew. Now I attack because I know it works.

— Gary Kasparov[2]

CHAPTER 2

MONDAY, MARCH 10TH, 2014, 3:47PM
CHARLESTOWN, MASSACHUSETTS
11 MONTHS LATER

"Goddammit!" shouted Tony Russo, "that little fucker just shot me!"

Finn Koenen couldn't keep a smile from his face as his partner unleashed a stream of invective through the earpiece in his right ear. Concealed about thirty yards behind the kid, Finn watched him sight the pellet gun at the corner of the brownstone Tony just ducked behind, after having taken a pellet to one of his beefy arms. Finn knew from long experience just how much Tony hated getting shot; he tended to take it kind of personal-like.

"That's it, Russo," murmured Finn as he slowly edged closer to the thirteen-year-old's back. "Keep squealing and hold his attention. I'm directly behind him."

"Fuck you, Finn," suggested Tony over the earpiece, "how about you get shot for a change?"

"Because," offered Finn amiably as he moved through the dappled sunlight up the narrow residential street to within 15 yards of the runaway teenager, "I'm not fat like you — I'm a lot harder to hit."

"You know what," said Tony, "That's it. I'm gonna teach this little bastard a lesson."

"Tony," Finn warned, "Don't even think about it."

"Too late. Done thinking," said the huge man as he stepped around the corner into view, one hand held up and the other behind his back.

The boy kept the pellet gun aimed at Russo but wisely didn't shoot him again. "Stay where you are, man!" he called out, high voice cracking slightly. "I don't know who you are or what you want, but I'll do it, you fat fuck! I promise. And this time I'll take out one of your eyes, so fuck off!"

Tony smiled. "Hey Brian, I got a question for you."

"How the fuck do you know my name?" the kid demanded, both wary and angry.

"Since you shot me, do I get to shoot you back?"

With that Tony whipped his hand out from behind his back, dropped into a shooter's stance and pointed his Glock 22 at the kid's head.

"Goddammit," Finn said under his breath.

Brian bolted, air rifle gripped in his left hand.

Conveniently, he bolted right at Finn, who stepped aside to make room, then grabbed him as he ran by, greatly surprising the wayward teen. Finn spun him around and in a flash had him on the pavement, arm twisted behind his back, the air rifle well out of reach a few feet away.

"Relax, Brian," Finn said to the back of the teen's head, "we're the good guys."

CHAPTER 3

EAST CAMBRIDGE, MASSACHUSETTS

An hour later found Finn and Tony in the anteroom-slash-reception area of their small private detective agency in East Cambridge. They could see Brian's silhouette, simultaneously angry and defeated, through the frosted glass window of the door that led into Tony's office, just to the right of Finn's. Finn was pacing back and forth on his mobile and Tony was lounging against the old wooden receptionist's desk that sported a monitor, computer tower, keyboard, and little else. They didn't have a receptionist, but Tony had insisted that they pretend to have one, 'for appearances'. Off to the right and separated from the reception area by a short half-wall was a small kitchenette with a refrigerator-freezer, microwave, coffee machine, several red-painted cabinets, a sink and a cheap but useful wooden drying rack for mugs and plates. Between Tony's office and the kitchenette was a hallway that led to a small conference room on the left and rest rooms on the right.

Finn hung up his cell phone and put it away in his pocket. "He'll be here in about three minutes," he informed Russo.

"Why'd we put the kid in my office and not yours?" asked Tony, only half joking.

"Because I don't want him stealing all my stuff,"

"What about my stuff?" demanded Tony.

"You don't have any stuff worth stealing," snorted Finn. "Except maybe for that bottle of Jameson's I gave you for your birthday in the bottom right drawer of your desk…"

"Ah, shit!" exclaimed Russo as he quickly stepped over to his office door and yanked it open. Brian sat right where they left him, staring with equal parts malevolence and shame at the men who had tracked him down for his father. They all glared at each other for a few moments until Finn got bored of the 'mine's bigger' game and broke the tension.

"Tone — how's the arm feeling?"

Tony turned and ambled back over to lean again on the edge of the reception desk next to Finn so he could have a clear view of the sullen runaway through his open office door. He rubbed his left forearm ruefully. "It's alright. Stings a little," he griped peevishly.

Finn pulled a sad face. "Aw. You want me to call the school nurse? "

Russo refused to take the bait and played along instead. "Would you? And can you make her look like that Air Force nurse that patched up your leg back at LSA Anaconda in Belad?"

"Fran?" Finn's brow wrinkled as he thought back. "Or was it...?"

"Nan!" exclaimed Tony with a lascivious grin.

"Yes! Nan The Night Nurse. God, she was cute."

"Very cute," agreed Tony, laughing, "and very fierce, like a polar bear."

"Not to be messed with."

"No!" agreed Tony wholeheartedly, "You remember what she did to Rodriguez?"

"He got what he deserved," opined Finn.

"And then some," added Russo, straightening up and walking over to an auxiliary mini fridge nestled between the two bland but comfortable armchairs that, along with a wood and glass coffee table, completed the furniture in the reception area. Tony had argued with him in the middle of Jordan's Furniture for twenty minutes one night several years ago before caving in in and allowing Finn to purchase the two armchairs rather than a suspiciously comfortable couch that, once spotted, he had been loath to give up on. Finn was confident that the arm chairs — perfectly comfortable themselves — had seen many fewer Russo afternoon naps than the couch would have.

Tony bent over, pulled a bottle of Dr. Pepper out of the dorm fridge, popped his head up and turned towards Finn. "Hey — I forgot to tell you earlier. Your new friend Crazy Krafty called for you again." Finn grimaced as he reached for the soda. Tony handed it over and grabbed another. "Yeah. Like, three times today alone."

"On top of the four other times earlier this week"

"You better watch out, man. I think you may have a stalker," warned Tony theatrically, hand in a fist, forearm making a stabbing motion.

"Ha, ha," replied Finn drolly

"No, seriously, man. Shh. Listen..." Tony cocked his head towards the hallway outside the office, then spoke in a stage whisper, "I think she's out there right now, getting ready to bust in here and carve you up with her machete."

Just then the door banged open, startling them greatly. Instead of a crazy woman with a machete, a short, barrel-chested man in his mid-fifties with a military style buzz cut came in and immediately shook their hands. "Thank you. Thank you both for finding Brian and bringing him back to me."

"Of course Alex," said Finn warmly, hoping their client hadn't seen the two of them jumping at shadows. "That's why we charge the big bucks."

"Hey Stevens. You know, your kid shot me out there," Tony declared plaintively as he rubbed his forearm gingerly.

Alex looked to Finn and gestured with his head. "Is he gonna make it?" he asked gravely.

Finn replied in kind, "God willing, he'll pull through. He's a fighter, that one."

"Does it cost more if he dies in the line of duty?"

"Actually, I'm offering a discount this month," replied Finn laconically.

"Ha, fucking, ha," chimed Tony, unamused.

Alex's face morphed from mischievous to apologetic as he took Tony's hand to shake it a second time. With all trace of mockery gone he said, "I really appreciate you helping us out, especially on such short notice." He then shot a decidedly less warm look at his son Brian sitting sullenly in Tony's office a few yards away. "And I am sorry he shot you," he said to Tony. "I owe you one."

"You could give me that pellet gun and let me use him for target practice," grumbled Russo.

"I'm seriously considering that," said Alex, loud enough for his son to hear. "You had a sharpshooter designation in the Rangers, right?" He winked at Tony then asked, "You guys mind if I have a few minutes alone with my son before I take him back home? These sorts of discussions upset his mother."

"Be our guest," offered Finn, glad he wasn't about to be on the receiving end of Alex's impending and very justifiable diatribe. Brian, who had lately been running with some of the less reputable townies, had recently been the lookout on a little shoplifting crew that had, inexplicably to Finn, stolen from the only convenience store in Charlestown — the very same one that they frequented every single day to get coffee they didn't need, cigarettes they weren't supposed to be smoking and lottery tickets they were too young to buy. An off-duty cop happened to be in the store at the time and grabbed one of Brian's 'buddies' after he stuffed a package of Ho Hos into his jacket pocket.

The other four immediately scattered, and Brian hadn't been home since. That was almost 72 hours ago, and Alex, who had come to Finn and Tony two days ago, had been working himself up into a lather ever since. Finn only knew the fellow Army vet peripherally (a friend of a friend), and didn't think he was the kind of guy who would hit his kid, but you never knew. Finn could tell that Tony had arrived at the same conclusion, because he left his office door ajar after ushering Alex in with his son.

Alone again in the reception area, Finn and Tony exchanged an amused look as they realized they weren't sure what to do with themselves while Brian got reamed out. The sitting around lasted much shorter than expected as, after about five or six minutes of quiet conversation, Russo's office door opened to reveal a much less sullen and significantly more hangdog Brian Stevens and his exhausted looking father. Alex thanked them again and Brian apologized to Tony for shooting him in the arm.

"I don't think that's the last time we'll see the two of them," said Tony with a bemused chuckle a couple seconds after the door clicked shut behind the departing Stevens.

Before Finn could say something snappy, the moment was broken by an unexpected knock on the office door. Finn and Tony exchanged a look — they almost never had unannounced visitors.

"You think they're back?" asked Finn, worried Alex had heard them laughing.

"Nah," said Tony, "That's your stalker with the machete!"

*   *   *   *   *

The door opened hesitantly to reveal a trim, well dressed woman in perhaps her late fifties. Her blond hair, streaked with lowlights that suggested an expensive salon visit, was held away from her face by a pair of oversize black Gucci sunglasses. She wore a dark blue knee length dress with tiny white and pale yellow flowers on it, and a pair of fashionable – but functional – heels. She started a bit, surprised to find two men standing just inside the doorway but quickly composed herself. With her right hand holding the door open, she looked each of them over in turn.

"Good afternoon," she said formally.

"Good afternoon," replied Finn in kind.

"Is this, '*Rogers Investigative Services*'?" she asked, tentatively.

"It is," confirmed Finn. "Can we help you?"

"I'm actually looking for Finn Koenen. Would that be either of you?"

"Maybe," he said evenly.

"Maybe?" she questioned, eyebrow arching at this hint of insouciance. Apparently she was a woman used to getting respect.

"Maybe," Finn confirmed, cheeky. For him, respect had to be earned before it was given, and he didn't know anything about this woman.

Her eyes flashed for just an instant before she decided to play along. "But maybe not?"

Finn gave her points for that and decided to push the button again. "Maybe not, but it's highly likely one of us is Finn."

Dismissing Finn, she turned to Tony and asked, "So would that make you Mr. Koenen?"

Russo gave a derisive snort. "I certainly hope not."

"Well. Perhaps I should just speak directly with," here she rapped the door with her knuckle, "Mr. Rogers then," she stated, attempting to go over their heads. "Is he here?"

Tony guffawed and Finn couldn't resist a grin either. Frustration bloomed on her face along with wounded patrician pride and something else Finn couldn't quite identify. Suddenly, he regretted giving their odd, unexpected visitor a hard time and decided to take the sass down a few notches.

"There *was* a Mr. Rogers," explained Finn gently, "but this isn't his agency, it's mine." He pointed to the letters on the frosted glass behind her. "Our firm's not named either of us. I named it after one of the original founders of the Rangers."

"The ice hockey team?" she asked, confusion momentarily overcoming frustration.

"The U.S. Army Rangers," Finn clarified.

"Ah," she said, like she understood. Finn wasn't sure she did.

Gesturing at Russo, he said, "We met serving in the 75th Rangers Regiment back in the day, and I thought it would be nice to pay homage to Major Robert Rogers, who founded it back in the 1700's, before the Revolutionary war, along with a Captain Benjamin Church."

"Aha," said their visitor, comprehension dawning.

"And, well, calling ourselves, *'Church Investigative Services'* sounded like we might specialize in exposing pedophiles."

She stared blankly at this.

"You know, like priests and stuff?"

"Hmm," she frowned.

"So I went with 'Rogers' instead," concluded Finn quickly, making a mental note to stay away from clergy pedophile jokes in future.

The woman shook her head as if to slough this last comment off, and said, "I'd like to start over." She extended her hand to Finn, and said. "Hello. I'm Zoe. Zoe Kraft."

Finn took the proffered hand and noted a surprisingly firm grip. "Finn Koenen," he said, appreciating the reset, "and this is my partner, Tony Russo."

"I'm so glad to finally meet you both," she said, shaking Tony's hand as well. "I trust you got my messages?"

"Oh, we got 'em," replied Tony, perhaps a little gruffer than strictly necessary.

Finn cringed at Tony's olive-branch-stomping even though he well knew that Russo's rough-around-the-edges nature was part of the package — one that included a sharp mind, uncanny street smarts, and a fierce determination to complete the mission. In fact, it was precisely these qualities that allowed Russo to save Finn's life once, many years ago, on one of their Rangers Missions gone wrong.

Tony loved to play Bad Cop to Finn's Good one, and in truth it was one of their most effective strategies for extracting information from uncooperative subjects. Finn just didn't think it was the right play here, as this woman wasn't an uncooperative subject. Rather, she fell more into the 'stalker' camp, given her persistence in trying to track them down over the past week. *Rogers Investigative Services* did not advertise, was not listed in the phone book and certainly didn't have a website, so her presence in their offices merited some caution.

"Mrs. Kraft, I apologize if we've been a little rude. You see, we don't get a lot of..." he paused to find the right word, "...walk-ins, here. Our little agency specializes in doing very high quality, very sensitive work for our clientele. Because of this, it is imperative that we begin every case with a certain minimum level of mutual trust, and trust is not something you can just fake or manufacture on short notice. As such, we decided early on that we would only work for people we knew, or who were trusted friends of trusted friends. As a result, we keep sort of a low profile and work only on referrals."

"Well," she said, cocking her head to the side like a bird of prey contemplating a stray mouse, "would you consider Officer Patrick O'Sullivan a trusted friend?"

"Um, yes," responded Finn slowly, caught off guard by the question about his old friend in the Boston Police Department.

"Good," she said immediately, a satisfied smile on her face. "Because he sent me here."

"Bullshit," spat Tony after a moment's silence. "No offense ma'am, but Sully wouldn't have sent you over without checking with us first."

Finn nodded in agreement. "He's right, Mrs. Kraft, he wouldn't."

"And yet here I am," she responded, unperturbed. "Shall you at least hear me out? I promise I won't take up much of your time."

Finn saw Tony's exasperated, 'why are you entertaining this horse-crap?' look and concluded he wouldn't likely be much of an asset for the rest of this conversation. "Okay, Mrs. Kraft," he said, "I'll bite. Why don't we go into my office? It'll be much more comfortable in there, and my partner here has a few things he needs to attend to before we wrap up for the day."

The victory of securing an audience with him flashed briefly across her face, gone almost before Finn could register having seen it. He ushered her into his office and invited her to take a seat in one of the two black Captain's chairs in front of his desk.

"I'll be right with you," he said, half-closing his office door before leading Tony over to their little kitchenette. "Listen," he said in a low voice, "I know this is weird and something doesn't smell right."

"I hear a 'but' coming," growled Russo.

"But..." continued Finn, "what can it hurt to hear her out? Let me find out what she wants and more about how she found us. If Sully really did send her over, he must have had a good reason."

"Or perhaps she's full of shit," countered Tony plaintively.

"Perhaps," allowed Finn, "but think of it this way. If it turns out she's lying, or nuts, then all it cost me was a few minutes of my time. But if she's legit, and Sully sent her over here with a real case, then we instantly backfilled the Stevens case you just solved — all without lifting a finger."

Finn stole a glance towards his partially-closed office door while Russo mulled that over. Finally, his doughy face broke into a grin and he said, "She's all yours boyo. Have fun taking notes on her sob story while I'm drinking with all the hotties down at the Tavern."

With that he clapped Finn jovially on the back and headed out, leaving him alone in the office with their odd visitor and an uncomfortable, growing sense of buyers' remorse.

*   *   *   *   *

"Thank you Mr. Koenen," said Zoe Kraft as Finn entered and closed his office door behind him. "I very much appreciate your willingness to hear me out. Oh, thank you," she said again as he handed her a small bottle of Poland Spring water from the little dorm style fridge he kept stocked in his office for just such an occasion.

"Earlier, you said that trust was very important to you and your partner."

"It is."

"And you also said that you and Mr. Russo only work with 'trusted friends of trusted friends'," she continued. "and I wanted to confess that I may have have implied something that wasn't technically true."

"Go on," said Finn, neutral despite mounting misgivings.

"While it is true that Officer O'Sullivan recommended I come see you if I needed a private investigator, I am not sure it would be quite accurate to say that he would consider me a 'trusted friend'," she admitted, giving Koenen a look equal parts guilt and defiance.

Sully and Finn had helped each other out on cases a couple dozen or more times over the years. Finn sometimes needed access to information the Boston Police Department would have that he couldn't easily get, like tracking down license plates, or a quick peek at a file or two; and Sully sometimes needed information he couldn't easily — or legally — get as an officer of the law. This informal and under the radar quid pro quo had worked very well for both of them over the years, but this here was something different. It was highly unusual that Sully would send a random stranger to Finn without a heads-up, and Sully knew perfectly well that Finn didn't take walk-ins, so what was his old friend up to?

"Okay," replied Finn, settling back into his incredibly comfortable high-backed black leather desk chair. "Would you care to elaborate?"

She shifted in her own seat and leaned forward ever so slightly, posture erect and alert, eyes a little over-bright. "Officer O'Sullivan mentioned that you often worked for families who were having..." she looked around the office and waved her hand lazily in the air, "...troubles."

Finn considered that for a second, then nodded his agreement, saying, "I guess that's pretty much true. I mean, people don't generally hire a private investigator when their lives are filled with rainbows and unicorns."

"Touché!" she said with a brief chuckle, the unexpected humor briefly erasing the fine worry lines on her face. "Let me put it another way. Patrick implied that you had some experience working with families that have gone through some trauma?" She pitched her voice up at the end of the sentence, making it a question.

Finn raised his eyebrows a fraction. "Well, we do work almost exclusively for military families, given our Army backgrounds and policy of only working with trusted referrals. In addition to all the pressures every normal family is under — money, wandering eyes, kids getting into drugs, et cetera — military families also have to deal with the constant additional pressures around deployment, moving every couple of years, and of course, somebody who might leave in the morning and never come home again."

"Exactly," agreed Mrs. Kraft, as if Finn had asked for her concurrence. "I knew you would understand."

"Mrs. Kraft — is someone in your family in the military?" Finn had to ask, though she didn't strike him as the military family type. She struck him as more Wellesley School Board than Washington Draft Board.

"No," she said, looking down at her hands, folded neatly in her lap, "no one in the service."

After a quiet moment's contemplation she raised her eyes to meet Finn's.

"But we do have a casualty."

*   *   *   *   *

For the next fifteen minutes, she told Finn all about her daughter, Amanda. Zoe explained that, like a number of kids, Amanda had seemed a little lost and depressed after college, directionless when so many of her friends were working in banks or attending law school or joining tech start-ups. She had always been a strong student and reasonably well-rounded, but had yet to find something that really ignited her passion.

Then Amanda had taken a job, almost on a whim it had seemed, with one of the many small biotech firms popping up all over the Boston area like mushrooms after a summer rain. She had never shown more than a passing interest in science or medicine, but the founder was young and charismatic, and he needed someone competent to be his personal assistant. Plus, Amanda had needed the money, since Zoe and her husband Will made it clear they expected her to support herself now that she was in the real world.

After a few weeks of working there (Capteryx, Zoe said it was called), Amanda had begun to change, to become more of the person she used to be, only more so. Her mood, self-confidence and focus all improved significantly. While she may not have been on the same level, science-wise as many of her colleagues, it turned out that she was excellent with people, details and managing projects in a way that they were not. It was a perfect fit, things were really starting to work out for her, and she took on more and more responsibility as time went on. She soon moved out of the family house in Sudbury, started dating again — only occasionally though, because she was working so hard — and even set herself the goal of finishing the Boston Marathon.

Finn was impressed. He'd done his fair share of running and had a pretty good sense of just how difficult traversing 26.2 miles through the hills of Boston and its suburbs was. As he processed this, a piece of the puzzle clicked into place, and he interjected, asking, "Zoe, was your daughter Amanda one of the people injured in the Marathon bombing last year?"

"Fate is a funny thing, Mr. Koenen," she said after a moment, her voice brittle. "If Amanda had been a single second-per-mile faster that day, or just one second slower, she would not have suffered cranial shrapnel damage and permanent loss of certain cognitive functions."

She pressed on, not giving Finn a chance to express his sympathies, to say anything, not giving herself the chance to falter in the telling. "She has trouble remembering words, or perhaps she remembers them but can't get her mouth to say them when she wants, in the way she wants. Or perhaps it is something else altogether. The doctors argue about that a lot, it seems. Regardless of what the issues are, she'll never have the life she was building for herself."

Like most who had spent time in forward combat positions, Finn had seen his fair share of life altering injuries and knew just how brutally devastating they could be, sending shock waves through entire communities as the victims, their families, and friends all adjusted to a grim new reality. And while the physical damage itself presented all sorts of obvious challenges, the attendant mental and emotional struggles were often much worse, all the more difficult to address for not being visible to the naked eye. While a few hardy souls found ways to rally and master their new lives, many, many more fell into depression, despair and, all too often, addiction.

"Zoe. I am truly sorry for what happened to your daughter," Finn said with a sincerity that must have caught her off guard, because her eyes misted up and her voice got tight, leaking bitterness through the cracks as she carried on with her terrible story.

"Of course, she had to quit her job at Capteryx. They were very kind and said she should come back," Zoe said, shaking her head sadly, "but she couldn't. She'll be able to do some sort of work, and live on her own, eventually, though it's unlikely she'll ever drive again," she said with a small, humorless laugh. "It amazes me how quickly things can change so drastically. In the blink of an eye, we've gone from helping her purchase her first home to helping her bathe herself in ours." She took a deep breath and wrapped herself in Yankee stoicism.

"And perhaps the cruelest twist of all, is that those animals," she bit this last word off, "damaged her just enough to ruin her life, but not quite enough so that she would be blissfully unaware of what she'd lost."

Finn stayed quiet, letting her bleed the poison out.

She continued, anger and frustration giving way to a seemingly infinite sadness. "She knows her dreams are all dead and the life she wanted is gone forever. And she feels like a terrible burden on her father and me, and frankly, she's right." Her wet eyes fixed Finn across the desk, challenging him to judge her as tears streaked her cheeks. "Do you think that makes me a terrible mother, saying that? Why shouldn't I? It's the truth — she is a terrible burden, and will be forever. Denying it would only be lying to myself."

She went on. "But since she can't really have children now she'll never truly understand that we would carry that burden and ten more just like it because *she is our child*." Zoe shook her head slowly. "Once we knew she would survive her injuries, I wasn't afraid anymore. I just wanted to help her get better, and she has, in many ways," she said, voice cracking. "But I'm getting scared again now, because I think she's starting to give up. I can see it in her eyes. And if she gives up,…" she broke off, dabbing at the corners of her ice-blue eyes with a tissue that had magically appeared in her hand. She tried to finish the thought, couldn't, then folded her arms across her chest and started sobbing.

Finn hesitated, then stood up, walked around the desk and put his arms awkwardly around the grieving woman. She leaned into his shoulder and after a moment gave one of his arms a quick squeeze and sat back, breaking the embrace. She quickly dried her eyes and composed herself.

"I like you, Finn Koenen. You have a hard face with kind eyes, and you were nice to me just now. I think I will hire you."

*   *   *   *   *

Finn could tell she was simply stating a fact rather than being overly presumptuous, but he certainly wasn't going to agree to take a case he knew nothing about from a woman he had just met, no matter how miserably sad her story was.

"Um, that's very kind of you to say, but I'm not sure what it is you want to hire me for."

Zoe looked surprised. "Well, to find the men responsible for injuring Amanda," she said, "And all those other poor people as well, of course," she added quickly.

Finn was starting to think he understood why Sully hadn't given him fair warning. "Zoe," he said carefully, "they got the guys responsible for what happened to your daughter. The Tsarnaev brothers?" he offered helpfully. When she neither replied nor changed her expression, he went on, "Zoe, the older one is dead, run over by his younger brother during a firefight with police last year, and that younger brother is currently in Federal custody facing the death penalty. My understanding is that there is more than enough evidence to prove that they planned and executed the attack. They got 'em. Case closed."

Mrs. Kraft continued staring at Finn in silence, unmoving.

"So… there isn't really anything for me do here," he concluded.

"It wasn't them," she declared patiently, but with a hint of condescension, as if she were the one catching Finn up to speed on the facts of the case and not the other way around.

Uncertain of what to make of this, he decided to keep his mouth shut and see what happened next. He'd learned long ago that silence was a powerful tool for getting people to explain themselves. The longer it went on, the heavier the pressure to speak, to fill that vacuum, became. It served him well again.

"Well," she went on somewhat fussily, "*of course* they were the ones who planted the bombs, but they did so at someone else's request and with someone else's assistance. That's who I'm hiring you to find — the person or persons behind the scenes. The ones ultimately responsible for maiming my daughter."

Finn looked down at his lap and ran a hand through his still thick though recently edging into salt and pepper hair. "Mrs. Kraft…"

"Don't," she said immediately, accurately reading the patronizing tone of his voice. "Don't do that."

Finn sighed inwardly. "Zoe. Law enforcement officials are highly incented to make sure there isn't anyone else out there planning additional attacks. The Boston Police Department, the FBI, CIA, NSA, ATF and the local dogcatcher went over every single piece of evidence related to this case with a fine-toothed comb and they didn't find any indication that the Tsarnaev's were working for or with anyone else. Not Al Qaeda, not ISIS, not Kim Jong-un, not anyone. They were just a couple of disaffected assholes, pardon my language," she waved the apology away with a dismissive flick of her hand, "who didn't have any idea what the hell they were doing. It was effective, and devastating for people like you and your daughter, but as far as international terrorism goes, it was amateur hour."

Undaunted, she asked, "What if I told you I had evidence that the police and the FBI didn't have? Evidence that suggests that the Tsarnaevs had a, what do you call it, a handler?"

Finn did not love this part of his job. People often thought they were hiring him to uncover evidence of something — an affair, a crime, the whereabouts of some money — but what they actually got was the truth, and that truth didn't always fit with the narrative they had constructed for themselves. If your husband isn't cheating, then the marriage problems must lie elsewhere, for example, and he often found himself forced to disappoint his clients when reality and expectation went their separate ways.

"Well, to be perfectly honest, I would find that exceedingly unlikely."

"But would you dismiss it out of hand?" she asked, pushing back.

"I wouldn't be a very thorough investigator if I dismissed things out of hand," Finn replied, "but I trust Officer O'Sullivan's skills and experience. He knows a heck of a lot more about the Marathon bombing case than either of us do, and if he's sent you to me, then I have to assume it is because he's done everything he can for you."

When she made no move to correct this assessment, he went on. "I am going to further assume that you shared this piece of evidence you claim to have with Officer O'Sullivan?" Her head bobbed once in agreement. "And what did he say about it?" asked Finn, trying to involve her in the logic of the argument so that she might better see the validity of it.

"He found it unconvincing," she replied, emphasizing '*he*' to indicated her disapproval of Sully's conclusions.

"He found it unconvincing." Finn repeated, shifting the emphasis to the final word. He let that hang in the air between them for a few moments, hoping the implications would sink in for this poor, grieving woman.

Instead of folding up her tent and leaving, she dug in her heels. "Is Officer O'Sullivan a better investigator than you?" she challenged.

Finn smiled. Appealing to his ego wasn't a bad move, it just wasn't going to work on him. "Actually, he is."

Undeterred, Zoe went on. "Even though we've just met," she said, taking a new tack, "I can tell that you are not the kind of man who is driven by money alone, so I don't need to mention that I am willing to pay anything, give literally anything, to get what I need."

Finn scored her a point for that one. She managed to flatter him for his ideals while simultaneously dangling a large paycheck in front of his nose, in a clever attempt to appeal to both his vanity and his greed. She may be a little blind to the facts around the Marathon bombing that injured her daughter, but she wasn't stupid. His impression of her went up a couple notches.

She must have sensed this, because she pressed on. "I know you don't believe me. You probably think I'm a little bit crazy, just like the FBI and the police do. But I assure you, Finn, I am not crazy. If you agree to take my case, I promise you that I have evidence that will change your mind. Help me find out who did this to her. Help me bring them out of the shadows and into the light."

Before he could decline, she continued.

"Just promise me you'll think about it," she requested. "If you do take my case, and I'm wrong, then you spend a little time and earn some money helping to prove it to me. I'll be able to get on with my life knowing that all of the perpetrators have been brought to justice. I'll be able to look my daughter in the eye and tell her she has been avenged, and that life isn't random, that there is a purpose for her, and that she shouldn't give up."

Her voice wavered at the end, and she paused to snuffle and wipe a tear away before it fully manifested itself.

"And while I know that having this sort of closure would be lovely for me, I completely understand that it may not be enough of a reason for you to take an unconventional case from a strange woman you just met."

She paused.

"But what happens if it turns out I'm right, and you didn't investigate?"

CHAPTER 4

8:13 AM, SATURDAY, MARCH 15TH, 2014
DAVIS SQUARE, CAMBRIDGE, MA

A horrible noise dragged Finn unwillingly from a deep sleep. He grudgingly cracked his left eye then quickly shut it against the unnecessarily bright sunlight streaming in through his third floor condo bedroom window. His left hand found its way out from under dark blue flannel sheets and slapped around on the bedside table until it located his phone. The screen was black and apparently not the source of the horrible noise, which — he now realized — was still buzzing on and off in a merciless, insistently cheerful pattern.

Groaning, Finn pulled the sheets off, swung his legs around and sat on the edge of the bed, elbows on his knees, forehead in his hands. As the fog brought on by babysitting Russo the previous night started to clear, Finn realized the goddamn noise was coming from down the goddamn hallway. He staggered to his feet and headed out down the hall towards the front of his condo, regrettably passing by the beckoning bathroom. Reaching the door buzzer panel, he pressed the button and growled, "What?" into the small metal grille.

"Morning sunshine!" his sister replied brightly.

"Goddammit, Heather. What do you want?" he asked, not bothering to mask his annoyance.

"Buzz me in," she demanded, so he did. While she climbed the two flights up, Finn unlocked and cracked the apartment door, threw on an old REM concert tee and some Army sweatpants and relieved the painful pressure in his bladder. Coming out of the bathroom brushing his teeth, Finn met his older sister in the living room where she was busily pulling items out of a large brown paper bag. As usual for an early Spring weekend, Heather was wearing a full complement of pink and purple Athleta workout gear, red hair pulled back in a ponytail from a face that mixed the best of their Dutch-Irish parentage.

"Please tell me those are Breakfast Grilled Crack sandwiches from Mike & Patty's over in Bay Village," Finn pleaded around a mouth full of toothpaste. "And a large black coffee with two sugars for me?" he ventured hopefully.

"Perhaps you should spit before engaging in conversation?" she suggested, never one to let a teachable moment go begging but nevertheless demonstrating she did indeed have said coffee.

Ten minutes later and they were eating, sitting across from each other at Finn's large well-worn wooden coffee table in his living room. He perched on the simple, dark blue Pottery Barn couch Heather had helped him pick out five years ago, immensely enjoying his food and hastily unthinking all of the horrible things her unannounced arrival had brought to mind. Mike & Patty's made the best hangover cure breakfast sandwiches in all of Boston, and to have not one but two of them — and coffee — delivered to your door on a Saturday morning was both a gift and a clear indication that his sister wanted something from him. Right about now he'd probably have given her the title to this condo, if that's what she were after. Just because a strategy is obvious doesn't make it any less effective.

Heather kicked off her neon pink and green New Balance running shoes and pulled off her fingerless gloves before eating her matching sandwich. She sat cross legged on the floor as had been her usual preference ever since they had been kids.

"Mfanks," he mumbled around a mouthful of fried egg, bacon, three kinds of cheese and buttered sourdough bread. A small piece of egg failed to cross the gap between sandwich and mouth and fell onto the floor between Finn's legs. Heather gave him a pointed look, uncrossed her legs, stood up and disappeared into the kitchen, returning a few moments later with a couple of plates and a roll of paper towels.

"Thanks again," Finn said, tearing one off and using it to clean the gooey yellow mess off the floor.

Once he was done, Heather tapped her sandwich against Finn's, said "Prost," and settled back onto the floor.

"Prost," he agreed, and they ate in companionable silence as Finn was perfectly content to enjoy these few precious moments of pampering before it came time to pay the piper.

"How's work?" Heather eventually asked, blowing on her coffee.

"Fine," replied Finn. "How's life at the 'Star Chamber'?" He made air quotes.

"Things at the *Center* are busy," she corrected, mimicking his air quotes and unable to hide her irritation at his continuing puerile refusal to call the Belfer Center for Science and International Affairs at Harvard by its proper name, "But fine."

"Great. And to what do I owe the pleasure of your company this fine morning?" he asked, deciding to cut to the chase instead of making her work for it. She had brought breakfast, after all, and from Mike & Patty's.

"Because I love my baby brother?" she suggested hopefully, tucking a few stray strands of straight red hair behind her left ear. Her hand brushed against the earpieces she still had spilling out of the neck of her sweatshirt, causing them to swing back and forth a few times before settling.

"Are you having a midlife crisis?" he asked unhelpfully.

"What?"

"I mean, now that you're fifty..."

"Forty nine," she corrected sternly.

"...Forty nine," he continued, "I expect you'll want to change jobs, buy a sports car and start dating a much younger man."

She thought about that. "Except for the job thing, I'm on board with the Porsche and the hot piece of ass. Maybe I will start having a crisis." They both laughed and Heather continued. "Speaking of dating, what do you have going on next Saturday night?"

Instead of answering, Finn said, "Alexa. Play Hard Bop Jazz on Spotify," exaggerating the clarity of his pronunciation.

A little round black plastic device in the corner by the front window overlooking the street lit up neon blue and spoke. "Playing playlist Hard Bop Jazz on Spotify," came the pleasant but slightly robotic female voice, followed momentarily by Cannonball Adderly's *"I've Told Ev'ry Little Star"*.

"Holy crap," said Heather incredulously. "You actually set it up!"

"I did."

"And you figured out how to connect it to Spotify and everything," she continued.

"I did, indeed," said Finn, openly pleased with himself.

"Well, I guess you can teach an old dog new tricks," she said as they tapped the remainder of their breakfast sandwiches together again.

"Take risks..."Finn began.

"...and if you win you can lead, if you lose you can guide!" they finished reciting in unison, smiling.

"Dad would be very proud of us," said Heather. "He always liked when we worked together as a team on something."

"Like the swan shaped rowboat thing we made for *Koninginnedag* that one time?"

"You must mean the one that required continuous bailing to keep it from sinking in the *Keisersgracht*? How could I forget?"

"Our parents gave us plenty of talents but boat building was not one of them," Finn observed.

"No, not an area of excellence for the Koenen children." Heather finished the last bite of her breakfast sandwich, made a ball of the foil and paper wrappers and dropped it on the coffee table next to Finn's. "You know what we *are* really good at doing for each other?" she continued.

"I have a feeling I'm about to find out," replied Finn laconically.

"Blind dates. We are really, really great at finding each other blind dates.

"Are we?" asked Finn, unconvinced, "I'm pretty sure we're terrible at that, too. And by 'we', I mean 'you', since this is like the eleventh time you've tried to set me up over the last couple years."

This got him a pout. "Am I a bad person for trying to find a partner my little brother?"

"No," he allowed, "you're a good person, just a bad matchmaker."

This got him a scowl. "I am actually known by my friends as quite a good matchmaker, thank you very much. In fact, I can name at least three couples who got married after I introduced them," Heather finished, a note of triumph in her voice.

"Well," Finn responded, deciding that if she wanted to play nursemaid, he'd play spoiled brat. "That hasn't been my experience."

"Well, given your general unwillingness to open up to anyone new, I'd suggest a look in the mirror might be in order," she retorted, eyes flashing with anger.

Finn regretted pushing her buttons and decided to make peace. "Fair enough," he said, holding his hands up, "I know I'm not the easiest person to date. Or be related to."

She chuffed at this but softened as they both sipped their coffees, his detente successful.

"So who is she?"

"Her name's Cat Rollins and she's a real catch — one of the good ones. We met at a Junior League meeting a couple months ago and we hit it off right away. She runs Marketing for a tech firm that does work in Artificial

Intelligence something, something and we talked about the role technology played in the Arab Spring uprisings a couple years ago."

"Sounds fascinating."

"It is, actually," she asserted. "You could do with some more book learning."

"Ever been married?"

Heather shook her head.

"Cute?"

Raised eyebrows and a nod. "Very."

"Batshit crazy?"

Another scowl, though without any bite in it this time.

"Okay, okay. I had to ask."

"Good!" exclaimed Heather, "because I already made reservations for you and Cat at Jae's for eight p.m. next Saturday night. She'll meet you there."

"I do like Jae's," Finn replied, finding his mood brightening, though from the prospect of the date or from the breakfast sandwich and coffee, he wasn't sure. Frankly, he didn't care. At worst, the date would be an awkward or boring meal at one of his favorite restaurants and at best, well... it had been a while since he'd — "

"Will you promise to give her a chance?," pleaded Heather, "Like, really try? I actually think you guys would be great together."

"I promise," Finn said, smiling.

"Good," Heather started, "because Koenens..."

They finished in unison. "...always keep their promises."

CHAPTER 5

11:30AM, MONDAY, MARCH 17TH, 2014
CHARLESTOWN, MASSACHUSETTS
ST. PATRICK'S DAY

Two days later Finn entered the Warren Tavern and found it packed, which he supposed was not surprising for lunchtime on St. Patrick's Day in Boston. Also unsurprising was finding Tony Russo hunkered down at his favorite seat at the far corner of the bar where he could command the best view of the many attractive women who made this their local. Charlestown, once a bastion of blue collar Irish-American families had in recent years accumulated the highest concentration of single, young, professional women anywhere in the Greater Boston area. In block after block, old condos and brownstones were being restored, fitted with all the modern conveniences and resold to people who didn't need a ton of space but who wanted a safe neighborhood, easy access to the rest of Boston, and some history & charm.

Charlestown's most historic bar, The Warren Tavern, was established in 1780 and poured beer for many of America's Revolutionary War heroes, including Paul Revere, Benjamin Franklin and even George Washington himself. It was a proper old English style (or perhaps more precisely, Colonial) tavern. Exposed beams, warped, wide-board floors, polished brass railings on the 'C' shaped bar and low ceilings made patrons feel like they had stepped back in time.

Finn loved the place and it showed, given how much time he and (especially) Tony Russo spent here. Just a short 15 minute walk over the bridge from their offices in East Cambridge, the pub featured above average food and an ever-present, happily buzzing crowd of twenty- and thirty-somethings which gave it the kind of upbeat vibe that Finn really enjoyed. It reminded him of the bars in Amsterdam he used to frequent as a teenager, back before…

"Finn!" Tony's shout cut through the St. Patrick's Day cacophony and broke Finn's train of thought. "Get the fuck over here!" Russo perched on his usual stool, an empty shot glass and half-full pint of Bud Light in front of him. Finn seriously doubted they were his first of the day. With no empty seats available, Finn squeezed in next to his partner while Sammy, the 24-year-old grad student and their regular bartender, placed a pint in front of him. Finn looked pointedly at the glass then at Sammy, eyebrows raised in question.

"Harpoon Summer," she said triumphantly. "Just put it on this morning."

"Summer?" sputtered Russo incredulously, looking down at his wrist where a watch would be if he had one. "It's the middle of March!" he griped.

"But don't you want it to be summer already?" she asked Tony. "Drink this and it is."

"Sounds like a bunch of marketing crap to me," grumbled Russo.

"Why do you care?" asked Finn. "You only drink Coors Light."

"Bud Light," corrected Tony, "And I don't understand why these goddamn beer companies can't just let winter be winter and summer be summer."

Finn ignored this annual refrain and thanked Sammy, who gave him a smile and a wink before heading back along the bar to take care of a group of friends that had just entered dressed as leprechauns, sporting shiny green blazers, oversized green top hats and full red beards, including the women. Finn suddenly felt like the oldest guy in the bar, which upon glancing around he figured might just be true.

Tony clinked his glass against Finn's. "Cheers buddy."

Finn clinked him back, careful to minimize spillage from the meniscus-full pint Sam had poured. "To solving the Stevens case," said Tony before draining the rest of his in one go.

Finn took a healthy sip of his own and said, "Cheers. Nice work on that one, Tone."

During his walk from the T station a few minutes ago, Finn had considered whether or not to chastise Tony for pulling his piece on Brian Stevens in broad daylight not three blocks from here, but had decided to let it go. Tony's mood could get pretty volatile once he'd had a few pops, so rather than cause a scene, Finn had opted for a different approach:

praise.

"Thanks," replied Russo, grinning broadly. "Ain't nobody who can hide from me, motherfucker!" he bragged, raising the empty pint glass above his head and pounding the bar several times for emphasis. "Sammy! Another round over here. We're celebrating."

Finn winced at Russo's demanding tone even though he knew it wouldn't bother Sam. This wasn't her first time dealing with a rude and inebriated Tony Russo and it wouldn't be her last. Beneath his overbearing nature nature, though, Tony was actually quite a good detective, and his boast wasn't an empty one — he really could find anyone, anywhere, anytime. If he'd seen him do it once, he'd seen him do it a hundred times, and if he were being honest with himself, Finn found it a little irritating that he couldn't figure out how Tony did it. His partner kept his own counsel and never explained his methods or thought processes, telling Finn to be happy with the results and to get comfortable not knowing how it was done. Koenen was pretty sure Russo took great pleasure in this refusal to illuminate him.

"So," said Tony, "I solved my case. Have you solved yours yet?"

"Negative," said Finn, sighing over the top of his beer.

"What the fuck are you doing all day, then?" asked Tony in mock reproach.

"Well, let's see," said Finn thoughtfully. "Last night I sat parked on Wadsworth Street across from Professor Richards' office at MIT for, I don't know, five hours? The guy's certainly not shy about working late on a Sunday, that's for sure."

"Any young birds fly into his office for a little extra credit?" asked Tony hopefully.

"Sadly, no," admitted Finn ruefully. "It would have made the time go by faster if they had. In any case, he leaves the office around quarter of eleven and heads straight home. Twenty minutes later, the lights went off and I called it a night."

"Did the wife text you?"

"Allie? She did, when she saw him pull in the driveway."

"What'd you tell her?"

"What do you think? I told her he'd been in his office all night and not so much as a pizza delivery guy went in there."

"You got no imagination," complained Tony. "It she thinks there's a chance he might be cheating, then she'll keep us on the payroll. You keep reminding her she's married to literally the most boring guy ever invented, she'll drop the investigation and we won't be making any money."

"So what? At least she'll have the comfort of knowing that her husband isn't cheating on her," responded Finn. "I'd call that a win, wouldn't you?"

"So you really think he's clean? No hanky panky?" asked Tony.

Finn thought about that for a second while he finished his deliciously hoppy Summer Ale.

"He looks clean but I can't shake the feeling that he's up to something. I just haven't figured out what it is yet."

"What makes you say that?"

"Well, first of all, it doesn't feel like a straight-up cheating situation to me. I've watched the two of them together and he doesn't act guilty around her. A little uptight, perhaps, but not guilty. He's not overly attentive, or overly distant. There's no defensiveness. The body language shows genuine affection, but still..." Finn trailed off into thought for a second while Tony drank off half his glass. "He's hiding something, though. Drugs? Trouble with the University? I don't know," Finn concluded, taking a sip of his own beer and shaking his head in frustration. "I've been on the guy for two weeks and have zilch to show for it."

"I always knew you were a shitty detective," offered Tony.

"You think you could do better?" challenged Finn.

Russo looked hurt. "Finn. We've known each other all these years and you still underestimate me."

Finn detected a note of true petulance in Tony's voice, despite his trying to play the comment off as a joke.

"And underpay me," Russo continued, the petulance more prominent.

This was familiar territory. Tony was just one of those people for whom the grass would always be greener over the next fence. Finn could be paying him a million dollars a year and Tony would want to know why it wasn't two. "Tell you what," declared Finn, "why don't you take the Richards case? I'm stuck, and if you're half as good as you think you are, you should have no trouble figuring out what the good Professor is up to."

Russo looked wary about this unexpected turn in the conversation.

Finn continued. "You solve it one way or the other before the end of June and you can collect for both your hours and mine. If it takes you longer than that, then you just collect for your hours. Deal?" Finn stuck out his hand.

Russo may have had a few drinks, but the prospect of making some extra money had no trouble piercing through the alcohol. He narrowed his eyes at Finn as he considered the proposition, looking for traps. Apparently not finding any, his wide face broke into a grin and he shook

Finn's hand enthusiastically. "Easiest money I've ever made," he declared happily, then drained the rest of his pint.

They drank side by side in companionable silence for a few minutes, a small island of contented quiet in the middle of an ever-growing sea of faux-Irish revelers.

Something occurred to Russo and he asked, "Wait a minute, if I'm taking the Richards case from you, then what the hell are you gonna work on?"

*   *   *   *   *

Before Finn could answer, someone smacked them both lightly across the tops of their heads.

"I thought I might find you two reprobates here," said Heather, dragging an empty stool she had magically found over to join them. She gave Tony a kiss on the cheek and then she and Finn did the Dutch left-right-left cheek-to-cheek kiss greeting that they'd picked up as teenagers living in Holland. She had her red hair pulled back into a ponytail held in place by a Kelly green scrunchy and sported a green and black plaid button down shirt untucked over jeans.

"You look like a leprechaun lumberjack," commented Tony.

"And you look like a grumpy drunk Italian guy," countered Heather with a grin.

Tony brightened. "You know what grumpy drunk Italians like? A round on the new guy." He waved Sam over and ordered the three of them beers on Heather's soon-to-be-opened tab.

"I'm only buying these because I feel bad for you," said Heather, handing Sam a credit card and asking her to keep it open. "My people get St. Patrick's Day, but your people just get Columbus Day. That must be hard on you."

"Even Mexico gets a better holiday than you guys," Finn chimed in.

"Yeah, but we got Sinatra," said Tony, defending his lineage. "And you have Conan O'Brien."

They all laughed and continued chatting and bantering for a while as the already full Tavern managed to get fuller and the noise, noisier, a hundred conversations punctuated with peals of laughter and shouted orders to Sam and the other four already over-stretched bartenders.

Russo was more like a cousin than a friend to the Koenen siblings. He had saved Finn's life once when they were back in the service together and of course they'd worked together for years. Finn was pretty sure he would not have been friends with Tony had they not shared the intensity of combat together. They called it, 'brothers-in-arms', not, 'buddies-in-arms' for a reason. Like most familial relations, there were good days and some not-so-good days, the highs and lows moderated somewhat by the knowledge that they were all stuck with each other now.

They ordered another round and Tony returned to his earlier question. "So what are you going to be doing while I wrap up the Richards case for your sorry ass?"

Finn had spent the last week debating whether or not to take Zoe Kraft's on as a client. On the one hand, it appeared that her grief and frustration had blinded her to the proven facts around last year's Marathon bombing. On the other hand, what if she were right, and there really were someone else out there who had put the Tsarnaev assholes up to the attack? If this were true, then not only had they gotten away scot-free, but they may also even be up to more mayhem. This possibility was remote, though — so remote in fact that Finn had gone so far as to dial Mrs. Kraft's number on his phone a couple of times to tell her he was declining to take the case. In the end though, he hadn't made the calls. As always, he couldn't ignore the tiny but insistent voice deep inside that told him to keep digging; to *keep looking*; that *something was missing*; that *something here just doesn't add up*.

"I've decided to take on the Kraft case," he declared, looking down at the three-quarters-full pint glass cupped between his palms on the dark wooden bar top.

"You did?" asked Tony, incredulous.

"What's the Kraft case?" asked Heather at the same time.

"I did, and I'll tell you in a second," replied Finn.

Tony was looking at him like he'd just announced he was becoming a Vegan, so Finn decided to provide his partner with a little more context for this unexpected decision.

"I know she seemed a little loopy, but surprisingly enough she made a rather convincing argument. I also texted Sully and he confirmed that she's legit serious about pursuing her theories — and that she can definitely pay us. Plus, there's something about her story that sets off my radar. I figure, why not take the case and see where it goes? What's the worst that could happen?" he finished, shrugging theatrically for effect. Heather laughed and Tony shook his head in mild disbelief but for once kept his tongue.

Finn spent the next fifteen minutes catching them up to speed on his conversation with Zoe Kraft and what had happened to her daughter Amanda.

After he finished, they sat there in silence for a while, each lost in thought, sifting through the facts they'd just learned, looking for anything shiny.

"So what's this magic piece of evidence she has that proves someone was helping the Tsarnaev's?" asked Tony.

Finn raised his eyebrows. "A witness. Someone who claims he saw Tamerlan Tsarnaev meeting with his 'handler' over in Harvard Square just two days before the bombing last year."

"A witness?" asked Heather, a little thunderstruck. "That's kind of a big deal. If that's true then why aren't the cops all over this guy?" she demanded.

Finn gave a thin smile. "Because he's a drug addicted, homeless beggar."

*   *   *   *   *

As St. Patrick's Day continued ramping up around them, Tony and Heather huddled closer to Finn as he recounted what Zoe Kraft had told him about a certain Mike Miller, currently residing (if you could call it that) on the streets in and around Harvard Square.

"So did this Mike Miller guy ever talk to the police?" asked Russo skeptically when he'd finished.

"Apparently he did," replied Finn, " but not until a few days after the bombing. He spoke to anyone and everyone who would listen to him but no one took him seriously."

"Because he's homeless?" asked Heather.

"Because he's homeless and because he's a junkie. Apparently he was pretty manic and not scoring so high on the believability meter at the time."

"Stoned?" asked Heather.

"Heroin," suggested Tony.

"Probably both and more from what Zoe tells me," confirmed Finn. "Sounds like the poor guy has had a pretty tough go of it and he maybe isn't making the best decisions all the time."

Over the years he and Russo had both known vets who ended up homeless – men broken by their time in the service, unable to transition back to civilian life. A few had been broken before they saw battle, but many more were invisible casualties of the crucible of violence that spared few and scarred all.

"So what happened when he went to the cops?" Russo prompted.

"I guess he was pretty insistent they listen to him so they took his statement, more to get rid of him than anything else, I'd guess. Zoe said the cops never did anything about it but I find that very hard to believe," Finn concluded. "In my experience, most cops are hard-working, tenacious, and pretty serious about things like bombs going off in their backyard. They're not the types to leave any stones unturned no matter how sketchy or bullshit a stone might seem."

"Well, it was pretty chaotic in Boston after the bombings," Heather recalled, voice raised above the ambient St. Patrick's Day roar. "I remember the news saying that thousands of leads came in, most of them well-intentioned but some of them malicious, racist, or just plain loony. I wouldn't be surprised if they put the homeless guy's story into the latter category."

"It's what I would have done," agreed Tony. "Homeless junkie overhears a conversation between the marathon bomber and his mysterious handlers? In Harvard Square of all places?" He shrugged. "Sounds pretty fucking unlikely to me."

No one had anything to say to that so the three of them contemplated their pints.

"So how'd this fancy pants woman from Sudbury run across a homeless vet in Harvard Square?" asked Heather, breaking the silence. "I'm guessing it wasn't at book club."

Finn laughed. "Long story short? Zoe Kraft is all over the cops, already convinced that someone helped the Tsarnaev brothers pull it off. They tell her a thousand times that the two pricks acted alone, but she clearly wasn't having it because she ends up bribing someone to give her a copy of the Marathon Bombing case files."

Tony and Heather shared a look, impressed at Zoe Kraft's balls.

"Eventually, she runs across a copy of Mike Miller's statement, tracks him down, and spends a bunch of time and probably some money to gain his trust. Once she gets this Miller guy to share his story, she redoubles her efforts trying to get the cops to investigate further."

"So why now?" asked Heather, breaking in.

"What do you mean?" Finn had to raise his voice to be heard over the braying laughter coming from a particularly intoxicated group directly behind them.

"Why is she coming to you now? Why not five months ago, or six weeks from now? Something must have changed," she clarified.

"Bingo." Finn clinked his glass against his sister's "You're wasted at the Star Chamber."

"Is it that the homeless guy disappeared?" asked Russo while Heather made a face and stuck her tongue out at Finn. "Does she want us to track him down? I got some contacts might be able to help," he offered, the free drinks making him generous.

"Thanks Tone but no, she knows where he is."

"So what changed, then?" asked Heather impatiently.

"Miller called her in the middle of the night a little over a week ago and said he had something very urgent and important to tell her about the case, but by the time she found him early the next morning he had clammed up tight and now won't talk to her at all."

"That's weird," observed Heather.

"Drugs fuck up your brain," asserted Tony. "Dude's probably losing it — or more likely running some sort of scam."

Heather seemed faintly disappointed by this conjecture. She looked at Finn and asked, "Do you think this Miller guy is scamming the Kraft woman?"

"It's a distinct possibility, and if he is, I'll suss it out pretty quickly. And put an end to it," glowered Finn, who wasn't a big fan of people preying on the weak and vulnerable.

"And if he's telling the truth?"

Finn looked his sister in the eyes.

"Let's hope he's not."

CHAPTER 6

6:15AM TUESDAY, MARCH 18TH, 2014
RELIABLE TRUCKING, CHELSEA, MA

"Understood," said Ruslan Kadyrov quietly into his mobile. "I am aware you have specified thirteen men and I am interviewing someone for the final spot this morning." He ran fingers holding the stub of a hand-rolled cigarette through his thinning hair. The expression on his dark, craggy face waxed angry as he listened. "Understood," he said again, trying hard to mask his irritation. "I don't make mistakes." He took a sharp drag and aggressively exhaled smoke into the cab of the parked pickup truck. "I'll text you once I can confirm I have the right man."

Scowling, he hung up, dropping the phone into his shirt pocket and shaking his head in frustration. "Fucking towel-heads," he spat, gravelly voice loud in the empty cab. They were excellent trouble-makers, but terrible insurgents. This one though was smart, ruthless and had very, very deep pockets, so he was willing to put up with a lot.

One thing the old freedom fighter did not put up with was being told how to do his job. Kadyrov and Kadyrov alone decided how best to pull off an operation. It was how he survived his teenage years fighting the Russian Army in and around Groznyy and it had served him well in America up to now. His newest client had insisted he stick exactly to his overly-detailed instructions but Kadyrov had decided to modify a few of them to better suit his purposes.

For one thing, Ruslan was pretty sure he could do the job with just ten men, rather than the thirteen stipulated by the mysterious Iranian. On something as… dramatic as this, he planned to keep the circle as small as humanly possible. Plus, he liked dividing the money between ten better

41

than thirteen.

Unfortunately, he currently only had nine on the crew and needed to find the tenth. He considered, not for the first time, trying to do the job with nine but he just couldn't get there. Ten was tight but doable. Nine was a no-go, he convinced himself again.

A tentative knocking on the side panel of the F350 brought him out of his reverie. As expected, Vakha was here to collect him so he opened the door and climbed down. His man gestured towards Reliable Trucking's offices and Ruslan followed him across the yard which, even at this early hour on a Tuesday morning, was busy to the point of being frenetic.

Delivery trucks of all sizes came and went seemingly at random. He had been there long enough that he knew the rhythm of the place like his own heartbeat. There had been some bad weather in Atlanta last night and a lot of luggage didn't make it to Boston on time. People could get from gate to gate a lot faster than luggage, even these days, and so Reliable Trucking was employed by Massport (which owned and ran Logan) to deliver lost luggage to passengers across New England. It was a shit job and an even shittier company, but neither Ruslan nor his crew cared about that. They did much more interesting things for their alternate employers and for far more interesting paydays.

What Reliable Trucking lacked in ambiance and quality it more than made up for in anonymity, freedom of movement, and a conveniently ambivalent attitude towards background checks, which (ironically, due to 9/11) were expensive and therefore to be avoided whenever possible. The owners of the firm would rather keep that money — and any questions — to themselves. And since the job was to drive all over New England in bland, forgettable delivery trucks, it gave Ruslan and his crew a ready excuse to literally go anywhere at any time. So long as they had some packages or a few pieces of lost luggage in the van along with the requisite paperwork to back them up, they could assess targets, collect intelligence, and time their routes without anyone being the wiser.

Ruslan made sure he and his crew were all better than average at their day job delivering legitimately lost luggage so as to avoid giving the owners any reason to come poking around. He also made sure they were exceptionally good at their *actual* jobs, which typically required a certain, shall we say, morally-lax attitude. He made a point to handpick and personally interview each and every member of his crew, all Chechens like himself, all people he knew, or who were known by at least three other people he trusted. The problem was that Shamil, unlucky goat fucker that he was, had gotten pinched last week when the cops raided a Southie whorehouse he liked to frequent. The Boston police may be stupid, but even they can see when a work Visa is four years expired. So now Shamil was presently locked up pending deportation, leaving Ruslan down an engineer at a particularly tricky time. Their Persian employer had a tight deadline and Ruslan didn't have time to find a proper replacement for Shamil. Instead, he'd have to find someone who could make do long enough to complete the job and then Ruslan would probably dump his body in the Atlantic.

Almost unconsciously dodging trucks, vans and forklifts, they arrived at the yard's offices and Vakha, five foot five, broad chested and serious, held the door open for Ruslan, who towered over him as they both went into the warmth and relative quiet of the small, two story building. Vakha led him to one of the stark windowless rooms they used for meetings like these, opened the door, and nodded for Ruslan to enter.

Inside, he found a thin-faced man around Ruslan's age of 35, a few inches taller than Vakha, with close cropped hair and a hook nose. He immediately stood up from and strode around the small table. He bowed his head and offered his hand to Ruslan, who was surprised to find the grip strong for such a skinny man.

"Khasan Varayev, please meet Ruslan Kadyrov. Ruslan, this is the guy I told you about," said Vakha, clearly nervous. Khasan continued bowing his head deferentially to Kadyrov, who nodded, pleased at the man's manners.

"Sit, please," said Ruslan as he gestured broadly to the oval faux-wood conference table and several cheap metal folding chairs. He approved of Varayev waiting for Ruslan to take his own chair before sitting himself. Like many Chechens, politesse and respect were central to his core of being, and he hated how the temptations of the West corrupted the hearts and minds of his younger countrymen, who were so easily led astray. This one, at least, knew how to mind his manners. "Where are you from?" asked Ruslan.

"Argun," replied Khasan, naming his Chechen home town. "My parents brought my three sisters and me to the US when I was six."

"And here?"

"Chelsea. I take care of my mother and one of my lazy whore sisters."

Ruslan smiled — this one was a traditionalist. "What do you do?"

Khasan raised his eyes to look directly at the terrorist for the first time. "I throw bags at Logan."

That perked Ruslan's ears up. Access to the airport had gotten harder and harder since those idiot Saudis killed themselves and three thousand others on 9/11, which meant this man had passed an intense vetting by the US Government. Given Kadyrov's tight timelines, this prescreening jumped Varayev to the front of the list of possible replacements for Shamil.

Let's see how motivated he is.

"Pays well, does it?" he asked with a lift of his bushy eyebrows.

Varayev shrugged noncommittally. "I've made less."

Ruslan gave a hard stare to see if he could rattle the guy. Varayev's face remained open and passive.

"His mother is sick," chimed Vakha, clearly worried that the interview wasn't going well.

Ruslan turned to Vakha then back to Khasan, who shrugged and said simply, "Cancer. It is not good. She needs a lot of medicine, has many doctors."

"I am sorry to hear she is ill. I hope she is able to recover soon."

"Thank you," said Khasan gratefully. "I appreciate it." He hesitated for a moment. "She will also need radiation and maybe surgeries, and..." He trailed off.

Ruslan finished the thought for him. "And... 'throwing bags at Logan' isn't going to cover the medical bills." It wasn't a question.

"Correct," Khasan confirmed anyway.

"I told him you could maybe use someone," interjected Vakha again.

Ruslan raised his eyebrows and shrugged with his hands. "Maybe, maybe not," he allowed, "though if I were, I might be looking for a man who has a certain set of technical skills."

Khasan said nothing and waited patiently. Ruslan liked that, too.

"Skills, and a willingness to... do certain things," finished Kadyrov, his tone pregnant with meaning.

"I will do anything for my mother. I work hard, keep my eyes shut and don't ask questions," stated Khasan. "Anything for my family," he emphasized.

Ruslan nodded, reached across the table and clasped the newcomer's arm with a meaty hand. "I believe you," he said, looking the man in his eyes, trying to read them for lies. He broke the gaze after a few seconds and stood up. Vakha and Khasan stood hastily. Vakha came around and opened the door for Ruslan, who started out.

"Vakha will let you know," he said, "and many blessings on your mother," he concluded, then turned and strode off down the hallway, smiling.

CHAPTER 7

7:30AM, SATURDAY MARCH 22ND, 2014
HARVARD SQUARE, CAMBRIDGE, MA

Mike Miller hated Saturday mornings. The only people out and about were early riser soccer Moms and high-strung corporate types grabbing a quick run and a coffee before heading back to the safety of their perfect suburban lives. People paid him significantly less mind now than at any other time during the week and Mike saw more looks of disgust and pity between 6 and 10am Saturday morning than he did the other six days put together.

He wouldn't have minded so much if they took two seconds out of their *very busy mornings* to throw him some change or a buck or two. He understood the dirty looks – he was homeless after all. *They should be disgusted,* he thought, lying on his side facing into the bench, eyes closed. *I am pretty disgusting.* He hadn't been able to sneak into the Y this week — they had been more vigilant than usual because a couple other homeless guys had started a fight in the locker rooms the week before. And it was still way too cold to use the Charles.

So instead of panhandling on Saturday mornings, when despite the steady stream of people around him his prospects were the worst, he liked to find a nice comfortable bench and lie in the warming sun. Plus, he was invariably fighting a massive cheap whiskey hangover or shaking and nauseous from withdrawal. Or both. Thankfully today was just the headache, and he appreciated the early spring chill in the air which always seemed to help bleed the worst of the pain from his head. Plus, he had an old army blanket, so all things considered he was doing pretty well. *Maybe I'll stay clean today,* he thought to himself as he dozed off in the bright sun while Harvard Square came to life around him.

* * * * *

"Morning," came a voice from somewhere close by. Mike lay motionless and ignored it.

"You awake?"

Goddammit thought Miller, *he's back.*

"Mike?"

Two days ago, this random guy had just walked right up out of nowhere and started talking to him. Said his name was Finn something and that Zoe Kraft had sent him, which sounded like bullshit to Miller. If the wrong people knew what he knew, what he'd seen, then he'd be done for, and he had no reason to trust this fucking guy.

Still, he had given him a twenty that first day and yesterday left four fat burritos from Boca Grande sitting on the rain-wet bench after Mike refused to engage with him a second time.

What the hell does he want from me? Mike wondered, but not enough to turn around and engage with the guy. Of all the skills he'd learned in the Army, patience was the one that served him best these days. He'd just have to keep waiting this fucker out, and eventually he'd go away.

Suddenly, the guy started reciting in a loud, clear voice:

I pledge allegiance

To the flag

Of the United States of America

Before he knew what he was doing or could even stop himself, Mike swung around, stood up, faced the flag flying over the main gate to Harvard Yard, placed hand on heart and joined in.

And to the Republic,

A young couple out for a morning stroll with their black lab stopped and joined in, as had a number of other passersby.

For which it stands

One nation, under God

Miller was surprised by how cracked his voice was with disuse.

Indivisible

With liberty and justice, for all.

The people who had spontaneously participated clapped and high fived each other before heading off on their myriad journeys. That Finn guy who had started it all was standing there, grinning at him and holding out his hand. Finding himself moved by this public and unexpected display of patriotism, Mike hesitated a moment longer, then shook.

"You want some breakfast?" Finn asked him. "My treat." When Mike didn't immediately respond, he added, "Look, I just want to talk. I buy the food, you tell me what you know. It's a fair deal, no?"

Miller weighed this then with a shrug said, "Sure. Fuck it. It's just breakfast, right?"

*　*　*　*　*

"Never sat inside before," said Miller around a mouthful of egg, cheese and sesame bagel.

The pretty girl with green eyes at the Au Bon Pain counter hadn't given Mike and his bedraggled outfit a second look, but one of her fellow employees — a middle-aged balding guy with a serious paunch — had been eying them suspiciously since they'd entered the restaurant. The homeless vet sat hunched over, elbows on the heavily-scratched table, greedily eating the second of two breakfast sandwiches. Steam rose from Miller's uncovered large coffee which sat next to the remains of a bottle of Tropicana orange juice and his dirty black watch cap. Finn hoped Miller wouldn't get agitated for some reason and throw the scalding hot coffee at him.

Mike licked his fingers, pushed a few strands of long, dirty brown hair away from his face and picked through the assorted wrappers and bags on the table, reflexively looking for any uneaten morsels. He popped a few odd bits into his mouth, sat back and stretched, audibly cracking a few vertebrae in the process. Still leaning back, he snaked an arm out to grab his coffee, slopping a bit onto the table in the process. He tested the temperature with his mouth then brushed some crumbs out of his short, reddish beard before looking up at Finn directly for the first time since sitting down.

"So," he said warily.

"So," replied Finn amiably, letting Miller control the pace.

"So Mrs. Kraft sent you?" he asked, the gruffness in his voice sounding forced.

"She did," said Finn. "She hired me to talk to you."

"Why would she do that?" he asked, curiosity peaking through the wariness.

"Because she believes you," Finn said simply. "And then you stopped talking to her."

A few moments of silence while Miller processed this.

"How do I know you're telling the truth?" Miller asked, suspicion returning like a door slamming. "You could be a cop, or a newspaper reporter trying to screw me. Or maybe," Miller drew this last word out, "you're here to see how much I know and who I talked to before you take me out back and shoot me in the head, because you're one of the bad guys!" He was tensing up and looked like he might bolt, or perhaps even toss that coffee after all.

Deciding to nip this paranoia in the bud, Finn leaned in over the table. "If I wanted to kill you," he said softly so that only Miller could hear him, "you'd already be dead." Miller froze, balanced on the edge of fight or flight.

"If I wanted information from you, and I wasn't too particular about your well being, I would already have it." Finn kept his voice flat, matter-of-fact. "But I'm one of the good guys. Zoe Kraft hired me to listen to your story and to see if I could help her find the people that blew up her daughter."

"Amanda," said Miller, eyes still locked on Finn.

"Amanda," said Finn, agreeing.

"Army?" asked Miller.

"Hooah!," replied Finn. "The Three-Seven-Five."

"Where and when did you serve?"

"One deployment in Afghanistan, four in Iraq."

"Why'd you leave?" Miller asked bluntly, still suspicious.

"Let's save that for another day," suggested Finn.

"Dishonorable?" asked Miller, perhaps sensing he could score a point here.

Finn stared at him.

"Sorry," he said, backing down. "I don't mean any disrespect." He took his hand out from under the table and offered it to Finn. "Sergeant Mike Miller," he said.

Finn shook his hand warmly. "Sergeant First Class Finn Koenen."

"Sergeant First Class? And a Ranger? You must be some kind of badass."

"Everyone who puts on the uniform is a badass," replied Finn. "What about you? Where'd you serve?"

A shadow of pain flickered across Mike's face, and his head shook slightly from side to side. He seemed to be debating with himself.

Finn reached across the table and put his hand on Mike's arm. "Hey, I've been there. It's okay to talk about," he said reassuringly.

Mike looked down at Finn's hand on his arm. "Iraq," he managed, pain filling his face. "I did some bad things over there."

*   *   *   *   *

"I was with the Third Squadron of the Seventh Cavalry for the Third Infantry Division in Baghdad."

Finn nodded as he dug back into his memory. "Third of the seventh for third ID? Were you there for the Surge in 2007?"

"Yeah," Miller confirmed. "I originally came over in the first wave of the Second Gulf War in 2003 and we took the country in a few weeks. Saddam's troops fell apart like a house of cards. I don't think I fired my weapon once in anger before the official action was over. Weirdly, it was a great time — maybe the best time of my life, those first few weeks and months in Iraq." Miller stared wistfully into the middle distance over Finn's shoulder while he took another sip of his coffee and the busy restaurant faded away for them both.

"Sure, it was hot as hell and the sand got into everything, but we kicked some ass and showed those pricks what American military might could do to their little tinpot army. We had great guys in my platoon, plenty of really good chow at the DFAC, and emails and phone calls from home. They were easy days, especially since nobody was shooting at us. We owned the place. Hell, I even took a crap on one of Saddam's gold toilets! Mission accomplished!" he finished with relish.

Then his face turned sour. "*Mission Accomplished.* What a bunch of bullshit. Sure we crushed their army, but most of 'em — even the ones who surrendered — just took off their uniforms and melted back into the population." He got the thousand-yard-stare again.

"At first, we controlled the whole country. Then just the main cities. Then parts of the main cities. Soon enough we're stuck living in a highly-fortified military compound we can only leave in a fully-armored vehicle, covered in whatever Kevlar we could srounge." He shook his head in disbelief, catching Finn's eye. "The fucking patrols were the worst. You ever walk down a hostile street where literally every person you see has a gun and they're all staring at you?"

"And you got no way to tell who's about to get revenge for something you had nothing to do with?"

"Then you know what I mean," said Miller. "Every shadow down every alley could hold your death."

"And every step you take away from the compound you feel a little red dot dancing on the back of your skull."

"And every second you prepare yourself to feel it all end, and you just hope it's clean."

They sat in silence, each sifting through their own uniquely unpleasant memories.

Eventually, Miller continued. "I lost a lot of guys who didn't get it clean. Legs, arms, feet, hands, ears. Shit, it was awful. Good men and women cut down and maimed, and why? Because they were trying to help free those miserable fucking people? Trying to keep them safe, and build 'em schools and homes? We take that fat fuck Saddam out of power and they thank us by taking our limbs and our lives?" Miller's voice had risen throughout this diatribe and a few of the other patrons — and the disapproving guy behind the counter — were starting to eye the two of them with open suspicion.

Finn put his hand on Mike' arm again. "Hey," he said softly, "what say we continue this conversation outside. Maybe down by the river?" Mike clued in and looked around, noticing he was being noticed. He started to get a little bit of the 'trapped animal' look in his eyes, so Finn quickly stood up, grabbed his coat off the back of the chair and took Miller by the arm, guiding him out of the establishment before things went sideways.

Once back out in the open air of Harvard Square Mike regained his composure and pulled his elbow out of Finn's light grasp as they made their way down JFK Street to the park running along the northern banks of the Charles River. The morning was warming up, though there was still a bite to the air. Most of the snow had melted away but for some isolated clumps of dirty gray muck defiantly resisting the onset of warmer temperatures. The two men crossed Memorial Drive at a stoplight and headed east along the park, finally coming to an empty bench. They sat and watched a growing stream of joggers, young parents with strollers, speed-walking middle-aged women and gaggles of college students pass by in both directions.

"I lost some guys too," Finn began, hoping get the homeless man talking again. "And knew more who wished they *had* been taken." He stared out over the choppy slate blue river. "Some guys just get lost after they get saved," he finished, feeling Mike's eyes on him. "The crucible of combat takes its pound of flesh from everyone who ventures in. Ain't no one comes out the same, or even whole."

"Fuckin' A," said Miller.

"Fuckin' A," said Finn. Miller looked like he wanted to say more and Finn gave him the space to wrestle with whatever demons wanted out.

"Billy Harrison," he finally said to Finn. "Billy Harrison was in my platoon, and was my best friend in all of Iraq. Hell, he was my best friend in the whole damn world." His eyes clamped shut with pain. When they opened again, clear blue and looking straight back through time, he told his story.

"It was early 2008, and even Washington could tell the Surge wasn't working. We were doing a patrol in Fallujah one afternoon, maybe fifteen, fifteen-thirty. There were five of us out there, including me and Billy. It was never really safe to be out and about but things had been pretty quiet for a week or two and it felt like we were making some progress with the locals. We'd been handing out food, being real friendly and respectful so that we could gain their trust." He paused and shook his head, as if arguing with himself.

"So you could get intel?" asked Finn.

"Yup. Locals are always the best source of intel on who's in which militia, who's shaking who down, and with what scams."

"And who might be itching to take a shot at an American," Finn added.

"Usually," replied Miller, biting the word off. "Unless the guys giving you *intel*," he made air quotes, "are the guys who want you dead."

"Is that what happened to you?" prompted Finn.

Miller teared up and it took him a few moments to master himself. "No," he finally choked out. "It happened to Billy."

"Tell me how," Finn asked gently.

Miller took a deep, shuddering breath, and did. "I'm leading us down the main street in one of the nicer neighborhoods. Most of the buildings still have their roofs and doors, not so many bullet holes in the walls. Broad daylight. Nothing out of the ordinary going on, people milling around, mostly waving or smiling at us. We're being friendly right back but staying alert, you know? But I guess not, because all of a sudden I realize the street is empty and we're the only people left out in the open. Before I can shout a warning I see Billy jerk backwards and crumple to the ground, like someone had pulled a string from behind him."

Miller paused, anguish distorting his features.

"Someone yelled, 'Shooter!' and then the whole squad is running for cover, two of us dragging Billy inside the closest building. Based on how Billy went down we have a general idea of where the sniper is, but that wasn't much to go on, so we all hunker down as best we can and wait for the cavalry to come collect us — it wouldn't be more than five, ten minutes for the Humvees to get to where we were."

Finn nodded, having also been under hostile fire from unknown assailants on their home turf. He didn't recall it fondly.

Miller gave a slight nod in reply. "Poor fucking Billy from Altoona, Pennsylvania is alive in my arms, but screaming in agony. Someone covers the door and I take a few moments to assess the damage, see if I can triage his wounds. His head and chest are fine — somehow the sniper missed the kill shot on a stationary target in the open — but based on how he's doubled over, I'm guessing he took one in the stomach. So I finally get him rolled into a position where I can examine the wound and I realize that the sniper didn't miss his shot at all. Actually, he'd hit exactly what he was aiming for. Billy's balls."

Finn watched Miller struggle to control a mighty rage before continuing, his words clipped with the effort.

"The shooter wanted to maim Billy, not kill him. Take away his manhood and make sure he had to live the rest of his life like that, disfigured and unable to ever have kids." Mike swallowed hard before continuing. "Billy lost his balls and almost bled out just so some Iraqi asshole could send us a message: that we weren't welcome in his country; that if we stayed, eventually every one of us would be writhing on the ground, crotch shot. If not today, maybe tomorrow, or the day after that."

"I'm sorry," Finn said, gut wrenched both for Miller and for the things Miller's story awoke in his own past.

Mike didn't speak for a long while and when he did, his voice was flat, emotionless.

"It was taking a really long time for the Humvees to get to our position and Billy kept screaming and I couldn't stop thinking about how all those people on the street, waving and smiling at us a few minutes ago had all known — they had known we were going to be ambushed because they all bugged out right before Billy got shot, and I just snapped. I… I became someone else…" he trailed off. "No, that's not right. I was still me, but it was like I was outside of myself, seeing my body do things, you know?" He didn't expect an answer and pressed on, the words coming in a rush, the dam burst.

"I watched myself stand up, turn around and go deeper into the house we were holed up in. I found a family of five or six huddled together in a back room. I raised my M16 A4 and I shot them all. I walked out, went next door, and killed them too, maybe four or five more. Another family, I think. I guess my team was yelling at me, and trying to figure out what the fuck was happening, but I just kept going. I went into another building and out into the courtyard in the back and there was a big group of teenagers. I started shooting them too, until somebody hit me in the head with the butt of their rifle and knocked me out."

When Finn said nothing, Miller continued. "When I came to, I was lying on the ground propped up against some sandbags, with a pounding headache and my hands zip tied behind my back. I remember throwing up all over myself." He raised his bloodshot eyes to meet Finn's. "I was so ashamed."

"I get it," said Finn.

Miller's eyes widened. "No. No, you don't get it. I wasn't ashamed that I killed all those people, those kids. I was ashamed I hadn't been quick enough to spot the trouble and keep Billy safe. I was ashamed because I hadn't killed more of them before my guys stopped me. I was ashamed I hadn't started killing those fuckers earlier. I was ashamed I didn't feel bad about murdering them."

"Then what happened?" Finn asked, disgust, pity and understanding vying for primacy in his heart.

"Guess," challenged Miller.

"Court Martial?"

"Ha!" laughed the homeless vet mirthlessly. "I wish. At least then there might have been some justice for somebody. Nope, no trial for me. The Surge wasn't going well and public sentiment back in the US had turned against our presence in the sovereign nation of Iraq, and the Brass couldn't afford the PR nightmare of a Sergeant going apeshit and murdering a bunch of old women and children. They swept the whole thing under the rug, paid off the families of the people I'd killed, made me sign a bunch of paperwork promising never to tell anyone about the whole thing, gave me an honorable discharge and sent me back Stateside."

"Then what did you do?" asked Finn.

"I came back to Boston, got an apartment, and a job doing construction but neither of those lasted very long. I mean, how do you go back to sitcoms and TV dinners after you shoot a bunch of kids and get away with it? I guess I started drinking to cope with the guilt I felt. That I still feel." Miller looked at Finn, real pain in his eyes. "The drinking led to drugs, which led to to harder drugs, which led to me being where I am now," he finished, looking drained, exhausted.

"But I'll tell you what," he continued, eyes shining with a kind of fervor "I'd do it all over again and I'd pay the same price I'm paying now. Those people deserved to die for what they did to Billy, and to me, and all of us over there."

Miller stared defiantly at Finn, daring him to judge.

"You see, that's my real sin, Mr. Koenen — I choose to fight evil with evil."

*   *   *   *   *

"I hear you," Finn said quietly, offering neither absolution nor judgment. "I do."

In truth, the two of them were more alike than appearances suggested. Both had chosen to serve their country and made that choice multiple times, re-upping when asked. They both bore the scars, visible and invisible, of the horrible things they'd endured as well as perpetrated. In fact, the only real difference Finn could see between his being the owner of a successful Private Investigator's business and his being a junkie living on the streets of Cambridge was down to luck — miserable, capricious, fucking luck. So while he in no way condoned Miller's actions in Iraq, he knew now how he would earn the man's trust.

Finn leaned forward, put elbows on knees and, looking straight ahead at the sparkling waters of the Charles River, began to talk.

"Back in 2002 my Delta Force squad was sent...somewhere east of Iran," he said carefully.

"Afghanistan?" asked Miller immediately. "Pakistan?"

Finn gave him a look and repeated firmly, "Somewhere east of Iran."

Miller nodded, catching on.

"We assembled there to prep for an upcoming op to our west, somewhere we were definitely not supposed to be going."

"Somewhere we don't have a whole lot of assets, maybe?"

"Exactly. What we did have was intel about the location of an illegal cache of chemical and biological weapons being stockpiled by this country's government. This intel was rated B-2, '*a usually reliable source, probably true information*'. It was specific. And it was actionable." Finn produced a small bottle of water from a coat pocket and placed it next to Miller's right foot. Miller adjusted his slouch and reached down to snag it. Finn kept his gaze steadily forward and continued.

"The higher-ups back in DC needed eyes-on verification of these purported WMD before they would authorize a strike to take them out. They needed evidence, preferably hard evidence of some sort, so they would be able to justify what would essentially be a preemptive strike inside and against a sovereign nation, one who wouldn't take kindly to our actions.

"Low profile mission?" asked Miller.

"Ghosts in the night," confirmed Finn. "If we were caught, or if we left a bunch of corpses behind it could start a shooting war with a country we do not want to be in a shooting war with. It was the blackest of black ops, and we were flying without a safety net."

Miller sat forward, mimicking Finn's elbows-on-knees posture, though Finn didn't notice. He was suddenly 7,000 miles away and 12 years younger, reliving the doomed operation for the ten thousandth time.

Once again he stood in the back of the AC-130, now 240 miles south of their Shinand Air Base assembly point, as the rear hatch of the plane opened like the maw of some gigantic hungry beast ready to vomit fire and death upon those below. Once again the thin air whipped and howled around the fifteen members of Team Poleaxe, fully kitted in desert camouflage and wearing oxygen masks. Once again they made their HAHO jump at 33,000 feet, using ram air parachutes to glide fifteen miles through Afghani and Pakistani airspace before finally landing on Iranian soil.

After assembling in the high arid desert where there were no roads and no one to see them, they hiked a couple miles west up into the Zehedan Mountains, eventually coming to their target's first security perimeter — FLIR PTZ (Forward-looking infrared Pan-Tilt-Zoom) cameras and sensors. These they passed undetected thanks to their wearing a newly developed camouflage material made of graphene and gold which could adjust its temperature within seconds to match that of its environment, thereby rendering the wearer invisible to infrared.

Shortly after that they came upon the first set of active measures — Mon-50 mines, the Warsaw Pact's version of the Claymore. Using metal detectors and patient eyes, they easily spotted the rectangular, slightly concave mines sticking out of the ground on two spindly legs. Their somewhat haphazard placement suggested the Iranians didn't take the threat of incursion from the east very seriously. A few minutes' stealthy climbing brought Team Poleaxe to the final active defensive measure — a pair of DsHK 12.7mm machine guns set behind sandbagged emplacements flanking the door to a stone hut set into the side of the mountain and which covered the oval parking area and single dirt road leading down to the west.

" Anyway," continued Finn, skipping the operational details he couldn't share with Miller (or anyone else for that matter), "we eventually get where we're going without any trouble." Finn trailed off, the memory still baffling to him to this day. "And they'd left the front door open. Wide open."

"As in, literally?" asked Miller, surprised.

"Like they were inviting us in to take a look around," replied Finn,

"Which we did. The intel was good — we got in and confirmed the existence of the WMD. Mission accomplished," he finished, echoing Miller's earlier bitter exhortation.

"What happened next?"

"What do you think happened next?" asked Finn, eyebrows raised.

"Everything went to shit," stated Mike in a gravely voice.

"Everything went to shit," confirmed Finn. "We finally managed to get out of there, but without being ghosts, without our hard evidence, and without three of my guys." Finn turned, looked the homeless vet square in the eyes and ticked off fingers as he continued. "Diego Figueroa from outside Los Angeles, Malik Jackson from the Bronx and Oscar Holt from Saint Louis. They're not home playing with their kids or working the late shift because I got them killed in a place they never were, on a mission that never happened."

"I'm sorry," Miller said after a moment of respectful silence.

"And the worst part?" Koenen went on, "was that our fucked up op, combined with the growing mistrust in the intel community at the time between the CIA, DIA, FBI and everyone else, made Washington so gun shy that they refused to even consider running a similar verification op in Iraq the following year to get eyes-on the supposed WMD Saddam had been stockpiling." Finn paused to shake his head in anger and frustration. "So they authorized the clusterfuck that was Operation Iraqi Freedom — the very reason you yourself were in-country — based on secondhand intel alone which, as we all now know, was abso-fucking-lutely wrong."

Miller's eyes went wide. "So are you saying that the failure of your mission spooked Washington so much that we ended up declaring war on Iraq based on secondhand and inaccurate intel?" Miller asked incredulously

Finn nodded miserably.

"That might be worse than my story."

*   *   *   *   *

Finn chuckled at his fellow vet's gallows humor. "War fucks everyone," he observed.

"That it does," agreed Miller.

Finn rubbed palms on eyes and swiveled to face Mike beside him on the bench. "I'll make you a deal," he said. "You help me, I'll help you."

"Whatta you mean?"Miller's expression became guarded the second Finn said, 'deal'. Clearly, he'd been offered some 'deals' while living on the street he wasn't particularly keen on taking.

Finn held his arms up, palms out, professing innocence. "Nothing weird, I promise. Listen, Zoe Kraft hired me to look into who might ultimately be responsible for injuring her daughter. She told me you knew something important."

Miller folded into himself further. Finn needed to tread lightly.

"Zoe trusts you because you're still a soldier who wants to do right by his country. You trust her, because you can see she is pure of heart in a way that you no longer are. Well, now I'm saying you and I can trust each other, but for a different reason — because we've both done things we can't un-do, even if we wanted to." Finn paused and took Miller's silence as an encouraging sign.

"Here's my proposal. I'm getting paid to investigate this situation and I could really use some assistance, because, believe it or not, it's not my only case. So, you come on board like a freelancer to help me, and I pay you for it. It's not a handout — it's a job. You don't work, you don't get paid. You work, you earn. Capiche?"

Miller sat up straighter, cocked his head and started muttering, his internal dialog bleeding awkwardly into the external world.

"How much?" he finally asked.

"Hundred a day."

Miller's eyes lit up. "A hundred... every day?" he could scarcely believe it.

Finn pulled a crisp $100 bill out of his inner coat pocket. "A hundred a day, so long as you do the work, and believe me, I'll know if you did it." He let the bill in his hand drift towards Miller, whose arm twitched in anticipation of grabbing it. "This," Finn nodded towards the money, "is for your time and our conversation today."

Miller slowly reached out to grasp the bill between his thumb and forefinger, but Finn did not immediately relinquish the money. Mike looked up at him questioningly.

"No drugs," Finn said firmly. They stared at each other for a moment, Miller searching Finn's eyes for negotiating room. Seeing none, he nodded, reluctantly. Finn let go of the bill and it disappeared into Miller's coat in a flash. Finn grinned at Mike and after a few moments the vet returned it.

"Okay," said Finn, rubbing his hands together and leaning in. "Let's get to work. Take me back to last spring, just before the Marathon bombing. Tell me what you told the cops and Zoe Kraft about seeing Tamerlan Tsarnaev meeting with people in Harvard Square."

*   *   *   *   *

7:14AM, SATURDAY, APRIL 13TH, 2013
HARVARD SQUARE, CAMBRIDGE, MA
11 MONTHS AGO - TWO DAYS BEFORE THE BOSTON MARATHON BOMBING

Mike stood on the brick plaza just outside the Au Bon Pain seating area, annoyed. The Square was unusually busy for this early on a Saturday and some assholes just claimed his favorite bench.

Goddammit.

Now where was he going to lie down? He chastised himself yet again for having bought booze instead of food the previous evening. Scanning the seating area he spotted a large group preparing to vacate several tables, chairs and — best of all — one of the other benches further down the row. Mike quickly made his way over to claim it, bumping clumsily into the back of another patron's chair as he went by.

"Hey!" exclaimed the startled kid, maybe twenty-something with dark curly hair, sporting a neon green tank top and wearing a set of massive headphones that made him look like the world's ugliest Princess Leia. "What the fuck?"

"Sorry," Miller mumbled without stopping.

"Fuckin' bum," grumbled the kid as Mike brushed the bench clean and lay down. Getting into it with a customer would result in his getting booted from the bench or even worse, banned for good from the seating area, so he bit his tongue but kept one eye on the fucker just in case he decided to make trouble. Some guys just had a chip on their shoulder, always looking to prove how tough they were, and Miller had zero interest in giving him that opportunity.

Thankfully, someone appeared and sat down with the little prick before things could escalate. The newcomer was a large ominous-looking older man with a dark, sharp-featured face and Mike thought it odd that he sat next to, rather than across from, the youth. They also did not greet each other, and despite last night's mistakes beckoning him to fall asleep on the bench, Miller found his curiosity piqued enough to spy on the odd twosome.

After another couple minutes of stony silence, a young Middle Eastern-looking man joined them, placing 3 large coffees on the table and tossing a large bag from the COOP, Harvard & MIT's popular joint bookstore, onto the youth's lap before sitting across from the both of them.

"What's this?" asked The Kid in a loud voice.

"Put it on," Middle Eastern Guy said flatly, gesturing to the COOP bag.

"Do as you are told," commanded the burly, older man ominously in what sounded like to Mike like a Russian accent.

The Kid covered his neon green wife beater with a gray sweatshirt sporting the distinctive crimson Harvard logo across the front. Mike could see at least four others exactly like it from where he was lying. Thus camouflaged, the Kid glared while the Scary Russian's face cracked into a smile.

Middle Eastern Guy gestured with his chin towards the coffees on the table. "Drink some."

"I don't want any," replied the Kid, petulant. Apparently he didn't appreciate his free coffee and new sweatshirt.

"Drink it," growled Scary Russian.

"Let us pray that your arrogance and stupidity," Middle Eastern Guy said with barely-veiled contempt, "do not cause us any problems."

Scary Russian tilted his head in agreement. "He's right," he said to the Kid, "you'll need to blend in better than that on Monday."

The Kid sat back with poorly feigned indifference and took a sip of his coffee, as instructed. "My brother and I know what we're doing."

"We'll see," Middle Eastern Guy commented dryly. "You may be stupid but apparently you know when to follow directions."

The Kid pulled a face but kept his mouth shut.

"It's a go." said Middle Eastern Guy quietly, just loud enough for Miller to hear it clearly.

The Kid straightened up. "Are you sure?"

"Yes."

"Which way should it be done, David Bowie or Katy Perry?"

"Bowie."

The Kid grinned. "*Under Pressure*, then."

Ignoring this, Middle Eastern Guy reached into his jeans pocket, pulled out a small key and placed it on the concrete chessboard table between them.

"Go to the South Station bus terminal," he instructed the Kid. "This key will open a locker. In the locker will be two backpacks and a duffel bag containing everything you will need."

The Kid quickly put his hand over the key and then spirited it away into his pocket, his darkly handsome face shining with excitement.

Scary Russian spoke up. "Just do as you're told and follow the plan and your family will be taken care of for a long time."

"We know what we're fucking doing, man. It's not like — ."

"Any mistakes, however," interjected Middle Eastern Guy coldly, "and..."

"And you will find your mother raped and dead in a cold ditch," Scary Russian cut in, menace flowing from his complete lack of emotion.

Miller shivered despite the warmth of the morning.

The Kid blanched, then tried to hide his embarrassment at having done so by adopting a peevish sulk, which as far as Mike could tell was his default expression. *What an asshole.*

Scary Russian abruptly snatched his coffee off the table, stood up and left without another word, followed shortly thereafter by Middle Eastern Guy.

"Fuck off," said the Kid once the others were safely out of earshot. "Tsarnaevs don't make mistakes."

*   *   *   *   *

PRESENT DAY

"You're sure the Kid said, "Tsarnaevs don't make mistakes?" Finn asked, skeptical.

"Yeah! Yeah, he did, I'm sure of it!"

Finn wondered whom Miller was trying to convince, but kept his doubts to himself for the moment.

"Anyway," Mike took a swig, emptying the bottle Finn had given him and continued. "You hear a lot of weird shit living on the street, so I didn't think much more about it until I saw the pictures the police put out a couple days after the attack. That's when I realized the Kid from a few days earlier was one of the Tsarnaev brothers. Tamerlan, I think," finished Mike, a little awkwardly.

"Why didn't you go to the cops sooner?" Finn asked, causing Miller to flinch, "Why did you wait for four days?"

Mike seemed to be having another one of his internal arguments and finally he said in a small voice Finn had to strain to hear, "Because I made some pretty good money the morning of the Marathon — people are much more generous on holidays — and I... I scored some heroin and... well, I got high and didn't really get my shit back together for a few days."

"So what happened when you spoke to the authorities?" asked Finn, not interested in berating the guy. "Did they believe you?"

Miller shook his head emphatically. "No. They didn't, but I'm not sure I would have believed me either. I really was pretty filthy and raving like a lunatic about how they needed to get out there and catch the guys."

"Little did you know they were already conducting the biggest manhunt in history," observed Finn, "and just hours away from catching the younger Tsarnaev hiding in a boat in some poor bastard's backyard over in Watertown."

"Right? Anyway, the cops took my statement but probably just to placate me more than anything else." Mike tipped the bottle to his lips again, but nothing came out. Finn pulled another from his pocket and offered it to him. Mike took it gratefully. "I know I looked like a crazy junkie. I mean, I am a crazy junkie! But I also know what I saw. I swear to you on Billy Harrison's soul that I saw that Tsarnaev asshole meeting with some young Middle Eastern Guy and some older, Scary Russian-type guy, right over there!" Miller stood and jabbed his finger repeatedly back towards Harvard Square.

"I believe you," said Finn quietly, gently pressing Miller's arm down.

Mike let his arm be lowered, sat back down and struggled to master his suddenly ragged breathing. The homeless vet buried his head in his hands for a few moments then looked back up at Finn.

"You believe me?" he asked the detective.

"I do."

He studied Finn's face, looking for something he apparently found.

"Good. Because the Scary Russian guy is back."

"The Russian guy you saw in Harvard Square last year?"

"Yup," replied Miller, "at least, he was as of two weeks ago."

*   *   *   *   *

5:21 PM, SATURDAY, MARCH 8TH, 2014
CAMBRIDGE, MA
TWO WEEKS AGO

Miller shook the large plastic cup in his right hand, jingling the coins rhythmically, calling out every twenty or so shakes, "Spare change. Homeless veteran. Spare change please." He barely made it a question anymore. Why bother? People who were going to give him money would do so regardless of how clever or animated his patter was. Several coins dropped into his cup from the rough hands of a construction worker. "Thank you sir," said Mike, but without much enthusiasm. He truly appreciated the charity but today was one of those days when he was overwhelmed by the shame he felt for who he had become, and more so for the choices he'd made that put him here. he wished he could obviate his guilt by assigning responsibility for his actions to Fate or Predestination of just plain Bad Luck. But he knew at his very core that he had consciously *chosen* this path even if he hadn't really considered where it would lead him.

Though it was true that blind rage and frustration drove him to shoot those poor people in Iraq, he also knew that, in his secret heart of hearts, a small unforgivable part of himself had enjoyed the killing. The lava-hot release of anger and fury in a fusillade of bullets had felt uniquely and unexpectedly cathartic. It wasn't the "killing of innocents" that caused him so much humiliating pain — everyone who dons a soldier's uniform has to accept the painful reality that they may someday harm or kill an innocent. What ate away at him every second of every day was how *good* it had felt to do it. Despite everything he had believed about himself up until that life-changing moment twelve long years ago, Mike Miller was not, in fact, a good person. Never would be. Never could be.

"Get a fuckin' job, ya bum!" growled one of a group of teenage skater punks bulldozing their way down the sidewalk. The youth slapped at the cup in Mike's hand as he went by, knocking it to the ground and scattering his meager change all over the sidewalk. Laughing maliciously, another boy — tall and skinny with way too much nose for his thin, acne-scarred face — kicked the cup further down the sidewalk. Mike let the group pass by then sighed and shuffled after his cup, stooping to collect change as we went. *Still, this is better than I deserve*, he thought morosely.

Reaching where the cup had come to rest in an oily puddle of liquid up against the curb, he glanced up to make sure he wasn't about to get hit by any cars and froze.

Holy shit, is that…

Standing not ten feet away was the 'Scary Russian' he had seen meeting with Tamerlan Tsarnaev and that Middle-Eastern Guy just before the Marathon bombing, almost eleven months ago. Panic momentarily gripped him, turning his bowels to jelly. A moment later, Scary Russian, wearing a dark hooded sweatshirt, crossed the street at a break in traffic, never once looking in Mike's direction. Panic flipped quickly into determination, as Miller realized that he may now have a chance to rectify his inaction of a year ago — this could be his opportunity for a measure of redemption.

Snatching his cup off the ground and pouring the loose change into a pocket, he quickly wended his way through pedestrians as he followed his target from what he hoped was a discrete distance. The Russian wasn't hard to track, as the crowd seemed to instinctively shy away from the man in much the same way as a school of fish avoids a shark cruising through. What was he doing here? Was he just out for a walk? Grabbing a beer with some friends? Something about the way he moved, like a man trying to cloak purpose with casual indifference, put Mike on high alert and led him to conclude something more was going on. Was there about to be an attack? Right here in Harvard Square? This evening?

Tamping down the sudden return of panic, Mike told himself that the guy wouldn't be here to blow himself up — he got other people to do the dirty work, at least if his connection to the Tsarnaevs last year were any indication. *That's it! He's here for another meeting.* Mike was sure of it. Should he tell someone? Find a policeman? Start screaming bloody murder? Try to tackle the guy? He dismissed each idea almost as soon as it entered his mind. No one would believe he had magically spotted a terrorist in broad daylight just steps from Harvard Yard on a beautiful Saturday afternoon, and yelling or attacking the guy would only make him look like more of a crazy homeless junkie than he already did. No — the right play here was to employ patience, watch and wait, and gather whatever intel he could. He'd figure out what to do about it afterwards.

Course of action decided, Mike resumed picking his way along the sidewalk, eyes locked on the back of Scary Russian's head. Suddenly, instead of crossing Dunster Street, the Russian abruptly made an about face and started back towards Mike. Thinking quickly, Miller diverted left, going around the above-ground T entrance for cover. To his great dismay he spied the Russian making the same turn around the T entrance to follow after him. Remaining calm, Mike continued past the T structure, along a low wall separating him from a public seating area that sat a few feet below street level. He then went down the three shallow steps and began actively begging from the people sitting at the public tables. Ignoring their annoyance, his eyes tracked the Russian as he walked past, thankfully paying Miller no mind. *He must have circled back to check for a tail,* Mike realized. *Good thing us homeless are invisible.*

Miller trotted back up the three steps back to street level and headed across Dunster Street in time to see Scary Russian enter the Au Bon Pain a hundred feet away. After a few moment's hesitation, Mike decided to camp out just in front of the clothing store next to Au Bon Pain so that he would have a clear view of Scary Russian coming out of the restaurant without being in his direct sightline. A few minutes later he emerged with a couple cups of coffee and a bag and went over to sit at one of a row of metal tables running along a low, thick hedge.

Mike started halfheartedly panhandling as a way to quietly blend in to the crowd while he kept the bulk of his attention on his quarry who sat quietly with his head turning constantly to scan the passersby. Someone actually dropped a five in Mike's cup but he barely registered it, as right at that moment a tall, dorky looking blond haired, blue eyed white guy with wire rim glasses, probably in his early twenties materialized out of the crowd, pulled his sweatshirt hood over his head, sat down across from the Russian and grabbed one of the tall coffees. Without thinking, Mike started heading along the outside of the hedge. Heart hammering in his chest, he pretended to fumble his cup onto the ground, stooped over as if to collect it, then crawled along dirty bricks until he was just opposite the two men on the other side of the verge. He got into a squatting position, tensed and ready to run should he be discovered, and tried to filter out the crowd and traffic noise to focus on what he could hear filtering through the verge. The two were speaking softly, and Mike had to strain hard to catch anything intelligible at all.

Dorky White Guy: "No, at this point in the... process, he would prefer to step out of the loop. That's why I'm here. Trust me, I speak for him."

Scary Russian: "If I trusted people, I'd be long dead. And since I don't know you, I would prefer to to deal directly with my client."

Dorky White Guy: "Well, he told me to tell you that you work for me now."

Scary Russian: Laughing. "Bullshit!"

Dorky White Guy: —unintelligible—

Scary Russian: "Tell him whatever you want. I'll have the team ready to go, as promised."

Silence now from the other side of the hedge. Mike started to sweat. Had he made a noise? Has they heard him over there? Were they about to reach over and — "

Scary Russian: "I think we may have another mutual friend, you and I. Did you know that?"

Dorky White Guy did not reply but Mike could swear he heard him nod.

Scary Russian: "Like you, our friend was given a job to do — one that proved to be beyond his abilities. When things didn't go as planned, he found himself facing some... difficult questions."

A brief but pregnant pause.

Scary Russian: "I wasn't there at the end, of course, but I am told that, before the acid breaks you down into your component atoms, it is excruciatingly and exquisitely painful.

Miller shuddered. The Dorky White Guy did not reply.

Scary Russian: "So, everything else is on schedule?"

Dorky White Guy: "Yes."

Scary Russian: "Good. Make sure it stays that way. There can be no mistakes this time, for both our sakes."

Dorky White Guy: —unintelligible—

Scary Russian: "Please pass along that I will only be speaking directly with him going forwa—"

Scary Russian broke off mid-sentence and after a further beat of silence Mike's radar started going crazy. They knew he was there, listening, spying. Panic exploded in his belly and he fought to stay crouched and still — he *had* to know. He couldn't fail again.

The silence on the other side of the hedge was broken by a soft whisper and what sounded to Miller like the metallic snick of a pistol slide being racked.

Without thinking he snatched his cup off the ground and started making exaggerated retching noises. Chairs scraped on the other side of the bushes as the two men he'd been listening to hastily reacted. He retched noisily again and threw in a few groans for good measure. With his back to the men, he rose unsteadily and, with a final retch, wiped his mouth with the back of his right sleeve and, heart pounding and mind racing, staggered away to slip safely into the ceaseless river of humanity coursing through Harvard Square, his mind and heart racing wildly.

*   *   *   *   *

PRESENT DAY

"That was smart, pretending to be sick like that."

Miller looked pleased at the compliment.

Finn fixed him with an intense look. "So what did you do after you got away? Did you go to the cops"

Mike's face flushed again and after a moment he answered.

"No," he admitted, "I was so freaked out by having seen the Russian guy again that I kind of lost my shit."

"You got high?"

Mike nodded, miserably. "I shot up, thinking it would help me calm down, but it just made it worse. The harder I tried to calm down the more agitated I got. Eventually, I got so twisted up in my own head that I called Mrs. Kraft, thinking she would know what to do, how to get me out of the mental maze I'd created. But as soon as I heard her voice, all sleepy and confused, I got so ashamed and angry with myself I couldn't bear talking to her."

Finn gave him the space to gather his thoughts and plow on. "Suddenly, I was convinced I had invented the whole thing, that it was all a drug-induced paranoid fantasy, and here I was dragging this poor, desperate women down the rabbit hole with me. At the same time though, I was equally afraid that it *wasn't* a paranoid fantasy, and that these guys were still out there getting ready to blow some more people up, and the universe had given me this second chance chance to try and prevent it, but then I went and got high instead of going to the cops, so I... I was in a bad place the next morning, and I just couldn't face her."

"So why tell me and not her?" asked Koenen gently, the kindness in his voice bolstering Mike's resolve.

"Because you'll understand in a way she never could. Because she's a good person something bad happened to," he said, fixing Finn with clear eyes, "and you and me? We're the bad things that happen to good people."

CHAPTER 8

8:07PM, SATURDAY MARCH 22ND, 2014
THE SOUTH END, BOSTON, MA

Cat Rollins was pleasantly surprised. This Finn guy was handsome. Like, really handsome. He had steel blue eyes, short cropped black hair with a sprinkle of salt, a weathered face that was somehow simultaneously kind and hard, and a compact muscular body — at least as far as she could tell through his black v-neck sweater and chinos. Heather had said she would be pleased when Cat met her brother but Cat assumed that was typical blind date horseshit. She scored Heather a mental point while thanking Finn for holding the door for her as they entered Jae's Cafe, one of her all-time favorite spots.

Most of her recent first dates — there had been many more of these than of second ones — fizzled out at either (a) the stuffy old-school steak house chosen to impress her with how *Boston Brahmin* the guy was, or at (b) some pop-up / trendy / experimental place with *artisanal Mexican chocolate foam* and *deconstructed garnishes* to make sure she knew how hip and in-the-gustatory-scene he was. She hoped the choice of Jae's meant that this guy might be worth getting to know, unlike the insecure jackasses or baggage-laden drama queens she seemed to attract.

Her dark blond hair fell in a soft wave below her shoulders and she wore black pants and a chambray shirt with the cuffs rolled up over the sleeves of a tan blazer along with low but sophisticated heels. Attractive and five feet nine, she usually let her above-average, but not intimidating height and her slender, well-toned figure be a sufficient enough statement for most situations. Her makeup and jewelry selection were simple, classic and minimal, as she knew she wore the less-is-more thing pretty successfully. She wondered if she had looked as pleasantly surprised as Finn had when they'd first met out on Columbus Avenue in front of the restaurant.

The tiny hostess led them down an aisle between a double row of simple wooden tables packed with conversing, laughing and eating patrons all bathed in low, comfortable red and yellow lighting. The walk to their table was a cacophony of sights, sounds, and mouth-watering Asian spices all blending into that wonderful experience of being at a favorite spot on a busy night with a great vibe. Looking back to make sure he was still with her as they progressed through the restaurant, Cat watched Finn navigate through the narrow chaotic space, noting how careful and agile he was at avoiding the stream of waiters, patrons and trays of food. It made him look like a person who was observant, thoughtful and capable. She approved, and was intrigued.

Her most recent slew of dates had not lived up to expectations, so she was pleased to have already had hers exceeded before even sitting down. Being a successful, attractive, never-married woman in her mid-40s would seem like a strong position to occupy, but Cat had found the reality of it a tad tedious and disappointingly underwhelming. She wasn't one of those people who felt they just *had* to get married. Frankly, the few instances she had taken the time to contemplate the concept, she had found in a mildly surprising way that she was kind of indifferent to the idea. She knew she wasn't particularly interested in having kids, and now found herself at the point in life where biology would dictate that decision for her, but she *was* interested in finding a partner she could share the experience of her life with — someone strong, smart, driven, fun, well-off, and of course a great ass wouldn't hurt. Was it so much to ask for someone who could be her equal, if not a little more?

Finn held the chair her as she sat, then he snuck into his seat on the other side of the small table. His chair was already snugged up against the wall, leaving him not a lot of room in which to sit. As he swung his hips into the narrow space, he bumped the table and a tall, thin, teardrop shaped vase holding a several small, colorful flowers started to tip over. Before she could even raise her arm, Finn had the vase in his hand, catching it before it fell. He gently replaced it on the table between them and gave her a sheepish look.

"Sorry about that," he apologized.

Startled by how fast he had moved, Cat was a beat behind. "Oh. Um, no problem! No harm, no foul, right?" She gave him a warm smile now that she had recovered to assure him it was fine.

"Thanks," he said with a genuine smile of his own. "It's probably bad form to start the date by getting you soaking wet."

Eyebrows raised, Cat gave him a pointed look. For a brief moment he looked perplexed, then blushed — he actually blushed — and apologized again.

"Uh," he started, eyes on the white tablecloth, "I probably could have phrased that differently."

"Oh, no," she said mischievously, "I think you nailed it."

He stared at her poker face for a second, trying to decide if she were kidding or not, then guessed correctly. He burst out laughing and tipped an imaginary hat at her. "Touche," he said.

She laughed too, and she mimed a seated courtesy back. Their waitress appeared just as Cat asked, "Thirsty?"

"Very."

"Long day?"

"More intense than long," Finn replied with an enigmatic smile. Before she could pull that thread he gestured with his chin for her to order her drink.

She got a Manhattan and Finn chose a ginger Mohito, instantly giving Cat drink-envy. They chit chatted about where they each lived while waiting for their drinks to arrive, which they did surprisingly quickly despite the full house. Finn caught her staring at his glass.

"Drink-envy?" he inquired, perceptively.

"Ha!" she laughed. "Actually, yes. It's a much better order for this," she said, spreading her arms to indicate Jae's Cafe. "Than that," she concluded, pointing at her somber, dark brown Manhattan. He proffered his taller glass and she took it, sipping off the side, letting the several thin black straws rest against her cheek. "Oh, that's nice," she said wistfully.

"You can have it if you want. I'll just get another," he offered.

"Oh no, you don't need to do that," she said quickly.

"You sure?"

She took a long sip of her Manhattan and smiled. "No, I'm good. I might switch after this though. Thank you."

"No problem," he replied lightly.

They locked eyes for a moment and Cat felt her stomach jump a bit, in the good way. She gave him a sly smile, gestured to the menu on the table in front of her and asked, "what's your go-to appetizer?"

"What's yours?" he asked in reply.

"Together?" She suggested, and he nodded. "Okay. One, two, three…"

"Gyoza," they said at the same time, causing them each to grin in delight.

"Fried," Cat clarified.

Finn shook his head in mock disapproval. "Steamed, of course!" he admonished, adding a 'tsk-tsk". Cat swatted his arm lightly and they both laughed again.

The next hour and a half were a bit of a happy blur. The conversation was so easy and natural that she quickly forgot she was on a first date. It had that rare combination of all the curiosity and excitement associated with getting to know someone for the first time combined with the lazy comfort of having already known them forever. She got — and thoroughly enjoyed — her ginger Mohito, and Finn switched to Singha. They ordered both kinds of gyoza in order to determine which was better (fried, score a point for her), sushi (hamaki, smoked salmon and Uni), and spicy Korean pork, all of which they shared. He showed more interest in her than Cat's last five dates combined, and she reveled in the attention. His queries were good ones — either digging deeper on a topic (*'what does a tech CMO really do, anyway, like on a daily basis?'*) or challenging something she said (*'Are you really balancing your focus on your job at VersaTech with your focus on yourself?'*) — and she really appreciated that Finn was clearly listening and engaged, instead of just going through the motions to see if he could get her shirt off later.

That didn't mean he wasn't flirting with her though. She couldn't remember the last time she had felt this strong of an attraction, and she was pretty sure it was reciprocated. He kept eye contact, sometimes longer than was strictly necessary, gave her his full attention and occasionally brushed his hand against hers. She smiled to herself, realizing that she was seriously considering playing footsie under the table like she was a teenager! *Perhaps that was the second ginger Mohito speaking?* She considered that. *Fuck it, I'm having fun,* she concluded. *I think I could like this guy.*

She suddenly realized that she had done the majority of the talking so far, and that she didn't really know that much about Finn, other than what Heather had told her. She had met Heather through the Junior League of Boston and the two had hit it off right away. They were both no-bullshit, but not aggressively so, and shared the same wicked sense of humor, often earning glares from some of the more buttoned-up members of the organization when they couldn't keep their laughter, or snarky comments, to themselves. Come to think of it, Cat didn't know all that much about Heather's past either. She knew that Heather had grown up overseas, and had once been married but wasn't currently on good — or bad — terms with her ex-husband Paul. She knew neither Koenen had kids, and that they were tight despite not spending a ton of time together. Apparently Finn's job as a cop, or whatever he was, made for odd hours and occasional time off the grid.

"So, you're not a cop, are you?" she blurted out. "Sorry, Heather told me what you did once, but I forgot, and you don't really seem like a cop to me, but you also don't seem like not-a-cop, if you know what I mean." Now it was her turn to blush a bit.

He chuckled. "I'm not a cop, but I am a Private Investigator."

Her brown eyes widened. "You're a PI?"

"Yup"

"I don't think I've ever met a PI before."

"Well, now you can check that off your list," he said with a smile.

He had a really nice smile, and Cat wanted to learn more, but found she wasn't sure what to ask next — she had so many questions. "Do you... have your own firm? Or do you work for a company? Or how does that work?" she asked, knowing which answer she was hoping for.

"I have my own small firm, with just one other guy who works with me." *Right answer*, she thought.

"What's it called?" she asked, "is it, *'Finn Finds Friends'*?"

He laughed. "Ha! Actually I named it *Rogers Investigative Services* after one of the founders of the Army Rangers."

Cat's radar pinged pleasantly. A PI *and* possibly in the Special Forces, too? "So... you were a Ranger?" she asked.

"I was," he confirmed.

She took another sip and the cavitation of her straw indicated it was finished. "What was that like?"she asked, risking a venture into a potentially tricky subject area.

"Good and bad," he answered simply.

"Were you deployed overseas or were you mostly here in the US?"

"I trained here in the US but was deployed in the field most of the time."

"How long have you been out of the service?"

"Not long enough," came his reply, and he finished his beer, carefully setting the glass back on the table.

"Hmm," she mused, slowly stirring the ice in her glass. "So you didn't like it?"

"No, I loved it, actually," he said, pausing, perhaps reflecting. "But in the end, it was time to go."

"What happened? Did you shoot a bunch of guys you shouldn't have?"

she joked before she could stop herself, instantly regretting the question. He looked down at the table for a few moments, then back up at her.

"So, you enjoyed your dinner?" he asked, clearly changing the subject.

Flushing with embarrassment and not wanting to make it worse, she played along. "I did!" she replied with a brightness she didn't feel. "Did you?" she asked lamely.

"It was delicious, as always," Finn said with a wan smile, then signaled for the check.

Cat was furious with herself. After all those shitty dates with half-interesting, self absorbed assholes, she finally found someone she connected with and what does she do? Push it too far. *Goddammit*, she chided herself silently.

Finn paid the bill, helped her get her coat on, and waited with her on the sidewalk until her Uber came, but the spell had been broken. On the surface all was fine — he continued to be polite, even friendly, but now there was an almost palpable distance between them. Her Uber driver pulled up in his red Toyota Highlander and they hugged, said they had fun and would do this again, but Cat wasn't so sure he wanted to, now.

She tracked him in the side view mirror as her driver pulled away, hoping for a smile, a wave, anything, but all she saw was Finn's back as he stalked off the other direction, hands jammed in overcoat pockets, melting into the night.

CHAPTER 9

12:46PM, SUNDAY, MARCH 23RD, 2014
BOSTON POLICE HQ, BOSTON MA

Finn shook hands with Lieutenant Patrick "Sully" O'Sullivan of the Boston Police Department and then pulled his old friend in for quick hug and the requisite two or three pats on each other's backs. Greeting rituals complete, they settled into a couple of chairs, large fresh Dunkin' Donuts coffees nestled into the mass of paperwork on Sully's desk beside them. The cube farm, which filled a large part of the third floor, buzzed with activity around them, busier than Finn expected for a Sunday afternoon. Boston Police Headquarters, at 1 Schroeder Plaza in Roxbury, had been built just three years earlier and looked it — a modern, glass-fronted and energy efficient building that was by far the most well-appointed station in the city. It sported cutting-edge technologies, a fully equipped gym and spacious locker rooms so the officers could shower and change as needed without being on top of each other like at most other stations.

Despite rating a private office of his own as the leader of Tactical Operations, Sully had always preferred to sit amongst his officers rather than behind a closed door all day — one of the things Finn really liked about him. He was responsible for several teams of highly trained, specialized teams, including the Mobile Operations Patrol, SWAT, Negotiations, and a variety of other supporting roles. The nature of TacOps meant Sully's officers were called into the highest risk situations, and Sully needed to ensure his officers knew him well and trusted him implicitly, and he, them.

Besides, at heart he was more foot soldier than general. Organizationally, he reported to the Captain of Special Operations

Division, who reported up to the Superintendent of the Bureau of Field Services, who reported to the Superintendent-in-Chief, who reported up to Police Commissioner Edward Davis, who reported to the Mayor of Boston, Marty Walsh. Being buried deep on the org chart gave Sully exactly what he wanted — the opportunity to lead an elite team of officers without having to deal with all the political bullshit that came with the more high profile positions.

"I take it you're here to bust my balls," guessed Sully, "about sending Zoe Kraft over without so much as a watch-your-six?"

Finn gave him a pointed look.

"I am sorry about that," he said sincerely. "I really did mean to warn you but something came up and by the time that was over I'd completely forgotten about pointing her in your direction."

Finn hoped Sully's lingering guilt over this clear breach of their informal protocols would nudge him to be extra helpful, so decided to give him a pass.

"Don't worry about it," Koenen said, waving his hands dismissively. "Besides, I took the case, so you're actually going to make me some money."

"Holy shit! You took it?" Sully exclaimed, incredulous. "I definitely didn't see that coming. I honestly thought you would tell her to go screw, but nicer-like."

They both chuckled then Finn explained, "I came pretty close to turning her away, but something about her story stuck with me. Like… like having a splinter you can feel but can't quite get out."

"I hate that."

"Me too," agreed Finn, taking an exploratory sip of his coffee — Dunkin' Donuts gave it to you scalding hot — and got down to business, "So, tell me what you know about you-know-what."

"Let me just start by saying that," Sully caught Finn's eye, "we have one hundred percent confidence that the Tsarnaev pricks did the Marathon bombing. They made the pressure cooker bombs, they placed them near the finish line on Boylston Street, and detonated them, killing three and injuring 264 others. Next, they killed an MIT cop, jacked a car and got into a gun battle with us. Tamerlan then ran over his older brother Dzhokhar in an attempt to kill one of my fellow officers, who — even as that fucker was bearing down on him — was trying to save his older brother's life." Sully shook his head in disgust. "As you know, the trial is about to start and let me tell you, he's gonna burn for it. All of it. Fuckin' assholes."

"So you're saying they did it?" Finn asked, deadpan.

"Of course they fucking did it!" barked Sully, exasperated, before realizing Finn was messing with him. He brought his voice back to a normal level. "Of course they did it. We have video and about a thousand other pieces of evidence, both direct and indirect, that make this an open and shut case."

"I assume you said as much to Zoe Kraft?" asked Finn.

"I did," confirmed Sully. "But she's convinced herself the Tsarnaevs were too stupid and inexperienced to have pulled this off by themselves."

Finn tilted his head questioningly.

Sully shrugged and went on. "Yeah well, it turns out you don't need to be so smart to blow up a bunch of people and bring a major city to its knees for almost a week."

"All by themselves though?" Finn pushed back. "My understanding is that the devices they used were pretty sophisticated, and these two strike me as straight-up morons. I assume the Feds looked into this rather thoroughly and concluded the pair acted alone?"

"They did, and they did," confirmed Sully. "The Tsarnaevs worked alone. They didn't much like living in the US, even though it was thousand times better than living back in Shitbag-istan or wherever they came from."

"Dagestan," Finn corrected.

"Who fucking cares?" countered the officer, disdainful. "Anyway, they felt like America was screwing them over and they thought they would try to teach us a lesson."

Finn considered this for a moment. "Okay," he said, "So it's fair to say you're convinced they worked alone?"

Sully nodded.

"So why do you think Zoe Kraft keeps pushing the issue? She's clearly not stupid."

"Who knows?" replied O'Sullivan, leaning back and throwing his meaty hands into the air. "Grief does weird things to people. You've seen it." Now it was Finn's turn to nod.

Sully continued, waxing philosophical. "I remember reading once that stars, like our sun, are so heavy and massive that they can bend light itself. That's what grief is like — an invisible gravity that warps everything that comes near it."

Finn tried another tack. "How did she find out about that Mike Miller guy?"

Sully scowled. "Someone," he said in a low growl, looking around the room as if the culprit might be lurking nearby, "gave her access to some of the case files. And they're going to be pissing blood for a month if I ever figure out who it was," he finished menacingly. "It wasn't the main case files, but she got information on the thousands of leads generated in the immediate aftermath of the bombing. You remember how crazy it was? Everybody and their dear Aunt Sally was jumping at shadows and calling and emailing to tell us about it."

"I can imagine that was a bit of a cluster," agreed Finn.

"Don't get me wrong, we needed those leads, and a small percentage of them were extremely helpful. However, the bulk of them were false alarms, or people hoping cash in on the reward money. And more than a few were just bona fide nut jobs."

"Into which category would you put Mike Miller?"

"The homeless junkie?"

"The homeless *veteran*," Finn corrected.

Patrick waved a hand in surrender. "Vet. Homeless vet," he said. "Yeah, I'd place him squarely in the 'nut job' camp."

"Why's that?" asked Finn.

Sully gave him a pained look. "Dude. Have you met him?"

"I got the sense that he enjoyed the odd tipple."

"Tipple? What are you, an eighteen hundreds prospector? He's not a drunk, he's a junkie. A heroin junkie. And a drunk," he concluded.

"So what? A lot guys have problems," countered Finn, gesturing around the busy patrol room.

Sully nodded. "True, but this guy's problems have problems of their own." He grinned at his own joke. "He came in here a few days after the bombing, raving about having seen Tamerlan Tsarnaev meeting with a couple other sketchy guys just before the Marathon. His story barely made any goddamn sense, he stank to high heaven of booze, and if his pupils had been any more constricted he would have been blind."

"He was high when he came in?"

"As a kite being flown by another kite."

"And his story didn't make any sense?"

"Correct", confirmed the officer.

"But you checked it out anyway," said Finn.

"But I checked it out anyway."

"And?" asked the detective.

"And, bubble," replied Sully, making a zero with his thumb and index finger. "I asked around the other homeless guys in the Square and nothing. The Au Bon Pain didn't have any security videos, and none of the other cameras nearby cover that area. I re-interviewed Miller and, while he did mostly stick to his story, he didn't have any additional details I could check into, so I dropped it as a dead lead. Hell, I'd already put way more time into it than it was worth!" he finished, defensiveness creeping into his voice. "What was I supposed to do, track down and interrogate every 'Russian' and 'Middle Eastern' male in the greater Boston area?"

"Of course not! I get it, and I fully believe you invested more time investigating Miller's story than it deserved," placated Finn, who could only imagine the crazy amount of pressure that came with working a case under such an unprecedented amount of scrutiny.

"So…" drawled Sully.

"So?"

"Are we good here?"

Finn thought for a moment before responding.

"We are. We're good." They stood and shook hands again. "Thanks a lot buddy, I really appreciate it."

"Anytime," replied Sully. "Whatever you need."

Finn grabbed the remainder of his coffee and made to leave. He got a few yards away when Sully called out.

"Hey, Finn!"

He stopped and turned back, "Yeah?"

"You still like sushi?"

"Damn straight," replied Finn. "How long since you had any?"

"Must be six, six and a half months now."

"Well, lemme know when you wanna get some. I'm free anytime."

"I'll do that," said Sully. "Stay safe."

Finn tipped his head. "You too, Sully," he said, and left, suddenly unsettled.

What is it he can't he tell me here?

* * * * *

6:53PM, SUNDAY, MARCH 23RD, 2014
THE CORNER PUB, BOSTON MA

A little over five hours later, Finn drained his Tsing Tao, signaled to the bartender for another and checked the time on his phone. He thanked the heavily-tattooed 20-something woman as she slid his beer over and dropped an updated receipt, creased down the middle, into a lowball glass sitting in front of him. A neon, Chinese-style dragon light in front of the big mirror behind the bar bathed the small, basement space with red, green and blue hues giving it that dark and timeless feel every great dive bar had. It was 6:54pm; Sully was almost twenty-five minutes late. Finn took a long pull off his fresh pint and replayed their earlier exchange yet again.

"You still like sushi?"

"Damn straight. How long since you had any?"

"Must be six, six and a half months now."

"Well, lemme know when you wanna get some. I'm free anytime.

"I'll do that..."

Was it possible he'd misunderstood? That Sully hadn't meant to indicate getting together this evening? It certainly wasn't like him to be late like this. Uneasy and needing something else to occupy his mind while he waited, Finn let it drift back to when he'd first returned to the States.

After parting ways with the Army in 2005, Finn decided it was finally time to try living in the country he had been defending for the better part of the past fifteen years. His father Jan, though born in the Netherlands, had become a highly successful diplomat for his adopted country and as such, Finn and Heather had grown up overseas, spending very little time inside US borders before attending college. Finn's first eleven years were actually lived in Tehran, until the terrible events of 1979 forced them to evacuate.

The US State Department had then resettled them in rainy, relaxed Amsterdam, which Finn had loved after the heat, dust, strictures and relative poverty of Iran. His teenage years in the 'Venice of the North' were good ones, and he still had friends in the city to this day. Unfortunately in 1986, Finn's senior year in high school, an accident claimed his parents' lives, and he hadn't lived in The Netherlands since, though he had visited several times over the intervening decades.

Though he had spent four years in the US while at Georgetown and then a few more at Fort Benning, Georgia for his Basic, Airborne and Ranger training along with a brief stint at Freefall School in Yuma Arizona, Finn wouldn't characterize any of these experiences as 'living in mainstream America'. So, after his Honorable Discharge in 2005, he set off to see what the fuss was all about. He entered civilian life with a fairly respectable bank balance, as his spending needs in the Army had been sporadic at best, and the hazard pay all too frequent. Finn presumed it was his father's Dutch blood that led him to save more than technically necessary while in the service, but it was his mother Elise's free Irish spirit that took the reins now, inspiring him to crisscross the country for eight months before settling down.

He finally experienced firsthand all those places he'd only ever read about in books or seen on TV or in the movies. New York; Chicago; the Badlands of North Dakota; the sequoias of northern California; the endless Las Vegas carnival; the sheer monstrous scale of the Grand Canyon; the muddy Mississippi (and a week of Memphis blues); swimming with rays in the Florida Keys; and finally, New England, where his sister was attempting to put down roots.

Boston had seemed as good a place as any to settle, with easy access to Europe and even the Middle East if necessary, which he found unexpectedly comforting. His former Ranger brother Tony Russo had also just arrived in Boston, having recently been divorced by his wife, Sandra. As part of the settlement, she had offered to take less money from him if he agreed to leave New York City and never live there again. Most men would probably have been offended by this stipulation, but Tony agreed to it gleefully. He couldn't stand Sandra and was happy to keep more money for himself while never having to worry about accidentally running into her on the street. *I should have known it wasn't going to work*, he said to Finn that first night they'd gone out for beers together in Boston, *when she wouldn't let me call her 'Sandy'. What kind of person doesn't want a nickname?* he'd asked, incredulous. *She was insane in the sack, but unfortunately, she was even crazier out of it.*

Not that Tony himself had been blameless — the guy was unapologetically difficult to get along with and proud of it. It had taken Finn a long time to figure Russo out when they'd first met. He was often selfish about small stuff, like not sharing his food at the DFAC, always trying to get others to pay for the next round of drinks, and generally being squirrelly about his belongings. At the same time, though, Tony was generous about the big things, in that he would unhesitatingly lay down his life to save yours, which Finn had seen him do more than once. Just don't try to sneak some of his BBQ Pringles. These personality quirks and a dozen more like them sometimes made Tony a challenging minority partner in the Agency, but they'd mostly found their way through the bigger disagreements over the years. So, with Russo's strengths lying more in tactics and execution, Finn realized he would need someone to strategize with in order to figure out how to make his newly-formed small business successful.

For that, he reached out to his old friend Patrick O'Sullivan, a newly-minted officer in the Boston Police Department. They'd met a thousand years ago while undergrads at Georgetown studying International Relations. A couple seasons on the University's B-side rugby club gave them ample opportunity to bond even though Sully had been two years ahead of Finn. A Government major with a minor in Economics, Patrick already had his eye on law school and eventually a career at the FBI when his mother died of breast cancer. It had come as a shock to Finn because, despite all the hours on the rugby pitch and in front of the bar together, Patrick had never once mentioned that his mother was sick, even dying.

He'd also neglected to mention that his father was showing early signs of dementia — a condition that took a significant turn for the worse once his wife of 47 years was gone. Sully had only shared these painful details after finding out that Finn himself was an orphan. Something about this fact struck a chord with Sully, and he began to reveal some of the tremendous grief and anger and fear he'd been carrying around all by himself. Though never explicitly discussed, Finn started helping Sully with whatever he needed help with. Groceries need delivering to his father? Done. Need someone to take notes for you in a class you can't make because your father is having a fit? Done. Need someone to down a fifth of Jack with, no questions asked? Consider it quaffed.

In the end, Sully still managed to graduate Georgetown with High Honors, but had to forgo his law studies to take care of his father back in Boston, who was by then in need of pretty much constant care and supervision. Sully's requirement for seriously flexible hours had prevented his taking a job commensurate with his educational success, but he claimed he didn't mind waiting tables and tending bar so long as he could be there for his dad. But after his passing in 2002, Sully finally had the opportunity to pursue his passions and serve his community, so he'd joined the Boston Police Department, becoming perhaps the oldest and most overqualified rookie cop they'd seen in a long time. After working a beat for a couple years, he got transferred to the Special Operations Division where he worked his way up to Sergeant, and then, a couple of years ago, to Lieutenant, in charge of the entire Tactical Operations team. Genetically incapable of kissing ass, his success stemmed from working hard, playing well with others, and efficiently clearing cases. If he occasionally bent a rule here or there, it went unremarked upon — so long as he continued getting results and didn't let anything blow up in his face. He was sharp and had the respect of the men and women he worked with — both up and down the chain of command — and wasn't beholden to anyone but his wife and two kids, a notable rarity in a police department as politicized as Boston's.

Which was exactly why Finn had taken Sully out for drinks to get his thoughts and guidance on how to run his new PI agency successfully.

After several hours of drinks and discussion, Sully had given Finn two pieces of advice he'd taken and one he hadn't: (1) Don't waste money on advertising — it's a trust business and word of mouth is both free and effective; (2) only work for 'friends & family', meaning military folks or others he could trust implicitly; and (3) ditch Tony Russo, whom Sully had accurately assessed as difficult to manage, hard to control, and unrepentant about all of it.

Somehow, their evening ended up landing them in Chinatown at this very location, The Corner Pub, where — about fifty or so drinks in — Patrick suggested that they make an arrangement to help each other out, but under the table-like. Sully knew that Finn would often need access to official records or data, while he himself would need access to people, items, and information that Department policy would seriously frown upon. Finn saw the efficacy of this and readily agreed. Then Sully had drunkenly shouted that if they were going to be secret crime-fighting partners, they needed a secret crime-fighting code. After a number of highly amusing but unworkable suggestions, they'd hit upon a scheme that was simple enough to remember but effective enough for their purposes.

Since anonymity would be a key factor, The Corner Pub made for the perfect go-to meeting spot, as no one they knew frequented the place, and it clearly adhered to the sacred dive bar guarantee of anonymity. Next, they decided to use their newest inside joke as the foundation for their own personal code. Earlier in the evening, Sully had drunkenly complained that The Corner Bar didn't have sushi on the menu, and Finn had to work surprisingly hard to explain to him they were at a Chinatown bar that did not sell Japanese sushi. As such, they decided that, when one of them needed an off-the-books meeting with the other, the first person would ask;

"You still like sushi?"

And if the other person couldn't meet, you would just say;

"Nope. I don't eat that anymore."

But if the other person could meet, he responded with:

"Sure! How long since you had some?"

To which the first person would respond using the number of months to represent the time of day they should meet at The Corner Pub;

"Must be six, six and a half months now."

And if the other person said he was *"free anytime"* that meant today. Otherwise, he would say something like, *"how about next Tuesday?"* Their code was simple, elegant and reasonably hard to fuck up. That is, unless he had somehow fucked it up.

Coming back to the present, Finn saw it was seven pm; time to wrap it up.

As he reached back to pull out his wallet, a strong hand gripped his wrist and he felt something poke into his lower back.

"Gotcha," growled a deep voice behind him.

* * * * *

"Gotcha," growled Sully as he grabbed Finn's wrist and stuck a pair of chopsticks into his lower back.

"All you got is a case of the heavy footsteps," countered Finn, "I heard you coming a mile away."

Sully conceded the point with a grunt (he was thirty minutes late after all) and motioned for a round as he hunkered down next to his old friend. Greetings complete, they sat in silence while Sully contemplated his image, partially obscured by the necks of liquor bottles, in the mirror behind the bar. He drank off most of his beer almost as soon as it arrived.

"Sorry I was late."

"No sweat," Finn replied lightly.

Sully placed his now-empty bottle on the bar and after taking another long pull of its replacement, he shook his head in exasperation and finally turned to look at Finn for the first time. "Fucking FBI. I hate those assholes."

"Didn't you want to *be* one of those guys?"

"Jesus Christ,' sighed Sully. "Thank God I didn't end up going into the F. B. Fucking I."

"Amen to that," agreed Finn. "Just think how much bigger of an prick you'd be."

"Agreed"

"So. Dish."

"You're an Army guy, right? So you understand about bureaucracy." Sully rubbed his eyes as he spoke. "You can probably guess what a shitshow it was last year after the Marathon bombing. The Boston Police Department had to deal with the Staties, the FBI, NSA, The Army, The National Guard, FEMA, The Governor's Office, the White House, and Justin fucking Bieber!" he finished with exasperation.

"JFB?" asked Finn, with a smirk.

"He was the best of 'em," grumbled Sully.

"I get it. Lots of agencies, overlapping jurisdictions, massive egos."

"Exactly. Every single meeting with the Boston Joint-Terrorism Task Force devolved into the usual dick-measuring competition."

"Sounds charming."

"It wasn't," said Sully. "And it turns out the JTTF didn't much appreciate our moving in on the Tsarnaev kid in the boat in Watertown before the FBI had officially given us the 'go' sign."

Finn raised his eyebrows in surprised admiration. "Well, I wonder who made that call?"

"And I'd make it again today," cut in Sully defensively. "We had him in the boat, the neighborhood was locked down, and I was tired of waiting for those FBI assholes to finish jerking each other off. By the time they found out I'd given the order it was already over, and we had the kid in custody so they couldn't ream me out in public."

"The ends justify the means?"

"Sometimes they do," answered Sully, and they clinked their bottle necks in an X shape. "But that hasn't endeared me to our well-suited friends from DC, so they've gone out of their way to make my life difficult. They withhold information. They interview people without my knowledge, and I'm pretty sure they know I got an undercover operation going on.

"Ahhh. Now we get to it."

"What?" asked Sully.

"The real reason we couldn't talk about this back at your desk."

"Yup. The little bastards are all over me. They can tell I got something going on, and they think it's in their pumpkin patch."

"Is it?" asked Finn with a raised eyebrow.

"Fuck them. It's my city," spat Sully. 'Besides which, we might be on to something big, and I can't afford to have anybody raising a stink just now." He paused for a moment. "Honestly? It's the main reason I pawned Zoe Kraft off on you," he admitted with a small apologetic shrug of the shoulders. "She was threatening to go to the papers and tell them we were refusing to help the distraught mother of a maimed bombing victim. The second she does that, reporters like that Gabi Mendez are going to be all up in my ass, and I need to keep things quiet so I sent her over to you to get her out of my hair. I figured it would at least buy me a week or two of relative peace before you refused to take her case and she came back at me again."

Finn took a moment to consider this information. "So, tell me if I got this right. You're running some sort of top secret undercover operation that, and I'm reading between the lines here, is in some way related to the

Marathon bombings that the Feds feel might be their jurisdiction?"

Sully looked straight ahead and started peeling the label off his Tsing Tao.

"Okay, well, putting your inter-service etiquette issues aside for the moment, since one of the Tsarnaevs is dead and the other is on trial, I can only assume you must think someone else was involved but hasn't been arrested yet?"

A third scrap of label fell onto the bar top.

"Or maybe," Finn continued, clearly warming to the task, " you think they, or somebody else, might be planning something for this year's marathon?"

"I feel like it's getting warm in here. Do you feel that?" replied Sully looking around the otherwise empty bar area and fanning his face with a colorful, laminated menu, causing the scraps of label to skitter away and fall behind the bar.

"You have any proof of this?"

"Define 'proof'."

"As in, actual physical evidence you could use in a court of law."

"Well, no, not yet. But enough that I'm willing to put one of my TacOps guys out on the sharp end of the stick."

"But why lie to the Feds?" Finn asked.

"This is a particularly touch and go situation. I can't explain why, but just trust me on this. The stakes are high, and you know what a house of cards every undercover op is. One wrong word to the wrong person at the wrong time and I'm fishing my guy out of the Mystic River with a couple holes in his forehead. So I had to keep the circle small on this one and I don't trust the Feds any more than they trust me, so here we are, everybody lying to everybody. Especially those CIA pricks."

"There's CIA guys involved?" asked Finn, surprised. "I thought they weren't allowed to take action on US citizens inside the US."

"Yeah, well, welcome to the new world. Where's the line between a 'foreign" threat and a 'domestic' one? It's all gray area, and you know how the spooks love a good gray area."

"So what are they doing in this gray area?" asked Finn warily.

"Mostly just sniffing around, asking to be kept in the loop," here Sully made rather derisive air quotes, "and it doesn't smell like they are running any ops of their own. Yet."

"Curious," observed Finn.

"You know how it is. If you see a lot of vultures flapping around, there must be a body somewhere nearby." Finn laughed and Sully continued,

"The only good thing for me is that the NSA, CIA, FBI; they all hate each other more than they hate the Boston Police Department, so they spend most of their time stepping on each others' dicks, which creates some, shall we say, operational maneuvering room for me and my guy."

"And he's onto something?"

Sully hemmed and hawed for a few moments. "I should know more from my guy in the next few days but if his instincts are right? Let's just say our friend Zoe Kraft maybe isn't as crazy as we thought she was."

CHAPTER 10

8:29PM, MONDAY, MARCH 31ST, 2014
27 HANESBOROUGH STREET, DORCHESTER, MA

The voices below fell silent as soon as they heard his heavy tread coming down the stairs. Reaching the ground floor, Ruslan saw that three of them (Vakha, Timur and Makmud; his most trusted lieutenants) had commandeered the only proper seating — an oddly formal couch — leaving the other six to grab some floor, cross-legged. The modest living room of the Chechen's safe house had been cleared of all other furniture earlier that afternoon as they wouldn't be using it to play cards or host soirees. No, the nondescript single-family home at 27 Hanesborough Street, deep in the heart of blue-collar Dorchester and rented by a friend of a friend, would hide their true activities well. Situated just south of Boston proper, it was the kind of neighborhood where a bunch of young guys could come and go at odd hours in anonymity. People here kept to themselves and — more importantly — kept their fucking mouths shut, so long as you didn't go out of your way to piss them off.

Kadyrov stood in front of his men and carefully cracked the knuckles of his left hand, misshapen by the butt of a Russian Army rifle many years ago, each pop echoing like a gunshot around the otherwise empty room.

"Welcome to your new home away from home," he said, spreading his arms wide. "At least for the next few weeks. We have very little time and much to accomplish. I am not concerned, however, because I have personally chosen each and every one of you to be on this team." Ruslan locked eyes with several of his men as he said this, first Akhmad, then Timur, and finally the new guy, Khasan Varayev, before continuing.

"While our past endeavors have generally been blessed with success, they all pale in comparison to what we are all about to do. This particular job is..." the terrorist struggled to find the right words in English and settled on the Russian,'грязный' which mostly translated as 'messy', or 'dirty and filthy'. He was pleased to see that no one so much as blinked. "As such, our employer is providing each of us with compensation that recognizes the serious nature of this assignment. Pay close attention to what I am about to tell you. I will not tolerate any mistakes. Am I understood?"

"Yes sir!" replied the men as one.

Satisfied, Kadyrov began.

"Three weeks from today is Monday, April 21st; Patriots' Day and the running of the Boston Marathon. Thanks to the valiant but amateurish efforts of our fellow Chechen Tsarnaevs brothers last year, this is now the single most heavily guarded race in the world. Therefore, we will target the other big event in Boston that morning."

Ruslan grinned at the puzzled looks. Patriot's Day — always the third Monday in April — had been instituted in 1894 to commemorate the first battles of the American Revolutionary War in Lexington and Concord in 1775. Only a few states celebrated the holiday: Massachusetts, of course; Maine (at the time part of Massachusetts), and, randomly enough to Kadyrov, Wisconsin. The Boston Marathon itself was first run in 1897 to link the American struggle for liberty with that of the Athenians in ancient Greece. Then, in 1959 the Boston Red Sox began scheduling home games for the same morning. Since 1968, the first pitch had been scheduled for 11am which, given the race start time of noon, had generally allowed the game to let out before the winning runners reached the finish line a few blocks away from Fenway Park, usually around 2:00pm

Starting in 2007 however, the Marathon had pushed its start time a couple hours earlier which meant that the Sox game now let out well after the winners had gone home, though a large portion of the remaining runners would still be struggling towards the finish line. Tens of thousands of people would come streaming out of the iconic ballpark to join the hundreds of thousands already milling around the streets of downtown Boston. Despite all the extra security personnel that would be on, it was a logistics and security nightmare for the authorities and they would be overwhelmed from the start. And once the panicked stampeding began, Ruslan and his men could disappear into the mayhem like raindrops into a stream.

"The first runners start in Hopkinton, west of the city, at 10am," he continued explaining, "and the Red Sox first pitch is at 11am. The elite runners will finish sometime around 12:10pm - 12:15pm, depending on the weather. The Red Sox game, which always sells out and has a maximum capacity of just under 38,000, will likely end around 1:30pm - 2pm, just when thousands of amateur runners will be arriving in downtown Boston." He paused and Varayev offered him a bottle of water, which Ruslan stooped to grab with a nod. After a long swig, he continued.

"The ten of us will break into five teams of two and deploy to specific, designated rooftops overlooking each of the five major exits from the stadium. Each team is comprised of a pilot and a shooter. At exactly 1:12pm the pilots will launch their specially-modified drones along with their payloads. At 1:15pm, all 5 drones will be flown over the walls and into Fenway park, where they will hover above the crowds in the stands for thirty seconds."

The nine men stared raptly up at him, hanging on his every word. Ruslan loved this part, the anticipation from his men as he explained their plans; the looks of surprise and excitement and respect that always followed; the unwavering loyalty he demanded.

The former Chechen freedom fighter continued. "At 1:16pm the drones will begin to fly all around over the crowds, dispersing their payload on the fans below."

"And what is the payload?" asked Akhmad eagerly.

"Acid," replied Kadyrov with a grim smile. "Highly corrosive acid. The drones flying around and spraying the acid will cause a panic and people will surge out of the five exits, whereupon from the rooftop positions the second man in each team will gun them down like the cattle they are, using SAWs mounted on bi-pods." The Squad Automatic Weapons were reliable, accurate, sported a high rate of fire for a light machine gun, and were ideal for assaults like this one.

His men's eyes shone with excitement at the audacity of the attack. Even Ruslan had thought the Iranian's plan genius when he'd first heard it.

"At this point the first man will discard the drone controls, pick up his own weapon, most likely an assault rifle with a bump stock, I haven't decided yet, and either begin firing on the crowd himself or provide defensive cover for his partner if security forces are in the area."

"At 1:25pm, we will stop shooting and leave the rooftops, pulling off our masks and coats to reveal first responder uniforms. Waiting for each team at street level will be ambulances, into which will go all the guns and assault gear. By this point, the streets will be filled with a frantic mob, impossible to control or manage. By pretending to have wounded civilians in the back we will have no trouble getting out of any cordon that may have been set up and we will subsequently dispose of the ambulances and set them ablaze in several forgotten corners of the city. By 4:00pm we will be home drinking vodka on the couch while Boston tears itself apart."

"Won't they come looking for us?" asked Varayev softly. "I know the Americans don't trust us, especially after last year's attack."

Ruslan smiled again. This one was a thinker — he liked that. Plus, he was about to tell them anyway.

"The authorities will be much too busy," in a soft voice of his own, "looking for the Saudi terrorists."

"Sir?" asked Vakha, confused. "What Saudi terrorists?"

"The ones claiming responsibility for the attack as retribution for the assassination of their leader, Osama bin Laden in 2011, in a video that will be sent anonymously to the FBI while we are driving right past them in our ambulances."

His men stared at him, amazed.

"So buy yourselves a nice bottle to drink when this is all over. You'll have earned it."

CHAPTER 11

1:22AM, SATURDAY, APRIL 5TH, 2014
LANSDOWNE ST., BOSTON, MA
SIXTEEN DAYS UNTIL PATRIOTS' DAY

Sully stood in the shadows with Gate C of historic Fenway park directly behind him. It was times like these that he really wished he still smoked; three hours he'd been waiting since he watched his undercover man head inside the House of Blues across the street, with his Chechen tail right behind him not a minute later.

Fuck!

He hated the waiting. Actually, he didn't mind the waiting so much as he detested the not knowing. Did his man realize he'd been followed? When would he figure out Sully wasn't showing up? Was he even still alive or was his tail there to do more than just follow?

It was almost last call so Sully would find out soon enough. Even in just in the last five minutes the crowd out front had expanded to spill out into Lansdowne Street, people laughing and smoking and some even singing off-key. Sully considered breaking cover to go bum a cigarette but before he could betray himself, the door to the bar opened again and his undercover guy came out and immediately headed west towards Brookline Ave.

Sully knew he wouldn't have long before the tail followed suit so he quickly strode over and pretended to drunk-stumble into his guy which caught him off guard. Sully grabbed his jacket to steady him and quickly whispered instructions into his ear. Sully then smoothed the man's shirt and apologized loudly and with much exaggerated slurring before heading off up the street ahead. If they had any luck, the tail won't have noticed the interaction.

If not, well, that could be a problem.

Ten minutes later the door to the Men's room at the Cask 'n Flagon swung open and much to Sully's relief, his undercover cop came over and joined him at the metal trough.

"Room's ours," Sully confirmed. "And you've got a shadow."

"I know," came the reply in a tight voice. "He's been on me since Monday."

"What happened Monday?" asked Sully. His undercover guy looked scared. Very scared.

"I don't have much time. Listen carefully… "

Sully did, his stomach dropping with every word. Options flew around his brain like leaves in a dust devil, but he quickly selected one and spoke the words he knew his man needed to hear.

"Okay. Well done. I've got a plan."

CHAPTER 12

5:15PM, MONDAY, APRIL 14TH, 2014
ROGERS DETECTIVE AGENCY
SEVEN DAYS UNTIL PATRIOTS' DAY

Finn finished carefully pouring the tall Guinness can into a cold pint glass and handed it to his latest client. He'd started keeping a six pack in his office dorm fridge after he'd noticed she ordered one at The Sevens, a snug bar in the swanky Beacon Hill section of Boston, where they'd met to sign off on the Agency paperwork. Some clients wanted coffee or water or a Bud Light. Zoe Kraft wanted Guinness, so that's what she got. She sipped and wiped the foam away from her upper lip with a perfectly manicured index finger while Finn settled in behind his desk, across from her.

"So." she said after a few moments' silence.

"So," replied Finn, running a hand through his short hair. "So I really appreciate your turning me onto Mike Miller, and for your," here he patted the thick folder acquired that same afternoon at The Sevens, "meticulous and very well-organized notes and information."

"My pleasure," she said cautiously, "But do I detect a 'but' coming?"

Finn gave a wry smile. "But... despite all that, plus my best efforts over the three weeks or so, I don't really have all that much progress to report," he admitted ruefully.

She smiled at him in a 'we're both in the same boat' kind of way, rather than in the, 'I see I've made a huge mistake in hiring you' kind of way, which Finn appreciated.

"Just walk me through what you have," she suggested hopefully. "You never know." .

Finn started by recounting how he finally broke through to Mike Miller with the Pledge of Allegiance (a trick she thought rather clever) and went on to describe their subsequent conversations, though left out the bit about what Miller had done in Iraq. Zoe seemed very pleased Finn had solved the mystery of why Mike's late-night phone call and subsequent recalcitrance, and was quite interested to learn that Mike had recently seen The 'Scary Russian' again, this time meeting with a 'Dorky White Guy'.

"You've made quite a bit more progress than you let on." Zoe said with a smile. "I'm impressed."

"I'm not sure you should be," replied Finn, appreciating the praise but thinking it unfounded. "Once I got through to Mike, he turned out to be a pretty good guy at heart. He's got some demons, don't get me wrong, but he's had his share of bad luck too."

"As have we all," she added, with some gravitas.

Finn nodded in somber agreement. "As have we all."

They sipped in silence for a bit, then Finn said, "But now I'm stuck."

"What do you mean?" asked Zoe. "Aren't you looking for this, what did Mike call him? This 'Scary Russian' or the 'Dorky White Guy' Mike saw him with?" She pursed her lips in thought. "Or what about the 'Middle Eastern Guy' Mike saw meeting with Tsarnaev and 'Scary Russian' last year ?"

Finn spread his arms wide. "If only I could. Mike's descriptions of the three men were vague at best; 'Russian', 'Dorky' and 'Middle Eastern' are not details that filter the possible suspect pool in any meaningful way. I would need something more specific and verifiable like distinguishing marks, tattoos, clothing brands, addresses, names, anything. He's very clear about certain things, but frustratingly fuzzy about a lot more, so as of now I literally have nothing left to investigate," he lamented.

She furrowed her brow. "Could you, I don't know, stake out the Au Bon Pain in case there is another meeting?"

Finn shook his head. "No. It's a low probability event and besides, you need a lot of bodies to run a surveillance like that." Zoe opened her mouth to speak, but Finn raised his hand to forestall her. "However, despite considering it highly unlikely I'm not ruling it out. Our mysterious Scary Russian may use the Au Bon Pain location for all his meetings, though that would indicate a level of shoddy tradecraft that doesn't really align with his having gone undetected all this time. On the other hand, we know he has met people there at least twice now and I don't believe in coincidences, so I asked Mike Miller to act as my eyes and ears in Harvard Square."

This surprised Zoe. "Did he agree?"

"I told him I'd pay him to work for me so long as he stayed off the drugs. I figured he would still drink, but maybe we could meet each other halfway, if you know what I mean. I gave him some cash and a cell phone and a charger so he could reach out to me at any time, for any reason."

Zoe nodded. "I'm impressed again."

Finding himself mildly embarrassed, Finn pressed on. "So anyway, he'll let me know if he sees or hears anything." He took another sip of his stout. "Oh, I almost forgot. I also spoke with our mutual friend Patrick O'Sullivan from the Boston Police Department. We had a chat about your case — " Finn could see Zoe getting a little agitated at this so he quickly assured her, "Just so I could pick his brain about it. I'm a big believer in getting as much information firsthand as possible. If his story had been different from yours, or Mike's, then I would have learned something, perhaps something I could follow up on."

She nodded her understanding, relief showing on her face. Finn made a mental note that not far beneath her put-together persona and Boston Brahmin coolness was a torrent of grief and anger and fear. It was the kind of thing that led people to act irrationally, and there was a reason Rule 3 of 7 for his Delta Force squadron had been, *"We don't do crazy"*.

"Unfortunately, your story, Officer O'Sullivan's story and Miller's story all more or less match up. Again, I didn't get anything I could go on, so I really am stuck."

She smiled thinly through her disappointment. "I'll bet you don't say that very often."

"You'd be surprised," he replied kindly. "It happens all the time."

"So what do we do now?"

Finn blew out a deep breath. "Well, I still have Miller covering Harvard Square so we'll know if anything happens there. As for the race next week, Sully assured me up and down that the Boston Police Department, the Joint Terrorism Task Force and about 17 other acronymed agencies were embedded all over Boston like ticks, just in case someone really was stupid enough to try an attack."

She looked unconvinced.

"Trust me. If I could do something, I would. If I thought for a second that I could in any way help the authorities secure the Marathon, I'd do it. You have my word."

She looked like some of those roiling emotions might be making her seasick. "But what if this Russian guy does something next week at the Marathon anyway?"

"I'm sorry, Zoe, but for now there's nothing we can do," Finn said, not without empathy. " It's just out of our hands."

CHAPTER 13

3:45PM, FRIDAY APRIL 18TH, 2014
27 HANESBOROUGH STREET, DORCHESTER, MA
THREE DAYS UNTIL PATRIOTS' DAY

"Let's go!" bellowed Ruslan Kadyrov angrily. He'd been trying to rattle his men like this for the past two and a half weeks, and no one had failed the test yet. If they couldn't handle the pressure here in the safe house, they'd never perform in the chaos they would incite around Fenway Park in just three days. He carefully picked his way through what, until three weeks ago had been the living room but which was now a makeshift chem lab, with lots of plastic sheeting, five sturdy folding tables, piping, glassware, Bunsen burners, gas masks, beakers, an eye wash station and a range of chemicals you couldn't find at Home Depot.

Well, some of them you can, Ruslan thought with some amusement. It almost wasn't fair waging war inside the enemy's belly like this. If they had been back in Chechnya, he wouldn't have been able to take a shit without sixteen Russian Army fuckers asking him questions about what he'd eaten yesterday. But in America he could use freedom — their greatest strength — against them: freedom to move around without checkpoints; freedom to purchase things like lab equipment and chemicals; freedom to connect anonymously (anonymously!) with others on-line. He knew the NSA was watching the wires, but so long as they were careful to avoid certain words and subjects, like 'bombs' or "President', it was unlikely they would be found out.

Heading upstairs to check on the remaining team's final preparations, Kadyrov stole a glance at his watch — 3:50pm. In just over six hours the first of the vans would arrive to distribute the men and their materiel to a series of temporary safe houses squirreled away all around the city, where they would hunker down, not even going out for food until go-time on Monday morning. They would have operational silence from tonight onward so this was his last chance to ensure that everything was prepared, everyone knew exactly what to do and when to do it, as well as what to do if things went to shit. *When don't they go to shit?* he thought, characteristically pessimistic right before a job.

He reached the landing on the second floor where he had men in each of the three bedrooms assembling the drones they would use to drop the acid on the baseball fans at Fenway. In the basement he had two more men unboxing, assembling, disassembling, cleaning and reassembling the SAWs and ARs. They were also managing the ammunition and filling the extra clips they would need, taping them together head to tail so that they could easily flip and reinsert them without wasting any time.

"Faster!" he screamed in Russian at no one and everyone at once. Nothing blew up, so that was another good sign.

He looked into the first of the bedrooms on the right and found the new guy, Khasan, three-quarters of the way through building his drone. Ruslan liked Varayev but hadn't fully trusted him at first. Vakha was a solid guy, and his vouching for Khasan meant a lot but Vakha also wasn't the sharpest tool in the box and Kadyrov hadn't lasted this long by trusting anyone completely. So he'd had the new guy followed for a while, just in case. Other than sometimes heading out for drink late at night a couple of times, the guy had been either at Logan throwing bags or home taking care of his sick mother. And with that to look forward to at home every night, who wouldn't need to go out for a few drinks once in a while?

"You're well ahead of the others."

"I like putting things together," said Khasan simply, "it's like a puzzle."

Kadyrov nodded. This one was smart, worked hard, kept his mouth shut and was motivated. He could use twenty more just like this baggage handler. "When you are done, double-check your work and then go help the others. They could use your assistance."

"Yes sir," Khasan replied, lowering his eyes in respect.

He had proper manners, too. Cared for his elders. This Khasan Varayev was cut from a different cloth than so many of these spoiled second generation Chechen-Americans who had no respect for their old country and a deep hatred of their new one. If only they had met a few years ago, then Kadyrov wouldn't have to give him the 'loose end' treatment now. But if Ruslan wanted to get to the deep wilds of British Columbia so he could live the rest of his life in peaceful solitude, then that's what had to happen.

Such a shame, thought the old terrorist as he left the room and headed off down the hall towards the next, *that I have to waste this perfectly good soldier.*

CHAPTER 14

"He's up to something," Russo declared over the early Friday evening hubbub at their local, "though I haven't figured out what it is yet."

Finn and Tony were catching up on their respective cases over a few beers, as was their practice when jobs kept them apart for more than a couple days at a time. Despite their personality differences they had always worked very well together as a team, and these informal bull sessions where they discussed each others' cases often resulted in new ideas, lines of inquiry and solved problems. Finn had just finished recounting his progress on the Kraft case and Tony had concurred that there really wasn't anything else to be done. As such, it was now Russo's turn to provide an update on his investigations into the supposed infidelities of MIT Professor of History, Greyson Richards.

His wife, retired Marine Allie Richards, approached them back in February. As a very pretty, petite, feisty, blond-haired, blue-eyed Minnesotan, Finn had no trouble understanding why she'd initially caught Richards' eye, but it baffled him a little as to why the bookish academic had caught hers. Not because of his looks — Greyson was a decently handsome guy at maybe five-ten, slender with a ginger beard and heavy black glasses. Actually, Finn thought he looked exactly like who central casting would send over if your scene needed an approachable young History Professor. It was more that their personalities seemed so different to Finn. Greyson appeared to be a slightly befuddled bookworm while Allie was all energy, hard-assery and deeds-over-words.

The night she and Finn first discussed her case over beers at The 21st

Amendment, he'd returned from a bathroom trip to find four or five young investment banker types circled up around her, sensing fresh meat. Out of curiosity, Finn hung back to see what would happen. He didn't have to wait long, as within just a few minutes she had demolished the Alpha of the group who clearly thought he had another easy notch coming for his belt.

"Listen Sparky," she'd started, holding up her left hand to demonstrate both diamond ring and gold band. *"I'm not sure you're hearing what I'm saying, so let me make this crystal clear for you. I like my drinks the way I like my men — hard, straight and neat."* She paused to look him up and down before concluding, *"Not soft, bent and sloppy."*

They shared a laugh about the asshole's bruised ego and then she'd gone on to explain why she wished to hire Finn. Allie Richards loved her husband completely. She knew they didn't look like a good match for each other on paper but her heart wasn't made of paper. As corny as it still sounded to her, she told Finn it had been love at first sight for both of them. Greyson Richards, Associate Professor of History at MIT, had somehow managed to overcome his obvious innate shyness to initiate a conversation with her at a party held by a mutual friend, and she'd felt something fundamental slide into place as they'd chatted about the mistakes America may or may not have made in the Bosnian intervention back in the 1990s. Though not the sexiest of topics, he impressed her with the way he analyzed complex situations, and clearly appreciated her boots-on-the-ground first-hand knowledge as a Lieutenant Colonel flying AH-1 SuperCobra helicopters.

She asked him out on the spot and he accepted almost before she'd finished asking. They dated for a few months and then she asked him to marry her and he'd accepted without hesitation or reservation. Greyson was meticulous and patient and Allie knew that if she left it up to him it might take years before he felt everything was properly planned, double-checked and organized enough to pop the question. Besides, he wasn't the kind of guy who cared about all that 'who asked who' stuff. They were equal partners on this journey, and they were very happy together.

Over the course of the next few years, like most couples, they settled into their daily routines. She was still in the Reserves and worked at the Wounded Warrior project in downtown Boston and Greyson had risen quickly through the History Department ranks to become Assistant Chair despite his relatively young age. Her husband was excellent at teaching, writing and researching and had made a bit of a name for himself in the academic world with his theories around insurgencies and guerrilla warfare. Surprisingly little attention had been paid to the topic despite its obvious relevance in the post 9-11 world. By analyzing insurrections from around the world and across the millennia, Greyson identified patterns that suggested certain counterinsurgency strategies were significantly more effective than others. The New York Times had somehow got a hold of his papers (all published in the obscure but well-respected *War In History* journal), and gleefully pointed out that the US Government had, with a few exceptions here and there, consistently pursued the worst possible counter-insurgency strategies. At least, as elucidated by MIT Professor of History Greyson Richards. The resulting furor and publicity had been kind to the shy professor and he could have taken a job teaching at any University in Boston or anywhere else that caught his fancy.

Allie had asked him once why he chose to stay at MIT, a school synonymous with science and math geniuses, not history buffs or Humanities majors. He'd replied that (a) MIT had taken a chance on him as an untested, unpublished first-year professor fresh out of grad school and (b) he really liked having the opportunity to inject the lessons and perspectives of history into minds otherwise completely focused on the abstract symbols of math and the cold data of science. *"History is a story about people, and people are messy,* he'd said, *"and these kids are not comfortable with 'messy'. I want them to know that the equations they write and the inventions they create will change history, but that history is nothing but the story of people, and so I want them to remember that they are affecting people's lives, not just solving tricky equations."* That made sense, so she'd dropped it and they'd continued on happily together.

But something had changed after the Marathon bombing the previous year. That the fear, violence and anger he'd dedicated his career to analyzing were suddenly and viscerally in his own backyard deeply unnerved the professor, especially because he had known MIT Police Officer Sean Collier, who was shot and killed by the Tsarnaevs as they tried to make their escape. For the first time since she'd known Greyson, he'd become moody and markedly more introspective. Recently he had taken to working later and later at the office, with one key consequence being that they spent much less time together. She felt him withdrawing into himself and it scared the hell out of her.

One night after Greyson had called to say he'd be working late yet again grading papers, she'd decided on a whim to bring him some food from their favorite Thai place up the street. However, upon arrival she'd found his office dark and empty. She'd gone home, troubled by this, and when he finally got home later that night she'd casually asked if he'd had a chance to eat any dinner and he'd lied and said no, he'd been too busy to leave his office all evening. The next morning she'd reached out to some friends from her time in the service and they'd recommended she contact Finn, so she had.

"What makes you think he's up to something?" Finn asked Tony as he placed his pint on the bar.

Tony grinned in that way he did when he had something salacious to share. "Well, I didn't for the first two weeks. The guy's routine didn't vary an iota and he never did anything even remotely interesting. I mean, if I were him, I might shoot myself just to spice things up a bit."

Finn laughed, accidentally spraying some foam off the head of his pint. "Ha! Sounds about right. But then?"

"But then, he did something different. I mean, I almost fell out of the fucking car I was so surprised. As you know, he usually finishes teaching around 4pm, takes a walk around campus, grabs a bite to eat and heads to his office to grade papers or write papers or wipe his ass with papers or whatever the fuck it is these guys do, until around 8:30 or 9:00pm, then heads home to his hot wife, watches some TV and goes to bed. But last Wednesday he comes out of his office just after 4pm like usual, but not like usual he's carrying a black gym bag. And, instead of taking a walk and grabbing dinner he stops and looks around all nervous, then heads off down the sidewalk."

"What do you mean, nervous?"

"Like, looking up and down the street all shifty-eyed, and then he heads off down the sidewalk at a guilty clip."

"Where'd he go?"

"He heads a few blocks away up into Kendall Square and hails a taxi, which takes him out to some residential neighborhood out near Davis Square." Tony grinned.

"How very curious."

"Isn't it though?" replied Russo, draining the last of his beer and signaling Sam for another before continuing. "He exits his cab, gives another nervous look around then walks up and rings the bell at one of the houses. Unfortunately, we're on a quiet street so I had to park pretty far down the block so he wouldn't make me. Because of that, I couldn't see who answered the door and let him in, but in he definitely went."

"Pictures?"

Tony nodded and tapped two fingers on the phone sitting on the bar next to his empty pint glass.

"Go on," prompted Finn.

"Unfortunately, all the curtains were drawn so I couldn't tell which room they went into or what they were doing in there, but I do know that he came out about an hour and fifteen minutes later, jumped in an Uber and headed back to campus."

"Did he still have the gym bag?"

"He did."

"Was he still acting nervous?"

"You bet. If he got in that Uber any faster he'd have shot out the other side."

"Interesting," said Finn slowly. "He never did anything remotely like that when I was watching him."

"What can I say? I have a gift," said Russo, puffing his chest out theatrically.

"A gift for getting hammered," countered Finn. "So have you had a chance to check out who might own that apart—"

He broke off, attention caught by a 'BREAKING NEWS' alert which had just interrupted the Sox pregame report. An aerial shot showed cops and SWAT guys swarming around a residential neighborhood somewhere. Finn's called down the bar for Sam to turn the music down and the TV volume up. She fiddled with a number of remotes behind the bar while a Smoky Robinson tune continued to blare, the cheerful audio entirely at odds with the jerky helicopter shot on TV of figures running around, weapons drawn, in tactical formations around a house in flames, with blue and red lights flashing from dozens of vehicles in a wide perimeter around it.

Finn couldn't take it any longer. "Sam! C'mon, you're killing me here!"

"Easy there, Chief! These goddamn things are— ah, there we go," she finished triumphantly as *Tears of a Clown* cut out and a breathless on-the-ground reporter scuttled to safety as the sounds of gunfire and an explosion rolled out of the TV.

"That's probably not good," said Russo, understating it.

CHAPTER 15

27 HANESBOROUGH STREET, DORCHESTER, MA
THIRTY MINUTES EARLIER

Ruslan Kadyrov stood in the back yard of the safe house smoking, a moment's peace before the coming storm of activity, stress and violence. His men were all inside finishing up their tasks and beginning to prepare the house for their departure around 10pm, roughly three and a half hours from now. Enjoying a precious few moments of solitude, he waited quietly for Timur to bring him Khasan Varayev, which he did several minutes later.

"Here you go, Boss," Timur said as if delivering a package and not a person.

Ruslan gave Timur a nod of thanks and the heavyset man grunted, turned and lumbered back across the yard and into the house leaving the two men alone in the lengthening early-evening shadows.

Varayev stood, quiet and attentive, to Kadyrov's left. Did he look nervous? Or was Ruslan imagining that? Though still too new to be fully trusted, the man had indeed been true to his word: he in fact did work hard, keep his eyes shut and didn't ask questions.

And yet…

Following his instincts, Kadyrov decided on one last test as he finished his American Spirit cigarette.

"Khasan."

"Yes sir?"

"Do you believe in God?"

"Sir?" asked Varayev, clearly off put by the question.

Kadyrov turned to look more closely at the baggage handler,

preternaturally alert to any weakness, fear, betrayal.

"Do you. Believe. In God?" he asked, creating tension by drawing out the words.

The baggage handler paused, almost for too long, before replying,

"I do, but I am not sure he believes in me."

Kadyrov pierced Khasan with a sharp stare for a long moment before bursting into a long, loud laugh, throwing his head back and even slapping his knee. "You are a funny guy," he said, nodding approvingly at the man, who smiled back. "I'm glad you're on my team."

Ruslan stubbed the cigarette butt out in the grass then picked it back up and placed it in his pants pocket (no DNA could be left behind) before pulling a half-crumpled pack from his shirt pocket. He shook one into his hand and tried to get a second one to appear but to no avail. "Ah, fuck," he said under his breath as the empty pack joined the spent cigarette.

He looked back over at Khasan. "I've been watching you. You work hard. You help the others and you don't cause any trouble. I never have to tell you anything twice. But..." Kadyrov trailed off.

"But, sir?" asked Khasan, clearly worried he had done something wrong.

"But... I think you can do more. You've impressed me, and so I want you to go with Vakha's team and be his number two."

A brief flicker of relief shot across the thin man's features. Kadyrov was glad to see he could still generate fear with just a single word.

Though Khasan seemed surprised at the battlefield promotion, he quickly regained his composure and replied. "Thank you sir. But, are you sure? I am new, and others have been here longer. Like Makmud, or Timur. Wouldn't one of them be a wiser choice?"

Ruslan chuckled amiably. "Makmud is reliable but has no imagination — he is a good soldier. Timur is too stupid to be scared, which makes him a bad leader. I think you will do fine." He offered his last cigarette to Khasan to seal the arrangement.

Varayev took it and Ruslan lit it for him.

"Yes sir, thank you sir. I won't let you down."

"I know you won't," said Kadyrov with a paternal smile. He patted Khasan on the back on the neck with one meaty hand then turned and headed back to the house. "Come in when you're done smoking, and help Vakha with the final preparations."

After the back door closed behind the terrorist leader, Khasan Varayev slipped his phone out and dialed a number from memory.

Someone picked up but didn't speak.

"I'd like to order sushi for nine," he said quietly.

"Pick up, or delivery?" came the reply.

"Delivery. As soon as possible."

"Ten minutes."

*   *   *   *   *

27 HANESBOROUGH STREET, DORCHESTER, MA
NINE MINUTES LATER

Sully used a small mirror at the end of a long, thin, telescoping metal rod to peek around the corner of the high fence. Though there were three commercial vans out in front of the house, no one was in sight. He motioned for the rest of Team 1, clad in body armor and Kevlar helmets, to join him, which they quickly did, weapons ready, safeties off and cameras on. Less than a minute after the call from his undercover guy he'd deployed his three teams of five around the house in Dorchester. A couple of minutes after that, his man had come strolling casually out of the front door of 27 Hanesborough to head up the street the other direction as if he didn't have a care in the world. *That guy has some serious balls*, Sully thought to himself, and not for the first time.

He spoke into his helmet mike, "All teams, check in."

"Team 2 in position."

"Team 3 in position."

"Team 1 in position," Sully said tersely. "On my mark." He checked his watch. It had been ten minutes… now. He said a silent prayer and hoped these Chechen fuckers wouldn't go down swinging.

"All teams go, weapons free. Repeat, all teams are a go, weapons free."

It started well. Sully crouch-ran Team 1 across the lawn right up to the front door without anyone shooting them, which was always nice. The conspicuous absence of shouts or gunfire meant his other teams had approached undetected as well. He waved Burroughs forward with the heavy battering ram, and he positioned himself on the front stoop. Sully dropped his arm and Burroughs swung hard, shattering the door inward and off its hinges. Sully's team poured into the living room, automatic weapons at the ready, shouting "Police! Down! Everybody down!"

A large, dark haired man wearing a dust mask over his face froze and slowly put the four full black trash bags he had been carrying down onto a floor covered with plastic sheeting. There were several tables and what looked like lab equipment in the room. The man in the dust mask carefully raised his hands over his head as Sully's men fanned out into the first floor of the house, checking the doorways and corners.

Then all hell broke loose.

The bay window behind Sully and his men quite unexpectedly blew inward with an explosion of glass as bullets strafed the room from outside. Burroughs went down face-first while Sully and the other three on his team dove for cover. The large, dark haired Chechen grabbed some glass jars off a lab table and dashed up the stairs in all the confusion while Sully, crawling over to where Burroughs lay, yelled into his helmet mike, "We're under fire in here! Coming from outside the house, out front!"

Another staccato fusillade of gunfire swept across the room as Sully dove on top of Burroughs' prone form. Wood chips, drywall, bits of plastic and shards of glass flew through the air and rained down on Sully and his men, pinned to their bellies on the gritty plastic sheeting.

"Goddammit!" roared Sully. "Somebody take that fucker out!"

Several short, sharp bursts of gunfire from outside resulted in a strangled cry and an end to the strafing. "Sorry," came a voice over the open channel, "He popped out of one of the vans. He's down now. Repeat, subject is down."

"Fuck," growled Sully as he got back up to a crouch position, sweeping the room with his gun while he felt around on Burroughs' back for blood. He found none but did locate where a round had flattened on impact with the back of Burroughs' Kevlar vest. Sully heaved and rolled the bigger man over onto his back, causing Burroughs to groan in pain.

"You'll be fine, you big baby," said Sully, relieved. "Stay here." He then motioned for two of his team to cover the stairs heading up while he and the fifth member of their team cleared the rest of the first floor and linked up with Teams 2 and 3. From the chatter over the open channel and what he could hear from the back and side of the house, it sounded like the other two teams were taking heavy automatic weapons fire from the second floor and had been repulsed from entering the house as planned. It looked like Team 1 would need to break the deadlock.

In a random moment of silence from the shooting upstairs, Sully heard a creak come from the kitchen out back, so he threw in a flashbang, covered his ears, closed his eyes and shouted, "Incoming!"

The sound was deafening even from a room away and Sully knew it hadn't been a pleasant experience for the Chechen terrorist who was now writhing on the kitchen floor in pain. Sully kicked an AK-47 away from him and swept the room with his own weapon before alerting the other teams, "Kitchen clear."

No sooner were the words out of his mouth than Team 3 piled through the smashed back door. He sent four members of Team 3 to the back stairs and took the fifth to join the rest of Team 1 at the bottom of the living room stairs. Sporadic gunfire continued above and out on the other side of the house, with Team 2 apparently still taking fire.

Sully motioned for one of the guys from Team 3, he thought his name was Chavez, forward to take point on the stairs. Chavez popped his head out into the stairwell opening and right back. No one shot at him. Crouching low, he spun around to point his automatic rifle up the empty, narrow stairwell. Johnson from Team 1 swiftly took Chavez's place at the side of the stairwell. After a moment, he, too, spun around the corner and tapped Chavez on the back. They both started mounting the stairs, guns trained up at the second floor hallway.

Johnson only made it two steps up before Sully heard the shattering of glass, followed almost immediately by an horrific scream as Johnson leapt backwards down out of the stairwell and Chavez came staggering back after him, clutching at his face and head. He fell onto his back screaming in a high, keening wail that made Sully's skin crawl. Team 1's second in command, Gabe Larson, grabbed Chavez's boot heels and dragged him into the living room proper and away from the bottom of the stairs. Not two seconds later, a jar shattered on the floor right where Chavez had just been lying. Wisps of smoke, an acrid smell and a nasty hissing came from the floor where the glass had broken.

"Holy shit!" yelled Sully into his mike. "They're throwing acid! I repeat, they are throwing acid. Do not let any of it get on you!" *Fucking Chechens. Why couldn't they just shoot at the cops like normal criminals?*

Despite some sporadic shooting, it seemed they were in a bit of a stalemate for the moment. The terrorists couldn't get out without being riddled with bullets, and Sully didn't want to risk sending more men up the stairs in case they had more acid up there. On cue, another jar came hurtling down the stairwell and shattered against the floor, splashing up onto what looked like a pile of trash and debris pushed up against the wall which immediately began to smoke and hiss.

Sully peered closer at the smoking pile of trash. Was it trash? The closer he looked at it, the more it looked like...

"Abort! Abort!" yelled Sully. "All teams pull out. Now! All teams pull back now!"

His men obeyed instantly and began retreating in a swift but professional fashion. Two men carried the still screaming Chavez out by the legs and shoulders, and Sully himself helped pull Burroughs to his feet, throwing an arm around the man for support. Just as Sully got the two of them to the front door the 'pile of trash' behind them burst into searing white-hot flames, sending streamers of magnesium fire shooting around the room, one or two of which bounced off Sully's back. They staggered out, down the three concrete steps and got about five yards away before the first floor of the house exploded, throwing them both into the air and into oblivion.

CHAPTER 16

10:45PM, TUESDAY APRIL 22ND, 2014
MASS GENERAL HOSPITAL, BOSTON, MA

Sully motioned with his head for Finn to shut the door to his hospital room. Finn rose from his chair and pulled the door free of its stopper so that it would close on its own. Once it had clicked into place, Sully pulled his left hand, and the flask that had magically appeared in it, up from behind the side of the bed so that he could pour some Dewar's into a paper cup, which he offered to Finn. Finn took it and sat back down in his chair while Sully poured a cup for himself.

"Where do you hide that thing in here?" Finn asked. "I mean, it's hard to hide stuff in a hospital room, and I'm pretty sure you're not allowed to have booze in here."

"You have your secrets," replied Sully dryly as he screwed the cap back on the flask and squirreled it away somewhere on the other side of the bed. "And I have mine."

"Ah, goddamn that's good," sighed Sully after sipping gingerly. "Almost makes me forget that everything hurts."

"Stop whining," said Finn. "It's just a couple of cracked ribs, some barely burned skin and a fractured ankle."

"And a bad concussion," grumbled Sully.

"Your brain was jelly anyway," observed Finn lightly, patting his friend's good ankle. At least, he thought it was his good ankle. "You're lucky to be alive, old man," he said, all joking aside.

Sully nodded and they sat in silence for a few moments. Finn was anxious for details about what had happened four days ago in Dorchester but waited patiently. Sully would recover, but it had been a closer-run thing than he would ever admit. The firefight and explosion over in Dorchester had cost one cop part of his face and resulted in a wide range of injuries from cuts and bruises, to a bullet graze, to Sully's stay in the hospital. It had also apparently cost all of the terrorists their lives, at least if the news reports could be believed. The dramatic and explosive raid on a terrorist den in the heart of an old Boston neighborhood had dominated the airwaves in New England and around the world for the last four days and, almost anticlimactically, the Patriots' Day events had gone off yesterday without a hitch.

"When you getting out?"

"Couple of days," replied the cop, falling silent, then, "We got lucky. Real lucky. It could have been a lot worse."

"I have no doubt," replied Finn, knowing first-hand how quickly things went sideways once bullets started flying.

"My guys did great, though. They got the job done."

"They sure did," Finn agreed, then snapped his fingers. "Speaking of, I checked on Chavez this morning. He's stable, and they think they can repair most of the damage with grafts and reconstructive surgery. He won't win any beauty contests, but he wasn't that pretty to begin with." That got him a chuckle. "Seriously though. He'll be fine in a few months."

"I'm glad," said Sully, who then shook his head in bewildered frustration. "Who the fuck throws acid, Finn? What is wrong with these people?"

"It's a good question," said Finn seriously. "What were they doing with acid in there in the first place?"

Sully shot a look at the door to make sure it was still closed (it was) before answering. "You're not gonna believe this shit. It's so bad that the government will never release the full details of what they were planning, and you sure as hell didn't hear anything from me."

Finn mimed zipping his lips and crossing his heart, which seemed to satisfy the officer.

"So the story we're telling the press is that a terrorist cell had been using that house as a base where they were planning for an attack on the Marathon using AK-47s and homemade bombs." Anticipating Finn's question, he went on. "We believe they were all Chechen nationals, though due to the explosion and the high heat of the magnesium-induced fire, we'll need DNA confirmation before knowing exactly who was in the building at the time."

"I read all that in the Globe. Well, except for them being Chechen. Or the fact they had magnesium-based incendiary devices. Neither of those things have been reported yet."

"They will be," said Sully.

"Wait," interjected Finn, "You said that was the story you were telling the press. Do you mean it's not true?"

"It's mostly true," replied Sully. "They were indeed a bunch of Chechen terrorists who were definitely planning an attack for Marathon Monday."

"On what? The finish line again? The starting line, maybe?" asked Finn.

Sully shook his head, which must have aggravated his concussion because he grimaced in pain before answering. "Worse," he said. "Much worse." Sully went on to explain the plot to use drones to drop acid on the fans at Fenway in order to drive them like cattle to the slaughter.

He finished, and Finn just stared at him in shocked disbelief.

"Holy shit," he said under his breath, then reiterated Sully's question from earlier; "What the fuck is wrong with these people?"

"Right?" Sully replied. "And can you see why we can't share all this with the public? There'd be a total panic."

"Yeah, I get that," agreed Finn quickly. "Don't worry, I never heard anything."

They sat in thoughtful silence for a few minutes, Finn absently fiddling with his visitor's badge and Sully nursing his scotch.

"So," said the injured cop, "there's more." But instead of continuing he just stared off into space until Finn impatiently rolled his hand in the air for him to continue.

"It's about our mutual friend."

*   *   *   *   *

"Zoe Kraft?" asked Finn, after a moment's thought.

"Yup," Sully managed through a wracking cough, "One and the same."

"Care to elaborate?" asked Finn.

Sully smiled and adjusted his pillows. "I could tell you, but then I'd have to shoot you."

"Ha, ha."

"Smart detective like you oughta be able to put it together."

Finn organized his thoughts before responding.

"Okay. So, am I to conclude that this group of Chechen terrorists — the ones who threw acid at you before blowing themselves to smithereens in Dorchester four days ago — were perhaps involved in helping the Tsarnaevs bomb last year's Marathon?"

Sully pursed his lips and shrugged. "I could never confirm such a wild theory without direct approval from my supervisor," he said, deadpan. "I also wouldn't be able to tell you that the leader of these asshats was a nasty piece of work named Ruslan Kadyrov, and I'm pretty sure he's the 'Scary Russian' your boy Miller observed having a couple meetings in Harvard Square."

"You have proof of this? Evidence linking this Kadyrov guy with the Tsarnaevs? Other than the word of a homeless junkie, I mean?" he challenged, playing Devil's Advocate.

Sully almost managed to hide his irritation. "Nothing concrete yet but the circumstantial is pretty strong."

"Such as?" Finn asked. When Sully declined to elaborate further, he wheedled a bit. "C'mon, you brought me this far…"

"Fine. Well, for starters, do you recall where the Tsarnaev pricks originally came from?"

"Dagestan, right?"

"Correct. But their father was from Chechnya, and the Tsarnaevs always self-identified as Chechen, not Dagestani."

"So?" replied Finn, "Identifying as Chechen doesn't make you a terrorist."

"No, but the Chechen community doesn't consider people like the Tsarnaevs true Chechens, because they never actually lived on Chechen soil."

"Okay, seems a little tribal, but how is it relevant?" Finn asked.

"Imagine we have two disaffected youths living in, but not fully accepted by, their adopted community — one that, by the way, has been waging a centuries-long insurgency against the unholy Mother Russia. Basically, their entire culture is based around resisting the invader and puts great stock in acts of violence against the oppressor. A kind of guerrilla machismo, if you will."

"Did getting blown up make you some kind of a professor?" joked Finn, getting a wry smile from his friend. "But the Tsarnaevs chose to emigrate to the US. Why would they then turn around and attack it? That doesn't make any sense."

Sully held up a finger so he could self-medicate with the Dixie cup before continuing.

"So the Tsarnaev father takes the family and flees the Caucuses for America, where he claims political asylum so that they can live a better life. But then they find out the reality about being a Muslim immigrant in post 9/11 America: that you can't get a good job, or even a shitty one when you're a filthy, swarthy foreigner who speaks English with a thick accent and prays to Mecca a hundred times a day. And so you find yourself sitting on a cheap couch in your tiny apartment that's home to just a few too many people, spending your days online or watching TV and you see the American government cozying up to your generations-long enemy, Russia. And you start to ask yourself, why isn't America helping us in our struggle for freedom? Where is America in our time of need? Do they not want us to be free? And finally, maybe America is secretly working with Russia to keep the Chechen people down."

"Sounds overly dramatic to me," Finn replied, skeptical.

"Sounds like a siren call for a couple of angry, disaffected kids already overly eager to prove how Chechen they are by lashing out at the country they feel betrayed them with false promises and left them with nothing but broken dreams."

"Well, when you put it like that…"

"Right? So in addition to your standard-issue Middle Eastern immigrants, we've also kept a surreptitious eye on the Chechen community as well," said Sully. "Actually, since just after 9/11."

Finn nodded and took another sip of his whiskey, enjoying the bite in his throat. "Makes sense."

"We've even come across some circumstantial evidence indicating that an element of the Chechen community in Boston may have been involved in a number of rather unsavory activities over the years. They're clever little bastards, though," spat Sully," never quite enough evidence to bring them in, especially with the Department's top brass always worried we'd get sued for being culturally insensitive and racist if we didn't have something rock-fucking-solid."

"I think this is the part of the story where you tell me you did something naughty," guessed Finn.

"Let's just say that I explored the edges of my authority and set up a little undercover op. The one I may have mentioned to you about a month ago." Sully grinned through another short spasm of coughing that took him off-stride. "My pitch was that, at the very least, the Chechen community could be a source of support or even recruits for terrorists trying to build networks of operatives here in the US. With the help of some like-minded civil servants like myself, I built an informal team so we could coordinate efforts with police in Detroit and New Jersey — the only other two places with any meaningful Chechen populations here in the US. Ultimately, I was able to place an asset undercover here in Boston."

"Pretty ballsy," Koenen observed. "How'd you get him in?"

"We placed him as a Chechen immigrant baggage handler out at Logan, overburdened by his mother's huge medical bills," explained Sully.

"Bait?"

"You bet, and they finally took it. A little over a month ago our man was approached by another Chechen named Vakha. In addition to his day job, Vakha drives and occasionally provides muscle for this Kadyrov guy, who, by the way, is not stupid. We've never been able to get anywhere near him even though we suspect he's been involved in dozens of crimes, thefts and murders. So anyway, this Vakha guy tells our undercover guy that Kadyrov has a thing coming up and would he be interested in a little side work? Our asset accepts, makes it through the interview process with Kadyrov, and joins his team."

"So that's how you know so much about their plan for Fenway," said Finn, impressed. "Did your guy get out?" he asked with sudden concern.

"He did," confirmed Sully, grinning. "He conveniently went out for a pack of smokes just before I went in with my TacOps teams."

Finn held his cup out and Sully refilled them both. "To the guy on the inside," he toasted. "Since your undercover guy has Kadyrov and his crew dead to rights on the Fenway plan... "

"No pun intended," quipped the injured officer.

"No pun intended," replied Finn with a wry smile of his own. "I take it you are looking for some sort of physical evidence to connect Kadyrov to the 2013 Marathon bombing so that you don't have to rely on the circumstantial argument? Or did you already find some?" he asked, excitement creeping into his voice.

"We are, and we haven't," answered Sully, partially dashing Finn's hopes. "At least not yet. The problem is that the Dorchester crime scene is a goddamn mess. What with the explosion, the fire, and who-all knows what chemicals, it's more like an EPA Superfund site. As a result, it's been wicked hard for our Forensics guys to get ahold of anything useful, but we'll get it locked down."

"But you're sure it was Kadyrov?" asked Finn, reconfirming. "For last year and this?"

"100 percent," said Sully definitively. "Our guy delivered incontrovertible proof Kadyrov was running the Dorchester operation, and he had to be the one giving help to the Tsarnaevs as well. It's the only explanation that makes any sense. I mean, the only other alternative is that there's some other secret terrorist cabal operating in Boston? I mean c'mon, what are the chances?"

"Occam's razor, right?" agreed Finn.

"The simplest explanation is usually the right one," paraphrased Sully.

Finn knocked back his whiskey, crumpled the empty Dixie cup and tossed it into the small rectangular trash can next to the bed. "Alright. That's good enough for me," he said, standing.

Sully leaned forward and clasped Finn's hand in both of his. "Thanks for coming in Finn."

"My pleasure, amigo. Thank you for..." here he waved his hand in the air to indicate their discussion. "You rest up and get your ass back out on the street where it belongs."

"You bet," said Sully, sinking back into the nest of pillows. Just before Finn stepped into the hallway, he called, "Hey Finn, tell Zoe Kraft that I'm sorry I didn't believe her."

"I will, buddy."

"Tell her she was right. She was right all along."

CHAPTER 17

9:15AM, WEDNESDAY APRIL 23RD, 2014
SUDBURY, MA

The next morning Finn peered through the windshield of the rented white Ford Focus, trying to figure out where he was, house-number-wise, as he drove slowly down the pleasant tree lined street with its tasteful homes set back on expansive and exquisitely manicured lawns. There sure was a lot of money out here in Sudbury. Finn had not grown up poor by any stretch, and after his parents' accident he and Heather had inherited a more than comfortable amount, so money had never really been that important to him. He wasn't sure if this was because he hadn't ever actually *needed* money and thus didn't truly know how hard it was to get your hands on it; or because he was just the sort of person for whom money didn't hold a lot of sway. He hoped it was the latter, but suspected it was at least partially a little of the former. Whatever the reason, he'd started his adult life with more means than most and had earned and saved well over the years as, generally speaking, he rarely spent money on himself except for necessities. Unlike many other single men his age, he didn't have any expensive cars (he had no car, in fact), sailboats, ski houses or alimonies. And when he did decide to buy something substantial, he made sure to pay for quality rather than for brand names or status symbols.

The numbered mailbox just ahead read '38' which would put the Kraft's house a couple more down on the right. Bright sunlight flickered cheerfully as it filtered through the massive oaks and maples which were just starting to throw buds into the warm spring air. He shook his head. Even the trees looked expensive out here.

However, the little time he had spent with the fabulously rich had revealed a grim reality behind the shiny facade: that one day you might wake up and realize that the thing you put your faith in couldn't truly help you when you needed it most. *All the money in the world won't un-injure your daughter's brain,* he thought as he pulled into the driveway and parked next to a steel-gray Lexus sedan. Although Zoe's money, in the form of having hired Finn, would at least bring her a measure of revenge and hopefully maybe some closure.

She was waiting at the open front door as he strode up a brick walk snaking alongside a meticulously maintained garden currently featuring a variety of red and pink tulips and bright yellow daffodils. Smiling and looking more relaxed than Finn could ever recall seeing her, Zoe wore a light green dress of some flowy material that swished somehow more sophisticated than flirty as she led him through the house to the back flagstone patio. Black wrought iron chairs sat next to an umbrella table of the same material and which boasted a clear Lucite tray holding a coffee thermos, two oversized mugs, spoons, sugar and a small white pitcher that likely held cream. A few feet away was a separate seating area with wicker couches and chairs arranged around a well-used fire pit. Finn sat while she busied herself pouring them each a mug of coffee; black with a little sugar for Finn and some cream and one Equal for her.

"So, any updates?" she asked eagerly.

"Actually, yes." said Finn, unable to suppress a smile.

She lit up. "And?"

"And… it's over. You were right."

"I was?" she asked, somewhat disbelievingly. "About what, specifically?"

"All of it. This case. Your theories. What Mike Miller told you. Everything." Finn gathered her hands into his and gave them what he hoped was a celebratory squeeze. "You were right all along."

She sat very still, cup and saucer halfway to her mouth, almost as if afraid that any movement would shatter the moment, the one she must have dreamed of so many thousands of times over the past year, the one where someone in authority told her she was right. And being right meant that she wasn't crazy after all.

"Zoe?" asked Finn gently, starting to worry that perhaps he should have chosen to ease her into this cathartic revelation with a tad more finesse. He started to reach for her cup and saucer, afraid she might drop them, when she finally spoke.

"Well," she said in a soft, calm voice, stopping his hand. "Isn't that extraordinary?" She lifted the coffee the rest of the way to her lips and took a deep sip of the steaming liquid. Fortified, she now turned to look Finn directly in the eyes. "Tell me everything," she commanded.

Finn did, after making her also promise not to divulge any of what he was telling her to anyone except her husband Will. Keeping certain key details to himself, he told her what he could about the Chechens; their likely connections to the Tsarnaevs; and that Sully was convinced they were behind the attack last year as well. When he finished they both sat in silence, contemplating the entirety of it all. Finn took a sip of his coffee, now lukewarm.

"Is he dead?" she asked in a small voice.

"Yes," said Finn, knowing who she meant. "The man who hired the Tsarnaevs to hurt Amanda is dead."

So much existential weight lifted off of Zoe Kraft's shoulders that Finn thought she might just float up into the mid-morning sky like a distracted child's party balloon.

"Thank you Detective. Thank you for everything." Tears of relief fell gently down her high cheeks.

"I'm sorry no one believed you," he said, including himself.

"There's no need for apologies, Detective Koenen. You took my case and now it's solved. Lieutenant O'Sullivan did his job and now the terrorists are dead. I think that's a pretty good ending to the story, don't you?" she asked with a sad smile, her words tinged with the bittersweet knowledge that while the death of her enemies was a victory of sorts, it would never undo or compensate for what they had done to her daughter.

"I can think of worse endings," agreed Finn.

"So can I, Detective. So can I."

PART THREE

The way to gain a military advantage, therefore, is not necessarily to be the first to produce a new tool or weapon. Often it is to figure out better than anyone else how to utilize a widely available tool or weapon.

— Max Boot[3]

CHAPTER 18

11:39PM, FRIDAY, APRIL 25TH, 2014
EVERETT, MA

Anderson Pierce reached high above his blond head, stretching his lanky six foot frame as he strolled across the dead-empty headquarters of Bay State HazMat on 15 Robin Street, where he'd been since five-thirty that morning. His spine cracked several times, the sound echoing around the quiet stillness of the loading bay, and he removed wire rim glasses to rub tired blue eyes. He'd spent the bulk of the last 18 1/2 hours doing his 'official' job, and the last few his 'actual' job. In fact, he was working on his final item right now. While making for exhaustingly long days, just a few more weeks at this pace and he will have siphoned off more than enough materiel for his purposes.

A blue collar town just west of Charlestown and north of Cambridge, Everett was home to hard-working families, recent college grads sharing cheap apartments and a fair amount of industrial activity. Anderson had been working at Bay State for the better part of a year now, his Environmental Studies-Chemistry double major from Brown making him completely overqualified for the loading dock job he'd taken. However, that same double major, supported by hard work and a 'go team!' attitude had allowed him to rapidly progress up the ladder and into a lower level management position. He was now second in charge of the loading bay / storage facility containing the hazardous and toxic chemicals Bay State HazMat collected and either disposed of or redistributed.

The twenty-five year old had quickly picked up how to use the inventory & shipping software and in no time was logging barrels, completing DOT shipping manifests and printing MSDSs (Material Safety and Data Sheets), as well as uncovering all sort of other software bells and whistles the old guy running the loading dock didn't know anything about but which had made everyone's lives easier. Anderson was careful to act humble and to deflect any credit to other people on the team and as a result was popular, respected and — most importantly — trusted.

How ironic, he thought, rolling a newly-filled drum along its bottom edge before setting it down next to the computer workstation set atop a sturdy wooden podium, *that the software used for safely tracking these chemicals can also be used to make them disappear without a trace.* He carefully applied a new label (K004 - wastewater treatment sludge from the production of zinc yellow pigments) on top of the one previously affixed to the drum (nitromethane with warnings for Health, Flammability, Instability). He checked the new label against what was showing in the inventory database, tapped a few keys, then smiled. *Another one for my cache. Another one closer to teaching everyone a lesson they will never forget. Another contribution to agony, death, and mass casualties.* He ran his fingers lovingly, possessively, around the top edge of the lid.

Bay State Hazmat had benefited from Boston's pharmaceutical and biotech boom in the late 1990's and early 2000's. The development and manufacturing of medicines at scale had both hazardous and biohazardous chemical byproducts (including his beloved Nitromethane) all of which naturally had highly-regulated disposal requirements. After all, it wasn't the 1930s anymore when you could just flush your waste down a pipe into the Charles River.

Bay State's founders had earned their chops working for national waste disposal giant Waste Management Inc, and had correctly ascertained that the burgeoning life sciences industry in Boston would need a waste partner who could handle their somewhat unique and specific needs. They quit WM, took out second mortgages, and sold their cars to start Bay State HazMat, initially marketing it as a 'specialty niche provider of waste management solutions, purpose-built for the biotech industry.' It had worked out better than they could have ever imagined and the firm had quickly grown into adjacent markets, like servicing the many university and government labs around the greater Boston area. Ten years later the two founders had happily sold the firm to their former employer who had finally concluded that if you can't beat 'em, buy 'em.

Now just another cog in the great WM machine, Bay State HazMat's high margins and ongoing profitability kept Corporate out of day-to-day operations, as they had other more troublesome business units to attend to. This laissez-faire attitude provided Anderson the operational freedom he needed in order to do what his patron wanted done in Boston. Well, *to* Boston, to be more precise. Hell, what they were about to do — what *he* was about to do — would rock the entire United States and change the course of world history. It would also erase the memory of Kadyrov's abysmal and very public debacle a week ago. Anderson knew he would succeed where the Chechen had failed. He had to. It was his destiny.

Though worried that the authorities might somehow connect him to the foiled plot, Anderson also felt no small measure of schadenfreude at the terrorist's downfall, given what a smug prick he'd been during their last meeting in Harvard Square a few weeks ago. Pierce hoped his old college friend Hamid had laughed uproariously at seeing Ruslan join him in Hell. Regardless, It was now Anderson's turn to prove himself

"You're special," he whispered lovingly to the nondescript gray metal drum filled with colorless, oily, liquid Nitromethane. "But you'll be so much *more* special when you meet my other friend, Ammonium Nitrate." Anderson usually capitalized the first letters of chemical names in his head as oftentimes they felt more real to him than the people around him. Ammonium Nitrate Nitromethane (more commonly known as ANNM) was the explosive used by Timothy McVeigh and Terry Nichols in the Oklahoma City bombing of 1995, which killed 168 people and injured more than 680 others. Even though they would be using only around 40% more product than McVeigh and Nichols, Anderson had his sights set on an exponentially-higher body count.

Initially, his Mentor had argued against Anderson's suggestion that they utilize this tried and true combination of chemicals, saying, *'it's been done before'*, and, *'I require something spectacular and impressive'*. Anderson countered that the impressiveness of his Mentor's plan would be exactly zero if he blew himself to smithereens utilizing an unstable, untested and unfamiliar formula. Eventually, Anderson's patient arguments using statistics related to detonation velocity, shock sensitivity and enthalpy of combustion convinced his Mentor that the mixture of ammonium nitrate fertilizer, nitromethane, and diesel fuel would provide the best ratio of potential damage inflicted to total accidental detonation risk incurred. In other words, ANNM provided Anderson with the best chance to kill as many people as possible without accidentally vaporizing himself first.

Anderson saw the fact that he had been able to change his Mentor's mind as high praise. The man was as smart as he was ruthless and terrifying, and for Pierce to have convinced him of something spoke to the high level of trust he had earned in the past year since...

An involuntary shiver derailed his thoughts, but he forced himself to finish them.

Since his best friend Hamid Farhadi had... died badly.

Hamid's choice of the Tsarnaevs had proven rash, and he'd paid for his mistake in a terrible way the previous July. Failure of any sort would elicit their Mentor's wrath, which was the stab of ice rather than the burn of fire, and he reminded Anderson of the Night King from Game of Thrones, his favorite show. Until the Tsarnaev debacle last year, He had communicated with Hamid and Hamid alone and that honor fell to Pierce afterwards. And though he still did not know his Mentor's real name or what he looked like, Pierce did know the man was deadly serious and wanted what he wanted; to bring down the West.

Once on board with Anderson's plan to utilize ANNM however, his Mentor lost no time putting things in motion. Somehow he arranged for the procurement of the thousands of pounds of everyday fertilizer they would need (for its ammonium nitrate), apparently through a dozen shell companies, all of which were making regular orders of amounts well under the levels that would alert authorities, who obviously kept a close watch on such purchases specifically to prevent exactly what they were doing. The fertilizer P.O.s specified delivery locations scattered all over Boston and beyond so as to make it even harder for anyone to catch a whiff of trouble.

Meanwhile, at BayState Hazmat, Anderson was busy skimming all the nitromethane he could get his hands on. Given that the compound's ability to efficiently donate nitrogen made it a key component in pharmaceutical manufacturing, a fair amount of it flowed through their doors. Bay State's trust in Pierce, plus his mastery of the waste inventory management and shipping software, made it laughably easy for him to slap fake labels on drums to ensure they ended up at the rented warehouse where Anderson would ultimately use the chemicals to build something historic, beautiful, and terrible.

He took a deep, fortifying breath and let the thick scent of oil mixed with harsher notes of astringents and other faint but nasty chemicals fill his lungs. He reveled in the heady brew. It smelled to him like he was making forward progress, getting closer to settling old scores. It smelled like victory. Thinking about how blissfully unaware everyone from his parents to his capitalist pig employers to the FBI were of his extracurricular activities, he laughed and said, "And, they'll never know," loudly into the still, cool air of the loading bay.

"They'll never know what?" asked a voice out of the shadows behind him.

*   *   *   *   *

Anderson jumped. *What the fuck*?

He spun and peered tensely in the direction the nasally voice had come from as a figure stepped into the moonlight spilling through the high windows.

Pierce relaxed. It wasn't the Feds. It was just the kid.

"Hey Carl!" he called with forced cheer. Carl Nowak was just a year or two younger than Anderson — a top-knot sporting, Gender Studies-Environmental Studies double major just out of Skidmore so overflowing with enthusiastic self-righteous optimism it made Anderson want to hit him with a wrench. "What are you doing here at," Anderson checked his watch, "almost midnight on a Friday night?"

"I was drinking with some buddies at Backbar over in Somerville and realized I'd left my phone charger plugged in at my desk. I'm driving down the Cape early tomorrow so I figured I'd just grab it on my way home." He pulled an iPhone with a cracked screen out of the front pocket of his skinny jeans and wiggled it around to indicate it was dead. "So, who'll 'never know' what?" he repeated, much to Anderson's annoyance.

"Nothing," said Anderson, sidling a step to his left to block Carl's view of the laptop. "I was just daydreaming out loud," he finished, trying to sound sheepish.

About what?" Carl inquired, the liquor making him jovial to a fault as he approached Anderson to give him one of those awkward "bro" handshake-with-a-shoulder-bump things.

Anderson smiled and looked down, feigning mild embarrassment. "Sometimes when I'm working late I talk to myself out loud, and I was just daydreaming about asking my girlfriend to marry me and then eloping so my parents would never know."

Carl laughed conspiratorially, as Anderson had previously told him (and everyone else at Bay State HazMat) that he didn't speak with his parents (true) because his father worked for Big Oil (false) and because Anderson was committed to helping to save the planet (definitely false). The real reason he didn't speak to his parents was because they were the epitome of everything that was wrong with America and the West. They had thousands of times more wealth than the average Indian, Chinese, Iranian or Ghanaian, but it was never enough for his social climbing mother who constantly berated his weak-willed father for not working harder, or being smarter, or having better connections so that they could live 'the good life'. And, whatever the fuck she thought that that was, she knew it wasn't in Stamford, Connecticut. Greenwich, maybe, or Rye, New York would do. But Stamford? *"Jesus Christ, Phillip, the* WWE *is based in Stamford. I would think we could do better"*, she had said on more than one occasion. And unfortunately, as an only child he had to bear the full brunt of his mother's remonstrations that nothing was ever good enough and his father's pathetic attempts to bond with a son he knew so little about.

So, he determined at a young age to get good grades so as to get into a good college (with at least a partial scholarship) so that he could get the hell out of his house and away from his sad little parents and their sad little lives that revolved around such sad, little things like who made more money, got a promotion, or drove a better car. His hard work and focus paid off with a full ride to Brown, provided he worked 15 hours a week and maintained his GPA. Successfully escaping Stamford, however, also left him unexpectedly adrift: unable to slack off on his studies thanks to his OCD-like approach to life, but also not entirely sure anymore what it was he was working so diligently *towards*. At the same time it also led to his meeting Hamid Farhadi (also an outsider, also working in the dining halls) — someone who understood Anderson's antagonistic feelings not just towards his parents or his town, but towards America as a whole, as a concept.

Hamid was also an only child from a similarly middle-class Persian family (he never called himself Iranian and bristled when anyone did) in Tehran. His father Dariush died fighting for the Iranian Army when Hamid was just five and his mother Anahita never remarried, which explained why he didn't have any siblings. A family friend had taken Hamid and his mother under his care and eventually sent (and paid for) Hamid to attend the prestigious Rugby School in Warwickshire, England, about 85 miles north-west of London. There, Farhadi learned that no good deed goes unpunished, as the generosity that made this world-class education possible also exposed him to other, less enjoyable things.

Dark-skinned, foreign, and exponentially poorer than his privileged classmates, Hamid had spent four years enduring a never-ending stream of jokes about 'the brownie' and had been called 'towel head'more times than he could count. This particular jibe especially rankled him because Persians didn't wear turbans, so these stupid fucking rich white kids couldn't even get their racism right. Hamid hated the UK for its smug colonialist, xenophobic superiority and hated the US because he claimed his father had somehow died fighting the Americans. Farhadi had never explained to Anderson what he meant by this other than to bitterly repeat his mantra that America had been starving and murdering his people since the 1979 revolution.

One night over cans of Narragansett and bowls of ramen, Hamid explained that he had grit his teeth and borne all of it — the abuse, the condescension, the frequent loneliness — because he had his eyes set on a higher prize: getting revenge and restoring his homeland to its former glory. Not that Hamid agreed with the religious fanatics who ran Iran today. He had been clear with Anderson that he thought they were venal, stupid and on the wrong side of history. The Mullahs' Republic of Iran was but a shadow of the great Persian empire that had once stretched from the Balkans in the west to the Indus valley in the east. Hamid believed in a new Persia which would unify the fractious governments of the Middle East into a single polity.

Not surprisingly, Farhadi fully blamed the West for the current mess in the region, claiming (accurately) that at the conclusion of World War I the western powers had carved up the Middle East with no regard to shared history, language, culture or religion. They had uncaringly lumped Kurds, Sunnis and Shias together in Iraq; forced Jews, Muslims and Christian Druze to all live in tiny Lebanon; and most egregious of all, enshrined a Jewish homeland in the heart of Palestine via the Balfour Declaration of 1917.

Much more scientist than historian, Anderson had soaked in Hamid's passionate, big-picture, long-term view of global politics, absorbing a range of perspectives he had never considered before meeting the Persian youth: that the Jews were pure evil; the Arabs stupid, medieval and short-sighted; and the Russians weak, corrupt and arrogant — an unsteady house of cards ready to fall at the first timid footsteps of the future. China had its sights set on dominating Asia and removing American influence. India was too much a chimera of a nation to ever function properly, and was for good measure terminally corrupt. Africa and South America were riddled with tin-pot dictators. Only the Persians were strong and smart enough to become the global power needed to counteract the predations of America and Europe.

So, bonded by common grievance and shared hatred, Hamid and Anderson had quickly become close and Anderson learned more from Hamid in four years than in all his Chemistry, Biology and Calculus classes put together. And when out celebrating their graduation together in Providence, Rhode Island three years ago, Hamid had asked Anderson to help him strike a blow against rotting corpulent America, Pierce had readily agreed. In fact, he had instantly felt a deep and profound sense of purpose, order, and worth he had never known before. Farhadi's trust in him had galvanized a million little thoughts in his brain, like a magnet brought near a confusion of metal filings, instantly aligning them all in the proper direction, ordered and full of intention. And now here he was, turning all those words into action, even though sadly Hamid was no longer around to appreciate it.

The job at Bay State Hazmat afforded Anderson access to trucks and other heavy machinery; a machine shop; storage drums, and a reasonably up-to-date lab. Also, he could get his hands on just about any nasty, toxic, flammable or explosive chemicals he desired, via the waste they picked up, treated and disposed. It was the perfect situation for what his Mentor needed him to do. And now this fucking dip-shit Carl, who had inexplicably walked in on Anderson while he was switching the labels and paperwork on his final barrel of the day, was perilously close to screwing everything up.

"You should totally elope, man," pronounced Carl, raising his hand for a high-five Anderson was compelled to complete. "That would really chap their asses!"

"We'll see," replied Anderson quietly. "I don't want to start another fight with them, I just don't want to deal with them at all."

"Don't be such a pussy, man! They're the ones killing the planet! Dude, you remember what you told me the first day I started here? *'Each of us has a responsibility to change the world, one act at a a time.'* So do it! Do this act and throw it right in their faces!" suggested Carl with great enthusiasm.

Like so many middle-class white Americans, Carl was full of hope and righteous indignation. *What a load of shit,* thought Anderson. *It's easy to be a rainbow warrior when you haven't sacrificed anything to the fight.* People like Carl drove Daddy's Saab to the political rally right before they flew to Aspen or the Florida Keys to drink $14 Margaritas and take selfies with a cardboard cutout of Jimmy Buffett. These self-absorbed, armchair intellectual Millennial losers would get what's coming to them soon enough. *Let's see how they handle a kick in the teeth,* thought Anderson, though what he said out loud to Carl was, "Ahh, maybe you're right. Thanks man, I'll think about that."

Carl grinned, came in for another boozy 'bro-hug' then headed off into the offices to collect his phone charger. "Don't work too hard, man," he called as he headed across the empty room to the far door into the offices. "You're gonna make the rest of us look bad."

Anderson smiled and called back with false jocularity, "Don't worry. You do a great job of that all by yourself!"

"Ha ha, screw you," Carl replied just before the heavy door slammed shut, the thunder of it reverberating around the loading bay.

Anderson quickly rolled his barrel over to its new temporary home next to the other two barrels slated for an early Monday delivery — one that Anderson himself would offer to make, in order to, 'give one of the drivers a break'. The address on the invoice was for a fictitious third-party distributor named Integrated Logistics Solutions, a firm that Hamid had incorporated in Delaware last spring so that it could rent warehouse and office space in the upscale Back Bay neighborhood of Boston, over across the Charles, south of here. Pierce had started storing the chemicals there a few months ago and the dipshits he worked for were none the wiser. He used money from his Mentor to set up a business checking account for Integrated Logistics Solutions so that he could issue proper checks and ensure all the paperwork was on the up-and-up.

Anderson logged out of the hazardous waste information management software, softly closed the laptop lid and left the building — and Carl — behind.

I will indeed change the world, one act at a time, he thought as he strolled casually to his car. *For death is the biggest change of all.*

CHAPTER 19

7:03PM, SATURDAY, APRIL 26TH, 2014
SOMERVILLE, MA

Cat adjusted the strap on her red floral skater dress and squeezed between a couple of businessmen-types engaged in an animated discussion about whether Michael Scott or Dwight Schrute was the better character on *The Office*. She reached the bar behind them with a smile on her face that was equal parts eavesdropper's amusement ('*Dwight Schrute is the perfect blend of 'American Gothic' and Machiavelli!*') as it was the fact that, judging by the raised eyebrows, smiles and solicitous space-making as she passed, her outfit was having its desired effect.

Despite Heather's urging that she let it go, Cat was still mildly furious with herself for asking Finn such a personal, loaded question on their first date. She hadn't felt that strong an initial connection to anyone — emotionally or physically — since, well, Thomas, and she'd let her guard down, giving 'Clumsy Cat' a chance to assert herself. She generally preferred keeping her embarrassing alter-ego under wraps until later in the getting-to-know-you process, given Clumsy Cat's unerring ability to say just the wrong thing in just the wrong way at just the wrong time. It wasn't that she *wanted* to blurt things out, it's was just that when she was happy, relaxed and excited, things had a way of going directly from her brain (overclocked to begin with) to out of her mouth, bypassing the higher cognitive functions entirely.

Catching his eye, she ordered a white wine from the very cute hipster bartender and wondered why so many men in their twenties sported such large and immaculately-groomed beards. She preferred the clean-shaven look herself, as beards tickled and stubble chafed when kissing. Finn was clean-shaven, and definitely kissable, and she'd ultimately decided on this particular outfit to hopefully facilitate that happening at some point this evening. Well, she corrected herself, he had been clean-shaven for their first date a little over a month ago and ideally he still would be. She'd most likely kiss him either way if things went well, but she would much prefer he sported smooth cheeks to scratchy.

Cat hadn't realized how much she had been hoping Finn would ask her out again until he'd called about a week or so after their dinner at Jae's. The conversation had been short but pleasant, and left her almost giddy with excitement and anticipation. 'Composed Cat' had chided herself for acting like a love-struck teenager, but Clumsy Cat has enjoyed the thrill and anticipation immensely. Unfortunately, her work commitments, including a conference in Singapore, had pushed their dinner into late April, an annoyingly long wait.

Nonetheless, here she was now at Dali, her favorite Spanish restaurant, wearing her go-to 'I'm interested in you, can you tell?' dress, and looking forward to putting the end of the last date behind them as they got to know each other better. *Just try not to talk about shooting people*, she reminded herself for the hundredth time that day.

"What's that?" asked the taller of the two businessmen that had let her through a few moments ago. "Did you say you wanted to shoot some people?"

Dali was, as always, crowded, chaotic and cacophonous, so much so that Cat hadn't realized she'd spoken her last thought out-loud. "No! Far from it," she replied, slightly embarrassed. "Just talking to myself."

"Happens to the best of us," the man replied, returning her smile and offering his hand. "I'm Glen. Glen Upton." He gestured to the other man. "And this is Teddy."

"Cat Rollins," she said, shaking each hand in turn, and watching Glen check out her left hand which bore rings only on her thumb and middle finger. "Nice to meet you."

"I know this is going to sound cheesy," Glen started, "but humor me."

"Okay," she said, mildly curious, "hit me."

"I feel like we've met before. Not in a past lives kind of way or anything like that," he added hastily. "You just look really familiar to me, but I can't quite place how we might know each other."

She appreciated the compliment of his hitting on her, especially because he was being sweet and dorky about it, and now that she looked at him a little more closely, she found he looked vaguely familiar as well. She was here to meet Finn of course, and didn't want to hurt the guy's feelings, but networking was a huge component of her job as a CMO, and she met literally hundreds, if not thousands of new people each year, so she wanted to sort out whether or not they actually did know each other. "Where do you live?" she asked.

"Davis Square?" he offered hopefully.

"South End," she said, and his expression fell for a second before rebounding.

"What do you do for work?" Glen asked. "Teddy and I are both Project Managers at Google in Kendall Square."

"I'm in Marketing at VersaTech. We're also in Kendall Square."

"Oh! I know you guys, but no," he said, shaking his head slightly, "I don't think I've seen you around Kendall." He furrowed his brow and swirled the beer in his pint glass as he concentrated, and Cat took a sip of her wine. "I know!" he said, suddenly, snapping his fingers. "You spoke at our Marketing Tech Stack Conference at the Ritz downtown last Fall." He grinned triumphantly while Teddy nodded his agreement.

"You talked about 360-degree engagement models that were coming to the fore thanks to advances in the Internet of Things, sensor deployment, and AI," recalled Teddy, eyes closed, two fingers against his temple.

Cat found herself both taken aback. She knew she was a good speaker, and thanks to VersaTech's position in the IoT market people generally listened to her, but still, she rarely got the fanboy treatment. She found she kind of liked the recognition, and if she weren't already about to start a date, she might have considered giving Glen a chance.

"Well that's very kind of you to remember. Honestly, I assume that people forget everything they hear at a conference the second they walk out the door." The three of them shared a laugh and Teddy started to say something but just then the door opened and Finn entered the restaurant, eyes scanning the bar for her. She craned her neck a bit and tried to catch his attention.

"I'm sorry," said Glen, following her gaze, "you're waiting for someone, aren't you?"

"No need to apologize," she said, "I am actually, and he's just arrived. It's been lovely meeting you both, and you're very nice for recalling my talk."

"Well," said Glen, giving it one last try with a mischievous smile, "you make quite an impression."

She smiled and squeezed his elbow. He was actually pretty attractive, with short, curly dark hair, a strong Roman nose, intelligent blue eyes and cute dimples. Six weeks ago she would have definitely engaged him in conversation, but at the moment…

Finn appeared at Glen and Teddy's elbows and Cat leaned in between them to greet him with a hug and a kiss on the cheek. "Finn, this is Glen and his friend Teddy. We were just talking and they very nicely remembered me speaking at a conference their company put on about a year ago. Glen, Teddy, this is my friend Finn Koenen." The three men shook hands, and Cat's ego puffed a bit when she saw her fellow tech execs slightly intimidated by Finn's unnervingly calm demeanor. Lots of so-called tough guys walked with bluster, gave crushing handshakes and took offense to anyone chatting up their lady friends. Finn's relaxed confidence, friendly grip and rugged good looks clearly spoke for themselves.

Showing some class, Glen offered to buy a round for Finn and Cat while they all waited for their tables. Dali did not take reservations, but the food was so good that it was not uncommon for people to happily wait sixty to ninety minutes at the bar drinking (the dangerously excellent) sangria and chatting with other patrons. This dynamic only added to its authentic European feel, and which made the inevitably long waits an integral part of the experience rather than something to be endured.

Before Cat could respond to Glen's kind offer, a short, stocky man in perhaps his early sixties came over and gave Finn a big hug followed by a kiss on each cheek.

"Buenas noches, mi viejo amigo!" he rumbled more than said in a deep, accented baritone as he clasped Finn's hand in both of his meaty paws. With his short stature, bushy dark beard and twinkling eyes, he instantly reminded Cat of a Spanish Gimli from the *Lord of the Rings* movies.

"Buenas noches, mi amigo mucho mayor!" Finn put his hand on the man's shoulder and turned him to face the others. "Sebastian, please meet Cat, and my new friends Glen and Teddy. Everyone, this is Sebastian Sanchez, he owns the place."

Impressed, Cat said, "It's a pleasure to meet you, Sebastian. I've always loved eating here." Dali's owner somehow found room in the crowded bar area to bow theatrically, making Cat, Glen and Teddy laugh. Sebastian motioned with his head and Finn and Cat excused themselves. As Sebastian led them away from the bar to their table, Glen slipped Cat his business card.

"In case this doesn't work out?" he said sheepishly in a voice only she could hear.

Cat squeezed his arm again and smiled. He had some balls for a Google tech geek, and she liked guys with some balls. Not more balls than sense, but certainly more than none.

As they threaded their way through the crazy melee of conversations, laughter, garlic, steaming plates and eclectic decor that was Dali on a Saturday night, she heard Finn asking after Sebastian's wife Lucia and their daughters Carolina and Alessandra ('*Wonderful! Beautiful! In love, every week someone new!*') and he in turn asked Finn about Heather ('*busting my balls*') and work ('*great, just solved a case*'). "So, we celebrating tonight?" Sebastian asked, his twinkling eyes looking past Finn to his date. "You are punching above your weight these days, my friend," he said in a lower voice, admiringly. Cat still heard him, and tried to hide her smile. Apparently she really had made the right outfit decision.

Sebastian deposited them at a small table in one of the rooms deeper into the warren-like restaurant, shook Finn's hand again, kissed Cat's in the old fashioned way, then waded back into the fray to keep the place from going off the rails.

"Hey there," she said, leaning in to be heard over the raucous din.

"Hey," he replied warmly, taking her hand in his over the middle of the table, already crowded with a small vase holding a few fresh wildflowers, salt, pepper, plates, silverware, water and wine glasses. "You look stunning," he said, giving her an exaggerated once-over.

The date was off to a solid start. "You don't look to shabby yourself," she replied, liking the way he filled out the arms and chest of his pale pink Oxford shirt, open at the neck. She'd definitely appreciated the view of his khakis on the walk to the table and, she was pleased to note, his face was freshly shorn. "Can I get you a drink?" she asked, blushing slightly at the look he was giving her.

Before he could reply, a waiter bustled up out of the crowd and put a couple more wine glasses down into which he poured a red liquid, replete with several chunks of fresh-cut fruit, out of a large yellow-orange earthenware pitcher. Finn waved his hands to indicate that the drinks were *a fait accompli* and they both laughed.

"It's not your first time here, is it?" she teased.

"Let's just say when I find something I like, I stick with it."

She raised an eyebrow at this and they clinked glasses. "Amen to that," she said and they sipped. "Damn," she said, "that's good!" She closed her eyes and allowed herself a moment to soak in the sensation of the sangria entering her system before addressing the elephant in the room. To her surprise, they both spoke at once. Her, "I'm sorry for asking that stupid question" intermixed with Finn's "I'm sorry I was so rude to you." They laughed awkwardly at this exchange then Finn indicated she had the floor, so she continued.

"I should have thought before I asked something like that," Cat went on, "or at least eased into the subject a little more carefully. Of course that's a…" she paused, looking for the right words, "…a tricky area for you. But there I was, throwing it out on the table right in the middle of what I thought up until then had been a pretty successful first date." She turned her voice up a bit at the end, making it a half-question.

"Best date I'd had in years." agreed Finn.

Her eyes flicked to the table. "Well, I'm sorry I ruined it," she said, overly self critical.

"You didn't ruin anything," Finn said quickly. "And I'm the one who should be apologizing. What kind of guy treats an intelligent and beautiful woman rudely just because she catches him off guard?" He shook his head at his own misbehavior. "So," he said when she raised her eyes to look at him again, "I'm sorry. It takes a lot to knock me off balance. Thank you for giving me a second chance. I promise to be better behaved tonight."

She reached up with her left hand and gave Finn's a squeeze. "Fair enough. But maybe not too well-behaved," she risked saying.

Now it was his turn to raise an eyebrow. "Done."

"Good. And feel free to elaborate on the whole intelligent and beautiful' thing. That's my kind of conversation," Cat said playfully, leaning back in her seat and giving Finn a look.

Laughing, they grabbed their menus and spent the next ten minutes debating which tapas they would order — Cat extracting a promise that Finn would try a bite of her grilled octopus, and in return she would try his bacon-wrapped prunes filled with goat cheese and almonds. With the awkward bits behind them, she found they fell quickly back into that easy, open, teasey, flirty vibe again. The back-and-forth banter flew and before they knew it, their waiter reappeared, forgoing pad and paper as he took their tapas and sangria refill order.

Fifteen minutes later found them digging into their first round of food, immensely pleased. After a few appreciative noises and a satisfied smile, Finn said, "I'm ready," and pointed with his fork at the small plate in front of Cat covered in reddish-brown chunks and a few curled, heavily suckered mini-tentacles. "But you have to admit," he continued, face screwed up, "it looks like somebody forgot to go to the market for a couple of weeks, so they threw whatever they had lying around onto your plate and called it 'Pulpo A 'Feira'." She snorted around a mouthful of the aforementioned octopus, and he finished, " More like, 'Bunch A' Crapola', if you ask me."

Cat laughed hard enough that a couple small flecks of octopus flew out of her mouth before she could get her hand up to cover, which got a look of amused surprise from Finn that made her laugh even harder. She realized delightedly that she hadn't actually guffawed like this in months. Maybe years. She made a mental note to thank Sebastian for his excellent sangria.

But it wasn't the sangria, or at least, it wasn't *just* the sangria. Cat realized that she liked this guy, that she felt like they connected, that they were on the same wavelength, despite being so different. *Or were they?* She also realized that, while it may feel like they were old friends when talking, she really didn't know that much about Finn's upbringing other than that Finn and Heather had grown up overseas somewhere and that their parents died a long time ago. Her analytical mind had a lot of questions, but she was determined not to screw this up by coming at Finn full force. If she were right about her feelings for him being reciprocated, they'd get to know each other better in due course. For now, she was content to bask in that rare but highly pleasurable feeling of new friends bantering like old ones.

Almost before she knew she was doing it, her right foot slipped out of its shoe and found his ankle under the table. Finn leaned his shin into her foot and they smiled at each other. They may banter like old friends, but Cat was starting to consider doing some things with him she wouldn't typically do with her old friends. And even though Finn was charmingly out of dating practice, Cat could tell he was seriously interested. As long as she could keep Clumsy Cat under wraps, things were looking pretty good.

"Everything okay?" Finn asked, giving her a quizzical look.

Cat grinned. "I'm just thinking I need to thank Heather for putting us together. I'm not much for blind dates, but she was quite insistent that I meet you."

Finn laughed, "I think you mean that my sister is relentless."

Cat agreed with a laugh of her own, then said, "Seriously. I'm enjoying this."

"Me too."

Cat took his right hand in both of hers and ran her foot up and down his shin a couple times and they locked eyes for a good long moment before she broke away, cheeks flooding with heat. Getting a hold of herself (*Down girl!*), Cat stood, announcing, "I need to powder my nose. And also make room for more sangria." Finn also stood (*Good manners, check*), and she headed around the corner to the bathrooms, miraculously finding one of them free. She did her business, made some minor makeup adjustments, and settled herself down. *C'mon, Cat. Act like you've been here before.*

* * * * *

Excitement and impulses now under some semblance of control, she returned to find Finn looking intently at something on his phone.

"Whatcha got?" she asked, leaning in by his left ear and placing her right hand lightly on his right shoulder.

"Hey," he said, "Sorry. Just got a news alert related to something I was working on, so I thought I'd check it out while you were in the loo."

"No worries!" she said brightly as he stood while she took her seat. She liked that and the fact he called the bathroom a 'loo' — it was sort of cute. "So, what's it about? Can you share?"

"Well, they released the identities of the dead terrorists from that shootout over in Dorchester last Friday. Apparently, they were all Chechen immigrants."

That explained the photo grid of nine scary looking Eastern European-type men she'd spotted on his phone screen. "Chechen?" she asked. "As in, from Chechnya, like in Russia?"

"Precisely," declared Finn, happily snagging the last scrap of octopus off her plate and popping it into his mouth. He wiped his fingers on the white cloth napkin. "Nasty place. Nasty guys."

She had no doubt he knew something about nasty guys, and she wanted to know more but didn't want to repeat her mistake from their last date. "Do you mind if I ask you a work question?"

"Sure. Go for it."

Cat took a sip of her sangria while formulating it. Well, she tried to take a sip, but her glass was empty. Finn grabbed the pitcher and refilled while gallantly ignoring her fuzzily sheepish look.

"You don't have to answer if you don't want."

"I know. Shoot."

"Were you by any chance there? At the shoot-out?"

"No," he said with a little laugh. "Thankfully"

She found herself both relieved and a little disappointed by this. "So were you helping the police in some way? Or did you have like, a private client?"

Finn hemmed and hawed for a few moments.

"Ooh," she said, eyes sparkling with candlelight and curiosity. "Whatever it is, it must be good, otherwise you would have just said." She leaned in over the table and he followed suit, clearly amused by her unabashed interest. "Do tell! Or is there some sort of client-investigator privilege thing?"

"Something like that," he replied vaguely.

"Hmmm" she said, frowning with dissatisfaction. "You know that's super annoying, right?"

His smile widened. "I do. But I take confidentiality pretty seriously. I'm also not really a, 'telling tales out of school' kind of guy."

Well, frustrating as she found that attitude at this exact moment, she couldn't fault him for it, and she had to admit it was refreshing.

"Plus," he went on, now sporting a wicked grin, "there are few things more enjoyable than keeping information from a curious woman."

This, she could fault him for. She smacked him playfully on the arm, hard enough to rattle the many small plates on the table. She'd had older brothers, after all, and she wanted Finn to know she wasn't one of those damsel in distress types. She knew how to take care of herself and was damn good at it. His grin widened as he rubbed his arm theatrically, and she knew her message had landed as intended.

He put his hands up in mock surrender. "Okay, okay. You win. I'll explain what I can without giving away anything I shouldn't. Sound fair?" he asked.

She gave him a mock piercing stare before capitulating, "Sounds fair."

Finn explained that he had a client whose daughter had been injured in the Marathon bombing last year and who hired him to find prove that others had been involved, despite all evidence to the contrary.

"So why investigate if you didn't think you were going to find anything? You don't really strike me as someone who makes a habit out of taking money from crazy old ladies."

He laughed. "Glad to hear it, and I'm not. And she's not an old lady. I mean, she's older than us, but not 'old' old, if you know what I mean. Though initially I did think she might be a little kooky."

"You didn't answer my question, Detective," she countered with a wry smile.

He fixed her with a keen, appreciative look and said, "I took the case because my gut told me to. And because I thought that, as a disinterested third party, if I could prove to her that no one beyond the Tsarnaevs had been involved, she could begin to move on with her life."

They sat in silence for a few moments, and she took his hand in hers over the table again, out of feeling though, not flirtation. Finn went on, explaining how he had reviewed all her evidence and chased every lead, including an eyewitness who turned out to have some unfortunate credibility problems. Eventually, he'd run out of things to investigate and had told his client that she could consider the case closed, though neither of them had been satisfied with that outcome.

"I should have known better," he finished, shaking his head.

"What do you mean?"

"It is extremely difficult if not impossible to prove a negative, but that's the position I put myself in when I took the case."

"How so?" she asked, intrigued.

"Well, answer me this: what would you need in order to prove that a man is cheating on his wife?"

"Easy!" she said, immediately. "All I'd need is a single incriminating photo or maybe a video."

"Perfect. So how would you go about proving that another man *isn't* cheating on his wife?"

This gave her pause, and he sat sipping his sangria patiently while she mulled this over.

"Hunh," she finally said. "I guess I couldn't. I mean, you can't."

"Really? Why not?"

"Because the absence of evidence today is not the same thing as the evidence never having existed," she replied.

"Explain," he prompted, a smile ghosting the corners of his mouth. She was on the right track.

""Even if the guy only cheated once, if you had evidence of it then it's been proved that he's a cheater. On the other hand," she went on, leaning into the table again, "proving that the guy *isn't* cheating essentially requires an infinite amount of evidence, as in, he's not cheating at this moment, or the next one, or the next, and so on."

"That is one hundred percent correct," he announced, clearly pleased by her logic. "If you ever get tired of tech marketing, you should consider a second career as an investigator," and gave her a high-five over the table.

She laced her fingers into his, making it look like they might start arm wrestling. "Well, I am kind of a prodigy," she announced, solemnly, getting another laugh from him. He was damn handsome when he smiled.

"So, I unwittingly placed myself in the position of having to prove a negative to this client; that there wasn't then or even now some other person or people behind the bombing that injured her daughter." They simultaneously sipped their sangria and Finn went on, "She fully believes that there *is* evidence, just that we hadn't found it yet. As such, she refused to close the case, but with nothing left to investigate, we ended up in this weird limbo, at least for a little while."

Something about the way he phrased that caught her ear. "For a while, until…" she probed.

"Until last week's raid in Dorchester," he said with a little relish. Cat could tell Finn was enjoying the conversation. He probably didn't get many opportunities to talk about his work.

"Aha!" she declared with triumph, now that they had now come full circle. "So… the raid in Dorchester is related to the Boston Marathon bombing last year?" she asked, putting it all together.

Finn looked around nervously and patted the air between them with his hands. "Hold on — I didn't say that. And I would appreciate it if you didn't say it again, either."

Cat was mortified. She'd let the moment distract her from keeping Clumsy Cat on lock-down, and she'd clearly spoken much louder than she'd realized. "Sorry," she said, lowering her eyes. "I get it. I won't say anything, I promise. Cross my heart. Scout's honor. In fact, I've already forgotten what it is I'm not supposed to talk about, so…" She trailed off, realizing that she was babbling.

She felt Finn's fingers beneath her chin as he gently lifted her face until they were looking into each other's eyes again. "I know," he reassured her. "And I apologize for the secrecy. I promise I'm not just being coy. I have a good friend inside the local law enforcement community and we help each other out from time to time." He paused to take his fingers from her chin, then continued, "I can, however, say that you might want to keep your eyes on the news over the next day or two. You might see something that…" waving his hands around as he searched for the right words, "…fills in some of the gaps in my story," he concluded, smiling kindly at her.

Relief flooded through her and Cat realized that she was, quite literally, sitting on the edge of her seat. She sat back, forcing herself to relax. "Well," she said, raising her glass, "Here's to nine dead Chechen terrorists."

"Here, here," he concurred, clinking her glass with his own, then downing the last of his sangria. He had a couple drops of red liquid sitting at the corner of his mouth and she reached over with her napkin to dab them off.

"Thanks," he said, "but enough about Chechen terrorists. I'm pretty sure Heather would smack me right now for talking about assholes like that on a date with you."

Cat laughed then said, with mock gravity, "You are not forgiven. For we must always speak the truth to each other about assholes. Especially terrorist assholes." Now it was Finn's turn to snort and laugh.

"Agreed," he said, composing his face solemnly. "Truth about assholes."

*   *   *   *   *

The next round of tapas appeared and they spent a while in happy, companionable silence, sampling and sharing the grilled pear skewers, sauteed mushrooms, and hot garlicky fried potatoes. Cat marveled at the flavors, and as usual found herself blown away by the food, the ambiance, the experience.

Finn finally broke their food reverie. "Tell me about your favorite book. Or movie. Or song. Or whatever. Tell me something about you that tells me something about *you*."

Delighted, Cat pursed her lips in thought. "Actually, 'book' and 'movie' are the same for me."

"*The Notebook*?" Finn asked innocently.

She laughed. "Hardly. It's pretty dorky, to tell the truth."

"Twilight?"

She pulled a WTF face. "Hardly. It's actually the *Lord Of The Rings* trilogy, which I realize isn't a single book, but I like to think of them as a single story over three volumes." She took a sip of her sangria and continued eagerly. "They've always been my favorites since I was a teenager, and I think the movies were just perfect. Like Peter Jackson had reached into my head and reproduced exactly what I imagined Tolkien's world would be like, but better."

Finn looked at her quizzically. "Actually, they're my favorite books too. Also since I was a teenager."

Cat continued, delighted. "For me, I just loved the multi-layered journey that took them from the peaceful gardens of the Shire to the fiery heart of Mount Doom; from sheltered innocence to facing the ultimate evil; from local boy to the greatest hero of the age."

"You keep talking geek to me like that, we may need to get a room," teased Finn lightly. Cat reached over and smacked his forehead with the back of her free hand. "Seriously, though," he continued, "I couldn't agree more. It's an incredibly powerful journey. But for me, it was always Sam, and his relationship with Frodo, that brought me back. About how, in the end, love triumphs over hate."

It was her turn to look at him quizzically. Was he mocking her? It didn't seem like it. Was he really for real? She could feel herself starting to get excited about the possibilities with Finn, which in turn ramped up her anxiety. In her admittedly checkered dating experience, there was always another shoe waiting to drop. *You know what?* she told herself, *who cares if there's still another shoe to drop? I like this guy, and he's hot, and he's into me. And… shit, did he just ask me something?*

Slightly flustered, she asked, "I'm sorry, what did you say?"

Finn smiled. "I said, 'love triumphs over hate'."

"Nothing after that?" she asked, mildly mortified.

He shook his head.

"You and Heather grew up overseas, right?" she asked quickly, looking to get the conversation back on track.

"We did."

"How was that?"

"Bit of a mixed blessing."

Before she could dig deeper, Finn chimed in with a question of his own.

"You were just in Singapore, right?," he asked. "Do you like traveling or do you just endure it for work?"

"Honestly? I love traveling!" she replied enthusiastically. "Of course, business travel kind of sucks, but the *concept* of traveling is still great."

"Did you travel a lot growing up?"

"Well, we didn't have much money growing up. I mean, we were comfortable, but not a ton of extra cash for Caribbean vacations or skiing in Park City. I did get to do the requisite backpacking around Europe after graduating from Smith, and over the years my career has given me a lot of opportunities to travel. Being single with no kids means I can always tack a couple of days onto the front or back of a business trip and do some exploring, which, it turns out, I really love to do."

Finn sat forward, mirroring the posture she had unconsciously adopted while speaking. Their faces were getting dangerously close over the cluttered table. He held her eyes long enough to start her blushing before he leaned back and asked, "So what's your favorite thing about travel?"

"The differences," she replied, feeling the heat in her cheeks as she plowed forward. "Every single place you go, the people are different, the culture and language are different, even the smells are different. Also, it's hard to fully appreciate something if you haven't experienced it first-hand, and I've always felt this drive to truly understand how other people think, how they make decisions, what motivates them, and, you know, how they get through life being *them*."

"You should have been a psychiatrist," he observed.

"Actually, I double-majored in Psych and Econ, but quickly realized I liked deciphering people more than I did fixing them, so I got into marketing instead of becoming a therapist." She wasn't apologizing, just stating a fact. She could tell he approved by the way the corners of his eyes had crinkled when she'd said it. "Marketers spend a huge amount of time, money and energy trying to understand more about their customers and prospects. What do they want? What would make them happier? What scares them? What are they willing to pay for? Is it something that gives them joy? Mitigates a risk? Enhances their life?"

Had Finn's eyes gone a little distant? Was she boring him about her work? A pulse of relief ran through her when Finn rolled his hand indicating she should proceed, so she did.

"That's one reason why I love traveling so much; it feeds my passion for deciphering people, which, it turns out, is sort of what I get paid to do."

He raised his glass in toast. "To getting paid to do what you love."

She sipped then decided to brag a little bit. "You know, a couple of years ago I was a finalist for an Effie award for successfully connecting with a global B2B target audience."

"You'll forgive me for not knowing what that is, but it certainly sounds like a big deal," commented Finn.

"It is," Cat replied, enjoying the feel of being a little cocky about it.

"Well, color me impressed."

"You know what I think is impressive?" she countered, wanting to return the compliment. "People like you who voluntarily put themselves out on the sharp end of the stick for the rest of us. Like what the police did over in Dorchester the other day," she said, gesturing vaguely towards the east.

Finn chuckled ruefully. "Well, there's a reason they recruit nineteen-year-olds to be in the armed forces. That's the age where you really believe that you (a) are invincible and (b) need to prove yourself to the world. Once you get to be my age, "he pointed to his salt-and-pepper hair, "you realize how 'vincible' you actually are and just how little you need to prove."

Cat laughed. "Fools rush in where angels dare to tread," she said, quoting the old maxim. Her smile faltered a bit as Finn's face went blank all of a sudden, and after a few seconds of his staring into space over her left shoulder, she leaned her head into his line of sight and waved her hand at him. "Hello? Finn?"

"Sorry," he said, eyes refocusing on Cat. "I haven't heard that phrase in a long time. It's something my mother used to say. She was Irish," he concluded somewhat incongruously.

"Were both your parents from Ireland?" Cat asked, trying to tether him back to the conversation.

"No," he replied a tad vacantly. "My father's Dutch."

"Oh!" she said brightly. "How did they meet?"

"At a party at Yale back in 1954," he answered absently. "She was down visiting from Vassar with some friends, and... Could you say that phrase again for me?"

"Fools rush in where angels fear to tread?" she said, tentatively.

He stared through her for a few moments before shaking his head as if to clear it. "Sorry. Occupational hazard. Sometimes ideas and connections come at you kind of sideways-like, and something about what you just said..." He smiled and took her hand over the table again. "Whatever it was, it'll have to wait. Right now I'm in the middle of a fantastic date."

The warm, tingly feeling returned and she squeezed his hand. "Me too!" she said, pleased to be back on track. "Tell me more about your parents."

And so he did, explaining that his mother Elise had been published in the prestigious *Atlantic Monthly* at the tender age of 16 in 1951 with a scathing comparison of J. D. Salinger's recently-published *Catcher in the Rye* with the tumultuous state of European politics after the war, in which she characterized many leaders as 'phoneys' and 'adolescent navel-gazers' who, like Holden Caulfield, whined, flip-flopped and castigated when they should have been helping to rebuild a better Europe. She guffawed at Finn's rendition of his mother's Dubliner accent and his father Jan's use of Dutch swear words around the house while they were growing up, incorrectly assuming the kids didn't know what they meant.

They finished the last of their tapas and Sangria, forwent desert, and suddenly they were out on the sidewalk in front of Dali, standing very close to one another.

Cat stared up into Finn's eyes, turned gray by the night, reached up around behind his neck and kissed him for what seemed like a long time and no time at all.

"That was really nice," he said afterwards, in an adorably awkward way.

Quelling her impulse to tease him for this somewhat underwhelming assessment, she said instead, "It really was," and kissed him again, deeply, happily. After a respectably long time they disengaged and she called an Uber. Thirty minutes after that they were taking each others' clothes off in her front hallway, the door barely having closed behind them.

Nice job, dress, she thought as it slipped to the floor and she stepped a little drunkenly out of it and into Finn's waiting arms.

*   *   *   *   *

Early Sunday morning Cat cracked an eye and even before coming fully awake she knew he was gone. The apartment felt somehow diminished without him there. She rolled onto her back and threw off the sheets, which were in a twisty mess anyway. It had been fun — very fun — getting them into that state the previous night, and she sat up, looking around for a note or a flower or something from Finn. Nothing.

She checked her phone and found a text from him with a 5:34am time stamp:

Hey - last night was amazing. Sorry Im leaving early but a work thing came up and I didn't want to wake you. I know we discussed hanging out today - rain-check on that? Followed by three emojis: a smiley face, a sleepy face and a thumbs-up. *Such a great nigt*

For some reason the misspellings aggravated Cat, as well as the somewhat abrupt ending of the text. And of course Finn's disappearing act. Hadn't he been different than other guys?

You forgot, Clumsy Cat. That's what the other shoe dropping sounds like, Composed Cat told her.

"Well," she said, throwing herself back onto the pillows. *"Godverdomme!"*

CHAPTER 20

6:57AM, SUNDAY, APRIL 27TH, 2014
ROXBURY, MA

Finn followed Sully across the third floor bullpen at Boston PD HQ, quiet and mostly empty as usual for this early on a Sunday morning. He checked his phone for the hundredth time since slipping out of Cat's apartment ninety minutes ago but no response yet.

After getting to know each other a whole heck of a lot better (and several times at that), they'd both fallen into a deep sleep around two am. Unfortunately for Finn, when he got up to use the bathroom three hours later, his brain finally figured out what it was about the conversation at Dali that had tweaked his radar. Cat had said, "...fools rush in..." and that sounded like, '...fools Russian...', which reminded him of the nine dead Chechen terrorists because technically Chechnya is part of Russia, and its citizens are therefore Russians. Not that any self-respecting Chechen terrorist would admit that, though. More than likely if they self-identified as anything else, it would be as Caucasian, as in, 'from the Caucasus Mountains' (as were the Ingush, Circassian and Georgian peoples, among others), rather than as European or Middle Eastern.

And, standing there naked and frozen in thought just outside Cat's bathroom at 5:25am, it hit him. They had all missed something. Something potentially very important.

He'd immediately texted Sully to ask how soon they could meet. The cop happened to be heading in for the morning shift and had a few minutes he could give Finn at 7:00 am, so the detective had quietly dressed and cast about for a pen and some paper to leave a note but (given he was dating a tech executive he should not have been surprised) came up empty. Knowing it was a poor substitute, but worried about missing his window with Sully, Finn decided to do the 'modern' thing and send a text instead. He knew he wasn't nearly as in tune with digital etiquette as Cat would be, so he could only hope his message struck the right balance and delivered the intended meaning: that he'd had a blast, felt badly about leaving unexpectedly early and wanted to make it up to her. However, reviewing what he'd sent from her point of view left him with the uncomfortable feeling that he may have made a bit of a mistake with the way he…

"Take a seat," Sully said gruffly, breaking into Finn's thoughts as they entered a well-worn interview room. The officer closed the door and motioned for Finn to use the perp side of the scarred and dented metal table sporting nothing but a ring bolted onto the top for shackles. The room also contained a couple metal chairs, several video cameras providing multiple angles of coverage, and in the corner by the door, a black plastic wastebasket overflowing with disposable coffee cups.

Finn placed a single sheet of paper facedown on the table and a small paper bag with a folded top next to it. He waited patiently while Sully ambled over and sat across from him. "You still remember how to read me my rights after a few days in the hospital?" Koenen joked.

"Yeah," Sully replied petulantly, "you got the right to bring me coffee when you text me at 5:30 in the morning."

Finn enjoyed watching Sully's mood brighten significantly when he produced a large, steaming cup of Dunkin Donuts coffee from the paper bag for him.

"Well, that's more like it," O'Sullivan said as he carefully pried the lid off and blew across the top. "I'm all yours for the next fifteen. What's up?"

Finn leaned forward in the purposefully uncomfortable perp chair and placed his elbows to flank the shackle ring while he thought about how to say what he came to say without sounding crazier than Zoe Kraft or Mike Miller probably had when they'd come to see Sully. *Well*, he thought, *everyone likes apologies.*

"First off," Finn began, "Sorry for bugging you so early this morning. Something popped into my head when I went to the bathroom and I didn't want to forget so I texted you while it was still fresh."

"I don't think I like where this is going," the cop said warily.

"Sully. You know me. I wouldn't be here if I didn't think it was important. And also potentially time-sensitive."

"Okay," said Sully, mollified by his favorite hazelnut coffee, "Whatta ya' got?"

Finn tapped tented fingers to his nose and started, "So I was out having dinner last night…"

"With who?" interrupted Sully.

"With a friend."

"You don't have any friends, except your fat slob of a partner, so this must be a new friend. Maybe a girl-type friend?"

Finn grimaced. Looked like the free coffee alone wasn't going to do it; Sully would apparently be busting his balls as well. Finn knew that Sully knew that Finn was a very private guy who didn't like talking about these sorts of things. Finn also knew from long experience that the cop took great pleasure in torturing the ex-Delta Force operator when the opportunity presented itself.

Finn took his medicine and answered. "A woman-type friend. And yes," he said, anticipating Sully's next salvo, "it was a date. A pretty good one, actually."

"Cute?"

"Very."

"She must be desperate then. Or perhaps she just has terribly low standards?"

"You forgot, 'just out of prison'," suggested Finn.

"You guys…" Sully made a fist and pumped his forearm back and forth.

"What are you, twelve?" retorted Finn. "And no, not that it's any of your goddamn business."

Sully gave Finn and his rumpled going-out clothes, way too nice for early Sunday morning, a once-over.

"Looks like maybe someone had a sleepover?"

Finn neither confirmed nor denied this conjecture.

Sully's face brightened as a thought struck. "Hey, you want to borrow my handcuffs for next time?"

"Settle down, Cupid. That's not really my jam."

"Jam? Nobody has a 'jam' at your age."

"Anyway," Finn drawled, trying to get his story back on track. "The date is going really well, right? I mean, like, really, really well. We're at Dali, hitting it off, the conversation's great, she looks great, she seems to be into me, the whole thing."

"And?" Sully prompted.

"And she makes this offhand comment that gets me thinking."

"About what?" asked Sully, curiosity finally overcoming his desire to bust balls.

"Answer me this: were all the terrorists killed over in Dorchester really Chechen?"

"Affirmative. Forensics somehow managed to confirm DNA from nine separate individuals out of that mess."

"Any other DNA on-site? Anything you couldn't identify? Maybe something additional or weird you didn't share with the press?"

Sully looked puzzled. "No. Nothing. Everything we found matched up with someone we could identify. Plus," he added, "my undercover guy who walked out five minutes before the assault teams went in independently confirmed the nine people we found DNA for. No one else was there, and no one escaped." He gave Finn a piercing look. "Why do you ask? And what's this have to do with what your sleepover buddy said?"

"Well," Finn began, "a little later on in the date, in the middle of some totally unrelated conversation she said the phrase, 'rush in', which made me think of, 'Russian' like the people."

Sully stared blankly.

"And I couldn't figure out why that caught my attention until I went to the bathroom earlier this morning."

"So you mentioned. This is relevant how?" asked Sully, irritation starting to show.

"Remember the meeting in Harvard Square that Mike Miller saw a few weeks ago? The one where a 'Scary Russian', presumably our friend Kadyrov, met with someone?"

"Yeah, what of it?"

"The guy Miller saw Kadyrov meet with was, and I quote, 'a dorky white guy'. A 'Caucasian kid' with short blond hair and blue eyes. 'Like a bowl of vanilla ice cream with vanilla sauce on top,' I believe is how he put it."

"So what?"

Finn flipped over the piece of paper on the table and spun it around so Sully could see the printout he'd grabbed off a bulletin board on his way up. Nine swarthy mug shots stared up off the page.

"Any of these guys look like a bowl of vanilla ice cream to you?"

Sully looked at Finn, then down at the pictures, then back at Finn again, this time with his hackles up. "No, but so what? Kadyrov probably met with lots of people, all the time. He was into a lot of underhanded shit," he said defensively.

"True, but remember, Miller also observed this same 'Scary Russian' meeting in Harvard Square a year ago with Tamerlan Tsarnaev and some other 'Middle Eastern Guy' discussing a terrorist attack just before it happened," countered Finn. "Then a few weeks ago, 'Scary Russian' threatens this 'Dorky White Guy' with something to do with acid. If memory serves, you and your men encountered some acid when you raided 'Scary Russian's' safe house over in Dorchester."

"So what's your point? We foiled the plot. Game over."

"For the Chechens, maybe, but I think someone escaped. Or was involved but not there when you raided. I think this 'Dorky White Guy' is still out there, and for all we know he's planning another attack, maybe even to get revenge for your ruining the last one."

Agitated, Sully abruptly stood up. "So you're telling me you think there's some secret 'dorky white' terrorist running around Boston who was working with Chechen gangsters? Jesus Christ, Finn, even if I believed you, what am I supposed to do with that? 'Dorky White Guy' describes a large number of the kids at Harvard, MIT, Northeastern, BU, BC..."

Finn waved his arms to stop Sully's rant. "I get it," he said, "but work with me here. I'm just following the evidence to see where it goes, and this is where it led me. Occam's razor."

Sully sighed and sat back down. "Okay, fine. For the sake of argument, let's assume that the homeless addict Mike Miller... "

"Homeless *veteran*," Finn interrupted.

"That the homeless *veteran* with a documented *drug problem* is telling you the truth, and not jerking you off under the table for more money and food." He held up his own hand to forestall Finn's impending interjection. "What do you want from me?"

Finn leaned in over the table again. "There's only one person alive who was in that house as part of Kadyrov's crew and who might know if anyone else was helping them, and maybe even who this Dorky White Guy is."

"No," said Sully immediately. "I will not reveal the identity of my undercover guy and I sure as hell ain't letting you talk to him."

Finn put his hands up in gesture of peace. "I'm not asking for that. I was just hoping you'd be willing to talk to him and find out if he saw or heard anything about this mysterious Dorky White Guy. That's it. Anything at all would help, and it can't hurt to check." Seeing that his friend still looked unconvinced, Finn decided to use the self-same strategy Zoe Kraft used on him a couple months ago.

"Think about it this way: if I'm right, and your guy gives us information that leads us to this Dorky White terrorist, he's all yours to arrest. Or shoot in the face. Whatever makes you happy, I'll stay out of it.

And if I'm wrong, and there's nothing to it, we can both sleep better at night."

"Oh, I'll sleep just fine tonight."

"But if another attack happens," Finn continued, undeterred, "and we didn't chase this lead down when we had the chance, that's gonna be on us."

Sully stared at Finn with equal parts annoyance, frustration and acceptance. Finn had hit the cop where it hurt most — right in his sense of duty. "Okay," he finally said grudgingly. "Give me a few days." He stood and Finn did too. "Come back on... say Thursday morning. I'll have had a chance to talk to my guy by then, and we can take it from there. Will that make you happy?"

Finn grinned, stood and shook Sully's hand. "Yes it will. Thank you. See? It's fun hunting terrorists together!"

CHAPTER 21

2:53AM, THURSDAY, MAY 1ST, 2014
TEHRAN, IRAN

Agitated ever since Kadyrov's سیاه بختی, his unmitigated disaster of an operation thirteen days ago, the Iranian had obsessively monitored the American and British news services, looking for any hint of a sign of an inkling that they were onto him. So far nothing even remotely close to the real truth had come out, so for the time being his involvement appeared undetected. The only potentially concerning detail so far was that the authorities claimed to have killed 'all nine' of the Chechen terrorists, but he had clearly specified 13 for Kadyrov's team. Had four men somehow escaped the assault? If so, when captured, was it possible one of them could provide a detail that might lead back to him?

He found this possibility disconcerting.

However, in retrospect it was clear the police had known in advance about the Chechen cell, so they also likely knew how many were involved, and if any had escaped the carnage in Dorchester then, based on last year's manhunt for the Tsarnaev idiots, the entire country would be out looking for them. Thankfully, the authorities' words and behaviors since then clearly demonstrated they believed all the perpetrators were dead. Given that, the Iranian concluded that Kadyrov must had modified his very clear and precise instructions without his approval.

What kind of a world is it, he thought, *when one businessman can't trust another?*

Unfortunately, if the Fenway attack fallout did end up blowing even remotely in his direction he would be forced to act. He could not allow Kadyrov's stupidity and poor judgment to jeopardize his ultimate objectives, even if it meant cauterizing this particular wound by abandoning the next carefully-planned attack and liquidating his remaining asset in Boston.

Speaking of... the Iranian leaned in over his desk and maximized a window on his laptop. He unmuted the live stream and spun his chair around to sit. Earlier in the day Pierce had alerted him to an upcoming ABC News report on the whole affair that he should monitor.

"And up next, an exclusive interview you won't want to miss," declared ABC studio anchor Bob Jenner from the laptop. "Gabi Mendez has that story."

Mendez appeared in a small window over Jenner's shoulder, sitting next to some woman in a fussy-looking living room. As he finished, Mendez's window expanded to fill the screen.

"Thanks Bob. I'm here in Sudbury, Massachusetts, a wealthy suburb about 23 miles north-west, and a world away from, the hardscrabble blue-collar neighborhoods of Dorchester. Yet there is an unlikely connection between this suburban oasis and the small, single family homes of Hanesborough Street." Gabi turned from the camera and faced the prim, late-fifties-something wealthy woman seated next to her.

Alarm bells started going off in the Iranian's head. This was heading in an unexpected direction, and he very much did not like surprises.

"This is Zoe Kraft. Homemaker, socialite, charity volunteer." A pause. "Mother." Gabi gave a warm smile. "Hello Zoe."

"Hello," said the woman, looking uncertainly from Gabi to the camera and back.

"Zoe's daughter Amanda," said Mendez, holding up a large silver framed picture of a young woman in Boston College graduation regalia, "was one of the more than 250 people injured by the Tsarnaev brothers last year when they bombed the Boston Marathon."

Mendez paused and gave Zoe Kraft a somber look that radiated deep sympathy. "Amanda was badly injured that day, wasn't she?"

"She was," replied Zoe in a tight voice.

"And while some of her injuries have healed, unfortunately there are others that never will."

"That's true," the distraught mother replied. "She'll never... She won't be..."

Gabi gave Zoe a moment to steady herself. Clearing her throat, she went on, "Thanks to the wonderful doctors at Mass General and Brigham & Women's hospitals, Amanda survived, despite suffering irreparable and irreversible brain damage in the attack. Among other injuries."

Gabi reached across and took Zoe's hands in her own, the very picture of empathetic support and care. "I'm so sorry," she said. "It must be so terribly difficult."

Zoe nodded. "It is, but Amanda's father and I are just happy we still have her. Three other families lost someone forever that terrible day. We feel lucky just to have the gift of more time with our daughter, despite the difficulties that come with her situation."

A look of annoyance flashed briefly across Gabi's face as she started to speak and it seemed to throw the Kraft woman off stride. "Excuse me Ms. Mendez," Zoe interrupted her, "but could you please repeat that?"

Face composed again, Gabi said, "Of course. I was just saying that you weren't satisfied with the official explanation that the Tsarnaev's were solely responsible for your daughter's injuries, were you?"

The Iranian froze. Was this reporter about to connect the Tsarnaevs and Kadyrov's crew together? And them both to him? He leaned in even closer to the monitor, unblinking.

"Yes, you're correct. I had some… theories about that," confirmed Mrs. Kraft.

"And you went to the police? Federal agents?"

"Yes, I went to all of them, multiple times after the attack."

"And what did they say to you?"

"They thanked me for my concerns, assured me they had the investigation well in hand and that the Tsarnaevs had acted alone."

"But you didn't believe them," prompted Mendez.

"Well, frankly, those two boys seemed way too stupid and arrogant to have pulled off something that sophisticated."

The Iranian might have laughed if it weren't so painfully true. Thankfully, the threat of unrelenting brutal torture for his parents would keep the younger Tarnaev's mouth shut all the way to the electric chair.

Gabi nodded, turning to face America through the camera. "Initially, a number of agencies had the same suspicions, yet for some reason discarded them. However, as the dramatic events of the past week have shown, there *was* someone else involved in the Marathon bombing, and consequently that you were right all along!" she finished triumphantly.

Zoe gave a weak smile and began to speak, "It's been quite a…"

"So here we are a year later," interrupted Mendez, a sudden edge in her voice, "and since neither the police nor Federal officials believed you, we came within a hair's breadth of another unspeakable tragedy, another Marathon Massacre many times over."

"Well, I'm not sure I…" Zoe tried interjecting.

"A year wasted," Mendez went on, righteous fury now blazing in every word. "A year in which we could have uncovered this cancer growing at the heart of Boston, a year in which we could have identified and arrested the nine terrorists. A year in which the police, and the Federal agencies sent to support them, could have been making America safer. But they didn't. They let their arrogance and greed for easy convictions and cleared cases blind them to the apocalypse brewing quite literally in front of their faces."

The Kraft woman seemed stunned by this sudden, angry change of direction from the interviewer.

"Doesn't that make you angry, Mrs. Kraft? That you were right, and all those patronizing officials who ignored you and your theories were wrong? Shouldn't they be held fully accountable for their dereliction of…"

"Actually," the Kraft woman interjected, "there were two people who believed me."

"I'm sorry, what?" stammered Mendez, clearly wrong-footed.

Zoe suddenly seemed more confident now that she had wrested control of the conversation away from the news anchor. "First by Mike Miller, who is a poor homeless veteran living in Harvard Square and then Finn Koenen, a former Army Ranger and private investigator I hired when the authorities were unable to assist me further."

The nondescript office, deep inside a secret government installation in Tehran, instantly fell away as the Iranian's entire being focused on the interview being conducted 6,000 miles away.

"And how were these two men able to help?" asked Mendez, quickly recomposing herself and pulling at this new thread.

"They did some legwork based on my ideas and were able to uncover the terrorist cell over in Dorchester," said Zoe.

"Go on," Mendez prompted with barely restrained excitement.

"Well," said the odd older woman with a guilty glance down at her lap, "of course once they uncovered the existence of the cell they contacted the Boston Police Department so that, with their greater resources and training, they could take care of it in an appropriate way."

"So are you telling me," Gabi asked slowly, "that not only did you suspect the existence of more terrorists in Boston almost a year ago — something the police explicitly and publicly discounted — but that you also hired the private investigator who then found the terrorist cell in Dorchester and told the authorities about it?" She seemed almost giddy.

"Um, I guess?" Zoe responded uncertainly. "I just wanted to thank these two men for believing in me and for helping bring these horrible people to justice."

"And what was that detective's name again?" asked Mendez.

"Finn. Finn Koenen," Mrs. Kraft replied haltingly, suddenly seeming unsure of herself.

"So how did you find this detective Finn Koenen?" asked Mendez.

"One of the Boston Police Detectives connected me with him." replied Zoe, almost absently.

Mendez's perfectly-manicured eyebrows shot up in delighted surprise. "The police sent you to the detective who then solved the case the police couldn't, or wouldn't, solve themselves?"

Zoe abruptly stood up and plucked the Lavaliere mike off the front of her sweater. She held it up too close to her mouth and said loudly, "This interview is over. I think it's time for you to go."

The broadcast quickly cut back to Bob Jenner in the studio and the Iranian minimized the window, staring off into infinity, thunderstruck for the first time in more years than he could count.

Finn Koenen?

He had known a Finn Koenen once. Many, many years ago. Several lifetimes ago.

Finn Koenen. We were friends once.

Brothers, even.

Once…

*   *   *   *   *

4:07PM, TUESDAY, MAY 22ND, 1979
TEHRAN, IRAN
35 YEARS AGO

Dust devils whirled around the courtyard, leaving a gritty taste in Reza Moradi's mouth that went all but unnoticed by the eleven-year-old. Equally ignored were the beads of sweat dripping down his spine under a thin white t-shirt, the afternoon sun unusually hot for late May in Tehran. Nor was he distracted by the frequent laughter emanating from the small round table ten meters away where his father and his American friend Mr. Koenen sipped bitter coffee from tiny porcelain cups.

The incessant sighing and fidgeting coming from the other side of the inlaid wooden chess board however, were another matter. Recognizing this for the gamesmanship it was did nothing to lessen its effectiveness in disrupting his concentration, and Reza was annoyed with himself for letting Finn's go-to ploy get to him.

With an effort he pushed these unproductive thoughts away, cleared his mind and reassessed the board. The game was well underway, with a roughly equal assortment of heavy stone pieces sitting captured off to the side. Reza (as usual) had taken control of the vital central area of the board, but his American friend had (as usual) made a nuisance of himself around the edges as he probed for weakness.

Just a few moments earlier, Reza had spotted it — the path to victory. Keeping his face composed, he worked quickly through the implications, assessing Finn's possible counter-moves, and his own in reply. Tamping down a rising excitement in his belly while Finn sighed theatrically (again), Reza rechecked the permutations and probabilities. Finn had indeed made an error with his last move, overplaying his position and exposing his Queen to a forked capture in three moves. It was *right there*. He was going to win. He was finally going to win.

Reza and Finn had known each other their whole lives. Other than spending the first six months of his life in Washington DC where he had been born, Finn had grown up in Tehran. His mother Elise taught Irish Literature and his father Jan worked for the U.S. State Department, posted the last 14 years to the American mission in Tehran. Uncharacteristically for Embassy staffers, Jan and Elise's best friends were not other Americans but rather an Iranian government official and his wife, Amir and Fairuza Moradi. Their youngest son Reza, born just a few weeks after Finn, had been a welcome surprise to their other children: Narges, Jalil, Parvaneh, and Mas'ud. Thanks to the parents' close relationship, the two boys had grown up more like twin brothers than friends.

Both were highly intelligent, hard working, athletic and competitive, but where Reza was structured, methodical and intense, Finn was unstructured, creative and generally easier going. Too young yet for jobs of their own or to be off together around the city unsupervised, they often accompanied their fathers for endless hours of conversation and political arguments in boring government buildings, crowded coffee shops, and, most often, this very courtyard behind the Moradi residence. Looking for ways to corral the boys' rambunctious natures, Jan and Amir had early on introduced them to the game of chess as a way to sharpen their minds while quietly wiling away the long, hot afternoons of sonorous discussions.

And in all those many hundreds of hours of chess, Reza had never beaten Finn. He had forced a fair number of draws, but had never handed the American boy a proper defeat. Not one time.

Until today.

Reza rested a finger tentatively on top of his Queen's Bishop and was rewarded by a smile ghosting across Finn's face. Sliding the Bishop diagonally looked tempting but was in fact a trap laid by Finn and spotted several moves ago by Reza. He removed his finger from the piece and faked a minor show of frustration, shaking his head in mock annoyance. Acting impatient, he made what he hoped looked like an inconsequential pawn move instead; the stalling move of a player unsure of his plan. Reza was secretly pleased with his performance — he was getting pretty good at playing whatever role circumstances demanded.

Nothing to see here, Reza thought, *that's just me getting spooked by your trap.*

Finn grunted and studied the board for all of about ten seconds before decisively moving his own remaining Bishop into a mildly threatening but well-protected spot.

Hope flared in Reza's chest. Finn had ignored his last move entirely! Two more moves and Reza would have Finn's Queen and soon thereafter, his first victory over the American. Reza again forced himself to calm down and focused on reviewing all likely possible scenarios again, arriving at the same conclusion: he had Finn dead to rights. Accordingly, Reza moved his King-side Knight into position.

"Hunh," said Finn, cocking his head first one way, then the other, as if the different angles would reveal different games. A few seconds later he moved one of his pawns forward, away from its protection, to vaguely threaten one of Reza's pawns.

Reza hesitated. He hadn't expected Finn to make that particular move. Frankly, it wasn't a very good one, as the pawn being threatened was currently protected by two of Reza's other pieces, so as threats went it was kind of hollow. *In the land of the blind, the man with one eye is king!* he thought gleefully, having waited a long time to best his friend on the chess board.

Reza couldn't resist taking the free piece, which wouldn't affect his main strategy other than to delay it by a move. He decided he could wait to watch the realization dawn in Finn's eyes that he was beaten and reached out to move his Queen across the board to capture the isolated pawn Finn had arrogantly left unprotected. In one smooth motion he deftly placed his Queen and snatched up Finn's piece, a grin lighting up his face.

Finn looked stonefaced at Reza's move, then up at his triumphant smile, then down to the board again. Bellows of their fathers' laughter echoed around the courtyard and yet another dust devil whirled its mischief through the lines of laundry hanging to their left — the boys paying none of it any mind as they sat intense and motionless over the chessboard, as do all who have reached the denouement.

"That's your move?" asked Finn, eyes again coming up to meet Reza's.

"It is," replied the Iranian triumphantly.

Finn smiled. "Are you sure?" he asked condescendingly.

Reza was irritated. Did the idiot not see that he was finished? "Of course that's my move!" he snapped.

Finn shrugged. "Okay," he said resignedly and moved his knight, attacking Reza's Queen while simultaneously revealing an attack on Reza's King. "Check," he announced smugly.

Reza stared at the board in disbelief. *This can't be*, he thought, desperately looking for a way out, a mistake, an illegal move, something, anything.

"It's checkmate in three moves, if that helps," offered Finn, unhelpfully.

Reza cursed in Persian and unceremoniously swept the pieces off the board, scattering them across the yard. His father's laughter cut off abruptly.

"Reza!" he called sternly, the sunny courtyard now dark and chilly to the frustrated youth. "Come here."

"Dude!" said Finn, shocked by the outburst. "Don't be such a spaz! It's just a game." He held out his hand to shake. They always shook at the conclusion of every game. Their fathers had instilled a strong sense of etiquette and good sportsmanship in their sons, and shaking hands was the way temporary opponents remained permanent friends.

Screw that, thought Reza, pushing past Finn with a scowl and skulking over to receive a tongue-lashing from his father.

"I mean," Finn called to Reza's back, "It's a game you never win, but it's still just a game."

We'll see about that, thought the young Iranian. *We'll see who wins in the end.*

*   *   *   *   *

PRESENT DAY

So.

His childhood friend had resurfaced, apparently blundering into Reza's Marathon operation and fucking everything up. Reza had long ago chosen to forget about Finn, despite what his honorless snake of a father had done to the Moradi family. Finn may have been an arrogant prick of a boy but his father's sins were not his own, so Reza had been content to not think on him anymore. Besides, truth be told, Finn had been there for Reza when his Iranian schoolmates routinely teased and ostracized him for his father being friends with Finn's father, an American pig. In a weird way, for those years they had known each other back in the 1970s, they had been more like fiercely competitive brothers than friends.

Despite coming from two very different worlds, they shared much in common: their fathers worked closely together for their respective governments; both were athletic, intelligent and competitive; and, as it turned out, neither had many friends. Reza was always so quick to remind everyone how much smarter he was than they and Finn was an American whose government propped up the Shah and his vile secret police — the *Savak* — who killed at will without compunction or repercussion.

One day, when he had been but nine or ten, an older schoolmate had attacked Reza out of nowhere, shouting that his grandfather had been taken by the *Savak*. Reza had badly beaten the much larger boy and been sent home, unfairly in his opinion, where he found his father Amir waiting for him with a sad smile. Instead of punishment, his father gave him the truth. Before doing that though, his father explained that the truth was often unpleasant, sometimes terrifying, but always clarifying, and also that a thing once known cannot be *un*known, so Reza should be cautious in its pursuit. In addition, he counseled Reza never to ask him a question he wasn't ready to hear the answer to. Reza decided then and there that he was ready, so he asked was it true? Had the *Savak* taken Farshad's grandfather? If so, why? And what had happened to him?

Amir looked into his son's eyes and searched them for a few moments, apparently finding what he sought. "Mohammad Reza Shah Pallavi is the leader of our country. He is a good man at heart." Amir smiled and tousled Reza's unruly mop of curls. "Good enough that we even named you after him." The smile faded and hardness crept into his father's eyes. "But even the best of men make mistakes and choose the wrong path now and again."

Reza nodded, "Yes, Papa. I understand."

"Good. Because this is what has happened to the Shah. He has let fear make his choices for him, and the only thing fear wants to see is more fear, so yes, there is a secret police called the *Savak*. Yes, they kidnap, torture and kill people, like Farshad's grandfather. And yes," he continued, anticipating Reza's next question, "sometimes those people are innocent. Does this bother you?"

Ignoring the question, Reza asked a more important one. "Do you help them?"

"What?" replied his father, surprised.

"Well, you work for the Government, you're friends with Americans, you always defend the Shah, and you didn't want your children to know that bad things were going on." There was no judgment in his voice, only a thirst for the truth.

"Well, that's a complicated thing," said his father, eventually.

"Can you explain it to me?"

"I can try." Amir shifted position until he was sitting down on the smooth wooden plank floor next to crosslegged Reza. And, looking intensely at his youngest through swirling motes of dust caught in the afternoon sunlight, he did.

"I do not directly help the *Savak*, or have anything to do with any of that. Do you believe me?"

"I do Papa," he replied.

"Good. Now, I could just leave it there," he went on, "but reality always has subtlety and layers. Let me explain. I believe the Shah is a good man in here," he reached across and tapped Reza on his chest, over his heart. "But he has lost control of here," and Amir tapped Reza's forehead. "Under normal circumstances, we would find a way to have him step aside, or we could minimize his influence. But these are not normal times. You see it. Religious fundamentalism is on the rise and religion cannot be reasoned with. Because it is always based on faith, it is by its very nature not rational."

He paused and Reza nodded for him to continue.

"If the Shah falls, it will be bad. Very bad. The zealot exile Ruhollah Ayatollah Khomeni will return to take over, many will lose their lives, and all will lose their freedoms. I am working to find another solution that will prevent Khomeni and his fanatics from gaining power while removing the Shah so that he can do no further damage to the country he loves but is ruining. This is a very difficult balancing act, and a much bigger problem than one man can handle alone."

A light bulb went off. "So that's why you are working with the Americans," Reza declared.

Amir smiled, clearly pleased. "It is. The Americans are not our enemies, as the Mullahs would have you believe. They are not quite our friends either, but for now our interests in a stable, reasonably democratic Iran coincide."

Reza quoted, "The enemy of my enemy is my friend."

"I see you *have* been studying!" Another hair tousling. "But understand this, my son. An alignment of interests is not the same thing as trust. Trust is only for a few special people who have earned it." He patted Reza meaningfully on the knee, making him beam with pride. "In a happy quirk of fate, it turns out that Finn's father, Mr. Koenen, is one of those people we can trust."

This both did and did not surprise Reza: surprised because Finn's parents were Europeans who had chosen to become Americans, and forsaking the country of your birth felt somehow like a pretty big breach of trust; but not surprised because anyone could tell that the families were tight (not that Finn's attractive older sister Heather ever said a word to him) and that his parents trusted these Americans implicitly. Family was sacred in Persia, and the Koenens had clearly been invited into the Moradis'.

So, like their fathers, Reza and Finn had spent many, many hours together, unlikely friends who became brothers of circumstance. At least until the 1979 Revolution. And what happened after...

Reza drained the crystal tumbler and put it heavily down on the desk.

Fate has put you back on the board for a reason, he thought, *so I must reassess and perhaps reposition some of my own pieces.*

Reza stared off into space, swirling the remains of the ice around in his glass as he sifted through a three dimensional matrix of possible moves, feints, sacrifices and end games. After a while, he concluded that he had too many variables and not enough data, so he decided to acquire additional intel on Finn and what he had been up to since they'd last seen each other. The mention in the news story of his having being an Army Ranger in particular gave Reza pause for thought. Pulling a small metal key from his pocket, he used it to unlock one of his desk drawers. He reached into the back and hunted around until he found what he was looking for. Pulling out a secure SAT phone, he powered it up and selected the only number saved on it. It was answered on the second ring.

"Yes?" said the deep male voice on the other end, with just the trace of a North Carolina accent.

"I need information"

"Well, 'the work of a nation' truly never ends," replied the man, quoting the official motto of his long-time employer.

"I need everything you have on a Finn Koenen. He's just been interviewed on your ABC News about his involvement in the incident in Boston last week. Including his time as an Army Ranger. I want it all, especially anything classified," he demanded.

"Is that so?" inquired the American lazily, "As it turns out, not only is my right-hand man an ex-Army Ranger himself, but he also happens to be in Boston as we speak. Perhaps they know one another."

"I don't care how you get it," interrupted Reza, "I just need it ASAP."

After a pause, the American asked in his infuriatingly slow manner of speaking, "And for delivering this sensitive information ASAP, you will provide me with…?"

Reza counted to five then said, "I will give you proof that, earlier this year, Syria used chemical weapons on its own people."

"Did they?" asked the CIA man, mildly surprised.

"Does it matter?" snapped Reza.

Reza heard the American's laughter echoing hollowly around his tiny office in far away Langley, Virginia. "I guess not," he finally replied, his voice close to the phone again.

"We have a deal?"

By way of answer, the American quoted the CIA's unofficial motto:

"And you shall know the truth, and the truth shall set you free."

CHAPTER 22

7:03AM, THURSDAY, MAY 1ST, 2014
ROXBURY, MA

Finn slipped into Boston Police Headquarters in Roxbury, hoping the early hour would lend him an anonymity he could already tell he wasn't going to get. Zoe Kraft's surprise assertion last night on ABC News that he had done the BPD's job for them was unlikely to earn him any friends on the force, despite the fact that it was patently false. Any protestations he made today, after the fact, were unlikely to ring true. No one would believe he hadn't asked Zoe Kraft to make him look good on national television to maybe drum up more clients for his P.I. business, or to grab his ten minutes of fame, or perhaps just to give the BPD the finger. Finn would have preferred to stay away from here altogether until things cooled down and he could work quietly to repair the damage.

Unfortunately, today was the day he had promised to meet Sully to get an update on what his undercover guy might know about the 'Dorky White Guy' that Mike Miller saw meeting with Kadyrov a couple months ago, so here he was. He hoped that his appearance at Boston Police Headquarters this morning would be interpreted as, *taking his medicine like a man*, which would help, but was afraid it was more likely to be seen as, *I'm here to gloat and rub it in your faces*, which would not. Trying to look both innocent and contrite at the same time, he achieved neither as he quickly worked his way over to Sully's desk which, unhappily, was empty.

"Shit," he cursed under his breath, having been afraid of this. Sully knew he was coming in early so hopefully he was just grabbing a cup of coffee or something and would be back at his desk shortly. Scanning the uncharacteristically quiet cube farm, Finn's gaze stopped on a glass-fronted office on the far side of the room which was packed to the gills with uniforms. Finn squinted and could just read the name and title on the door — *Capt. Edward Mussey, Special Operations Division* — Sully's boss. Finn had only met Ned once in passing, but had liked him instantly, his initial impression confirming Sully's comments over the years that the Captain was a good leader and boss. Finn deduced that (a) Sully was in there, and (b) they were talking about the Kraft interview from the night before. He knew a damage control meeting when he saw one.

A sudden flurry of activity inside Captain Mussey's office culminated a few seconds later with the door banging angrily open, revealing a man Finn had only ever seen before on the news, Police Commissioner William B. Evans, staring at him coldly for a few long, tense seconds across the empty space before stalking off deeper into the building.

Fuck.

People started pouring out of the office like angry ants from an ant hill and began heading across the room to where Finn stood at Sully's cube.

Double fuck.

Moments later Finn found himself facing a decidedly unfriendly phalanx of cops, Feds, and a few guys who looked like they might be spooks from Langley.

"Morning guys," he said, trying for light and amiable. It felt like throwing sunshine into an empty grave.

Hard eyes and closed faces stared him down as a broad figure in an expensive dark gray suit worked his way to the front of the crowd to square off against him. The man was around Finn's age, lantern-jawed, broad-shouldered, and with captain-of-the-football-team good looks currently twisted into an angry scowl.

No fucking way, thought Finn, stunned.

"You should be ashamed of yourself" the suited man said disgustedly.

"Nice to see you too, Zach," replied Finn, trying to keep his voice even, his mind racing. *What the hell was his old Delta Force and Team Poleaxe squadmate Zach Fisher doing here?* "Been a long time. You look good."

'You know each other?" asked an incredulous cop.

"Unfortunately," bit off the CIA man.

"I was his commanding officer," declared Finn, needing to claim some respect before the public steamrolling.

"That was a long time ago, Finn. Things are different now. Very different." Fisher made no attempt to hide the menace in his voice. "I'm in charge now and what I say, goes."

Unbidden, Finn's mind suddenly transported him back to 2002, to when he was regaining consciousness inside a secret WMD storage facility high up in the Zahedan Mountains of Eastern Iran...

*   *   *   *   *

2002
ZAHEDAN MOUNTAINS, EASTERN IRAN

A splitting, almost incapacitating headache. Something was wrong with his hearing — everything sounded distant, muffled, like it was filtered through a mile of cotton. Everything hurt, but thankfully no part of his body screamed 'serious injury'. Finn opened his eyes and the world shifted and morphed nauseatingly. He quickly closed them and focused on assessing the situation without their help. He was sitting on the floor with his back up against something hard, maybe metal. The smell of cordite, blood and his own sweat filled his nostrils. The noises around him rose and fell, slowly resolving into discernible words. It sounded like an argument. He chanced opening his eyes again and this time his vision settled down.

He was in the control room of the secret Iranian facility they'd raided but wasn't entirely sure how he'd ended up there. He did remember leading the six-man assault force of Team Poleaxe into the simple stone hut guarded by machine gun emplacements. At the back of the hut they found a heavy steel door sitting open, its biometric scanner panel thereby not providing much security. They entered cautiously and crept down a short hall into an open cavern that served as living quarters with bunk beds, card tables, footlockers and, incongruously enough, a StairMaster machine. They made their way across the space to the only other exit, another hallway leading deeper into the mountain that emptied into a control room where they'd found an Iranian soldier literally asleep at the switch.

After quietly disabling the soldier, Finn put Zach Fisher in charge of Malik Jackson and Diego Figueroa and ordered them to keep an eye on their terrified captive and cover their backs while he led Tony Russo and Oscar Holt deeper into the facility. At the end of a hallway leading from the Control Room further into the mountain they found an elevator and a stairwell, both of which led only down.

The three of them stealthily descended four flights of poorly-lit stairs until reaching a closed (but not locked) door. Worryingly, the stairwell continued down into the gloom, though their intel had suggested just the

173

one sublevel. They didn't have time to cry about this unwelcome complication so they'd opened the door and stepped into an empty hallway, a carbon copy of the one above except that instead of a control room at the end opposite the elevator, there was a serious looking airlock style door that turned out to require a handprint in order to work. They decided to go back upstairs to get the captured soldier and make use of his hand to gain access when a slightly pathetic 'ding' emanated from the elevator behind them.

The doors creaked apart to reveal three young Iranian army soldiers goofing around with each other. It seemed one of them had initiated the 'push all the buttons' game, and the other two were playfully punching and shoving him.

Finn, Tony and Oscar froze in the middle of the hall; sitting ducks with nowhere to hide and several yards from the relative safety of the stairwell. The Iranians stopped messing around and stared in shock at the three camouflaged and heavily-armed intruders standing unexpectedly fifty feet away. The elevator doors dutifully trundled shut before anyone could move but once closed, the Americans sprang into action, bounding down the hall and into the stairwell. Finn cursed as their comms channel gave him nothing but static as he tried to warn his men upstairs that they were about to receive some very unwelcome visitors.

They were halfway up when the door above them banged open and then the stairwell filled with bullets flying by to thunk into the concrete block walls, gray chips and dust exploding out in a hundred places all around them. They all dove for cover as something more substantial dropped, ricocheting off the metal handrails and careening crazily down the stairwell. Tony reached back down the stairs and grabbed Finn to pull him up as the grenade went flying past his face to explode two seconds later and half a flight below.

And now here he was, sitting on the floor of the control room trying to clear his head.

It looked like Zach Fisher was questioning the Iranian soldier they'd caught napping at the control panel while Tony Russo stood off to the side, his expression unreadable. As he readied himself to stand up, Finn registered the carnage and destruction that had taken place since he'd left the control room to head downstairs. Malik was dead, facedown on the floor of the hallway leading back to the cavern / living quarters and Diego's lifeless body sat slumped against the wall over to Finn's left. One Iranian lay dead on the floor and Finn could see several more down each of the hallways to his right and left. He couldn't see Oscar anywhere, which wasn't a good sign.

The captive shrieked in pain and rage as Zach Fisher did something to his forearm. He gave the Iranian a pointed look, waited for a moment then squeezed the arm again, eliciting another piteous wail. It looked like Zach was maybe making use of a bullet wound to motivate the guy to talk. This wasn't how they did things and Finn bellowed at his second in command to stop. He wasn't going to allow anyone to get tortured on his watch. Fisher ignored Finn and said something to the captive, then placed the muzzle of his pistol on the man's right thigh.

Finn staggered to his feet and yelled incoherently at Zach a second time. He took a few steps then stumbled to one knee, his head spinning, eyes seeing double. He shouted at Fisher to stop, what the fuck was he doing? But he must have sustained a bad concussion because he couldn't wrangle the words he wanted to use.

Concentrating as best he could, Finn ordered Fisher to stop what he was doing and start cleaning up this goddamn mess.

Fisher looked at Finn, shrugged, raised his pistol to the captive's head and did just that.

*   *   *   *   *

PRESENT DAY

The memory of Fisher's gunshot and Finn's answering roar of disbelief and anger echoed around his brain as he returned to the present to face the man who, twelve years ago, disobeyed his superior officer on the field of battle and gotten away with murder.

"Well then," Finn replied, "I'll be sure to give your orders the same respect you gave mine."

Fisher seemed to physically expand, rage radiating off him like heat. The room went unnaturally silent, the assembled cops enthralled by the manifest complexities reverberating through this simple exchange.

"You've got balls, I'll give you that," said Fisher, opting for a change in tack. "After that stunt you pulled last night I thought you might be heading for Canada to lay low for a while."

"First of all, I didn't pull any stunt," replied Finn, " and second…"

Fisher cut him off angrily. "How stupid do you think we are?" he asked rhetorically, waving his arms at the crowd assembled around them. "You put your client on national TV and told her to promote your little P. I.

Business and you threw the entire Boston Police Department under the bus. So yeah, I'd call that a stunt," he finished triumphantly. "And a pretty fucking pathetic one, at that."

Things were heading sideways fast and Finn knew he wouldn't be meeting Sully today or anytime soon. At this point he wasn't even sure he'd make it out the front door under his own power.

"I know you're not going to believe me," he said, trying to keep his voice even and calm, "but I had nothing to do with what she said."

Fisher pounced on that. "Oh yeah? Well here's some other things you'll have nothing to do with: the Marathon bombing, the Dorchester investigation, and the entire Boston Police Department." He shook his head in disgust then looked Finn in the eye. "Now get the fuck out of my sight and don't come back."

As frustrated as he was, Finn decided to take the hit to make the play, so he just shrugged, turned and left. Blue uniforms parted as he headed out, and he felt rather than saw every one of the dark scowls and middle fingers sent his way.

He put his aviators on as he hit the street and the sharp morning light, breathing deeply several times before sighing and saying to no one in particular, "Good talk."

CHAPTER 23

5:32PM, FRIDAY, MAY 2ND, 2014
THE WARREN TAVERN, CHARLESTOWN, MA

Russo requested a replacement pint from Sam and openly tried to catch a look at the side-boob just visible in her blue and white striped tank top as she reached out to place his refill on the bar. She caught him looking and gave her chest a coquettish shake.

"I still got it!" she proclaimed happily.

"That you do," he agreed wistfully, "that you do."

She flashed him a smile and moved off down the bar to attend to other patrons who were steadily streaming in to fill the cozy space.

"You have a way with women, Tony," opined Finn from the stool next to him. "I can see why they like you so much."

"I may not be all that great to look at, but sitting next to you I look like George Clooney."

They laughed and clinked glasses, sitting in companionable silence for a few minutes while conversations and laughter rose and fell around them, the after work crowd loosening up and settling in.

Deciding the time was right, Tony dug his phone out of his pocket and thumbed through a bunch of photos. "Hey Finn, you're gonna like this," he said before handing the phone over.

"Whatta ya' got?" asked Koenen, curiosity piqued.

"Richards case," Russo replied by way of context. He had taken a series of pictures with a telephoto lens of Greyson Richards standing on the porch of a perfectly nice, nondescript blue-gray house. "That's where he goes on his secret outings," he explained, "and now I know why."

Finn looked at him expectantly and Tony motioned impatiently for

Finn to continue swiping through the sequence of pictures, which he did. Like a slide show, the photos showed Professor Greyson heading up the walkway, gym bag over one shoulder; standing on the porch reaching for the doorbell; and jackpot! an open door revealing a strikingly attractive woman in maybe her mid-twenties with her straight blond hair pulled back in a short ponytail. She was barefoot, wearing black and red yoga pants and an old t-shirt that kind of fell off one shoulder.

Finn whistled. "The Professor has good taste," he observed. He flipped through a bunch more, which showed the pair hugging and then disappearing inside the house.

"Got him coming out?"

"Yup."

"Any shots of them inside? Maybe doing something they shouldn't be?"

Tony grimaced. "No," he said, annoyed. "Every window in that place is covered, so I got nothing from when they go inside to when he comes out with his gym bag to head back to campus."

Finn flicked quickly through the pictures a second time then handed Tony his phone back.

"However," Russo continued, "I do know that whatever they do in there, he washes it off in the shower before he leaves."

Finn cocked his head slightly. "If you can't see inside, how do you know he showers?"

Tony grinned. "Because one day last week something fell out of his gym bag as he was getting into his taxi. He left a little later than usual and was in a pretty big hurry so he didn't notice. After the taxi left I went over and checked it out."

"And?" asked Finn, a little impatiently.

Tony really enjoyed dragging these things out for maximum effect, and was pleased he had Finn hooked. "It was a trial size Head and Shoulders shampoo bottle, half empty and still wet from the shower. Boom. We got him dead to rights."

"Hunh," said Finn, somewhat noncommittally.

"What?" Tony demanded, irked by his partner's lack of enthusiasm.

Finn hemmed and hawed for a few moments, and Tony took the opportunity to finish his pint, catching Sam's eye down the bar for another.

"I'd prefer something a little more substantive," said Finn cautiously.

"What do you mean, substantive? We have him lying to his wife about where he is. He sneaks out of the office to visit a hot young blond chick once or twice a week for an hour or so. He showers, then sneaks back to the office, thinking no one is the wiser."

"Yeah, but that's all circumstantial. We need actual evidence that the guy is screwing around on Allie. I'm not going to ruin their marriage without some hard proof that the Professor is dipping his pen in someone else's inkwell."

Tony could tell Finn was pleased with his little joke, which only irritated him further. "C'mon, man," he pleaded, "I got the guy dead to rights. Besides, what do you want me to do? Break in, hide behind the curtains and get pictures of them *en flagrante?*"

"I'm sure you'll think of something," said Finn in that infuriating way he had. "I just need you to stay on the case a little longer to see what you can document."

Tony couldn't hold back the annoyance any longer. "Goddammit Finn. You said I'd collect for both our hours on this if I solved it before July, and I did! We got what we need so let's wrap it up, get paid and move onto something more interesting!"

Finn gave him a condescending smile, angering Russo further.

"I say something funny?" he demanded, hackles rising. "Because I'm serious, Finn. I'm bored out of my fucking mind on this one. He does nothing for days, pops over to see his mistress for like an hour and then he's straight back to boring, Professortown for this guy. It's brutal! Like watching someone watch paint dry."

Finn laughed at that then said, placating, "I get it. I'm sorry the assignment sucks, but that's the job, you know that. We need proof, actual proof. Not guesses and assumptions."

Russo shook his head in exasperation then grabbed his fresh pint, sloshing some onto his hand and the bar top. "Fine, he grumbled into his glass, "I'll get you the goddamn proof."

They sat in silence for a few moments, each attending to his own thoughts. Sam came over and slid plates of food in front of each of them: fish and chips for Finn and pasta primavera with chicken for Tony. They each thanked her and Tony tucked into his with some gusto, the food on Finn's tab mollifying him somewhat, until Finn broke the silence.

"So... I saw an old friend of ours yesterday," he said casually, and something in his tone made Russo sit a little straighter on his stool.

"Who" he asked, already knowing he wasn't going to like the answer.

"Zach Fisher."

"Zach Fisher?" asked Russo incredulously. "Like, Team Poleaxe Zach Fisher?"

"Yup,"replied Finn around a mouthful of fried cod.

"As in, 'Got trigger happy in the mountains', Zach Fisher?"

"One and the same," confirmed Finn.

Russo thought about that for a minute, sipping at his Bud Light, the happy chaos of the bar fading into the background. He'd always assumed he'd run across that slippery bastard again. Some guys you just knew were going to cause you trouble forever. He hadn't liked Fisher from the first time they'd met, at the US base outside Kuwait City. His skill as a soldier notwithstanding, Tony had immediately sensed that Fisher was one of those guys who only thought about the team when it suited his purposes. Otherwise, it was *'me first, you second and fuck everyone else'*. Tony had made sure to keep his mouth shut and his eyes open the few times they'd had to work together, whether at the base or in the field, and the 2002 black op the three of them barely survived was seared into his memory like an angry brand.

*   *   *   *   *

2002
ZAHEDAN MOUNTAINS - EASTERN IRAN

Everything had gone smoothly — maybe too smoothly — until they'd hit their first real snag at the sublevel security doors that presumably led into the WMD storage rooms. The biometric scanner had been much more sophisticated than anticipated, and they had decided to make use of the captured Iranian guy upstairs to gain access. Just then, the elevator at the end of the hall had dinged open, revealing three Iranian Army soldiers who were apparently as surprised to see the Americans as they were to see the Iranians.

Once the elevator doors shut, they sprang into action. Oscar bounded up the stairs with Tony hot on his heels and Finn brought up the rear, covering their six in case any Iranian Army guys popped out of the elevator behind and below them. He could hear two versions of Finn trying in vain to warn Zach, Malik and Diego to prepare for company: one echoing crazily around the stairwell, intermingled with the frantic staccato clanging of their ascent, and the other mingled with the hiss of interference in his earpiece.

Suddenly, bullets ripped through the air from above, at least one catching Oscar in the face, killing him instantly. Tony dove back against the wall, then tried to pull Finn up to the next landing as a grenade sailed by to detonate half a floor below them, the explosion blowing them up to the next landing. Finn's body had taken the brunt of the explosion, shielding Tony from the worst of it, and his commanding officer was out cold, though still breathing. Tony fought against the shock he felt coming on, hoisted Finn's slack body onto his shoulder and continued up the stairs. He heard gunfire and shouts from above, but thankfully no further attacks rained down on them. Apparently the boys upstairs were keeping the Iranians' attention.

He carefully propped Finn against the wall, checked his M4A1 rifle. The magazine was full (he hadn't fired it yet) and stuck his head out into the corridor to see what was going on. He could see the backs of three Iranians, most likely the ones from the elevator a few moments ago, as they popped off rounds into the Control Room beyond. It looked like at least one of Team Poleaxe was down at the entrance to the other hallway at the far side of the control room. He snuck out of the stairwell into the hall behind the Iranians, and took them out with three quick head shots. They went down like puppets whose strings had been cut. He ran forward and crouched over the bodies, confirming they were dead.

Just then, three more Iranian soldiers appeared at the far end of the the hallway beyond the control room, leading back to the living quarters and the only exit. Tony raised the M4A1 to his eye and dropped them all, pop-pop-pop. They never knew what hit them.

Ten minutes later, while Zach zip-tied the guy they'd initially caught asleep in the Control Room to his chair, Tony dragged Finn in and propped him against the wall. He also confirmed that Oscar, Malik and Diego were all dead. He was filled with rage, pumped full of battle adrenaline, and itching to get some revenge for their losses.

But even so, he was still surprised and shocked by what Fisher did next, which was to point-blank shoot the poor bastard in the forearm. Russo tried to intervene, but Zach growled that with Finn out of action, he was in charge, and he had orders to find out who was responsible for this secret base using any means necessary. Russo hadn't liked that one bit, but the chain of command is inviolable, especially in the middle of a live-fire situation, so he'd held his tongue and covered the hallways in case any additional Iranians were dumb enough to show themselves. Finn regained consciousness and begun shouting and unsteadily waving his arms around, apparently taking exception to Fisher sticking his thumb in the bullet wound in the poor guy's arm.

And then, without warning, Zach straight-up executed the guy, a few bits of his hair and scalp landing on the toe of Russo's left boot. Tony hadn't much liked that either but had to quickly get between the two men before they killed each other. Extending his arms to separate them, Russo reminded them that their priority was to figure out what to do now that their stealth mission had gone tits-up, and fast. One of the Iranians had almost certainly raised an alarm, so the Americans should expect company any second.

Fisher had, unbeknownst to the rest of them, brought some high-powered explosives, enough for them to bury the secret WMD facility, its deadly contents, and all evidence of their having been there. So the three of them quickly set charges and reconvened out in front of the stone hut in the oval dirt parking area. Before Fisher could detonate, Finn staggered and fell down on his hands and knees, the exertion and concussion reasserting themselves. Tony hoisted Finn up over his shoulder again and set off down the mountain hoping like hell he didn't step on any of the Mon-50 anti-personnel mines while Zach stayed behind and set off the explosives. Several blasts shook the mountainside and almost brought Tony to his knees, but he kept his legs pumping as he struggled to carry Finn down the rocky slope.

The rest of the journey back to Afghan territory, which cut across a corner of Pakistan just for good measure, had been almost anticlimactic, and Russo had a lot of time to think about what had transpired back at that secret facility. He concluded that (a) he didn't like it, (b) it wasn't his job to do anything about it — that was Finn's responsibility as the assault force leader and (c) he resolved to stay as far away from Zach Fisher as possible, deciding that spending too much time with the man was likely to get him killed

*   *   *   *   *

PRESENT DAY

"Yeah, well, I don't trust that fucking guy," Russo said before aggressively draining half his pint.

"I wouldn't say we're best friends either," observed Finn, "at least based on the very public ass-reaming he handed me down at BPD yesterday morning."

Tony was taken aback. "What are you talking about?"

As Finn recounted the story, Tony felt himself getting more and more agitated. "Goddammit, Finn!" he shouted, though it was almost lost in the din of the now packed bar. "We need the cops to help us do our job! What the fuck were you thinking?" Tony's anger was rising, verging on rage.

Finn's Irish got up as well. "What was I thinking?" he asked, incredulity mixed heavily with defensiveness. "I didn't tell Zoe Kraft to go on TV and submarine the cops while praising us! Why in God's name would I do that? I have no idea what prompted her to make that up, but I do know that it makes our lives a shitload harder."

"Whatever," grumbled Tony, realizing he shouldn't have jumped to conclusions but not willing to admit it yet. "Maybe you put the idea in her head by accident, said something about how a little publicity might help the business."

"Are you kidding me? Publicity is the single worst thing for a detective agency! We can't do our jobs if everyone knows who we are. And we sure as hell can't do our jobs if the local cops freeze us out!" He paused and the two men squared off until Koenen relented. "Tony, I promise you that I had nothing, nothing at all to do with this. It's all a big misunderstanding, and I'll fix it. Somehow." Finn took a long pull off his own beer after finishing.

"Sure you will," said Russo sarcastically. As mad as he was about the situation with the Boston Police Department, he was significantly more worried about the reappearance of Zach Fisher in their lives, but he didn't want to share that with Finn just yet. Was he here to settle old scores? Or was he peddling some new kind of treachery?

Tony stood up, peeled some bills off a wad and tossed them onto the bar next to his half-eaten meal. "I'm calling it an early night, since I gotta get up early and go watch the Professor grade papers all day," he declared, then stalked off, pushing his way none too gently through the oblivious, happy crowd, his mind racing and troubled.

CHAPTER 24

8:05PM, WEDNESDAY, MAY 7TH, 2014
SUDBURY, MA

"Coffee? Tea?"

"Actually, some coffee would be lovely," said Finn, perched awkwardly on a pale green, overly formal sofa that probably had a special name. "If it's not too much trouble."

"No trouble at all," replied Zoe Kraft, beaming. "It's my pleasure," and she swooshed off into the kitchen humming a happy little tune.

"Why are you here?" asked a decidedly less accommodating voice from the armchair on the other side of an expensive looking mahogany coffee table.

"If you don't mind, I'd like to wait until your wife comes back. It's kind of a sensitive subject," explained Finn, treading carefully. Will Kraft had never been a big fan of his wife's obsession regarding the bombers, and his disapproval extended to Finn as well.

"The last time I let someone come in here without fully understanding their motives, we were humiliated on national TV. So, before my wife returns with your coffee, I would like you to tell *me* why you are here," demanded Will plaintively.

Finn shifted uncomfortably on the couch. He'd known this was going to be a tricky conversation but hadn't expected Will Kraft to corner him like this, without Zoe in the room. He gave an invisible mental shrug. What could he do? He had a point about that goddamn Gabi Mendez interview and besides, Amanda was his daughter too.

"I have reason to believe," he started, after taking a deep breath, "that at least one and maybe more of those terrorists are still at large."

"You what?" started Will, alarmed.

"Mr. Kraft, I realize this might come as a bit of a surprise..."

"I'll say it does," interrupted Will, openly displeased.

" ...and I am sure this isn't going to make you very happy..."

"But you came all the way out here to tell me anyway."

"...but I thought you and Zoe would want to know there might still be some bad guys out there and that they may still be up to something."

That gave Will pause for thought. "You're serious?" he asked, edges softening slightly.

Finn nodded. "I am. I'm sorry, but I am."

Will rubbed heels of palms into eyes and then stood up. "Finn, do you have any idea what this will..." Before he could finish, the door to the kitchen swung open and Zoe came bustling back into the living room bearing a silver tray laden with cups, saucers, a silver sugar dish replete with spoon and a small delicate pitcher of cream. " 'Any idea what this will', what?" she asked brightly.

"I was just telling Detective Koenen here," said Will, spreading his arms to indicate their house and everyone in it, "that he had no idea what the resolution of this whole affair means to our family."

Zoe beamed at her husband, then Finn, as she poured coffee for all three of them, apparently having forgotten that her husband had not asked for any. "Well," she said, offering a bone white china cup and saucer decorated with delicate dark blue scrolling to Finn, "it certainly has been a relief to know that we can put this horrible chapter of our lives behind us so that we can focus on healing as a family." She patted Finn's arm, then sipped her coffee.

"I'm sure it is," agreed Finn carefully.

"I just feel like an enormous weight has been lifted off our shoulders," she went on, happily. "Of course, we still have our challenges, but there are a lot of other families in a lot worse shape than ours. At least Amanda is still alive." Zoe shuddered a bit and with a visible effort composed herself. "Thanks to you, I feel like me again. I feel hope. Do you know how wonderful that is?" Her eyes pleaded with him.

Finn took her hands in his own and said softly, "Actually, Zoe, I do."

She wasn't making this easy. Was he really going to tell her, without any actual proof, mind you, that her nightmare may not be over? And yet... she had a right to know that one (or more) of the bad guys might have gotten away; that his job wasn't over yet; that there was still justice to serve. "And I just,..." he started, then stopped.

He could sense Will's eyes on him, feel the warning in them.

"You just, what?" asked Zoe, puzzled.

"I just..." he stopped again, unsure how to proceed. This sort of indecision was rare and made him supremely uncomfortable. She had paid him for the truth so she could have the justice she so desperately needed. *And yet...* he thought, *doesn't she already have what she wanted? What she paid me for?* He sighed and decided.

"I just can't find the words to tell you how happy I am for you and Will. And Amanda." Will Kraft visibly relaxed in Finn's peripheral vision though Zoe seemed oblivious. "And I'm glad we were able to work together."

"Me too," echoed Zoe, beaming

The invisible tension had drained from the room and after a few more minutes of pleasant chatter Finn said, "Well, I guess I should be on my way."

They all rose and started towards the door. As they got closer, Will turned to Zoe and said, "I'll see Finn out, honey. Could you check on Amanda and see if she wants any desert? I have a hankering for some mint chocolate chip myself."

Zoe's face lit up. "Oh Will, she'll love that." She turned to Finn, gave him a brief but powerful hug, then disappeared, leaving the two men alone.

Will gestured *after you* towards the door with his arm and followed Finn out onto the front porch where the two men shook hands.

"Thank you Finn."

"Of course."

"Not just for taking my wife's case when she clearly seemed, well, overly fixated on her theories, but also for what you did back there," Will jerked a thumb back towards the house.

Finn still wasn't sure how he felt about that. "To be honest, I think she should know the truth. But I guess she doesn't need to know just yet."

"I'm glad you see it that way," said Will quietly, pulling a folded piece of paper from his pocket and locking eyes meaningfully with him. "This is to thank you for your help, and to ensure that you never make contact with my family again. Ever."

Finn took and unfolded the piece of paper to find it was a check made out to Rogers Investigative Services and sporting a shockingly hefty sum. He quickly refolded it and thrust it back towards Will Kraft. "I can't take this," he said.

"Yes you can," replied Will firmly.

"No, I can't," countered Finn, just as firmly. "You've already compensated me more than fairly for my work on the case. We're all square."

Finn's refusal apparently caught Kraft off-guard, and he seemed to be struggling with something.

"Take the money, Finn. Take the money and never come back."

When Finn neither moved nor replied, he went on, pain and worry lacing his words. "My only daughter is permanently disabled. My wife's sanity has been hanging on by a thread for a year. A year!" he exclaimed before pausing to gather himself. "I don't think I can take any more of this. Zoe definitely can't. She's only just now coming out of a fog of fear and confusion and anger and if you drag her back in... If you do that, then she will lose her mind for good, and I won't allow it." Now he was pleading with Finn. "Please. Just take it and don't come back."

Finn's stomach churned but he didn't argue. Accepting that Will wouldn't take the check back, he placed it carefully in his front pocket, resolving to donate it to One Fund Boston, the charity set up by Governor Deval Patrick and Mayor Thomas Menino to benefit victims of the Marathon bombing. Nodding to Will, he turned and headed down the stairs, along the walk, back into his rental and out onto the genteel Sudbury streets.

"Well," he proclaimed to the universe at large, "it's been a good week for burning bridges."

CHAPTER 25

1:24AM IRAN STANDARD TIME, FRIDAY, MAY 9TH, 2014
TEHRAN, IRAN

The treadmill beeped plaintively and slowed to a cool-down walking pace. Reza Moradi wiped the sweat from his brow with a small towel and drank deeply from a liter bottle of spring water. Two hours at a punishing pace had burned off just enough of his excess energy that he felt he could focus again. Unfortunately, he was now focused on the fact that no matter how hard or how long he ran, he would not out-distance the past.

The sudden reappearance of Finn Koenen in his life had unsettled him to a disturbing and unexpected degree, unleashing a string of powerful memories Reza found he could no longer control. This both interested and concerned him. On the one hand, Reza detested that which he could not control, but on the other, these memories quite literally made him who he was today, sustaining and focusing and propelling him with singular purpose through all the long years since... late 1979, when he had been but 11 years old.

* * * * *

OCTOBER 31, 1979
TEHRAN, IRAN
THE START OF *EID AL ADHA*, THE FEAST OF THE SACRIFICE.

One of the holiest days in the Islamic calendar, *Eid al Adha* celebrated the willingness of the prophet Ibrahim to sacrifice his son Ishma'il to Allah, as per Allah's request. Satisfied with Ibrahim's faith and devotion, Allah stopped him at the last moment, providing Ibrahim with a sheep to sacrifice instead. Muslims across Iran and around the world prayed, ate savory kabobs and spent time with friends and family to honor Ibrahim's offer of sacrifice and Allah's mercy.

1979 had been a particularly difficult year in Iran, especially for those, like Reza's father Amir, who had supported or worked for the Shah, himself deposed and exiled ten months earlier. As his father had predicted, Ayatollah Khomeini's triumphant return to Iran and his subsequent consolidation of power had led to the restriction of freedoms and the loss of lives at home, disruptions to the oil supply abroad, and increasing animosity towards America most of all. Even as an eleven-year-old Reza could almost physically feel the tension ratcheting up daily, pushing the country to its breaking point.

That evening, after a brief but intense argument between his parents (something Reza had not seen in many years) his father abruptly left and his mother retired to their bedroom, weeping and inconsolable. Playing a hunch, Reza slipped out during all the commotion and surreptitiously followed his father as he wound his way deep into the heart of Tehran. It had been a chaotic and supremely intense surveillance as the streets heaved with revelers enthusiastically enjoying a rare opportunity to celebrate while wild-eyed zealots stalked the shadows for any prey they could find. Reza felt scared and guilty, determined and enervated all at once by the emotions coursing through the city in waves of electricity that ebbed and flowed along with the scents of grilled mutton and the rich soup called *haleem*. At one point after about half an hour, Reza completely lost sight of his father and panic gripped him. Frantically whipsawing his head back and forth and even jumping up and down to get a better view only served to intensify his blooming fear.

When he did finally spot his father speaking with another man under the shadow of a shop awning a ways down the street, confusion abruptly replaced Reza's anxiety. *Why was Finn's father here? Had Amir planned to meet with Jan Koenen or was this an accident of fate?* It was certainly easy enough to spot the tall, blond European-turned-American in the densely packed crowd of Persians, so perhaps they just ran into each other by accident?

Whatever the reason, Reza had no trouble tracking the two men as they headed off together, shortly rounding a corner and stopping to talk halfway down a narrow alley. Boxes, trashcans and other detritus provided Reza with ample cover as he crept closer and found a spot within earshot.

"I can't do it, my old friend," Jan had said with finality. *"I won't."*

"You must," replied Reza's father, almost too softly to hear above the din in the street behind them. *"You promised, and Koenens always keep their promises."*

"There has to be another way!" Jan was pleading, almost frantic. *"There must still be time to..."*

Amir cut him off, steel in his voice. *"There is no more time. They will be coming for me soon. Maybe even tomorrow."*

"No."

"You must do it now," his father commanded, stern and unyielding. *"For my family. Do this for Fairuza and my children."*

A chill ran down Reza's spine as questions roiled around his head: who was coming for his father? What won't Finn's father do? And why does Reza's father want him to do it? He decided to risk poking his head out to see what was happening and was shocked by what he saw.

The two men were standing very close and facing each other. Finn's father appeared to be holding a handgun loosely by his side. As Reza watched, Amir gently reached over and pulled Jan's arm up until the muzzle of the pistol was pressed up against his stomach.

"We planned for this day," Amir said with a sad smile, *"though I rather hoped it would not come to pass."*

Finn's father just stood there, frozen in place, gun pointing at his old friend's belly, looking ill and unhappy.

Reza's father placed an arm over Mr. Koenen's shoulder and drew him closer, the pistol digging deeper into his gut, as he continued. *"They know I work with you. If I do nothing, they will come for me and then they will torture and kill my family to try and get me to talk. If I disappear they will torture and kill my family, assuming they know where I have gone. If I take my own life, they will torture and kill may family, assuming they know more than they do."* Amir paused, gave Finn's father a pointed look until he nodded miserably, conceding.

"However," Reza's father continued, commanding in that soft yet firm way that he had, *"killing me now, in this dark alley during the mayhem of Eid al Adha, will lead the Revolutionary Guard to conclude that the Americans have cleaned up their mess, tied off the loose end that is me. And they will also conclude that if the Americans left my family alive, it must be because they know nothing of value. As such, they will therefore also leave my family alive. So you must do this. Fulfill your promise to me from so many years ago. Cauterize the wound I have become and save my family from what comes next if you don't."*

Reza froze, skewered by an overwhelming fear. The crowds behind them on the streets, the noise of a hundred conversations, the smells of a thousand small charcoal grills all fell away as Jan Koenen's eyes hardened, his grip tightened, and he pushed the gun even harder into Amir's belly.

And then he dropped his arm, defeated, unable to pull the trigger, and pulled Amir into a hug that Reza's father did not return. After a few moments Jan Koenen let go and stepped back.

"There is another way. There must be." His voice was shaky. *"I will find it. One where we both keep our heads and our families."*

And with that, Jan shoved the pistol into the waistband of his pants, turned and walked off down the alley away from Reza as Amir slumped heavily to the ground, his back against a stack of wooden pallets, and began to weep.

Reza had crept away, not wanting to abandon his father in all his misery but knowing instinctively that he was never meant to play a part in this scene. He'd returned home 45 minutes later to find no one had missed him and that he could not make sense of what he'd observed, eventually falling asleep on the cool floor of his room with tear-streaked cheeks and a nasty pit in his soul.

His father awoke him early the next morning and told him to pack his things, they were leaving Tehran that very morning. Before Reza could even fill a duffel bag with clothes, there came a knock on the door that made Reza think of his schoolmate Farshad and his grandfather.

Before the Revolutionary Guard soldiers took Amir away he managed to steal a moment to whisper a few brief, urgent instructions to his youngest son. He told Reza that he had been wrong about the Koenens, that they could not be trusted, and to be strong in the coming weeks and months.

"You need to be prepared, to be strong and do whatever is necessary to survive, and to help your mother, sisters and brothers to survive. Do you understand? Whatever it takes to get revenge on the Ayatollah and the faithless Americans, who abandoned your family in its greatest time of need."

And then he was gone, stuffed into the back of a nondescript black government car, staring at his family through the back window as it drove away, never to return.

By the time Reza saw his father again and for the final time four months later, his oldest brother had been executed and his mother and two older sisters raped, tortured and killed by the Revolutionary Guard. He had not been able to protect them as his father had charged and was more than a little relieved when they finally came for him and his last remaining sibling Ma'sud early one cold winter's morning. As expected, they were taken to what was clearly a secret prison, most likely one used by the *Savak* before the Shah's deposition.

The irony of this was not lost on Reza, but instead of the expected sweet release of a courtyard firing squad, they were instead led into a dank, subterranean chamber where they found their father Amir, emaciated and battered, sitting in a metal chair above a drain, the concrete surrounding it stained an ominous rusty brown. One of the four Revolutionary Guard soldiers, just a few years older than terrified 18-year-old Ma'sud, had pronounced their father a traitor who had conspired with the Great Satan America against the Islamic Republic of Iran. For this, the sentence was death.

"*It is true,*" Amir had said in a cracked, raspy voice the boys could barely hear. "*I conspired with the Americans. I am a traitor to the Islamic Republic of Iran.*" Amir's gaze lingered on Mas'ud, then switched to Reza. "*For I am a child of Persia, and the Ayatollah is right to fear me.*" He then asked for and was surprisingly given a couple of minutes with each of his sons, to say goodbye.

What happened next set the course of Reza's life.

Reza remembered gingerly hugging his father's thin frame and leaning in close.

"*Reza. My son,*" Amir croaked, "*Never forget this moment. Burn every detail into your memory: the coppery smell of my blood; the sound of the uneducated Parsi spoken with peasant accents by these young* madar ghahbe. *Feel the ragged stubble on my cheek scratching against your smooth one. And most of all, never forget the rage you are about to feel.*"

Amir had taken a deep, ragged breath before continuing. "*Reza. You are my youngest, but in some ways you are also my oldest. You are still a boy, but you have a very old soul. I love all your brothers and sisters equally, but in my secret heart of hearts I knew you were special, I knew you would be the one, the one to make a difference. You have the heart of a lion, and the brain of a fox,*" he paused for emphasis, "*but so do many. What you have that they don't, is the will.*" His father put special intensity into these final two words.

"*You have the will to do what must be done. I see it. Will is not a thing you learn. It is a thing you are. Or are not.*" And here Amir flicked his gaze towards Mas'ud, standing stiff and uncomfortable several feet away.

"*And it is what will allow you to pass the test in front of you — one that your brother will not. Take care of him. He has too much of your mother in him to survive in this new world on his own. Do what must be done today but make them pay for it tomorrow. No matter how long it takes, no matter what the cost, make them pay."*

"*Yes, Baba,*" Reza had whispered, "*I will Baba.*"

"*And then,*" hissed Amir with an unexpected ferocity, "*you can lead Persia back into the light of day.*"

"*Yes Papa, I will,*" Reza confirmed, then added with emphasis, "*Unlike other friends of ours, when I make a promise, I keep it.*"

Amir's surprise at this comment quickly morphed into a crooked smile as comprehension dawned. Reza's heart leapt in joy that his father understood that *he* understood, even as it sank in anticipation of what was about to transpire.

Knowing the value of symbolism, the Ayatollah himself had ordered that Amir's execution be done by his oldest remaining son, as a way to prove his loyalty to the new regime and that the stink of the traitor did not stick to him as well. But poor, gentle Ma'sud, who, of all the Moradi children had the biggest heart, enjoyed making others happy, and was the first to take in a stray cat or dog, could not do it. He had pointed the Head Guard's pistol, unsteady and shaking at the back of their father's skull before dropping his arm with a strangled cry.

Before the Head Guard had a chance to react or rebuke his older brother, Reza broke in, saying, "*We will do this together, my brother! Together we will wipe the stain of this traitor from our family name, and prove ourselves true to the Ayatollah and to his Great Revolution. With this act we will commit ourselves to a lifetime of uncovering Persia's enemies and making them pay for their crimes.*"

And with that he had wrapped his much smaller right hand around his older brother's larger one, raised the barrel of the gun until it was pointing back at their father's skull and, unleashing a massive crack, pulled the trigger for all three of them.

*   *   *   *   *

Reza sat at his desk and let the echo of that 1980 gunshot reverberate around his soul. Both the greatest and worst moment of his life, he revisited it often, for this was the moment that had made him, given him purpose and charted the course of his life. He wondered sometimes whom he would have become had Finn's father Jan possessed the strength of character to kill his father Amir so that neither he nor his wife and children would have to face the horrors provided so enthusiastically by the Revolutionary Guard. Would his brothers and sisters still be alive? Would his mother have remarried? Would Reza be a successful bureaucrat, currying favor with the Mullahs as they slowly ground Persia into dust?

Or would he have ended up where he was right now, even if via different paths? His character, his will, would be constants regardless of how life unfolded. Reza rather thought that, in the end, he was destined to be here, now, about to change the world forever.

And despite what the Koenen patriarch's failure of character had done to his own family, Reza had been content to forget about the Koenen children. However, now that Finn had unwittingly stuck his nose into Reza's business, he might have to be dealt with. In particular, it bothered Reza that he couldn't figure out how Finn had caught wind of the Chechens' plans, given that, as far as he could tell, Anderson Pierce remained undiscovered. This implied that neither the impending July 4th attack nor Reza himself had popped up on anyone's radar.

And yet…

And yet, Finn's interference had already dealt him a serious and unexpected blow, and Reza liked surprises even less than he believed in coincidences. He needed to decide whether to ignore Koenen's involvement and stick to his original plans or alter them to take Finn off the board and make him pay for his interference. This indecision irritated him greatly, as it hearkened back to the same unpleasant and almost-forgotten feeling he used to have sitting across the chessboard from the American when they were boys. He'd underestimated Koenen before and had long ago promised himself never to do it again.

He sat stock still for several more minutes while his clever and unique mind sifted through unnumbered branching future pathways searching for clarity. Finally, he concluded that he should stick to his plan rather than add the risks and complications associated with trying to neutralize Koenen. Decision made, Reza began tidying up the myriad of printed reports, photos, and handwritten documents strewn across his desk; details on his old friend's life courtesy of his CIA contact, as requested.

He picked up the large manila envelope the paperwork had arrived in and was surprised to feel something small and hard stuck down in one of the bottom corners. He turned it upside down and shook out what looked like a small thumb drive wrapped inside a folded piece of paper secured by a green rubberband. Setting the thumb drive to the side, he unraveled and read the note:

2002 — Zahedan Mt. Raid. Thought you would find this interesting.

Reza felt like he had been punched in the gut. *What was this?* How would the CIA know about the destruction of his secret WMD facility twelve years ago? He had always assumed the Israelis had destroyed it —

they were infamous for violent and irregular tactics, like when in 1996 their internal security service *Shin Bet* rigged a cell phone to explode, killing Hamas' chief bomb maker, Yahya Ayyash in the Gaza Strip.

Had it been the Americans after all? Or was his CIA source sharing something they got from the Israelis?

Reza carefully slotted the thumb drive into his highly sophisticated, uniquely hardened laptop. It contained exactly one file — a video, by its extension. He double-clicked and began to watch.

* * * * *

An hour and twenty minutes later, after having watched the video file several times and trembling with a rage he wasn't sure he wanted to control, Reza shut the laptop and dialed a number on his mobile.

"Yes?" came Anderson's slightly nasal voice from thousands of miles away.

Waves of anger prevented Reza from speaking.

"...Sir?" came Pierce's concerned voice.

Reza mastered himself and spoke. "I have new instructions for you."

"Go ahead."

"I want you to get eyes on a Finn Koenen. He's the private investigator who claims to have uncovered the Chechens. Observe his every move but do not under any circumstances initiate contact until I say so. He is well-trained and very dangerous. Do not underestimate him."

"Y-Yes sir," Anderson replied, hesitantly. "But what about... "

Reza interrupted his protege. "This is in addition to your other duties. Do not let them suffer."

"Understood," said Anderson. "But..."

"Hamid always spoke so highly of you. I hope I wasn't wrong to trust his appraisal. After all," he continued, voice low and menacing, "Hamid did make some mistakes assessing people, for which he paid very unpleasantly."

"I understand," Pierce said shakily. "Tell me what to do."

"Excellent," said Reza, his hot rage already starting to coalesce into shards of black ice in his heart. "Listen carefully..."

CHAPTER 26

10:13AM, FRIDAY, MAY 9TH, 2014
ROGERS' DETECTIVE AGENCY, EAST CAMBRIDGE, MA

For the third time in the last hour, Finn erased a text he'd composed for Cat and put the phone face-down on his desk in exasperation. He was now convinced his clumsy but well-intentioned departure after their incredible night together had sent Cat the wrong message and he was quite keen to find a way to repair the damage. Unfortunately, their respective schedules had conspired to keep them apart the past couple weeks and he was understandably a little gun-shy about relying on texting for such a delicate situation. A phone call might have done the trick but he kept getting voice mail, which would not.

Taking a sip of water and (once again) deciding to park this problem for later, Finn returned his attention to the the large case file Zoe Kraft gave him back in March. Despite multiple reviews since, he hoped this particular stone still had a drop of two of blood he could squeeze out. Besides, what other choice did he have? He was *persona non grata* with the relevant authorities, banned from talking to Zoe Kraft, and even his own partner thought he was on a fool's errand.

Flipping open the cover revealed a 4 x 6 color picture of Amanda smiling with a bunch of colleagues in front of the Capteryx headquarters. She radiated happiness and confident anticipation, a young woman with nothing but success and great times ahead. Stapled beneath the picture was a copy of last year's hospital report from her stay at Mass General after the bombing, detailing the irreparable damage done to her. While some heavily-modified version of success and happiness may yet be in store for Amanda Kraft, the Tsarnaevs and their sponsor(s) had put her on a very different and unwelcome path.

"Alright, already," he grumbled, turning the page to get away from her accusing, pre-bombing stare and digging in to the file. Two hours later he sat back, rubbed dry eyes, cracked sore knuckles and stretched his legs. He was mildly disheartened to see that he was only about a fifth of the way through Zoe's documents and impatience with his lack of progress pushed his mind back to more personal matters.

He really liked Cat. A lot. He found her interesting, playful, confident and very attractive, but so were lots of women, so there was more to it than that. Cat somehow combined all these qualities and a hundred more in an unique and persuasive way that he found magnetic. At the same time he wasn't quite sure what to make of the fact that in many ways she combined the best qualities of both his parents: self-sufficient, strong-willed and mischievous like his mother; intelligent, analytical and clever like his father. Was that weird? It felt a little weird.

It was also weird to think that he'd lived many more years of his life without his parents than with them. He'd been just eighteen in 1986 and it was what, 2014 now? That made it twenty-eight years — almost three decades — since their car crashed in Switzerland on that terrible day.

"Jesus Christ," he complained to the empty office. "I'm fucking old."

Without over-thinking it, he grabbed his phone off the desk and sent Cat a text.

Hey - sorry it's been hard to connect - I'd really like to get together. Have you seen Blue Man Group? If not, let me take you. Charles Playhouse. You pick the night and I'll make it work. Psyched to see you again.

Though he knew full well it was foolish, his mood still dropped markedly when she didn't respond immediately. That uncomfortable feeling in his stomach started growing again when his phone vibrated, startling him.

Traveling overseas next couple weeks. Rain check when I get back?

Finn brightened. That sounded hopeful, though he didn't feel like waiting two more weeks to see her. He considered writing something snarky back but ultimately decided against it. *Never push a bad position*, he told himself and typed instead:

Of course. Let me know when you're back. I'll be here. Safe travels!

His phone buzzed again with Cat's reply of the thumbs-up emoji. He took this as an encouraging sign and made a mental note to check in with her in a couple weeks. Spirits thus lifted, Finn finished his soda, settled into his desk chair and dug back into Zoe's files.

5pm found Finn stiff and sore from poring over endless police reports, interview transcripts, surveillance photos, phone logs, witness statements and inter-agency memos. Tony hadn't stopped by or called in once, but Finn hadn't really expected him to. He'd cool off eventually. Or not. He'd cross that bridge another day.

It had been a brutal slog, but his dogged focus had surprisingly yielded a couple of new leads. They were kind of shitty leads, but at this point he would take two shitty leads over the exactly zero leads he'd started with. And there was always the chance that one of them might turn out to be a lot less shitty than expected, and he could actually make some meaningful progress on the case, which might just help him repair his relationships with Tony, the BPD and perhaps even Will Kraft.

Hope is a dangerous thing, he thought ten minutes later as he locked up, *but it sure does feel good.*

CHAPTER 27

10:15AM SATURDAY, MAY 10TH, 2014
CAMBRIDGESIDE GALLERIA, CAMBRIDGE, MA

Finn held the door as he exited the mall so that three moms and their ten children could enter and was pleasantly surprised by how many of the kids thanked him for doing so. Mood buoyed, he ambled left through dappled sunlight around the man-made pond and canal connected to the Charles River just to the south, the walk easing the disappointment of his visit to the GO! Wireless kiosk a few minutes ago.

The first of his two tenuous leads revolved around the fact that the Tsarnaevs had, in the course of planning their attack last year, utilized a 'burner' cell phone; one with prepaid minutes and a brand new SIM card, making it it effectively untraceable. They'd purchased said burner phone from the GO! Wireless kiosk in the Cambridgeside Galleria shopping mall just east of the MIT campus and next to a burgeoning biotech corridor that included, among others, Biogen, Novo Nordisk, Genentech and Amanda's old firm, Capteryx.

The police recovered the burner phone, registered to a 'Jahar Tsarni', when they captured Dzhokhar Tsarnaev hiding in a boat in a Watertown backyard, six or seven miles west of here. Zoe's case file had included transcripts of interviews with a number of GO! Wireless employees that (at the time) yielded nothing useful. But last Spring the authorities had been looking for information related to the Tsarnaevs, not for information related to Ruslan Kadyrov. Since Sully was convinced Kadyrov had trained and backed the Tsarnaevs, Finn's thin hope was that others from Kadyrov's crew, or perhaps even Kadyrov himself, had purchased other burner cell phones there as well, ideally recently.

Connecting Kadyrov or one of his guys to same the GO! Wireless store that the Tsarnaevs had used would have given Finn something of value to trade with Sully in return for his sharing the subsequent details his officer would uncover using their much greater resources and authority. Just pulling information about the phone's position, movements, calls made, texts sent, etc. would have been a treasure trove of information for them all, and it would materially mend his fences with the BPD. Eager to make some progress, Finn had arrived five minutes before the mall opened and had been the first, and only, person awaiting the sullen teen sporting an ill-fitting button-down shirt and deliberately off-kilter navy blue tie to open the kiosk. The kid didn't recognize any of the men in the pictures Finn showed him and his terse responses to Finn's politely-worded questions dripped with adolescent disdain. Lead number one met a swift and relatively painless death.

Finn worried his second lead would fare no better, given that it was predicated on the same premise: that even clever, paranoid people unconsciously fell into habits, occasionally recycling trusted locations, methods and people. As such, his current destination was the Au Bon Pain that Ruslan Kadyrov used for meetings at least twice, according to Mike Miller. As he headed over to the Lechemere T stop he said a silent prayer to the Detective Gods, asking them to let someone catch his final hail Mary pass.

Thirty-five minutes later found Finn standing in line at Au Bon Pain in Harvard Square. He'd chatted with Mike out front on his usual bench for a bit and they decided Mike should stay outside just in case the unfriendly guy was working. Sure enough, Finn spotted the balding head and impressive paunch manning the till as soon as he entered. As Finn's turn came he put on his winningest smile and approached the counter.

"Welcome to Au Bon Pain, can I help you?" asked (according to the name tag) Assistant Manager Gary Brown, without looking up from his register.

"Morning!" Finn said brightly.

"What can I get you, sir?" asked Gary, understandably keen to keep the long line moving.

"I'll take an Everything bagel, toasted, with some cream cheese, and a large coffee, please." As the man rung him up, Finn asked, "Gary, you're the Manager, right? 'Cause if so I have kind of a random request for you."

Gary glanced warily at Finn. "I'm the Assistant Manager of this store. Is something the matter?"

"No, not at all. I'm just looking for a little help. A small favor, actually."

Eyes narrowed in suspicion behind the counter.

"My name is Finn Koenen and I'm a Private Investigator.' He offered his hand but Assistant Manager Gary looked down at it as if it were a dead fish, so Finn just plowed ahead. "As it turns out, I'm working on a case that has led me to believe that you may have a crucial piece of evidence on your security footage." Finn pointed back over his shoulder to indicate the several CCTV cameras mounted on the wall outside the restaurant. "Specifically from a day a few weeks ago, and I was hoping you might see your way clear to letting me review the tapes for a few minutes?"

Gary stared blankly.

"Because if so, I would really appreciate it."

"I know you," accused Gary abruptly, eyes somehow narrowing even further. He pointed a meaty finger at Finn's chest. "You're that PI that lied about solving the Chechen terrorist case so you could get famous, right?"

Uh oh. "Well, not really… " he started, but Gary talked over him.

"And that," he said, pointing behind Finn to where Mike Miller was conspicuously looking through the plate glass front window, hands cupped around his eyes like he was holding binoculars, "is your homeless buddy! I've seen you in here with that filthy drug addict before. My cousin," he went on, voice rising with his anger, "is a cop on the Boston Police force. He's tight with some of the guys who were on that raid, and they said you didn't have anything to do with it, and that you were a money-grubbing fame whore who was full of it."

The other customers and the rest of the staff were staring at them now, but as this was his final lead, Finn bit the bullet and gave it one last shot.

"Listen, Gary, I promise I didn't try to take any credit for that raid. I have nothing but the utmost respect for the Boston PD. I have good friends there too, and we work closely together all the time. I would never screw them over." Gary clearly wasn't convinced yet, so Finn leaned over the counter and spoke in a softer voice only he and Gary would hear. "This thing I need help with? It's kind of related to the Dorchester thing, and I'm taking anything I find right to the police. Scouts' honor."

Gary wasn't having it, his eyes hard. "Sounds to me like you're just trying to grab the glory for yourself again by beating the cops to the evidence, whatever it is. So no, you can't see my security 'tapes'," here Gary made derisive finger quotes, "because (a) they're digital now, and (b) I don't trust you." He handed Finn his bagel and coffee and with a wave of his hand said, "You're money's no good here. Please leave and do not come back. You are no longer welcome at my establishment."

Finn felt dozens of eyes on him as he took his items. "Thank you for the

food and I'm sorry you see it that way. I hope you'll change your mind."
As Finn turned and made his way out of the restaurant, he could see Miller standing outside at the plate glass window grinning and giving him a big thumbs-up.

Oh yeah, thought Finn, *I crushed that.*

*   *   *   *   *

Finn stepped aside to allow a couple of students in Harvard Tennis t-shirts enter then donned his shades against the bright morning sunlight. Miller appeared at his side and gratefully accepted the last food either of them would get from Au Bon Pain, at least so long as Gary was around. They made their way to an empty concrete chess table and sat across from each other.

"So," asked Miller eagerly, "what did he say?"

"Let me see," said Finn, "I think he said I could go fuck myself."

Miller's surprise quickly turned to anger. "Screw that guy. He's a dick. He never lets any of us use the bathroom or wash up in there, and he always throws away the food he doesn't sell instead of giving it to those of us less fortunate, like some of the other places around here do," he said, gesturing towards Mr. Bartleys' down the street; a Harvard Square institution noisily cranking out burgers, fries and frappes to students, professors, tourists and locals for decades.

"I don't know if he's a dick," said Finn, shaking his head, "but he sure took a mean dislike to me right off the bat." That got a laugh from Mike. "You think that's funny? He called you a 'filthy drug addict'."

"Well," said Mike. "at least he's a good judge of character — I am a filthy drug addict!"

Their laughter was interrupted by a voice from behind Finn.

"And Gary really is a dick."

They turned towards the voice to find a young woman, maybe in her early twenties, five-eight with a pretty face, shaggy fake-blond bangs, green eyes and an Au Bon Pain apron that, while utilitarian, somehow still came across as sexy. "I'm Sue Frost," she said, and both men stood. She extended her hand to Mike first, and he shook it with a slightly dazed expression on his face.

Finn liked that she did that, shook her hand next and said, "I'm Finn Koenen and this here's Sgt. Mike Miller." Her grip was warm and firm. "You work here?"

She shot a glance back towards the restaurant and said, "Yeah, since the beginning of the school year," she said, forcing Finn to revise his age estimate downward. She shrugged. "Grad school's expensive. A girl's gotta eat, you know?"

Finn nodded, nudging his age estimate up a bit. "I do."

"So anyway," she continued," I heard what you said in there. About how you were working on the Dorchester terrorist thing? Was that true or was that bullshit?"

"True."

Sue peered at him intently. "And you think there's some sort of evidence on our security logs?"

'That's what I'm trying to figure out."

"Hmm," she said, pulling her mouth to the side as she thought. "I'm not surprised Gary wasn't all that receptive."

"Why's that?" asked Finn.

"Mr. Haddad, that's the owner, put Gary in charge of the security system, and Gary takes being in charge of stuff a little too seriously. He never lets anyone touch the software, claiming it's too sophisticated for anyone else to master, but any two-year-old could figure it out." She shook her head and shrugged, "Like I said, he's kind of a dick."

The two men laughed and she smiled back, apparently coming to a decision. She put her hands on her hips and looked at each of them in turn, though her gaze lingered on Finn for longer than was strictly necessary.

"Come back on Tuesday afternoon at like five-thirty. We close at five and Gary has his Improv class on Tuesday nights so he lets us lock up without him."

"That guys does Improv?" asked Mike, incredulous.

"Not well," Sue replied sardonically. "Anyway, come around to the back door by the dumpster and knock. I'll let you in so you can look at the security 'tapes'. She made exaggerated air quotes, mocking Gary's from earlier, then winked at Finn, spun on her heel and left.

As they watched her go, Mike asked, "Did she just wink at you?"

"I believe she did," allowed Finn.

"She must *really* hate her boss."

CHAPTER 28

5:40PM TUESDAY, MAY 13TH, 2014
HARVARD SQUARE, CAMBRIDGE, MA

As instructed, Finn found himself standing in the grimy alleyway behind Au Bon Pain the next Tuesday evening, impatiently knocking on the service entrance door for the second time. He hoped this wasn't a wild goose chase, though given how well the last few weeks had gone, he wouldn't be surprised. Nonetheless, he could really use a win and this security footage represented his last chance for one on the Kraft case.

Just as he raised his hand to knock for a third and final time, the door swung open on groaning hinges, and Sue waved him in with a smile. They picked their way around stacked boxes of napkins, cups and straws as she led him down a dimly-lit hallway. Sue removed her Au Bon Pain apron as they entered the kitchen and tossed it on one of two spotless, stainless steel counters. Revealed beneath were a pair of (to Finn's middle-aged eyes) surprisingly short denim shorts and a pale green form-fitting tank top which showed off her athletic figure as she led him into an office containing a desk, computer, filing cabinets, and a bank of CCTV monitors. She scooted around to stand behind the desk, leaned way over and tapped a few buttons on the keyboard. Finn was pretty sure she was deliberately giving him a view of her cleavage, which her tank top conveniently pushed together and displayed. She moved the mouse around, clicked a few things, then finally looked up at Finn.

"Have you worked with digital video before?" she asked.

"Is that with the computer thingy there? Like, watching a cat videos on the YouFace?" Finn asked innocently.

Her eyes narrowed. "Are you making fun of me?"

Finn laughed. "A bit. I know I'm no Millennial, but I've learned a few things along the way."

"I'll bet you have," she observed coquettishly, one eyebrow arching.

"Shall I take a look?" he asked, motioning to the monitor and changing the subject.

"Of course," she said, standing up and sliding over so that Finn could seat himself in the deceptively comfortable old, wheeled desk chair with its upholstery repaired in a dozen places by duct tape. She leaned close over Finn's left shoulder and pointed to a folder on the screen. "These are the recordings from the last year. They're organized by month, then by day, and each file represents sixty minutes of video." As Finn clicked deeper into the folders, she pointed with her finger, leaning closer and disconcertingly resting her breasts against the back of his left shoulder. "You can see that the time stamp of each segment is designated in the file name... here."

Finn leaned closer to the monitor to distance himself from her flirting. "Thanks. I think I can take it from here." Her face started to fall and he quickly followed up with, "Hey, Sue. I really appreciate your help here. I know you could get in trouble for this, and I wouldn't put you in this kind of a position if it weren't important."

She gave him a wicked smile. "You're right. I am taking a pretty big risk here. I mean, I could lose my job, and I have tuition bills to pay." She bent down behind him and spoke low into his ear as Finn half-turned his head to look back at her. "Why don't you do what you need to do, and I'll think of an appropriate way you can repay me while I finish out front." She patted Finn on the left cheek and then stood up, twirled on one foot and left him sitting uncomfortably at the desk.

Her attentions were flattering to be sure, but he had to be more than twice her age and besides, he was dating someone, wasn't he? *I mean, I think I am.* Finn shook his head to dislodge a few impure thoughts and dug into the security footage on the computer. The menus were indeed easy to navigate, and Finn watched quick snippets from a range of files, trying to identify which camera angles would give him the best view of the outside table where Mike said he'd seen Kadyrov take his meetings. While none of them gave him the clear unfettered view he'd hoped for, he did eventually decide on which camera would likely yield the best outcome. That done, he quickly located the file corresponding to the day and time that Miller claimed to have seen Kadyrov meet with the mysterious Dorky White Guy, a little over two months ago on Saturday, March 8th.

Finn played the video at 2x which moved things along but not so fast he couldn't spot who was coming and going. Sure enough, at 17:25:17 a man in a dark sweatshirt sat at a table off to the side and with his back to the camera. A few moments later another man came into frame pulling a hood over his own head before sitting across from the first man. They clearly knew where the security cameras were and took care not to expose their faces, and the lack of an audio feed compounded the challenge for Finn, who leaned in until his nose almost touched the monitor, silently willing the men to pull off their sweatshirt hoods. To his surprise it worked, sort of. The newcomer suddenly sat back and laughed, changing the angle of his head enough that sunlight penetrated his hood and for a few frames Finn could make out a Caucasian guy, probably young, with what looked like blond hair and light eyes, though the poor resolution of the video at that distance prevented certainty. Zooming in only succeeded in making a blurry image larger. Not enough pixels, apparently. He de-zoomed back to the normal magnification and restarted the video.

Miller entered the bottom left of the frame, hunched over and pretending to fumble and pick up his change cup until he reached the hedge and ducked down behind it, out of sight of the camera. The men kept talking until the one with his back to the camera held up his hand to stop the blond kid from speaking. A few moments later, both men jumped up from their chairs, the bottom half of the young kid's face becoming visible, twisted in disgust. Finn smiled to himself, remembering that Miller must have just done his 'vomiting drunk' routine. A couple seconds later, Miler staggered up from behind the hedge, his back to the men and the camera, and made its way unsteadily back down the street and out of frame. The two men watched him go, then separated. Annoyingly, the one that mostly had his back to the camera managed to take a route that never revealed his face, and the other one pulled his hood tighter around his head, shoved hands in his jeans pockets, and skulked off the other direction, towards Central Square.

Frustration grew over the next twenty minutes as Finn tried vainly to find a camera angle that would either give him a less blurry view of the Dorky White Guy's face, or any view at all of the second man's. Unfortunately the other cameras were less helpful that the first one, and he was forced to admit that the security footage wasn't good enough to help him identify either man. He sat back, cracked his knuckles and rubbed his eyes. He took a deep breath and with stubborn determination tried to wring something useful out of his last and final lead before admitting defeat.

What had he learned so far? Well, the footage provided independent confirmation of Mike Miller's version of events, which was something. Second, whoever these two were, their body language certainly suggested they were up to no good. Third, even if the video resolution was too poor to make a positive ID, one of the two men was indeed a young Caucasian guy, which would seem to confirm that, if his unseen partner really was Kadyrov, there really might be a Dorky White Guy terrorist out there.

Sue's head appeared in the office doorway. "How's it going?"

"Well," said Finn , pushing back from the desk and standing, "I've got good news and bad news."

She looked a trifle concerned. "Which is?"

"The good news is I think I'm done, and it appears you didn't get caught letting me in, so I don't think you're going to get fired," he offered as a half-assed attempt at humor.

"What's the bad news?"

"I wasn't really able to get what I came for."

She mulled that over with just the hint of a pout on her face then said brightly, "You play your cards right, and I'm pretty sure you won't go away completely empty handed," a wicked smile teasing her full red lips.

Red lips? *Aw, shit,* thought Finn, *she put on makeup.* How was he going to nip this in the bud without offending her? She was sweet and had really put her neck out to help him, a guy she barely knew except to sell bagels to once in a while.

"Listen," he started, but she cut him off, stepping fully into the small office.

"Shhh," she said, wagging a finger at him playfully. "Don't be the nice guy who says thanks but no thanks. That's not you. I mean, I don't know you really at all, but I can tell you aren't the nice-guy type."

Finn wasn't sure what to say to that so he said nothing.

"You're gonna tell me you already have a girlfriend, right?" He nodded, but she still drew closer. "Guys like you always do. Guess what? I have a boyfriend. One who's my age. I'm not trying to date you, Finn, I'm trying to get in your pants."

Despite his best intentions, Finn could feel himself responding.

Sue came in close, placed her hands on his waist, and kissed him. He found himself kissing her back but very quickly came to his senses and gently disengaged.

"I'm flattered, really, I am," Finn said kindly, "and if circumstances were different..." He let that hang in the air between them.

Sue gave him an appraising look followed by a theatrical sigh as she took a step back and shrugged. "Well, can't blame a girl for trying!"

He laughed, relieved that she understood, then followed her back down the hall and out into the alleyway.

Sue gave him another wink and called out as the door swung shut between them, "Let me know if you ever get tired of doing the right thing. I might still be interested in having you butter my bagel."

Finn stood alone in the dark alley for a moment, a little dazed by what had just transpired.

Well, he thought as he headed back towards the lights of Harvard Square proper, *I guess it can't hurt to have a Plan B.*

CHAPTER 29

9:32AM Pakistan Standard Time, Tuesday, May 20th, 2014
Lahore, Pakistan

Reza covered his face with a red and white checked scarf to protect against the maelstrom of dust whipping around Allama Iqbal International Airport as he walked from the terminal to the waiting car. The private jet he'd taken from Tehran had been lucky to arrive just before one of Lahore's frequent summer dust storms descended, and he hoped they would escape it as they headed north then east on the three and a half hour drive to the small city of Shakargahr, right at the confluence of Pakistan, India, and the disputed province of Jammu. He had some important business to attend to as he began positioning his pieces in preparation for his Three Wise Men attack next fall. The recent Chechen fiasco in Boston would make this a trickier conversation than he'd hoped, but he had confidence he could convince his local partners to move forward and support his plans. The twin promises of money and Iran's support for Pakistan's annexation of both Jammu and Kashmir should outweigh any lingering reluctance; greed being an almost universal motivator, at least in many of the circles he frequented.

As the black Toyota Land Cruiser pulled away from the curb, Reza leaned back into his seat and let his mind wander. He allowed himself a small smile at having put himself in a position to be the person comfortably and anonymously sheltered behind smoked glass windows in a luxury SUV while others had to fight the raging sand and dust that blotted out the sun and penetrated every exposed opening with trillions of gritty brown particles. It had taken the full measure of his strength, mental acuity and hard work to get to this point, but it had all been worth it —

would all be worth it — so long as he stayed focused and pulled off his audacious plans in just under eighteen months.

He'd understood, even as a 12-year-old on that terrible morning back in 1980 in the basement of a former *Savak* secret prison, that his father wanted him to fight back from inside the new regime, not outside. As such, he'd dedicated the rest of his life to proving he was a hard-line and vehement supporter of the Mullahs, the regime, and the Ayatollah. He buried his almost incomprehensible rage and made himself mercilessly invaluable to the powers that be.

And it had worked.

He'd made sure to distinguish himself while in the army, catching the tail end of the destructive and wasteful eight year war with Iraq, and then, patient and calculating as a spider, worked his way up through the ranks of the Ministry of Intelligence & Security. Enigmatic, clandestine and powerful, the MOIS acted as a sort of combination NSA and CIA, responsible for eliminating opposition within Iran's borders as well as organizing and conducting terrorist operations abroad. MOIS agents had fanned out across the globe for decades, posing as students, merchants, employees of Iran Air, bank officials and even as members of Iranian opposition groups. Back at home, few Iranians returned from an encounter with MOIS agents unscathed. All feared them.

Most of Reza's peers near the top of this all-powerful organization were clerics who curried favor with the Supreme Leader, Ayatollah Ali Khamenei. He had taken the reins from the legendary Ayatollah Ruhollah Khomeini himself — the man who led the Great Revolution of 1979 and taken 52 Americans hostage for 444 days. He had also sanctioned the rape, torture and murder of Reza's mother Fairuza, his older sisters Narges and Parvaneh, and his oldest brother Jalil. And it was Khomeini who had given the order that led twelve year old Reza to help his only remaining sibling Mas'ud shoot their own father in the head.

The Land Cruiser rocked hard to the right, buffeted by a particularly strong blast of wind that forced Reza to brace himself while his driver fought to keep the SUV on the road as it crawled along at a snail's pace through the impenetrable and ever-shifting brown gloom. Setting back into his seat again, Reza continued reflecting on the journey that had brought him here, and to many other similar godforsaken places over the past 34 years.

Now the number three man inside this brutal organization, Reza would rise no further, since by law only a cleric was allowed to lead the MOIS. However, that fit his designs perfectly, for his position as Head of the

Department of Disinformation (and an unblemished record of ruthless success) allowed him to sidestep backroom politicking, access unlimited funds, travel freely outside of Iran, and enjoy a protective halo of fear that discouraged any audits or scrutiny.

Reza's hatred of the clerics and their never-ending lies, poison and sheer incompetence was only outweighed by his ice-cold determination to both avenge his family and restore his country to the greatness it deserved. In place of the decrepit, corrupt, backwards shell of a nation he had ostensibly dedicated his life to preserving, Reza had long envisioned a Third Great Persian Empire, stretching from the western shores of North Africa all the way to the borders of China in the east. An empire that only he could bring into being and then lead. No longer would America stand like a Colossus astride the Middle East. No longer would Persia beg for scraps from the West to feed her poor. No longer would she kowtow to Russians, Israelis, Saudis or any other peoples. She would seize her place at the table as the dominant power between East and West.

Not that he hadn't faced his share of setbacks over the years. Occasionally circumstances had required him to liquidate assets, cut losses and explore new pathways. Only once before, though, had he been caught truly off-guard, and it had cost him dearly. He had been close, so very close to unleashing his secret cache of chemical and biological weapons, carefully collected over many years and hidden deep inside a secret facility in the Zahedan mountains of eastern Iran. Their destruction (surprisingly not by the Israelis, as it turned out) had forced him to go back to the drawing board and start over. However, he had to admit that the new plan, his Three Wise Men, had emerged like a phoenix from the ashes of the old one, and was infinitely more unexpected, devious, and devastating.

Burying himself like a tick deep in the heart of the ultra-Machiavellian Iranian security apparatus had provided him with more than ample opportunity to manipulate his colleagues, superiors, mercenaries, foreign terrorists and, his crowning achievement, even the head of the CIA's Iran Desk. This last accomplishment had been so unexpectedly easy that he had a very hard time convincing himself it wasn't, in fact, a trap laid for him instead. In the end though, he'd finally concluded the CIA man's greed, arrogance and ambition were genuine and the two of them had enjoyed a long and fruitful partnership ever since — a partnership that Reza let the CIA man think he controlled even as Reza set him up for the impending *coup de grace*.

However, the grandiosity of his new master plan and its many moving parts meant that Reza would regrettably need to rely on a few, select outside partners for it to come off. Conveniently, his official job required him to make common cause with exactly the kind of unsavory and unprincipled people in key areas of the globe he would need to recruit to enact his more personal agenda. However, these people, while greedy and amoral, were not stupid, and they'd quite reasonably demanded some demonstration of his ability to inflict damage and create chaos from a distance and on such a large scale. Last year's bombing of the Boston Marathon had been an important trial run, a test case that had taught him much. The recent Patriots' Day / Red Sox game plot and the attack yet to come on July 4th were to have been the proof he needed to convince his partners of his ability to succeed.

The failure of the Fenway attack to go off as planned had not been a fatal blow, as he had wisely kept the details of his plans to himself. Who was to say that he hadn't generated exactly the amount of fear, hyperbole and racist anger he'd planned for? Also, he always had a Plan B and sometimes a Plan C, D and E as well, because these types of operations entailed tremendous and varied risks. Nonetheless, the Fenway operation had not even come close to generating the carnage he wished to demonstrate to his potential partners, so this increased the importance of his Independence Day attack going off successfully. His recruitment window was closing, and his plans could ill afford another catastrophe like the one in Dorchester.

Just then, they abruptly left the dust storm behind, forcing Reza to quickly shield his eyes from the brilliant sun, suddenly reappearing as if to say; *"Did you think I was gone? I am always here, even when you cannot see me. Never forget that I am the power that moves the world."*

Reza chuckled softly as the car SUV came up to speed.

He and the sun had a lot in common.

CHAPTER 30

8:29PM SATURDAY, MAY 24TH, 2014
THE NORTH END, BOSTON, MA

Cat frowned, frustrated by her lifelong inability to say hard things in the right ways. She took a long sip of the intense, multifaceted 2005 Chateau Margaux more to buy herself some time to think than to savor it, unfortunately. She wished she could give Finn's very impressive selection the attention it deserved but her stomach had been in knots all day anticipating this very moment, and all she could taste was the regret of her own decisions.

"I kissed someone," she blurted, as soon as the large yet delicately-stemmed glass left her lips.

"Um, okay," said Finn, who looked just about as shocked as she feared he would.

Setting the glass down, she let the words tumble out, relieved to finally get this over with.

"I'm sorry. It's a guy I kind of dated a long time ago when we used to work together and he was at the same Robotics and Automation conference I spoke at in Seoul, and he tracked me down at the cocktail reception afterwards and we ended up going out with this big group for Korean barbecue and a lot more drinks and then came back to the hotel for even more drinks, and…" She trailed off, realizing she was babbling. She couldn't read Finn's expression and decided that was probably not awesome, then finished. "And we kissed in the hallway outside my room. And then I said goodnight and went in alone." She caught Finn's eye. "Alone."

"Okay," he said, neutral, "I believe you."

"Nothing else happened, and we both apologized to each other in the morning."

"Okay."

"But I'd be lying if I said I hadn't initiated it, or didn't enjoy it, even if I really wish I hadn't done it, so I wanted to tell you so that, well, you'd know. Because I like you, Finn, maybe a lot. And I know it's early-on and I'm not trying to put pressure on you or anything but I just want you to know I'll be honest with you." She shrugged. "Even if it means you get mad at me."

Her heart froze as he just stared back for a couple heartbeats. She'd hoped for a better reaction but...

"Me too," he said, with kind of a lopsided half smile.

This confused her greatly. What did that mean?

"What do you mean?"

He shifted uncomfortably in his chair and took his own explanation-delaying sip of Margaux.

"Well, I have a somewhat similar confession to make."

"In what way?" she asked, with trepidation that quickly morphed into the beginnings of real anger as Finn explained how some young thing 'ambushed him' in the back room of a fast food restaurant in Harvard Square.

"I am very sorry," he said earnestly, "I like you too, Cat. A lot. And I don't want us to have any secrets."

She gave him a pointed look.

He reddened. "Well, you know I can't talk about work things, client things," he sputtered, flustered. "I mean between us."

She was surprised at how mad she was, given that she had just admitted to doing essentially the same thing herself. And now here she was having the exact reaction she had feared he would have to her own confession.

"Well I guess that makes us even,"she bit off, unable to control her emotions and getting even angrier at herself for it.

"It's not a contest, Cat," replied Finn, pained. "And I truly am sorry, but in the grand scheme of things, it's actually kind of funny, don't you think? Both of us excited to see each other again tonight but dreading to have to admit our mistakes..."

"Was it a mistake?" she heard herself asking. Why had she said that? *Dammit.*

Finn physically cringed. "I know my indiscretion was: a mistake I'm sorry for, but the amount of guilt I've felt since has only proven to me how much I want this," here he waved his hands in the air between them, "to work."

He looked so miserable that she relented, checking her jealousy with some effort. "I'm sorry, too. For what I did and then for getting mad at you for doing the same."

The waiter reappeared with desert menus and seemed a trifle miffed when they shook their heads and asked for the check instead. Finn held the door for her on the way out, they hugged, kissed without much passion, and went their separate ways.

Cat scowled as the Uber returned her to the South End. She'd expected that the truth, about what in the grand scheme of things were a couple of pretty minor indiscretions, to make them feel better, to bring them closer together but instead she felt just the opposite. Was this the first signal that they were not ultimately meant for each other? A year from now would she look back and identify this dinner as the moment it all started to fall apart?

She certainly hoped not, but her scowl deepened, and the pit in her stomach hardened, and she could almost hear the bricks starting to go up, one by one, around her heart.

*   *   *   *   *

Fuck! thought Finn as he strode irritably away from the restaurant, *I'm really on a roll.*

In addition to clearly screwing things up with maybe the most intriguing woman he'd ever met, he'd also managed to become personna non grata at the Boston Police Department, alienated his business partner and been banned by his last client. Oh, and he had exactly zero leads on what was probably at least one terrorist roaming freely around his city.

He continued heading straight up Prince Street so he could work his way over to North Station, where he would grab a Green Line train to Park, then the Red Line out to his condo in Davis Square. Disgusted with himself, he made a decision, pulled out his phone and placed a call to Russo.

"Tony. Listen, you were right. I was an asshole," Finn said as soon as Russo picked up. "The Kraft case is bullshit and I shouldn't have forced you to work the Richards thing. Let's get together Tuesday and you can catch me up and hand it off so you can work on something more interesting than the cheating professor."

"It's too late," came Russo's gruff voice, slightly slurred with drink.

"What do you mean?" asked Finn, suddenly worried.

"I already solved it."

"Wait, what? You did?" he managed, but the line was already dead.

Bad mood now worse, Finn found he had lost interest in going home to stew in an empty apartment and decided to jump in a cab sitting at a red light.

"Where to?" asked the cabbie, an older gentleman with unruly white hair just barely contained by a gray and brown Irish tweed cap.

"The Druid," said Finn, "Davis Square. I need to get my drink on."

As the Green Cab swallowed Koenen and drove him away, the figure that had tailed him from the moment he'd exited the restaurant stepped out from a shuttered sandwich shop doorway and silently watched it go.

After the taxi disappeared around the next corner, the figure placed a call of his own.

CHAPTER 31

10:30AM TUESDAY, MAY 27TH, 2014
ROGERS DETECTIVE AGENCY, EAST CAMBRIDGE, MA

"So does this mean you're not mad anymore?" Finn asked, only half joking.

"I'm not," Tony replied before popping a chocolate munchkin into his mouth. They were sitting in Russo's office for once, the government-issue gray metal desk between them. "I mean, you're still a prick, but I've known that since Ranger school." He grinned and washed the munchkin down with some black coffee.

Tony could tell that Finn ascribed his forgiving nature this morning to the extra large coffee and box of fifty munchkins brought in precisely (and transparently) for that purpose. While always appreciative of free food, today's buoyant mood sprung from an altogether different place. However, given that he'd clearly been avoiding Finn of late, Tony didn't begrudge the attempt to curry his favor; he would have done the same, if the situation had been reversed.

"So you solved the Richards case?" asked Finn.

"I did," replied Tony, smug.

"How?" queried Finn, always so keen for details.

Tony liked making him work for it. "Guess."

"Did you finally get a few pictures of them in an indelicate embrace? Making the 'beast with two backs', perhaps?"

"Negative."

"Incriminating texts? A tearful confession?"

"Nope."

"What, then?" Finn asked, exasperation finally showing.

Not quite ready to roll over yet, Tony popped another munchkin into his mouth and chewed leisurely before answering, "Heev not sleeving wif hr."

"Come again?"

Russo swallowed. "He's not sleeping with her" he repeated.

Finn's eyebrows shot up. "He's not?"

"Nope." Tony greatly enjoyed reminding Finn that while he might be pretty smart, he didn't know everything.

"Hunh," said Finn, clearly perplexed. "Then what the hell's he doing?"

"Jiu jitsu."

"Come again?" asked Finn, gratifyingly confused.

"He's getting jiu jitsu lessons. The hot blond's name is Jenny Evans. She's a 29-year-old martial arts instructor who works out of a, whatta ya' call it, a dojo over in Davis Square, by your place. Judging by her Facebook feed, she's kind of a bad-ass."

"That's it? Just Jiu Jitsu lessons? No hanky-panky?"

"Don't say that, it makes you sound like my grandmother. And yes, just lessons. He brings a change of clothes in the gym bag and showers afterward, before he heads back to the office."

"Why all the secrecy, then? Why the hell would he lie about that to his wife?"

"Beats the shit out of me," replied Tony, unconcerned. "Eggheads are weird."

"How'd you figure it out? You have evidence?"

Tony pulled open a drawer and threw a fat manila envelope like a Frisbee over to Finn, who took out a stack of photos and started flipping through them.

"Two weeks ago I got tired of waiting for them to make a mistake and leave the curtains open, or kiss on the porch or something, so I decided to follow the blond one morning to see what she did when she wasn't with the Professor. Turns out she goes to a martial arts studio on Summer Street in Davis Square. I came back later that afternoon to check the place out and confirmed she works there because they have framed pictures of all the instructors hanging on the wall next to the reception desk and she's one of them."

Finn nodded and kept flipping through the pictures.

"Remember last week when we had that really warm day? Well, they came out into her back yard for his lesson. As you can see, I could just catch the back corner of her yard from my vantage point and every every once in a while they'd come into view."

Tony watched Finn cycle through the photos he'd taken: Jenny Evans in a white Jiu Jitsu outfit tied at the waist by a black belt demonstrating some sort of throw; her grabbing Professor Richards in his blue sparring outfit; and her throwing him over her back shoulder to the grass. The next few showed partially-obstructed views of the Professor apparently trying to execute the same move on his instructor.

"Well, I'll be damned," said Finn. "I don't understand why he's doing this on the sly, but at least Allie will be happy to learn he's not cheating on her." He slid the photos back into the envelope and handed them to Tony. "You want to give her the good news?"

"Nah. I'm all set," demurred Tony, gratified to see Finn caught off guard for the second time that morning.

"Really?" asked Finn, standing up to go. "You solved it, you should get the glory."

"Well," said Russo, taking a long pull off his water bottle and leaning back in his desk chair, "it probably makes more sense for you to tell her."

"Why's that?" asked Finn, instantly guarded.

"Because I'm gonna be taking a break from the agency."

"You're what?"

"It's something I've been considering for a while, and now seems like a good time for me to branch out a little bit, if you know what I mean."

"Actually, I'm not sure I do," replied Finn, sounding a trifle aggrieved.

"Listen, it's nothing against you, you've always been good to me and I appreciate you brought me into the business." He paused, then decided to rip the band-aid all the way off. "But to be honest, I'm not comfortable with where things have been going lately, and some other opportunities have presented themselves, so..." he trailed off, not interested in sharing more.

"What other opportunities? Does this have to do with the Kraft case?" Finn demanded.

"Let's just say I've got some other irons in the fire," replied Tony vaguely "And yes, it has something to do with you getting mixed up with Zach Fisher. I'd prefer to stay as far away from that snake as I can."

"I'm not 'mixed up' with Zach Fisher," retorted Finn, frustrated. "It's not my fault Zoe Kraft made shit up on national TV about me."

Tony spread his arms wide. "And yet here we are."

The two men stared at each other for a few moments then Finn asked, "So what else you got going on, then?"

"I'm putting a little something together with Andy," replied Tony.

"Who's Andy?" asked Finn, baffled.

"Guy I met at the Warren Tavern about a month ago. Actually, I'm surprised you haven't met him, he's there all the time." He shrugged his meaty shoulders. "Anyway, good guy, you'd like him."

"Hmph." Finn responded.

Tony stood and offered Finn his hand. "I'll be back, Finn. I just need some time to recharge and a little space to take care of some things, and then I'll be back."

Finn was clearly struggling to process this unexpected news but to his credit, he took it like a man and shook. "Sure, Tony. Whatever you need. Do what you gotta do."

"Thanks Finn. For everything." Russo made his way out into the reception area and paused to look back at a stunned Finn Koenen. "You'll be fine, Finn, even without me to watch your six."

"The door's always open, Tone. Don't be too much of a stranger," offered Finn, his voice tight with confusion and concern.

"See you on the other side, Finn," Russo said, and left.

PART FOUR

Myths are precisely what give people the faith to undertake projects which rational calculation or common sense would reject.
— Thomas Friedman[4]

CHAPTER 32

4:30PM TUESDAY, JUNE 3RD, 2014
BACK BAY, BOSTON, MA

A week later, Anderson Pierce, still nursing a hangover from babysitting that fat fuck Tony Russo yet again the night before, keyed in the pass code and raised the security gate guarding Integrated Logistics Solutions' back entrance with a noisy rumble. It had been all too easy to earn Russo's confidence as 'Andy': some relatable gripes about an unappreciative boss, free drinks, and a willingness to put up with the older man's propensity to get legless drunk. In return, the former Army Ranger had been all too willing to bitch about Koenen's 'batshit crazy' continuing investigation into some 'phantom terrorists', in the process letting slip some valuable tidbits about what the detective did and did not know. This crucial intelligence, plus the raw, ragged adrenaline rush that had come from baiting the bear in his own den had more than made up for having to carry out his Mentor's last-minute order to somehow surveil Koenen without getting caught or killed himself.

Silence descended as the last clattering, metallic echoes of the door's rise faded away. Anderson didn't worry about noise because there wasn't anyone else in the building to hear. Integrated Logistics Solutions was the sole current tenant of a double brownstone converted many years ago into a long-departed company's offices and loading bays. For some inexplicable reason, the building's owners had declined to convert it into fancy retail/restaurant/apartment space like every other building on Newbury Street. Anderson had initially discounted using this location for his base of operations because he thought it stuck out like a sore thumb on the ultra posh street. However, he then noticed while scouting it out that the *very important and busy* people bustling by treated the vacant building the same way they treated the downtrodden homeless all around them; by not seeing. Pierce noticed how their eyes skipped from the Episcopal Church on one side directly over to the art gallery on the other, paying dark and lifeless 35 Newbury no mind at all.

As such, it suited his needs perfectly, allowing him to construct his beautiful creation right in the middle of one of Boston's many self-imposed blind spots. Sure, he found the profound emptiness of the building strangely oppressive, but he did appreciate being able to come and go at odd hours as he pleased. This anonymity also ensured that his rapidly growing cache of explosive chemicals would continue to go undiscovered.

He grabbed the handles of the hand truck waiting patiently to his right, used a foot to tip it and the heavy 55 gallon drum it cradled, and carefully pushed it inside. The lock clicked shut behind and the sloshing of nitromethane accompanied his footsteps as he rolled the drum along the smooth painted concrete hallway floor. He continued into the spacious loading area which now contained a shiny pumper fire truck, somehow procured and delivered by his Mentor last week. Pierce was smart enough not to inquire as to its provenance; all that mattered was that it was here, his to transform.

Pierce carefully unstrapped the 55 gallon drum and slotted it perfectly into place alongside twenty-five others to complete two neat rows along the far wall. He wrapped the straps and snugged the hand truck tight up beside the drums and stepped back to admire the fruits of his labor over the past year. It was finally all here; more than enough of the three main ingredients he would use: nitromethane, diesel fuel and ammonium nitrate from the bags of fertilizer stacked along the adjoining wall. Even factoring in minor spillage and some slightly under-filled drums, he'd procured a buffer of an additional ~30% over what was strictly required.

If it's worth doing, it's worth doing right.

"Shut up, mom," he said into the still air, though with less venom than usual. Unfortunately, he had to admit she was right about a few things. Besides, his parents didn't matter anymore. Only this mattered.

Once he mixed the ingredients and filled the 1,000 gallon tank, the fire truck would become a well-camouflaged bomb with roughly one and a half times more explosive material than had destroyed the nine story Alfred P. Murrah Federal Building in Oklahoma City back in 1995. And he'd finished a month ahead of schedule, making this whole endeavor even more lucrative and attractive for himself.

He just wished that his best friend Hamid Farhadi — the person who had recruited him to this life — could be here to see this, to share this momentous milestone in their shared vision for changing the world. Farhadi's *accident* last summer had shocked and deeply terrified Pierce, especially because he hadn't been sure whether he were still 'involved' in their cause or if he were next on the 'accident' list. After a stressful, nerve wracking week of twisting in the wind, a bike courier handed him a package containing a cell phone. Five minutes later it rang and he spoke directly with their (now just his) Mentor for the first time. Anderson had slumped to the floor in relief once he realized he was being promoted rather than executed.

Over the coming weeks and months, Anderson deduced that his Mentor was a meticulous planner. As such, Pierce bet that early completion of his tasks would help de-risk the entire operation, so he proposed an incentive for meeting the stretch goal of compiling all the requisite materials a full month early. That way there would be time to deal with any unexpected occurrences or screw-ups. It had taken all his courage to ask the scariest person he'd even known for a bonus, but Anderson had correctly surmised that his Mentor appreciated an employee with some balls. He'd made sure to very carefully and respectfully word his proposition, however. He was greedy, not suicidal.

Well, Anderson giggled as he stared in awe at the fire truck, *technically he was, but when it served a higher purpose, it was sacrifice, not suicide.*

His Mentor had agreed and Pierce's only regret now was that he hadn't finished sooner. The 25% bonus he'd earned would materially expand the options for how he would spend his last four weeks on Earth. Before he would allow himself to begin contemplating his rewards, Anderson wanted to run through the plan one more time to see how he felt about it. Until this moment, right now, the firetruck bomb had been theoretical. With everything in place, all here in the same room, the entire endeavor became suddenly real, substantive, tangible. All this potential energy he would flash into kinetic with the press of a button...

He walked over to the driver's side and clambered up into the cab, settled into the seat, shut the door and carefully placed his hands on the over-sized steering wheel. Closing his eyes, he played out how it would all go down just one month from today, as if he were watching a movie in his head.

Fancying itself the birthplace of American freedom, Boston put a lot of effort into throwing a serious Fourth of July party. Every year hundreds of thousands of people flocked to the Esplanade on the south bank of the Charles River to watch a Boston Pops Orchestral concert and fireworks spectacular at the Hatch Shell, listening to patriotic songs while barges in the river pumped several million dollars of pyrotechnics high into the air. That money could have been spent on food or housing or job training for the downtrodden *slaves* that thought themselves free but wandered sluggishly through their empty lives never realizing they were meaningless cogs in the broken American machine.

Revelers would begin lining up at 7am in order to be one of the first to claim, when the gates opened at 9am, their patch of grass in front of the raised stage with its distinctive quarter-sphere concrete 'shell' behind it, rust colored on the inside, dirty gray on the outside. By mid-afternoon the wide expanse of lawn would be covered by a sea of people from around the world. Hundreds of thousands more would be crowded around the Hatch Shell area and along both sides of the Charles river, squabbling over the best vantage points for viewing the gaudy and entirely unnecessary fireworks display that started at 10:30pm and which was timed to the music being played by the Pops. The grand finale of the fireworks was always set to the cannons of the 1812 Overture, and wrapped up at 11pm sharp.

His Mentor's plan — genius in its devastating simplicity — would take full advantage of the practiced precision with which the city executed this annual orgy of American over-indulgence. At around 8:15pm or so on the evening of July 4th, dressed as a Mass DOT worker, Anderson would casually walk up onto the Longfellow Bridge to the closest tower facing west back towards the Hatch Shell, where the festivities would already be well underway. Taking advantage of the setting sun blinding anyone looking his direction from the Hatch Shell, he would slip into one of the access doors on the tower. He would then climb up three stories and place a small but powerful bomb camouflaged as several bricks inside the top floor of the roughly square tower with window-like openings on all four sides.

Anderson would then return to Integrated Logistics Solutions and finish his final checks. At around 10:50pm, just as the Pops would be getting ready to play the 1812 Overture for the finale, Anderson would pull the fire truck — and its 1,000 gallons of explosive mixture — out of the ILS loading bay and into Public Alley 437. Sitting in his lap would be the detonator for the firetruck and a cell phone. At the end of the alley he would make a left onto Arlington Street and head north towards the Esplanade just six blocks away. The roads directly adjacent to the Hatch Shell would all be closed of course, blocked off with concrete Jersey barriers, but that's where the heavy cow-catcher Anderson had affixed to the front of the firetruck would come in handy.

At this point he would speed-dial the only number on the cell phone in his lap, remotely detonating the bomb in the Longfellow tower. The explosion on the crowded bridge high over the Charles River to the north was not intended to cause significant damage but rather to draw attention away from the concert, the Esplanade and, most importantly, the fire truck that he would be driving toward the concert from the south. Pierce wanted the police, first responders and National Guardsmen focused on the bridge over the river so that he could catch them unawares from behind. After ramming through the barriers, security cordon and temporary fencing, he would ruthlessly plow through to the center of the assembled masses, where he would detonate the 1,000 gallons of explosives for maximum effect.

He, Anderson Pierce, would become the clenched fist of Allah himself, ripping the heart out of the arrogant city of Boston. Of the United States itself.

Changing history, however, requires sacrifice.

That day, it would be his.

Anderson probed his feelings and found a deep, still calm. He smiled, proud that the prospect of his own death did not bother him in the slightest. He was serving a higher cause. Striking a mortal blow to this fetid, rotten republic that rewarded greed and punished kindness. Pushing the system inexorably closer to total chaos, which would lead to collapse, panic, more death and ultimately, true freedom when a new society arose from the ashes of the old America. His sacrifice would be the spark that set the world alight with the purifying flames of *jihad*, the holy war every Muslim, even secret converts like himself, had a sacred duty to wage against the infidels. And after his death he would ascend to *Jannah* to receive his rewards and his virgins.

And though Anderson was himself currently a virgin, he would not be for long. To date he had lived an entirely circumspect life, never drinking, smoking, doing drugs or having sex. He did his homework, his job, volunteered in the community, paid his taxes and rarely, if ever even jaywalked. He came from a respected middle—class family in Stamford, Connecticut. He got very good grades and excelled at Brown University. Hell, he'd even helped a few old ladies across the street. In short, he was a model citizen.

However, the real Anderson Pierce, the hidden one, had always been filled with self loathing, hating the parts of himself he had no control over: his never-satisfied, domineering mother; his underwhelming and henpecked father; the materialistic society that was Stamford, Connecticut; the 'keeping up with the Joneses' mentality that affected everything done or said; and his own reluctant complicity with the entire shitty system. He'd learned early on to keep his true thoughts to himself, to act the part of the dutiful son; the serious student; the dedicated worker-bee. Until he had met Hamid and been exposed to the enlightened teachings of the Prophet Mohammed, he'd had no outlet for his feelings, no direction to his life. But Hamid had shown him the way, taught him how he could simultaneously end his private torture and suffering while striking a mortal blow for *Allah* against the Great Satan.

Anderson came back to the present and climbed down out of the firetruck, surveying the elements of destruction laid neatly out around the spacious room. He grinned and pulled a burner cell phone from his pocket. He tapped out just two words: *It's done,* dropped the phone on the floor and ground the heel of his stained and pitted work boot into the device, crushing it.

Unable to stop grinning, he now let himself contemplate the four long weeks ahead in which he would spend his well-earned money on all the things he had denied himself for the past 23 years: wine, women and expensive meals. Fancy suits. Pointless electronic gadgets. More women. Bathtubs filled with champagne and hundred dollar bills to sleep on. He would enjoy his last month in a blur of conspicuous consumption, just like a real American. And then...

Then he would do what needed to be done.

He would give Boston a new massacre.

And it would be beautiful.

CHAPTER 33

10:20AM SUNDAY, JUNE 15TH, 2014
ALONG THE CHARLES RIVER
THREE WEEKS UNTIL JULY 4TH

Heather dropped back behind Finn to allow two bikers to pass by heading the other direction. Stepping forward to jog alongside her younger brother again, she nudged him with her right elbow.

"Aren't you glad I talked you into this?" she asked gleefully.

"Ecstatic," he replied, faux grumpy.

Since Finn moved to Boston they'd always made a point to spend time together, but with Russo currently on walkabout, managing the agency had temporarily supplanted hanging out with his sister. Ordinarily Heather would have harassed him about this but had decided to cut him some slack, given his difficulties over the last few weeks. So, looking to get some face time and also give him an opportunity to burn off some steam, she had suggested they meet for an early Sunday morning run around the Charles. She had a 3.5 mile loop around a segment of the river that she loved, especially on warm, beautiful days like today.

Finn readily agreed to the exercise though predictably protested about the 'early' bit. His counter-offer of noon was just lazy, so they'd compromised on meeting in Harvard Square at 10am. A perennially early riser, Heather had put in several hours of research at her desk in the Belfer Center for Science and International Affairs before meeting up. They'd kissed cheeks three times in the Dutch style and started jogging towards the Charles without any further preamble. After crossing over via the Harvard Street bridge they'd turned left to head east then south along the meandering banks of the cobalt-blue river, sparkling frenetically in the bright morning sun. Well familiar with the route, they unconsciously weaved their way though a steady stream of other joggers, rollerbladers, dog-walkers and cyclists.

"You know, if you want," Heather continued, keeping her tone older-sister-teasing light, "I could spend the next twenty minutes giving you shit for screwing things up with Cat…"

"Hard pass," said Finn. "I already have that well covered on my end."

They both chuckled and she maneuvered around an older woman walking an ancient Scotch Terrier.

"Besides," he continued, getting defensive, "she made the same mistake I did, so…"

"Fair enough," she said, taking the hint. "How's work going? Are you managing okay with Tony gone? Looking to bring anyone in to help share the load?"

He gave a short bark of a laugh. "Even if I had he time for that, I still have no idea when or if he's ever coming back, so I don't know if I should replace him or not."

"Anything I can help with? I'd waive my usual consulting fees for you," she offered. "Well, maybe not completely, but I'd give you the friends-and-family rate at least."

"Oh yeah?" he said, glancing over with mock suspicion, "what's it gonna cost me?"

She thought about that for a few strides. "Meet me for another run next Sunday?"

He shook his head immediately. "I'm not against going running with you but you know my schedule changes day to day. Sometimes even hour to hour. We have to play that by ear."

"Okay," she countered, sensing an opportunity, "how about instead you commit to doing fireworks on the Esplanade again this year?"

Finn had joined Heather in the Boston area nine years ago and to celebrate their first Independence Day together in over a decade they attended the festivities at the Hatch Shell. Though initially ambivalent about the idea, once on-site he'd quickly become enthralled by the entire spectacle. Walking home afterwards, Finn had waxed philosophical about the event, saying that it had done an excellent job of celebrating the essence of America that led their parents to become Americans themselves and to dedicate their personal and professional lives to helping the nation live up to its promise as a shining city on a hill. Had their car not slipped off that icy Swiss mountain road, Finn was convinced they would have finished out their lives skipping merrily every few years from post to post until the time came to hang up their passports and retire somewhere warm, breezy and off the grid. Heather agreed and thought they would have liked that ending very much.

But the last two years he'd begged off, claiming both times that he needed to babysit an aggressively drunk Tony Russo. Despite this likely being true, she found the excuse pretty lame. The shine of the annual celebration had apparently worn off for her brother but it hadn't for her and she wanted to re-establish this family tradition — one of the few they'd created since their parents died. And now with Russo AWOL and unavailable to act as Finn's get-out-of-jail-free card, she figured she wouldn't get a better chance.

It was a measure of his frustration level that he agreed to the stipulation without argument. They ran on for a bit in silence, him brooding and her a little giddy with this small victory, off the path, up a hill and through the well-used hole in a chain link fence used to access the BU Bridge. As they crossed the Charles and curved down onto the Cambridge side of the river to head back the other direction, he began talking about the Kraft case, one she had thought long closed. He spent the next half mile or so catching her up to speed and described how he now found himself in the worst possible place; an unsettled limbo filled with both tantalizing hints and dead ends, one where his head could not prove what his gut was saying.

She could sympathize. Her job at the Belfer Center as a researcher and writer often put her in a position where her instincts told her a regime was behaving (or going to behave) in a certain (usually bad) way, but the evidence just wasn't available for her to prove it conclusively. As one of few Americans who had lived in both Tehran and Europe, she was a perfect fit (and significant asset to) the Belfer Center's Middle East initiative of the Diplomacy & International Politics Program, and she loved trying to untangle complicated international knots. She decided to recap Finn's update on the case to ensure she had it straight.

"So you think, but can't prove, that there is someone affiliated with, perhaps worked directly with, the former Chechen terrorist cell in Dorchester. You also think that maybe this 'Dorky White Guy' is somehow connected to the Marathon bombing a year ago. And despite his possible involvement in these two major incidents he has, other than Mike Miller's eavesdropping, to date gone completely undetected."

"Correct on all counts."

"And you've thoroughly reviewed the case files the Kraft woman gave you, pulled every loose thread?" she asked, already knowing the answer but needing to cover the bases.

He gave her his, 'how stupid do you think I am?' look in reply. Fair enough. They continued jogging in silence, the river rolling inexorably along in the other direction to their left.

"So, let's assume this so-called Dorky White Guy is out there, and he's a straight-up terrorist somehow involved in all this stuff. And given that he's avoided detection so far, let's also assume he's at least pretty good at being a terrorist, agreed?"

"Agreed."

"Okay. Research shows that the most successful terrorists we know of share some similar characteristics, three in particular. First, their use of ideology and propaganda to motivate others to do their dirty work is unparalleled. Second, they excel at asymmetrical warfare and exploiting the chinks in the armor of their significantly better-resourced enemies. And third, they wield fear like a weapon."

"Okay," said Finn, cautiously.

"So it looks like your guy is pretty good at the first, because he apparently got the Tsarnaevs and a bunch of Chechens to take the fall for him. Second, he's clearly shown a facility for identifying chinks in our armor. And third, since no one other than Miller has ever caught onto the guy, my bet is that he's pretty good at using fear as a weapon. So that's your lead. That's what you should look into next."

"What are you talking about?" asked Finn, not following. "Look into what?"

Heather grinned as they approached Harvard Street again, signaling the end of their run. She stopped short, surprising him, and he took a few more strides before coming to a stop himself, several yards away.

"Fear is the key," she said, dropping into professor mode, "so what scares people?"

"I don't know, snakes? Heights?"

She made a face. "Try again, sport."

"Death," he said after a moment. "Avoiding it tends to put a jump in your step."

"Exactly," she replied. "So that's your next line of inquiry. If I were you, I'd look into any and all suspicious or unsolved deaths in the weeks following the Marathon bombing last year."

"To what end?" he asked, puzzled.

"One of the hallmarks of an organization ruled by fear is that it does not tolerate people who make mistakes or break ranks. It makes examples of them as a way to cull underperforming members of the tribe while simultaneously providing everyone else with a clear demonstration of what will happen if they don't succeed."

Finn nodded. "Got it."

"And I'd guess that the man behind the scenes here — and it's just about always a man — wasn't particularly happy about that shit show the Tsarnaevs put on last year. If I were him, heads would have rolled. And since the surviving Tsarnaev hasn't blabbed to the authorities, he may have been scared into thinking jail and a death sentence is better than whatever the bad guy has in store for him or his family if he sings like a canary."

Finn's face went a little slack and she gave him the space he needed to process.

"So you're saying…"

"Yup. Look at the unsolved murders from last spring and early summer to see if any of them would have made for an effective warning, especially anything particularly notable or gruesome that would have sent a clear message to a certain young bomber in Federal custody, perhaps?"

Finn grinned and gave her a sweaty hug. "You're a genius!" he declared happily. "Thank you!"

She squeezed him back, pleased about all of it: running together; securing his commitment for the Fourth; and helping Finn with a problem he hadn't been able to solve. Generally speaking, he wasn't great about asking for help.

"You're right, I am," she replied. "And you're welcome." She gave him a piercing look. "Now, about this situation with Cat…"

CHAPTER 34

HIGH RISK OF EAST COAST TROPICAL DEVELOPMENT THIS WEEK
ERIC HOLTHAUS – *SLATE.COM* – JUNE 29, 2014

What may become the first tropical system of the 2014 Atlantic hurricane season has begun brewing off the Carolina coast, and weather models show it may affect much of the East Coast for the July 4thholiday weekend.

In its 6 a.m. Sunday update, the National Hurricane Center said there is an 80 percent chance that the swirling mass of clouds will develop into a full-fledged tropical cyclone within the next five days.

Regardless of whether it meets the official criteriaof a tropical cyclone, wet weather is becoming increasingly likely along the East Coast later this week. If the disturbance reaches tropical storm strength it will be given the name Arthur.

In the current worst-case scenario, a strong tropical storm will rake the entire East Coast. Yesterday's European model showed just such a scenario, with future Tropical Storm Arthur tracking from South Carolina to Staten Island on a four-day tour from July 3 through 7.

In both cases, rain looks increasingly likely from the Carolinas to New England on the Fourth of July—it's just a matter of whether it's an afternoon sprinkle or a torrential downpour accompanied by winds strong enough to send your barbeque grills skyward.

With the first storm of the season potentially forming so close to shore, there may not be much lead time for those immediately in its path to prepare for its impact.

CHAPTER 35

10:30AM SUNDAY, JUNE 29TH, 2014
CAMBRIDGE, MA
FIVE DAYS UNTIL JULY 4TH.

Finn thanked the waiter for the tall glass of orange juice and turned back to his phone to continue slogging through email triage. Usually, Sunday brunch called for relaxing over a mimosa or two, but Tony's unexpected sabbatical (and his inability to let the Kraft / Dorky White Guy case go) left Finn working seven days a week with precious little time off for meals out or Sunday morning cocktails. The past month had tangibly demonstrated the depth and breadth of Tony's contributions to the Agency. In addition to running half the cases, he had also acted as the de facto receptionist / office manager in a way Finn never had. And despite Tony's grousing, he had nevertheless continued to answer phones, return messages, field emails and make appointments for them — all things Finn now remembered he despised doing.

Though always a very strong student, Finn had never taken much of a liking to classroom learning and fundamentally hated sitting in one place all day long. By extension, he also disliked and was indifferent at best to all things office related, like keeping the books, managing paperwork and dealing with vendors. He'd spent three days wondering why 'the service' wasn't replacing his two conspicuously empty large water cooler bottles before belatedly realizing that he would have to call the number on the side of the dispenser to accomplish that himself. He leaned back and took a satisfyingly deep drink of the freshly squeezed juice, allowing himself to forget about his depressingly long to-do list and just enjoy the moment.

Sunday brunch was serious business at the S & S Deli in Inman Square and Finn sat quietly, content to let the organized happy chaos of the place wash over him. Old married couples reading the Sunday Globe over coffee and bagels with cream cheese sat next to raucous clutches of recent college grads rehashing the previous night's questionable decisions while scarfing down corned beef hash and eggs and emptying a never-ending succession of Bloodies. Waitstaff in perpetual motion threaded their way through a maze of tables carrying impossibly overladen trays while animated chatter and the bright clink of cutlery cascaded around the upscale diner. Finn concentrated and found he could identify the scents of coffee, tarragon, butter, freshly-baked bread and, of course, bacon.

The last few weeks had been tough, with Tony's loud absence from the office and the consequently doubled workload; the uncertainty around his relationship with Cat; the growing guilt over not having spent any meaningful time with Mike Miller since early May, and impotent frustration about the Kraft case. Today, though, he was actually in a proper good mood. It had started to turn around two days ago, when Allie Richards popped into the office to deliver her final payment and thank him personally. This gave him the opportunity to close the loop on why it was the Professor had taken such great pains to hide his Jiu Jitsu lessons from her. It turns out that dorky, bookish Professor Greyson Richards had intended to prove to his ex-helicopter-flying, ass-kicking, fireplug of a wife that he could be tough too.

Though Allie had never wanted Greyson to be anything other than what he was — an adorable, bespectacled egghead with a kind heart and a sharp mind — he'd apparently always felt somehow like less of a man next to his wife. It was something he had never once mentioned to Allie, having brought it in secret to their marriage like a splinter in his ego. He'd finally decided to get martial arts training on the sly to surprise her, and she'd managed to pull off acting the part of a surprised and delighted wife. And despite feeling the gesture entirely unnecessary she found she loved Greyson all the more for having made it. For once, and something that was rarely seen in the PI business, all was well that ended well.

Then on the heels of Allie's visit he'd received a text from Cat (the first one in a couple weeks) saying she'd be back in town soon and asking what he was doing for the Fourth, and did he want to get together then? He definitely did, and decided to invite her to join him and Heather for some illicit drinks on a blanket, listening to classical music and watching the fireworks. She'd readily agreed — so readily, in fact, that Finn suspected Heather had put her up to it, especially given the level of shit she had given him the last couple times they'd gone jogging together. Whatever the reason, he was psyched to see Cat again and have a chance to get things back on track.

Good things happen in threes, he thought happily as he drank off most of the remaining orange juice. Just last night Sully texted to see if they could get together over brunch this morning. Though the officer had declined to explain why he wanted to meet, Finn was hopeful that Sully was delivering the information he'd requested a couple weeks ago. It also wouldn't hurt if this face-to-face meeting in public signaled the end of his exile from Boston Police HQ. Or, if not the end, perhaps at least the beginning of the end? Coming to a snap decision about how he would spend the rest of his Sunday, Finn flagged his waiter down.

"Any chance you could turn this," he asked, waggling his almost empty orange juice back and forth, "into a mimosa?"

"Of course, sir," replied the waiter, flashing a smile. "Wouldn't be brunch without it."

*   *   *   *   *

Sully snuck up behind Finn and clapped him on the shoulders, causing him to sputter into his drink.

"You didn't tell me you had a past with Fisher," Sully accused mildly as he settled into the straight-backed wooden chair across from Finn and placed his leather messenger bag down to lean against it.

"We don't really run in the same circles," replied Finn, recovering his composure and wiping a bit of orange juice pulp off his upper lip.

"You know, if I didn't know better, I'd say he's not your biggest fan," Sully observed dryly as he reached over to help himself to a healthy sip of Finn's drink.

Finn barked out a laugh as he took the half empty glass back. "Yeah, well, you might say we have some history."

Their waiter materialized and Sully ordered a couple more mimosas. When it became clear that Finn wasn't planning to elaborate, he rolled his hands to indicate he should.

Finn seemed to debate with himself before sighing heavily and leaning in over the table. In a low voice that forced Sully to also lean in, Finn said, "You know I was a Tier 1 Operator, right?" Sully nodded. "All I can say without getting us both landed in prison is that your buddy Zach Fisher used to be a member of the CIA's Special Operations group within the Special Activities Division."

"That sounds pretty special," Sully interjected.

"Indeed. So special, in fact, that Zach got assigned to one of our Delta missions. Don't ask me about it because I'm not telling you, except to say that it went poorly and he and I had some radically different opinions about a few important things. In fact, it wouldn't be wrong to say that his actions that day ultimately led directly to me leaving the service."

Sully was incredulous. He'd asked Finn about his time in Delta Force of course, but his old friend had never shared any details about why he left the Army other than saying, 'it was time'. Just then, something clicked into place. "So Russo must know Fisher too, right? Weren't you guys on the same squad or something?"

Finn gave a wan smile. "He does and we were," he confirmed. "And when Tony found out Zach Fisher had reappeared and was pissed off at me, he took a powder."

"Took a powder? What are you guys, Prohibition gangsters?"

"Seriously," Finn said, "He quit."

"Russo quit?"

"Well, took a sabbatical, I guess," Finn amended. "I mean, I think he'll come back, but for now he said he had some other irons in the fire he wanted to pursue."

Sully could hear regret in his friend's voice, and was that some loneliness, too?

"You okay with that?"

Finn shrugged and finished his first mimosa just as the waiter returned with the next round. After taking their food orders, he left them alone again. "So, does this," Koenen waved his arm over the table, "mean I'm off the 'Do Not Fly' list?"

Sully chuckled and shook his head. "Well, we rescinded the shoot-on-sight order, but I wouldn't expect too many Christmas cards." He was glad to see Finn laugh at that, then continued in a more serious tone. "Listen, most of the guys know you, so they're willing to give you a pass on the news story."

"I had nothing to do with that!" interrupted Finn, frustrated.

Sully raised his hands in a placating gesture. "I get it. And so do a lot of others, but you know how it is. Some guys are always looking to hold a grudge." Finn grunted his agreement and Sully continued. "Lucky for you the Captain's on your side, otherwise you'd probably be face down in a Mattapan gutter."

"Really?" asked Finn, his turn to be incredulous. "Ned's on my side? I kinda thought he'd be more protective of his guys. Like, circle the wagons and all that?"

Sully shook his head. "That reporter, Mendez? She's made her career going after cops, always trying to catch us doing something wrong. She seems to think we're all fascist thugs out to terrify and subjugate the common man." He didn't bother hiding his distaste. "All she cares about is juicy headlines and these days, police brutality sells. Fucking disgrace." Sensing a counter-argument coming from Finn, he headed it off; this wasn't what he'd come here to discuss. "Listen, I get it. There are more than a few bad apples out there that deserve to be tossed, but she bends the truth to make a name for herself, facts be damned, and that's flat-out wrong." He took another sip of his drink and counted to five to allow the surge of anger subside to more manageable levels. "Anyway, Cap pretty much can't stand her, and he likes you. You've always done us right and that counts for more with him than anything she'll ever say."

Finn nodded. "Okay. Thanks. Good to know."

"So," he said, getting to the point, "you want the good news first or the bad news?"

"Bad news first."

"I figured. My undercover guy says he never saw anyone or heard any talk about anyone that matches your description of this 'Dorky White Guy'."

"Really? That sucks but I guess I'm not surprised," Finn said resignedly. "Disappointed maybe, but not surprised. What's the good news?"

Sully leaned sideways to pull a thick folder out of his messenger bag that he handed to Finn with a smile.

Finn's eyes went wide as he accepted it. "Unsolved murders from just after the Marathon bombing?" he asked hopefully.

"Damn straight," Sully confirmed, "though you didn't get 'em from me."

"Understood," Finn said quickly as he opened the folder and began to peruse its contents. "This is great, Sully — thank you very much."

"No problem. I also included a few open missing persons reports that smelled funny, on the off-chance they're more than just missing. Make sure to let me know if you get any bright ideas. Helping us clear any of these would go a long way to rehabilitating your reputation down at the station."

"No doubt," replied Finn distractedly as he flipped pages.

Just then their waiter reappeared and deftly slid eggs Benedict in front of Finn and a western omelet in front of Sully.

"I think it's safe to say that I'm not a huge believer in conspiracy theories, and as such, I'm pretty sure you aren't going to uncover a secret super-terrorist out there planning some big attack." After taking a bite of eggs, diced ham, green peppers and onions, Sully continued, "But I also carry a healthy amount of paranoia around and I'm not particularly keen about the probability, however small, that there may in fact actually be a secret super-terrorist out there planning some big attack."

"Okay," said Finn, "and your point is?".

"Today is Sunday the 29th of June and in just five days we're going to have three-quarters of a million people down on the river for the Pops concert and fireworks display."

Finn blanched, immediately catching Sully's drift. "Oh shit," he said quietly, sounding far away.

"Oh, shit indeed," repeated Sully. "And do you have any idea what a fucking nightmare it is to secure an event like that?"

"I can guess."

"Well, it turns out I don't have to guess, because I've been tapped as the lead BPD representative on the Joint Event Security Task Force," he announced, "which is the main reason it's taken me so long to get back to you. And guess who is running said JESTF?"

Finn winced. "Zach Fisher?"

"Zach Fisher. And while I didn't quite trust him before, I *definitely* don't trust him after what you just told me."

"That's probably wise," opined Finn.

"So as you can imagine, this whole situation has me going a little nuts. And on top of everything else, your little theory about an unknown terrorist walking around with an ax to grind keeps poking me in the shoulder. No matter how outlandish the whole idea is, I'd never be able to live with myself if it turned out to be true, so will you do me a favor and really dig into those files over the next couple of days to see if you find anything sketchy-like? You're the one who brought this bogeyman to me so now I need you to either find him or put my mind at ease."

"Sure, Sully, I'll do that," replied Finn hastily.

"The whole idea is so ridiculous I can't allocate BPD resources to it, but I also can't get it out of my head, so I'm counting on you to do your thing here."

"Will do. Scout's honor," promised Finn. "I live here too, you know. In fact, I'll be at the Pops concert myself, with Heather and a friend, and I don't much fancy getting blown to bits or shot while we're enjoying the fireworks."

"That would probably ruin the evening," Sully observed sagely, then tucked into his food with gusto — he hadn't had a proper meal in days.

* * * * *

Thirty minutes later, Derek Wasserman collected the settled bill off of table 14 and began transferring two sets of plates, flatware and mimosa glasses onto an oversized circular brown tray. Looking up, he noticed that Table 15 (also in his section) was suddenly empty. He stood up straighter and craned his neck to get a better look through the bustle of patrons and his fellow waiters. *Huh*, he thought, *when did that guy leave?*

He grabbed Carli's arm as she cruised past. They had both been at the S&S for a couple years now — he taught Third Grade during the week and she was starting to get some traction in her acting career — and they had been fast friends right from the start, the way it happens sometimes. "Hey," he said.

"Hey," she replied. "What's up?"

"Did you see the guy at 15 leave?" he asked, "I haven't brought him his bill yet."

She looked over at the table set for one, with its empty coffee, half-eaten omelet, mostly full orange juice and a neatly folded white cloth napkin. The chair was carefully pushed in so as to be out of the way. "No," she said ruefully. "Dine and dash, huh?"

Every waiter understood that the occasional dine & dash was a small and unavoidable part of the job but it meant a loss of a tip for Derek, and as a primary school teacher, every tip mattered.

"I hope not," said Derek, dismayed. "I mean, he waited longer than he had to because he specifically wanted to sit at that table, which I thought that was kind of weird, but he didn't strike me as a dine-n-dash kind of guy."

They went over and found a crisp, new $100 bill sitting folded in half and partially tucked under the rim of the plate.

"Holy shit," Carli said. "How much food did he order?"

Derek was stunned. He couldn't remember the last time he had actually seen a bill that large. "Not that much!" He checked his pad and found the correct slip. "I don't know, maybe like fifteen, seventeen bucks?"

"Holy shit!" she repeated, with more excitement this time. "You just made an $83 tip! Who leaves a tip like that?"

Derek wasn't sure what to say. It felt kind of wrong to take a tip that big on a bill that small, but screw it, he wasn't going to look a gift horse in the mouth.

"What did he look like?" she asked. "I wanna make sure I get him in my section next time!"

Derek furrowed his brow. "Um. White guy, young, our age. Short hair, blond maybe. Glasses." He trailed off. "It's kind of hard to remember. He didn't really make much of an impression."

Well, apparently you made quite an impression on him!" exclaimed Carli. "Though, in my experience, when a man gives you a large and unexpected gift like that, he's either trying to get in your pants, or he already has and you just don't know it yet."

CHAPTER 36

12:05PM MONDAY, JUNE 30TH, 2014
EAST CAMBRIDGE, MA
FOUR DAYS UNTIL JULY 4TH

"Got it,… Thanks, I really appreciate the help and I'll be sure to let you know if I learn anything new… Okay. Thanks again. Cheers."

Finn hung up and slowly leaned back, tilting his chair as far as it would go without tipping over. He tented his hands and lightly tapped index fingers against the tip of his nose as he factored what he just learned into what he already knew. His eyes roamed around without seeing and he subconsciously mumbled half-words and ideas into the stillness of his office. After a few minutes he sat forward and began making notes on a pad of paper in his chronically erratic and mostly illegible handwriting.

After paying for brunch and parting ways with Sully, he'd dedicated the rest of Sunday and all this morning to reviewing and researching the fifteen or so unsolved homicides and three missing persons cases from 2013 contained in Sully's fat folder. Depressingly, most of them were black or Hispanic males in their late teens to early twenties and Finn knew many of these homicides would likely be drug- or gang-related. There was a Caucasian male in his mid-forties who looked like he had probably been homeless and three young women, one of whom had been found lying face down in a Mattapan gutter, an ugly and unfortunate echo of Sully's joke over brunch yesterday. Finn dutifully read through each of these cases carefully, though his gut told him none of these deaths were a terrorist sending a message. Unfortunately, he was unable to come up with any new thoughts or observations that might help Sully clear any of them. The victims faces, staring eternally frozen out of mugshots or clipped from social media posts, challenged him to do better, much as Amanda Kraft's did.

Each of the three missing persons cases, however, had required a more thorough review because, with no bodies having been recovered, they necessarily had less to tell him. There were personal details, of course, and transcripts of interviews with family, friends and coworkers along with some inter—agency communications, but precious little else of value. The dead left behind a treasure trove of information: time of death; cause of death; fingerprints; dental impressions; tattoos; dirt under fingernails, surgery scars and traces of childhood's broken bones. Missing persons left behind a vacuum; one that, unlike physical vacuums, stubbornly resisted being filled.

One of the missing was a 52 year old Irish-American guy from Charlestown. His file contained a rap sheet for a string of misdemeanor drug possessions and a couple felony theft and drug dealing convictions. Paul Denehy had clearly been a small-time player in the Charlestown Irish mafia. Finn could guess why Sully had included this file: Denehy was a morally-flexible guy who seemed like he wasn't too picky about how he paid the rent, but Finn couldn't see this two-bit Irish mobster having anything to do with a group of shit-scary Chechen terrorists. Finn had more overseas experience than Sully did, and he knew that different nationalities tended to stick together in ethnic clumps that didn't necessarily mix well with other ethnic clumps. No, in Finn's experience, the Irish would no more help out the Chechens than a Red Sox fan would hold the door for George Steinbrenner, and vice-versa. It wasn't personal, it was tribal.

The second missing person was Sania Al-Maghrebi, a naturalized citizen from Saudi Arabia. In her late twenties when she disappeared, Sania had emigrated to the United States on her own at age 17, found a job, an apartment, got a driving license and made many friends both in and outside the Arab community in Boston, based on the wide variety of people interviewed after she'd vanished. By all accounts, Sania had been a classic American immigration success story and had assimilated to her adopted country with few if any difficulties. There had been no signs of trouble, no abusive boyfriend, no excessive partying or secret gambling debts, no signs to indicate that anything was wrong. And yet, one day she just wasn't there any more. No signs of struggle, no large withdrawals of cash, no body floating in the Charles. It was if she had simply evaporated into nothingness.

Finn read her file several times over and dug around on the Internet as well, using one of the fake personas he'd created across multiple platforms for just this purpose. He'd seen first hand that terrorists were happy to utilize women and children to spread their death and mayhem. Ultimately, though, poor Sania had become the sole item in his 'Maybe' pile. Initially he had placed her in the discard pile, feeling that these Chechens in particular would not have included any women in their inner circle as (generally speaking) they were pretty old school about women, and besides, every single one of the dead terrorists in Dorchester had been male. It occurred to him, though, that Kadyrov had been a pretty smart guy, and Finn wouldn't put it past him to use a woman, perhaps as a cut-out or go-between with the Tsarnaevs? Maybe helping them scout locations? Whatever her story might be, she was at least a maybe for Finn.

Though Hamid Farhadi's file had been the very last one Finn reviewed, it jumped out at him immediately, and he'd gone from feeling mentally fried to focused and excited. Twenty four year old Hamid had been born in 1989 in Tehran, Iran but had incongruously done his high school years at the Rugby School in England. Very few Iranian youths left the country for any reason, much less to attend an expensive and exclusive Public School in the UK for four years. He graduated with distinction, achieving an A* or A on all four of his A-Level exams and gone onto a stellar academic career at Brown University in Providence, Rhode Island. After graduation in 2011 he migrated forty-five minutes north to work at Bain Consulting in Boston. And then last summer, he just vanished.

According to interview transcripts with colleagues and former professors, Hamid Farhadi had been a serious and driven young man who abstained from alcohol or drugs. Though Bain paid its junior associates reasonably well, Boston was expensive and Farhadi had lived modestly, based on the location and photos of his apartment. It appeared he had been well liked but not well known, in the sense that while everyone spoke fondly of him, no one seemed to be truly close to him. And while his fellow batch-mates at Bain had been particularly distraught by his sudden disappearance, Finn found it curious that no family members had been interviewed or even appeared to exist. If he had family, did they not know he was gone? Did they not care? Or was he an orphan? If an orphan, how had he secured permission to leave Iran for schooling in the UK, much less paid for it? For that matter, how had he paid for Brown? Had he been a scholarship student in both cases or was someone else footing the bill?

And — most importantly — why had he gone missing on or around the long July 4th holiday weekend in 2013, about a week before Dzhokhar Tsarnaev chose to plead 'Not Guilty' to some thirty Federal counts related to the Marathon bombing? Could this young Iranian be the same 'middle eastern guy' that Mike Miller saw meeting with Kadyrov and the Tsarnaevs last April? Whatever the truth, something about this felt like more than coincidence. So, Farhadi became the sole occupant of Finn's 'Interesting' pile, and he'd spent much of Monday morning digging deeper.

He started with some ultimately fruitless calls to a few of Hamid's Bain colleagues, knowing that they would be at work by 7:00am or 7:30am and wanting to catch them before they got swamped by their days. He then reached out to the Brown Registrar's office, which had been eager to help but unable to provide any new or interesting tidbits. Finally, he reached out to the Rugby School to see what they might be able to tell him. At first the woman he reached in the school's offices had been reluctant to speak with Finn, but softened when he explained he'd been hired to try and track down what happened to their former student. She'd heard about Hamid's disappearance and just felt terrible about it, so decided to bend their understandably strict rules around sharing students' information. It turned out that Hamid had not, in fact, been on a scholarship, and that his fees had been paid anonymously from a Swiss Bank account, which, given the background of most of the students at The Rugby School, she found not at all unusual.

Finn however, did.

He sat up straight, cracked his back and rolled the kinks out of his neck. He stared at the three notes he's circled on the page, slowly tapping each with a pen as he read through them. First, Hamid Farhadi was a smart, young Iranian who'd worked hard, kept his head down, and had no close friends. Second, he apparently had no family but had benefited greatly from an anonymous source of significant funds. Third, a week after he had gone missing, the surviving Tsarnaev plead 'Not Guilty' to a crime everyone in the world knew he committed.

Hamid Farhadi. Are you my canary in the coal mine?

CHAPTER 37

OFFICIALS KEEPING AN EYE ON ARTHUR
TOM BLACKSTONE — *THE BOSTON GLOBE* — JULY 1, 2014

State and City officials were keeping a wary eye on a major storm ahead of the July 4 holiday, as updated security measures were disclosed for the annual celebration on the Charles River Esplanade.

Tropical Storm Arthur formed off the Florida coast early Tuesday. It is expected to stream along up the East Coast and could bring heavy rain to New England by the Forth of July.

Mayor Martin J. Walsh and others did not rule out the possibility of moving the big event up a day; a pre-show concert is already scheduled for Thursday. But forecasters said that Thursday could be worse than Friday, as the front threatened heavy rain and even flooding.

"It's going to be a tough haul," said William Babcock, a National Weather Service meteorologist. "Unfortunately for everyone, the two days Boston will be most impacted are Thursday and Friday, the backup day and the prime day. That's just the way the weather works sometimes, I guess."

In a new restriction, bicycles will not be allowed into the oval and the lagoon/island areas of the Esplanade, as reduced bike traffic will allow the crowd to easily disperse if an evacuation is necessary.

"The greatest partner that we have in these major events is the public," said Colonel Timothy Alben, superintendent of the Massachusetts State Police. "We really need people to be vigilant, to pay attention to what's going on around them."

Boats will not be allowed between the Massachusetts Avenue Bridge and the fireworks barges, which have moved west for the show.

Backpacks, firearms, explosives, coolers on wheels, glass containers, cans, premixed drinks and alcoholic beverages will be prohibited. Bags and purses will be searched.

The show will be similar to last year's, with the traditional playing of the "1812 Overture" accompanied by a fireworks display beginning at 10:30pm. Around 12,000 fireworks weighing at least 3 tons will have been set off by the time the show concludes.

Between 600,000 and a million spectators are expected to attend the celebration, which Walsh called one of the country's greatest patriotic traditions.

CHAPTER 38

10:15AM TUESDAY, JULY 1ST, 2014
ROXBURY, MA
THREE DAYS UNTIL JULY 4TH

Cacophony reigned on the third floor of Boston Police Headquarters as a hundred cops, Feds, Harbor Masters, Firefighters, EMTs, liaisons from the Boston Pops, fireworks vendors and representatives from Mayor Walsh's office all reacted poorly to what Officer Patrick O'Sullivan just told them.

"That's right, you heard me," he bellowed over the unruly attendees at this hastily convened JESTF update meeting. "Due to the threat posed to the city by what will probably be Hurricane Arthur on July 4th, we have decided to move the entire event up a day, to Thursday, July 3rd. To be clear, that is two days from right now."

"You gotta be shittin' me!" complained a uniformed officer in the back, who only just remembered to add, "Sir." A low rumble of assent rolled around the already uncomfortably warm room jammed with far too many bodies.

Sully glowered and waited until the crowd facing him settled into an uneasy silence.

"Listen, I know this puts us all in a very difficult position, with 24 fewer hours to do something we technically need another week for, but goddammit we will not fail! This is Boston. If you think the work is too hard, then feel free to take a job guarding trees out in the Berkshires. Otherwise, shut your pie-holes and focus on what needs to be done in the next two days. If you have time to bitch, you have time to take on more work, capiche?" He appeared to have their attention now.

"Am I clear?"

"Yes sir," replied parts of the crowd, unenthusiastically.

"Am I clear?" Sully added some menace.

"Yes sir!" replied the room, speaking as one.

"Well?" he glared at the assembled masses. "What are you waiting for? You all have your assignments. Scatter!" he commanded, and they did.

As the last of the crowd shuffled out of the stifling conference room, Sully checked his phone and wearily contemplated the overwhelming plethora of emails, voice mails, news alerts, weather alerts, texts and missed calls. He felt a pang of guilt for not having responded to Finn's several texts and voice mails over the past 24 hours and a ripple of disquiet passed through his psyche. Had Finn really found something in those files? The chances were slim to none, of course, but isn't that why he'd given the files to Koenen in the first place? To make absolutely certain? Sure, the demands on his time right now were unforgiving but could he really just ignore Finn's remonstrations? He doubted Koenen would be this persistent without a good reason.

Sully finished his lukewarm coffee and dropped the cup into an overflowing trash can. Nothing would likely dispel the low buzz of exhaustion that had settled onto his consciousness sometime last night (early this morning?) after too many meetings and nowhere near enough sleep. Yet despite the hardships this assignment entailed, Sully was proud to lead BPD's efforts to secure the upcoming event. Although, truth be told, he hadn't realized exactly how much cat herding the job would involve. He had to plan for, meet about, discuss, ponder and make decisions on everything from where to store the obscene quantities of booze his officers would inevitably confiscate (empty coolers would be provided at each security entrance) to exactly how many patrons could be serviced by each Port-o-Potty before becoming problematic (not nearly enough, unfortunately), to whether or not the T trains should stop running across the MIT bridge during the fireworks (nope, never needed to before).

He sighed heavily as three more emails marked with red "Urgent" badges landed in his in-box. He knew he needed to get back to Finn and now may be his only opportunity given that the event had just been pulled forward a day. Alerts for two new texts and a reminder about his update call with his JESTF boss popped up as his thumb hovered over Finn's name in the Missed Call list.

"Sully!" came a voice from the chaos in the bullpen outside the now-empty conference room. "Fisher on line two"

"Coming!" he shouted back with a grimace as he shut the conference room door, then to himself, "Dammit."

Sully looked at Finn's name on his phone screen. "Sorry buddy," he said with a heavy sigh, "looks like it'll have to wait."

.

CHAPTER 39

N.C. BARRIER ISLANDS PREPARE AS ARTHUR GETS CLOSE
BRUCE SMITH, ASSOCIATED PRESS – *THE BOSTON GLOBE* – JULY 2ND, 2014

NAGS HEAD N.C. — As one of the year's busiest travel weekends approaches, so does another visitor: Tropical Storm Arthur, expected to grow into a hurricane by the Forth of July.

The first named storm of the Atlantic hurricane season prompted a hurricane warning for a wide swath of the North Carolina coast and had officials, hotel owners, and would-be vacationers as far north as New England carefully watching forecasts.

At a news conference, North Carolina Governor Pat McCrory advised residents, "Don't put your stupid hats on." With concerns of rip currents, he urged swimmers and surfers to stay out of the water no matter how good the waves might be.

"Our major goal is to ensure that no lives are lost during this upcoming storm, including those of emergency workers."

The National Hurricane Center predicted the storm would be off the coast of New England later in the day.

CHAPTER 40

Anderson Pierce had given himself precisely one month to live the American dream of self-indulgence and conspicuous consumption and now that it was over, he felt he had gotten his money's worth, both literally and figuratively. Sitting behind the wheel in the cab of the fire truck parked quiescently inside Integrated Logistics Solutions, Pierce assessed his experiences.

He found that alcohol agreed with him, though he'd just as quickly discovered that he was what his Brown classmates would have called, 'a lightweight'. Realizing he didn't need to buy a lot of drinks to get drunk, he'd quickly shifted to a 'quality-over-quantity' strategy which had served him well. For someone possessing exactly zero experience with any sort of alcohol, he'd become quite an expert on fine wines (Amarones in particular), scotches (Glenmorangie 18 his favorite), and Belgian Trappist Ales (the Westvleteren 12 a highlight).

As for the drugs he'd promised himself, those had been, well, disappointing. Smoking marijuana gave him a bout of violent coughing followed by several hours of deep paranoia that left him profoundly unsettled for a couple of days. He tried ecstasy once with a Coachella-type girl named Emma at a club somewhere in downtown Boston. He had very much enjoyed that experience — the sex had been mind blowing — but he must have mistyped her number in his phone because he couldn't reach her after their incredible encounter. Unable to track down the only person he knew who had Ecstasy, he found he was too rattled by his marijuana experience to try buying and using street drugs he didn't know anything about. At least Emma had taken the same pill he had, so he assumed it was safe. He knew too much about chemistry to trust the lab skills of some random stranger in some basement lab. He obviously wasn't afraid of dying but he certainly couldn't complete his mission if he was in a coma in Mass General either.

So in the end he opted to forgo further drug experimentation, instead taking his remaining Drugs budget and allocating it to his Sex bucket, a strategic shift of funds that paid off handsomely. He'd been with every kind of woman: white, black, Chinese, French, Thai, Russian, Venezuelan, you name it. He'd learned and then practiced every position under the sun it seemed and more. The inventiveness and creativity of these women (mostly professionals) was astounding to him and he drank it all in like the celibate sponge he used to be.

And despite all the wine, women and partying, he'd still managed to transform the firetruck from a magnificent machine designed to extinguish fires into one which would ruthlessly extinguish lives. His right hand reached over and caressed the dashboard lightly. The *piece de resistance* had been his inspired idea to tape bags of nails and ball bearings on the inside wall of the tank before filling it in order to generate significantly more deadly shrapnel from the blast. *Every little bit counts*, he thought, then frowned, annoyed that he'd recited yet another of his mother's many trite and meaningless sayings that passed for life wisdom in her sad little worldview. *Every little bit counts, Save your money; It never hurts to look your best.* What a load of crap. The worst had always been, *You're a Pierce, act like one,* because it presumed he should be more like the one thing he detested most about himself. Well, since he couldn't go back in time and change his lineage, he decided to change what 'acting like a Pierce' would mean in the future. After what he was about to do, when someone was told to *act like a Pierce!* it would mean, 'Emerge from the shadows. Strike without warning. Be the monster in the closet'!

His phone alarm went off, ending his daydream. Swinging his legs out from under the massive steering wheel he used the metal step on the outside of the cab to hop down to the spotless concrete floor. He jogged past the rows of now-empty drums and headed up the back stairs. The loading bay occupied the rear third of the building and extended upwards twenty-five feet or so to a ceiling that sported a complicated sliding block-and-tackle system the previous tenants had left in place. This meant that while the empty and unused third and forth floors ran the entire length of the building's footprint, the second floor (which he would shortly be putting to more productive use) only ran the front two-thirds and had a set of interior windows overlooking the loading bay with its firetruck below.

Exiting the stairwell on the second floor, Pierce headed down the long straight hallway leading to the front of the building and its several small unused offices, conference room and kitchen / break area. Turning left well before that, he entered the large open space that took up the middle third of the second floor. Formerly a machine shop of some kind, it sported regular dents, scrapes and marks where heavy machines once stood, their silhouettes still marked by yellow and black striped caution tape. Outlets hung from cables that ran overhead in ever-expanding bundles along exposed steel I-beams before disappearing through the floor. A series of windows ran along the exterior wall, mostly hidden behind shelves containing crates, boxes and a range of loose metal tools, chains and other industrial bric a brac. The wall to his left sported grimy windows overlooking the loading bay and it's now-lethal vehicle.

Anderson scanned the dimly-lit space to ensure he had everything in place before powering up the military-grade hardened laptop on top of a rectangular metal folding table set in front of said windows. After logging in using both his thumbprint and facial recognition he pulled up the secure conferencing link, smoothing his shirt and running fingers through his hair while it connected.

It never hurts to look your best, said his mother's voice in his head, unbidden.

Anderson winced. *Stow it, Mom.*

Encryption and decryption completed, a window popped up, which Pierce quickly maximized to fill the monitor. Anderson was once again struck by how handsome his Mentor was, transfixed by the charisma pouring out of the screen like heat from hot embers. Thick black hair sat above dark olive skin, piercing blue eyes, a sharp nose and an unsmiling mouth framed by a short goatee with just the hint of gray sprinkled in. Wearing a nondescript black zip-up athletic jacket, he sat in an office so utterly generic it could have been anywhere and Pierce could never quite shake the feeling that his Mentor was actually sitting just down the hall rather than 6,000 miles away. It creeped him out.

"Report."

Snapping quickly out of his brief reverie, Pierce did, providing an economical assessment of the progress made on both his original tasks as well as those more recently added.

"...so as a result, I have competed all pre-Zero Day tasks ahead of schedule, leaving me more than adequate time for the," Anderson searched for the right words, "icing on the cake."

His Mentor's smile made Pierce uncomfortable. Devoid of warmth, it evinced the languid pleasure of a snake contemplating a cornered mouse.

"Excellent. I am glad to see that my faith in you has been rewarded." The Iranian stared at Anderson, his gaze somehow intensifying until he filled the cavernous, dusty room with his presence.

"Are you ready to strike a mortal blow against our enemies? Are you ready to teach the world a lesson? Are you ready to become the hero you were born to be?"

"I am," replied Anderson, at once deeply confident. "I am the nice, quiet boy next door who kills thousands without warning. My name will inspire fear. My deeds will bring this country to its knees. America will fall!" he finished, eyes shining with fervor.

This time his Mentor smiled with what looked like genuine warmth. "You have done well. Very well."

Anderson could feel pride erupting in his chest like a sun going nova.

"It is a magnificent thing you are about to do, for you will be striking at the very foundation of their system. The West is spoiled and soft and naive, Americans most of all. They believe their system is superior because it is built on freedom, but what they do not realize is that their precious freedom is nothing more than an illusion built on top of something eminently more fragile: trust. Trust that their banks won't seize their money overnight; trust that their police won't extort and kidnap them; trust that their neighbor's son won't wake up one day and murder thousands." Now his Mentor's eyes were shining as well. "Freedom cannot live without trust, and tomorrow you will forever destroy theirs. That is why you are a true hero. Your sacrifice will destroy the foundations of freedom."

Anderson felt an almost indescribable joy, and he had to fight to keep from shouting with the pure energy of it all. This was the affirmation he had been looking for his entire life. He had been born to do this but until Hamid had opened his mind at Brown and their Mentor filled his heart with purpose, he had been lost, a tool without a task. He now knew with all his being that he was a warrior of *Allah* who would earn his place in Paradise tomorrow evening. Nothing could stop him now.

As if reading his thoughts, his Mentor cautioned, "But be careful, for there is still much to do, and great risk ahead. Many things can still go wrong, so do not let yourself be blinded by overconfidence, and do not let your guard down even for a second."

"Yes sir!" Anderson replied, like he'd heard soldiers do in movies. "I will not let you down."

"Excellent," his Mentor said. "Much beyond this week depends on your success."

"I will not fail," Anderson declared, daring to look his Mentor square in the eyes. "I swear my life on it."

CHAPTER 41

12:45PM — ROXBURY, MA
SEVEN AND A HALF HOURS LATER

Finn left police headquarters and sighed. He'd known the chances were slim he'd catch Sully in person, especially now that the concert and fireworks had been moved up to tomorrow, but it still sucked having your hopes dashed.

Accepting that he was effectively cut off from Sully for the foreseeable future, Finn began sorting through his other options: Tony was still incommunicado, Heather was flying back from DC at this very moment and Cat wouldn't return from Munich until later tonight. It occurred to Finn, and not for the first time, that he needed to get out and make some more friends. Well, he did have a bunch of friends, but they weren't the *good* friend types; the ones who would understand the strange and intense kind of life he'd led; who would be comfortable discussing crime, mayhem and death; and who wouldn't judge him for what he had and had not done.

Russo, of course, shared the Delta Force and private investigating with Finn. Heather, despite her attempts to gin up a 'white-picket-fence' life for herself as a reaction to their unconventional and somewhat peripatetic upbringing, understood in a first-person kind of way much of what made him, him. And Cat... Cat was the first woman he'd met in a long time who wasn't fazed by his life nor did she view him as some sort of curiosity to be picked up and examined.

He needed to make sure tomorrow night's picnic with the ladies went well and he planned to bring foul weather gear, umbrellas and some towels (kept dry in a cooler) to make sure both women were taken care of on the Esplanade. Having lived for several years in Amsterdam where it rained 300 days a year, the Koenens made a point of thumbing their noses at wet weather and carrying on regardless.

Heading up Tremont Street he turned left on Ruggles and made his way into a broad section of the Southwest Corridor Park, a ribbon of green running five miles from the South End all the way to the Forest Hills section of Jamaica Plain. A cloud bank had rolled in, giving the oppressive early afternoon air an ominous cast. A few minutes' walk netted him an empty bench under a massive oak, leaves rustling faintly in the breathless humidity of the impending storm. He sat, crossed his legs, sighed again, and made what was likely to be yet another unanswered call. To his pleasant surprise, it was answered on the second ring.

"What's up?" asked Tony Russo without preamble, as if they'd spoken recently.

"Hey Tony, how you doing?" Finn asked, deciding for pleasantries regardless. "Am I catching you at a bad time?"

"Nope. Just sitting on my couch eating lunch, watching the Sox-Cubs game," he replied, the words muffled by a mouthful of said lunch.

"Listen, can I bend your ear for a few minutes? I could really use your help thinking something through." Finn had really come to depend on their regular bull sessions over beers at the Warren Tavern to help him prune some investigative branches while nurturing others. Tony's keen eye and skeptical nature had definitely been felt in their absence over the past couple months, though Finn wouldn't necessarily have been able to articulate that until recently.

"Sure," replied Russo magnanimously. "Fuckin' Sox are getting shelled anyway. Shoot."

Finn spent the next few minutes catching him up on his search for the Dorky White Guy, walking Russo down each dead end until they arrived at Heather's inspired idea to look at unsolved cases that might actually be a terrorist sending a message. He finished by detailing his suspicions about the missing Hamid Farhadi and asking Tony for his thoughts.

Finn registered neither the harried looking couple walking by pushing a triple stroller containing three cooing babies nor the goofy black lab chasing a ball on the other side of the field in front of him while he waited anxiously for Tony's assessment. A faint breeze kicked up, carrying the unpleasant odor of cigarettes along with it. Finn looked around and spotted a couple high school-aged kids a little ways upwind sitting under a maple tree hacking butts. He stood up and walked across the lawn, orthogonal to the floating trail of smoke.

"Tone? You still there?" Finn prompted.

"What was the dead guy's name?" asked Russo.

"He's not dead necessarily, just missing as of now," Finn corrected. "And Farhadi. Hamid Farhadi. Why?"

"Hmm," said Tony, thinking. "I think Andy mentioned having a buddy named Hamid. Or some Arabic shit like that."

Finn slowed as the black lab raced by with wild abandon, barely noticed, five feet in front of him.

"What did you say?"

"What?" replied a distracted Russo. "Goddammit! Throw a fucking strike. You suck!"

"What did you say about somebody knowing a Hamid?" Finn asked, over-talking Russo's invective.

"I said I think Andy knew a guy named Hamid, who died last year. Accident or something. C'mon!" he yelled at his TV. "Fuck!"

"Andy who?" asked Finn, silently willing Tony to focus.

"Andy? You know Andy. He's the guy I've been doing some work with the last couple months."

'I don't," Finn replied slowly. "Tell me about him, and what he said about his friend Hamid."

"Andy. Anderson Pierce, I'm sure we all had drinks together," Russo insisted impatiently. "He's always at the Warren Tavern — that's where I met him. Anyway, one night he'd had a few too many pops and he asks me about being in combat and I said I'd seen some friends die, you know, the usual shit. And all of a sudden he gets all sad and worked up. I guess he had this good buddy, Hamid Falafel, Fahrenheit, something. Anyway, apparently he died last summer and Andy was pretty broke up about it."

"Was his buddy's name Hamid Farhadi?" Finn asked, now standing stock still in the middle of the field.

"Yeah, maybe," Russo said brightly. "Andy's not usually melancholy like that, though. Generally he's a pretty fun guy to hang out with, even if he is a huge geek."

"Geek? Like, what do you mean, a geek?"

"He's a geek, an egghead. A chemist or physicist or something. Smart kid. Works over at Bay State Hazmat cleaning up toxic chemicals and hippy shit like that. For a tree-hugger though, he's got a lot of great ideas about how we can make some money. Finn, you wouldn't believe what they can do in labs these days. Just the other night..."

"Tony," Finn cut him off sharply. "What does this Andy look like?"

"Jesus, Finn! Who pissed in your Wheaties?"

"What does he look like?" Finn insisted.

"I don't know... about six feet, blond hair, blue eyes, nerdy glasses, skinny. Why?"

Ignoring the question, Finn pressed on, a chill running down his spine. "And he had a friend who might have been named Hamid Farhadi who died in an accident last year?"

"That's what he said."

The verdant park, the oppressive humidity, the eager black lab, everything disappeared as Finn turned fully inward to focus on the pieces clicking ineluctably into place.

"Finn? You still there?" asked Russo, Remy and Orsillo's play-by-play banter floating faintly off the TV behind his words.

"Tony..." Finn started, then stopped, unsure of how to put words to what was coalescing in his head.

"Listen, you want I can ask him about this Hamid guy in about half an hour. He's coming over to pick me up and we're going out for a little day-drinking."

"Don't do it," ordered Finn, stomach dropping. "Don't go out with him."

"Why the fuck not?"

"Because I think he's the guy I've been looking for."

Russo laughed. "What, now you think Andy's your terrorist?" He didn't bother to hide his incredulity. "He's from fucking Connecticut for Christ's sake. I'm pretty sure he was literally an Eagle Scout."

Finn's mind raced. Hamid Farhadi, a young orphaned Iranian whose expensive Western education had been paid for out of a secret Swiss bank account; who unaccountably went missing over the long July 4th weekend last year, a week before Dzhokhar Tsarnaev pleaded 'Not Guilty' to the 2013 Marathon bombing; had been close friends with Russo's new buddy 'Andy'... 'Andy', who was a dorky white guy type scientist — maybe a chemist — had befriended Tony not long after the Dorchester terrorist plot had been foiled; where acid had been thrown at Sully's team; and just after Zoe Kraft had told a national television audience (and the entire Internet) that Finn Koenen had been instrumental in the foiling of said plot.

"Hey, it's been great catching up" said Russo, still chuckling. "But I gotta go. Listen, if you ever get tired of the detective thing, you should go into stand-up. You've got some great material."

"Tony, wait..."

But it was too late — the connection had been cut and he knew from experience Tony wouldn't pick up again for a long while.

Finn's eyes darted around, seeing nothing except trouble, as he tried to decide what to do. It didn't take long.

Anderson Pierce. Bay State Hazmat.

CHAPTER 42

Carl Nowak exited Bay State Hazmat and turned right on Robin then left up Mystic Street to make it look like he was heading for Mike's Roast Beef five blocks away, something he had just conspicuously mentioned to several people. He silently castigated himself first for feeling guilty about skipping out of work for a personal errand and second for likely drawing more attention to himself with his 'cover story' about grabbing a late lunch than he would have by just slipping out quietly. Switching gears, he replayed the last hour in his head as he walked, wanting to make sure he wasn't jumping to conclusions or being crazy-paranoid or anything. He had tried some coke for the first time at a friend-of-a-friend's apartment in Inman Square the other night and had worried ever since it had fucked up his brain in some unspecified but potentially permanent way.

A little over sixty minutes ago, an intense, stick-up-his-ass guy had come striding into Bay State demanding to speak with the manager or owner. Anderson had been busy chatting up the new receptionist, a blond, doe-eyed Nebraskan who had only recently moved to Boston, and offered to help the guy when his request flustered her. He'd checked with Ken Larson, the Waste Management SVP who ran Bay State's day-to-day operations, and then stuck around after bringing the stranger into Ken's office.

The guy, Finn Conan or something like that, had been super wound-up. He claimed to be some sort of private detective (Carl had thought those only existed in movies or books) and he started asking Ken a bunch of questions about Anderson Pierce. When Ken politely declined to answer, saying he wouldn't give out addresses, phone numbers or any other personal information about his employees, this Finn guy didn't do himself any favors. He got pretty worked up and even kind of threatened Ken, which went over poorly. Ken, a large and generally gentle man, had bristled and suggested in no uncertain terms that Conan see himself out.

Carl could see why Ken got angry and tossed the guy, but something about the newcomers' urgent pleading insistence that, 'lives might be at stake', seemed genuine to him. Nowak felt he had a pretty accurate bullshit detector, and this guy, whatever he was on about, wasn't setting it off. In fact, the tortured look on the poor guy's face as Carl escorted him out of the building onto the front sidewalk had softened his heart.

"Hey man," he'd said to the guy once they got outside, "I'm sorry Ken threw you out like that, but you did come on kinda strong."

The man sighed, his broad shoulders drooping slightly. "I know. It's just I don't know where else to turn." He lifted his head and asked with sudden hope, "Hey — did you know Pierce? Do you know where I can find him?"

"Why? What do you want from him?"

The man seemed to be have a brief internal debate before replying. "I have reason to believe he might be in some serious trouble. That he might be in some danger. I can't say any more than that, but I'd like to try and make sure nothing happens to him."

The man's intense sincerity got to Carl and he'd given him Anderson's address in Allston way over on the other side of the Charles. Not long after the stranger left, however, he'd begun to have second thoughts. What if this Finn Conan guy had been lying and his claim that Anderson was in danger nothing more than a douchy ploy to get Pierce's address? What if he was going there to hurt Anderson? Or worse? Eventually the worry of it all became too much for Carl and he made his excuse to step out so he could call Anderson and let him know what had just happened.

Glancing back over his shoulder, Carl determined that he'd turned enough corners that he wasn't visible from Bay State any longer, and he made his call.

* * * * *

Upstairs and no longer alone in the former machine shop at Integrated Logistic Solutions in Back Bay, Anderson Pierce assured Carl he knew 'Finn Conan' and that all was well. He thanked Nowak, hung up, and sorted out the implications of what he'd just learned.

The news that the ex-soldier somehow knew about and was openly hunting him down initially panicked Pierce, but by the end of the conversation with Nowak he'd started to calm down. Adrenaline coursing through his veins, Pierce turned the new information over and over in his head, sorting through options. After a few minutes' deliberation, Anderson concluded that, while Carl may be a pain-in-the-ass do-gooder, he also just handed him a significant gift. Now grinning, he surveyed the setup in the room, checked his watch, and turned on his heel to head out.

When life gives you lemons...

CHAPTER 43

7:55PM HARVARD SQUARE, CAMBRIDGE, MA
FOUR HOURS LATER

Finn thanked the old homeless woman and slipped her a folded twenty, soaked from the heavy rain that began soon after he left Bay State Hazmat. She accepted it gratefully, blessing him several times and disappearing the bill somewhere into her wet and filthy clothes. They shook hands awkwardly, Finn afraid he would crush the birdlike bones of her withered hand, and he made his way down Brattle Street back towards the center of Harvard Square.

Frustration and fear pulled at his mind with sticky fingers, as he had precious little to show for his efforts over the past few hours. His sole tangible accomplishment was collecting his Glock .22 out of the gun safe in his office. The safest firearm on the market, it was also lightweight, accurate and it never jammed. If Finn's concerns were justified, he'd be needing it tonight.

He'd then headed over to Russo's apartment and picked the lock to let himself in, only to find it empty with no signs of a struggle or anything even remotely alarming, other than the sheer number of empty Bud Light cans lying around. Still worried, but glad he hadn't found a cooling corpse with a small hole in its forehead, Finn tried unsuccessfully to reach Russo by phone and text. The radio silence didn't necessarily mean anything but Finn couldn't quite bring himself to believe that Russo was safely enjoying a friendly drink-up in some dive bar across town with his new friend Andy who was definitely not a terrorist.

He'd grabbed a taxi to Harvard Square to talk to Mike Miller but now had to conclude he had struck out here as well. None of the Square regulars had seen him since last night, though one guy thought maybe this morning, but the he had been six sheets to the wind when Finn questioned him fifteen minutes ago, so he took that sighting with a grain of salt. It was possible Miller had simply gone off the grid, which wasn't all that hard for people as tenuously tied to the grid as the homeless were, but, like with Russo, something just didn't *feel* right about Miller's absence from Harvard Square.

Ducking under the canopy of an ATM vestibule, Finn checked his phone — 7:58pm: five hours since he'd last had contact with Russo and less than 24 hours until the festivities at the Hatch Shell officially kicked off. Finn shook the rain off his soaked Red Sox cap and fought the feeling that events were spinning out of his control. Every instinct was telling him to get help, but he had no one to go to. Best case scenario the police would laugh at him; Sully was unreachable; Miller had gone AWOL and Russo might be out drinking with a terrorist.

Tick tock.

He couldn't just do nothing.

Tick tock.

Well, if the clock wasn't stopping, neither would he, no matter what the cost.

He'd go it alone.

CHAPTER 44

8:00PM EASTERN TIME THURSDAY, JULY 2ND, 2014
4:30AM IRAN TIME, THURSDAY, JULY 3RD, 2014
TEHRAN, IRAN

As evening passed into night and the front edge of hurricane Arthur soaked Finn Koenen in Harvard Square, Reza Moradi took a walk to stretch his legs after a sleepless night, the predawn Tehran air foreshadowing an oppressively hot morning. He'd chosen to monitor the day's events from his offices in the Ministry of Intelligence in the fashionable Mehran neighborhood of northeast Tehran. He'd found that strolling through the well—tended park on the west side of the complex soothed him, especially at this early hour when no one else was around.

His fingers played with the thumb drive in his pocket, the one sent to him by his CIA mole two months ago in a diplomatic pouch routed through the United States Interests section of the Swiss Embassy. As the current Head of the CIA's Iran Desk, his contact had the kind of security clearance necessary to access video footage like this — direct evidence of an illegal black op inside Iran's sovereign borders back in 2002.

The fact that the man had sent it to him at all confirmed for Reza that he continued to have no idea he was being played. Deciding many years ago to ingratiate himself with America's spy agency in order to ultimately annihilate it, he had chosen to initiate contact with a young, ambitious agent named Jameson Poole. Starting in early 2009, Moradi met several times with Poole and openly offered to help further US interests in Iran — a denied-area country — in return for eventually being installed as the leader once the Mullahs and their ilk were exorcised from power. He explained to Poole that they both wanted the same things: a stable, secular, rational Iran counterbalancing the chaos in neighboring Iraq and Afghanistan, and providing the U.S. with a second base of operations in the Middle East, allowing the Americans to hedge their bets against any future misbehavior from the fanatical and unreliable Wahhabis running Saudi.

Smart, arrogant and nakedly ambitious, Poole had asked Reza to substantiate his desire to collaborate with America. After making a show of hemming and hawing, Reza promised Poole that, as proof of his bona fides, he would arrange for the arrest and detention of Saeed Hajjarian, one of the founders of the very MOIS where Reza himself worked. Poole had been suitably impressed when, just a few weeks later, Hajjarian had indeed been imprisoned, but his masters back in Langley somewhat less so. Poole explained that they felt Reza's betrayal of Hajjarian, a reformer with poorly-disguised ties to British Intelligence, had merely accelerated the man's arrest by a few weeks and was therefore not a consequential enough gesture to earn U.S. trust. As a result, they'd demanded that Moradi provide something they considered to be, 'of real value'.

Reza, always the chess master and playing the long game in any case, had anticipated this. For his next 'investment in a mutually-beneficial relationship', Reza offered in early 2010 to hamstring his own country's illegal nuclear weapons program. That got Langley's attention, and he was able to extract promises for money, weapons and clandestine support from the US, contingent upon said promised sabotage.

On June 1st, 2010, Reza arranged for the STUXNET virus to be introduced into the computers and servers charged with managing Iran's secret nuclear material labs. Cleverly subtle, STUXNET targeted the programmable logic controllers that managed the automation of industrial equipment. Specifically, it gave instructions that caused the rapidly spinning centrifuges (used to separate out the fissable nuclear material Iran needed for its bombs) to speed up even further and ultimately tear themselves apart. The virus infected over 200,000 computers and caused the destruction of fully one third of Iran's centrifuges, at one stroke pushing their dream of a usable nuclear bomb back by years and simultaneously boosting Poole's reputation and career inside the Agency.

In addition to gaining the CIA's trust, Reza sabotaged his country's clandestine nuclear program for his own personal reasons. For one, he didn't trust the religious fanatics running Iran with a nuclear bomb, and two, it gave the Mullahs a massive and very public black eye, thereby weakening their position both at home and abroad. There was a third reason as well, but that wouldn't play out until next year, when his *Three*

Wise Men plan came to fruition and he changed the global balance of power forever.

The video on the thumb drive in his pocket proved that Reza had underestimated the Americans' willingness to take risks, but the bigger surprise had come when he saw who led the assault team. Finn Koenen had been easily recognizable despite the intervening years and damaged nature of the footage, but Reza had to re-watch it several times to convince himself he wasn't seeing ghosts. Once past the shock of realizing that Finn had been the one to destroy his secret facility twelve years ago, Reza had amended Anderson Pierce's orders to include a reckoning with his childhood friend, now his adversary.

Fate, it seemed, was not content to let what was left of these two families — Moradis and Koenens — go their separate ways.

He checked his watch. It would be just after 8pm Eastern Time July 2nd in Boston. A lot was about to happen in the next 26 hours. Promises would be kept, capabilities would be demonstrated, and scores would be settled.

How does it feel, being the isolated pawn, alone with no other pieces to protect you? Reza thought with a grim smile. *Not as good as it feels taking you off the board, I promise you that.*

And for the first time in a long time, as he strode alone in the early morning dark under the ancient chinar trees, Reza laughed with joy.

Pure, unadulterated joy.

Checkmate.

CHAPTER 45

10:00PM EASTERN TIME – WEDNESDAY, JULY 2ND
ALLSTON, MA

From his vantage point across the street, the place seemed empty. A voice in Finn's head told him he should wait longer, that fifteen minutes was nothing, a smoke break on the back deck, a long trip to the bathroom, a lot of things maybe. But, deeming the risk of letting more time slip by to be greater than the risk attendant to breaking into a potential terrorist's apartment, Finn left the capacious shelter of a huge red maple and crossed the street.

According to the kid at Bay State Hazmat, Pierce lived alone on the first floor of a three story detached duplex. Finn crossed the pavement, a hand shielding his eyes from fat rain droplets, and trotted up several brick steps. He stopped on the porch and stood listening for a full minute. If there were any noises coming from inside they were drowned out by the heavy downpour and splashing from the odd car driving down Allston Street behind him. He peered at the two buzzer buttons on the wall and the hand-written names taped alongside them. A dim yellow overhead bulb illuminated 'Pierce' in neat, fussy letters next to the bottom one. Finn took a quick look around behind him to make sure he was in the clear and took a long, deep breath.

I need to watch my own six on this one.

Stepping over to stand in front of Pierce's door, he pulled a rolled cloth pouch containing lockpick tools from his back pocket while carefully testing the doorknob with his free hand. He froze, senses hyper-alert, as it turned easily, apparently unlocked. He replaced the tools and quietly unholstered his Glock. With infinite care he finished twisting the knob and applied pressure to the face of the door with his palm. As it swung silently inward, he crouched and used the Glock to cover the opening, belatedly realizing the gun wouldn't protect him from getting a face full of acid like poor Chavez did back in Dorchester.

Thankfully, nothing happened. He bent his knees slightly, rocked up onto the balls of his feet and stepped over the threshold, quickly closing the door behind himself, cutting off the faint light from the porch. As Finn's eyes adjusted, details precipitated out of the darkness and he registered an empty living room off to his immediate left which, if this were one of the standard Boston apartment designs, would lead back to a dining room and then the kitchen. Directly in front of him was a hallway with three evenly-spaced doors along the right wall, likely a bedroom-bathroom-bedroom situation. The far end of the hall, which would lead to a back yard or deck of some sort, was shrouded in a deeper darkness that Finn was careful to keep an eye on lest someone or something materialize out of it. The place was quiet as a tomb and smelled of curry and... something faintly sweet and unpleasant that he couldn't quite identify.

He waited silently for a good two minutes, standing in a shooter's stance with one foot behind and offset from the other for stability, the Glock held at the ready, safety off. Taking a step forward, he thought he heard a faint noise coming from somewhere in front of him, Freezing again, Finn strained his ears. The noise came a second time and he pinpointed its origin as coming from behind the first closed bedroom door on his right. When it came again a third time, he identified it as a soft snore, and relaxed measurably. Information was by far the most important asset to have in any tactical situation, and Finn now knew where his quarry was and what he was doing. He quietly strode down the hall until he was standing with his ear leaned up close to, but not quite touching, the bedroom door. The soft, raspy snore was more discernible now, coming in a slow regular cadence telling Finn that Pierce was in a deep sleep.

Maybe he really was just out drinking with Tony, he thought, *especially when that probably isn't a scientist alive who could go beer for beer Tony Russo without soon passing out.*

However, needing to be 100% sure, he slowly cracked the door open and peered in to find the room — marginally lit by a string of red and green Christmas lights framing one of the windows — completely empty. There was a phone lying in the middle of the neatly-made bed, from which came the sound of a man snoring.

Finn spun around, only to feel something wet and sticky spray onto his face and neck.

"Hey," said a bland male voice, close at hand.

Blinded by the viscous liquid, Finn tried to wipe his eyes clear, only to realize his consciousness was slipping away.

Oh, shit, he thought as his knees buckled.

Anderson Pierce, still holding the spray bottle with finger on trigger at arm's length, watched the much larger and stronger man collapse to the floor.

"Shortcuts lead to long delays," Anderson said, sing-song, before he could stop himself.

Fuck you, mom.

PART FIVE

The great questions of the day will not be settled by means of speeches and majority decisions but by iron and blood.

— Otto von Bismarck

CHAPTER 46

A FESTIVE 3RD…OR 5TH
TRAVIS ANDERSON — *THE BOSTON GLOBE* — JULY 3RD, 2014

The Boston Pops Fireworks Spectacular, a tradition that has thrilled spectators on the Charles River Esplanade every Forth of July for four decades, will be held this evening, a day early, rescheduled to avoid Hurricane Arthur which will soak the region today.

"It's not optimal," said Boston Police Sergeant Patrick O'Sullivan, in charge of security for the event, of the rescheduling. "We wish it were, but we've got to deal with this."

With the heaviest rains forecast to arrive later tonight, Sullivan left open the possibility that organizers would postpone the fireworks portion of the show until Saturday. However, he said the Pops concert itself would take place Thursday Evening or not at all, due to 'contracts and commitments' that some of the performing acts have.

The National Weather Service said Wednesday that widespread showers and thunderstorms with locally heavy rainfall are expected to continue into Friday.

Bad weather has caused trouble with the Esplanade celebration in past years, spoiling plans for the hundreds of thousands of spectators who come to mark the nation's independence.

"We're keeping our fingers crossed that the weather cooperates tonight," said Kurt N. Schwartz. Undersecretary for Homeland Security and Emergency Management, last night.

"Our number one goal is keeping everyone safe."

CHAPTER 47

9:00PM THURSDAY, JULY 3ND, 2014
THE ESPLANADE, BOSTON, MA

Heather stole a glance over her shoulder before surreptitiously refilling Cat's water bottle with chardonnay, prompting a laugh.

"I don't think they're checking anymore," Cat said, gesturing around at huge crowd braving the pouring rain along with them. "I guess the cops figure if you're willing to stand outside in a hurricane to celebrate the Forth, you probably deserve a drink or two."

Heather grinned and handed Cat her now-full bottle and poured the rest of the wine into her own, topping it off just about perfectly. She hid the empty bottle under her raincoat as she traversed the ten or so steps to the nearest recycling bin to drop it in. The number of other empty wine, beer and liquor bottles greeting hers suggested Cat's assessment was right; enforcing the ban on alcohol seemed less important now that the concert was well underway. She returned to where Cat was standing, guarding their space, and they clunked their Nalgene bottles together.

They listened to the Pops in amiable silence, enjoying a movie medley (Star Wars; Superman; Raiders of the Lost Ark so far) and occasionally wiping water off of their faces. Hurricane Arthur had truly arrived in earnest just after the Pops started playing at 8pm, but the warmth of the rain offset the worst of the chill from the wind. So as long as you were well kitted (both were, with LL Bean foul weather gear) it was actually quite pleasant once you made peace with being soaked.

"Sorry my brother's an asshole," Heather apologized for the third time.

"I told you, it's fine," replied Cat with a wicked smile. "Now he's got two women mad at him. Whatever he's doing now, I hope it's worth the price he's going to pay later."

"Ha!" agreed Heather, "though to be honest with you, blowing us off like this is a little more dickish than I'd expect. I mean, he promised me not two days ago that he'd be here, and then nothing but radio silence since. Usually he'd have the stones to man up and let me know he wasn't coming."

Cat frowned. "You know him better than I do, but this does seem a little weird. You think everything's okay?"

"Please. The guy's a former Army Ranger. I think he can take of himself."

"Well, maybe he's here but having trouble tracking us down?" Cat suggested, sipping wine through her straw.

"Maybe," Heather replied, surveying the sea of humanity around them, with most heads and faces obscured by hoods, hats or umbrellas. "But there's nothing stopping him from texting or calling us to find out where we got to."

"Maybe his phone died, or he lost it," offered Cat, clearly inclined to cut Finn some slack.

"Well, then I guess he's shit outta luck," Heather proclaimed. "If he can't find us, he'll have to enjoy the show all by himself."

*   *   *   *   *

9:30PM ET

The wind howled its soaking wet fury in increasingly uneven gusts that kept threatening to tear Sully's police cap off his head and send it up over the crowds and into the trees, or perhaps out into the Charles River, currently roiled to a frenzy of whitecaps by Arthur's intensification. He stepped aside to let a young man pushing a pretty woman in a wheelchair get by. Wife? Sister? Coworker? Sully would never know, as they quickly melted into the unending stream of people converging on and dispersing from the Great Lawn along dozens of paths, like blood flowing through arteries and veins into and back out of the heart.

Sully observed that the weather was changing in inverse proportion to his mood. With every incident-free minute that passed, the constricting worry in his chest loosened, even as Arthur began to have at it in real earnest. So far, the worst they'd had to deal with were drunk college kids (the paddy wagons coming in handy); some relatively minor injuries due to the rain-slick footing (a couple twisted ankles, a fractured forearm and one possible concussion); and overflowing Port-a-Potties (he'd fruitlessly but presciently argued they wouldn't have enough). If that's as bad as it got, he'd count them all very lucky indeed.

He checked his watch: 9:33 pm. The fireworks would start in around an hour and then ninety (hopefully boring, uneventful) minutes after that, he would release the bulk of his officers and thank them for a job well done. An hour after that, he'd be home on the couch: clean, dry and enjoying a Macallan 18 he saved for just that sort of moment.

"Boring," he implored the ceaseless storm as he threaded through the crowds.

"Uneventful."

*   *   *   *   *

9:47PM ET
TEHRAN, IRAN

Reza checked the time and noted he still had thirteen minutes. He pulled up the video conferencing software MOIS's Digital Espionage department had ginned up for him. It was surprisingly easy to use as well as fully encrypted in real time with zero lag, at least as far as he could tell. In fact, it was so well designed that he'd thought more than once about trying to figure out a way to monetize it. In his weaker moments, he'd even dared to imagine selling it to the general public through some complicated set of shell corporations, knowing it would make a fortune given how shitty Skype and WebEx performed in comparison. In this increasingly global economy, providing real time, unpixelated, lag-free communications would be a goldmine. Alas, nothing MOIS did ever made it into the public eye, even under an assumed lineage.

This minor disappointment was, however, greatly overshadowed by what Reza *could* do, given his position inside the agency. He had authority over three key MOIS portfolios: (1) tracking and neutralizing dissidents both at home and abroad; (2) maintaining support for terrorist organization such as Hezbollah and Hamas; and (3) cyber-terrorism and cyber-warfare, a group he himself had founded and grown exponentially. Direct control of these activities afforded Reza a number of rare commodities: the freedom to travel internationally, access to virtually unlimited funds, and complete control over some of the most powerful and technologically-advanced information weapons in the world. Responsible for much but overseen by few, Reza Moradi spent years controlling thousands of the "unknown Soldiers of Imam Zaman" (as they had been pretentiously christened by that asshole Khomeini), spending hundreds of millions of dollars' worth of unaudited funds, and building dozens of networks around the world as he wove an invisible web throughout the West like an industrious spider.

He doubted anyone would ever know the full extent to which he had subverted the people, money and actions of the Islamic Republic of Iran over the past 25 years to serve his own personal designs. His unblemished record of ruthless success provided ample cover for his true aims, and now, after all the planning, decisions, and ruthless calculations, his life's work was finally coming to fruition. Today's attack was the opening gambit in a game of chess that would play out over the next eighteen months and which would leave the world a very, very different place.

Today America would learn just how weak and ineffective She was, and the ensuing panic would lead Her to make some desperate choices; ones which would unwittingly facilitate a reforging of the world order into one more to Reza's liking.

But, *first things first*, he thought. *Pleasure before business.*

CHAPTER 48

9:55PM

A blur of gray in the darkness slowly brightened, expanding to fill his head. Muffled sounds, like someone speaking through a pillow. Cool air pushing against his face, beckoning Finn back into consciousness.

A vague, dark shape appeared and quickly grew larger. Finn wondered if he should flinch, then felt a burning fire race up into his skull as the smelling salts that had been shoved under his nose did their work. He tried to rub suddenly watering eyes only to find he couldn't move his arms, as they appeared to be tied behind the back of the chair he found himself sitting in. Instead, he sucked in a deep gulp of clear air and tried to stretch his cramping legs but found them also bound to the chair. As his nostrils recovered, he found he could now detect the smells of fuel, dust and sweat.

Three banks of construction-quality klieg lights illuminated with an unforgiving glare the large, mostly empty industrial-looking space that may have once been some sort of machine shop. About ten feet in front of him and off to the right, Tony Russo stood on tiptoe, pulsating with rage. His arms were pulled straight up over his head by chains that looped over a steel beam and which were anchored by some sort of a winch contraption over by the wall. His pelvis kept snapping forwards and backwards as he tried to get better purchase on the ground in order to take some of the weight off his arms and shoulders. Finn knew this was even more painful than it looked, having tied a few enemy combatants up like this himself in order to facilitate 'information sharing'.

To Finn's left, and in direct contrast to Tony's frantic rage, former Army Sergeant Mike Miller hung limp in his own identical chains-and-winch setup as if he were out cold. Finn knew Miller's arms weren't going to feel so great once the smelling salts that prick Pierce was administering to him hit his brain.

Anderson's face bore a disgusted expression as he stood well inside Miller's homeless-guy funk zone. He tossed the broken ammonia-and-perfume capsule over against the wall then walked behind Finn and out of his field of view. It sounded like he were heading off down a hallway.

Finn rapidly scanned the room as best he could, collecting data and looking for anything at all that might help him. While there was a lot about this situation Finn didn't yet understand, he was pretty sure that Tony and Mike were only here because of him. Replacing anger with resolve, Finn focused on the mission: free his friends, help them escape and stop whatever the fuck was going on here.

Directly in front of the bizarre triangular tableau made by the three captured men was a large metal table, on top of which sat a fancy looking laptop and an enormous monitor next to what what appeared to be a digital camera of some sort. The monitor was dark but the camera, pointed directly at Finn, had a steady red light shining on top of it. *Must be on standby, but standby for what?* he wondered, not liking any of the answers that sprang immediately to mind. The wall behind the long table had a set of dirty windows that, based on the dim light coming through them, appeared to look out over some other large interior space. Uneven rattling coming from behind some shelves off to his right suggested windows being buffeted by Hurricane Arthur. The intensity of their shaking, along with the fact that it appeared to be dark out, led Finn to surmise that it was probably the evening of July 3rd, which meant that, (a) he'd been out cold for almost a full day which meant, (b) some very bad shit was about to go down and, (c) that a lot more was at stake than just the three lives in this room.

He tested his bonds and found them solid but not particularly tight: a respectable but amateur job. Given fifteen or twenty minutes, he ought be be able to free his arms. However, Finn guessed Pierce wouldn't have roused them unless something was imminent, so he probably didn't have that long. Nonetheless, he immediately began rhythmically flexing his muscles and jerking his arms around to try and loosen the ropes as much as possible before the asshole came back. Finn glanced at Miller, groaning and trying to get up on his toes and then at Russo, whose eyes shone with murderous rage as unintelligible invective forced its way past the rag stuffed in his mouth. Finn somberly nodded his agreement with Russo's clear intent — *let's kill this fucker.*

Footsteps returned and Finn redoubled his efforts to free himself. He had to find a way to save his friends and everyone else. His ears felt a sudden shift in air pressure as a random pocket of calm was replaced by the full fury of the storm outside.

Pierce, now dressed in a Boston Fire Department uniform, strode into view and over to the long table, where he typed rapidly for a few moments before locking eyes with each of the three men in turn.

"I don't think you're going to like this," he said in a droll voice, "but I know I will."

*   *   *   *   *

10:00PM ET

The tiny light on the camera began blinking and the monitor sprang to life, displaying a frozen, snowy, distorted image. A deep, rich voice unfolded into the spacious room, loud enough to be clearly heard above the fury of the storm outside.

"Excellent," said the disembodied voice. "You have done very well."

"Thank you sir," replied Pierce, standing off to Finn's left, partially blocking his view of an increasingly agitated Miller.

This must be the Man In Charge, thought Finn, straining and failing to glean anything from the vague trace of an accent in the voice.

"Mr. Miller, Mr. Russo." A pause. "And Mr. Koenen. Welcome."

Though Finn wasn't necessarily surprised the mysterious Man in Charge knew their names, hearing them spoken still sent a chill down his spine. He was clearly at a significant informational disadvantage that needed rectifying, somehow. Then, he suddenly realized that, unlike Tony and Mike, he wasn't gagged.

"Excuse me," he said loudly, "I don't believe we've been properly introduced."

A soft chuckle floated across the room, the fidelity almost hyper-real.

"Are you sure about that?"

This wrong-footed Finn. It had never occurred to him that the person he'd spent the last three months trying to find — who had until just now been technically hypothetical — might actually be someone he already knew. He had, of course, made enemies over the years — some of them pretty serious people — so it wasn't out of the realm of possibility that this ass-hat was telling the truth.

"This will be a little trip down memory lane for both you and Mr. Russo," said the mystery voice as the frozen image on the screen sprang into motion, "but I fear it may go over Mr. Miller's pay grade."

Finn's blood went cold as he recognized the scene in the video almost immediately.

How the hell?

Helplessly, he watched as their ill-fated 2002 raid into the Zahedan mountains played out in jerky, pixellated snippets on the screen: their approach up the mountain; entering the stone hut and then through the unexpectedly open security door. Passing through the living quarters. Surprising the lone soldier asleep at the switch in the control room. The gun battle that followed, then the video stuttered badly and they were suddenly outside of the stone hut again, and the sound was back as the perspective suddenly shifted to what must have been 2002 Russo's feed.

The odd assemblage of people in the old machine shop was dead silent, transfixed by the scene unfolding in its disjointed way on the monitor. They watched as 2002 Tony and Zach propped a clearly disoriented Finn in the dirt up against the machine-gun emplacement's sandbags before leaving him behind to run back inside the cave to set charges.

Another cut, this time to a jarringly erratic sequence as 2002 Russo double-timed it down the brown and dusty scree, until a series of muffled explosions off-screen caused him to lose his footing and begin tumbling nauseatingly down the mountain.

The video froze mid-somersault and the disembodied voice returned.

"That facility you so recklessly destroyed? It was mine."

Now the video disappeared, replaced with what looked like a live feed of a dark figure sitting in the shadows behind a desk in a completely nondescript, anonymous office somewhere.

"You did not know it was mine, but you do know me."

The figure slowly leaned forward, bringing his face into the pool of soft yellow light cast by a lamp on the desk.

Finn gasped as a face, both familiar and strange, materialized out of the darkness.

"No. Fucking. Way."

*   *   *   *   *

10:06PM

Reza? Reza Moradi?

His long-lost childhood friend from Tehran was alive? And was, what, a terrorist now? Finn's mind reeled.

He'd lost touch with Reza and the Moradis after being exfiltrated mere days before the storming of the US Embassy in 1979. Despite being resettled in the relative safety of Amsterdam it had been a very tense time for the Koenen family. His father had frequently been away that first year, out of touch for long stretches while working all available diplomatic angles to try and secure the hostages' release. His mother had been fraught with worry, as many of the hostages were good friends, and she'd had a hard time keeping her emotions in check, her Irish anger always close to the surface. But then, just minutes after Ronald Reagan's inauguration, the hostages were freed. The tensions that had strained the Koenen household for the previous sixteen months evaporated, replaced by the more ordinary sort of concerns attendant to any busy family with two working parents and two mischievous teenagers.

Initially, Finn had been very concerned about what might have happened to the Moradis, especially Reza and his next-older brother Mas'ud, who had often played soccer with them in the courtyard behind their house. At the time there was literally no way for Finn to contact Reza so one day he'd asked his father if he knew anything. Jan Koenen had just shaken his head sadly and told Finn that the Moradis were gone, consumed in the religious fire sweeping across the world's newest Islamic republic.

This had upset Finn greatly and for a long time he could not shake the horrible images his imagination conjured up concerning Reza's fate. But life continues on like a river taking a leaf to the sea, and at thirteen years old there had been no shortage of enticing distractions for a gregarious, confident, good looking American boy on the streets of Amsterdam. Truth be told, Reza and his family had eventually slipped from Finn's mind.

Apparently, the reverse wasn't true.

However, Finn now knew who his adversary was, or at least, who he had been once, many years ago.

Let's see if I can still rattle your cage.

*   *   *   *   *

10:09PM

"No. Fucking. Way," came the shocked proclamation from his childhood friend, six thousand miles away, bound to a chair in an old machine shop in Boston in the middle of a hurricane.

"Unfailingly eloquent as always, I see," Reza replied, adding just a touch of disappointment into his voice. "The world will indeed miss a poet such as you."

"Well," countered Finn, "it won't miss a mediocre chess player like you."

Irritation and anger blossomed unbidden in Moradi's chest. He'd expected Finn to react with his trademark arrogance, but something about being face to face with it unexpectedly brought out the frustration of Reza's eleven-year-old self. Could Koenen not see that he was finished? The game — their final game together — was over, and Reza had won, as he'd always known he would. He calmed himself with a simple truth: *Checkmate in three moves.*

"Remind me," Koenen went on, annoyingly derisive, "is this how your father Amir taught you to treat your friends, *Zaza?*"

Reza now had to fight very hard to master his fury — he would not take the bait — but Finn's mention of his father, and of his Father's nickname for him…

"Because I don't remember him drugging his friends and hanging them in chains, do you?"

Hands shaking, Reza was surprised to find that he didn't trust himself to speak.

"Or blowing up women and children like an honorless coward."

Just before succumbing to rage, his father's voice spoke in his head, a clarion call from the past, saving him from himself.

"In my secret heart of hearts I knew you were special, I knew you would be the one, the one to make a difference. You have the heart of a lion, and the brain of a fox. But so do many. What you have that they don't, is the will. You have the will to do what must be done. I see it.

Will is not a thing you learn. It is a thing you are. Or are not.

Do what must be done today but make them pay for it tomorrow. No matter how long it takes, no matter what the cost, make them pay.

"Maybe you're right," Moradi said softly, back in control again. "Forgive me. I would of course never treat friends in this way. You and I though were not really friends — we were brothers."

That caught Koenen off-guard, and for once his trademark sarcasm failed him.

Reza shook his head. "Sadly, the story of Cain and Abel suggests that brothers don't always end things on good terms."

*   *   *   *   *

10:13PM

"You know," Reza went on after a pregnant pause, "I long ago made my peace with you, Finn Koenen. You were a spoiled little shit, of course, but just a kid when everything happened. We both were. And besides, you didn't betray my family, your father did, and I have never believed in punishing the son for the sins of the father."

Finn kept his face neutral as he tried to figure out what the hell Reza was talking about. *'Sins of the father?' What does my father have to do with this?* He honestly couldn't recall a single slight that his father would have ever given Reza, his father Amir, or anyone else in the Moradi family.

"But then, 34 years after your family abandoned mine to the wolves, there you were, brought back into my life by some strange orbit. Suddenly you're involved in uncovering my Chechen friends? And you start sniffing around my plans for tonight? Even if I believed in coincidences, I wouldn't believe in that one. No, our paths have crossed again for a reason."

"Don't forget, you always did have a hard time seeing my attacks coming," jeered Finn, probing for the rage he had seen a few moments ago.

Unperturbed, Moradi continued, almost languidly. "Unlike you, I think before I act and I did my research to find out who this adult Finn Koenen was, and how he had gotten there. Despite what you might be thinking, our separate paths have had some striking similarities."

Reza paused, looked at something off camera.

"And then a little birdie of mine deep within your CIA sent me this," here he held up a small black USB drive, "and much to my surprise I learned that you had in fact contributed to the single greatest failure of my adult life."

The old machine shop on the second floor of Integrated Logistics Solutions was dead silent below the low thrum of the wind and rain on the windows. The faintly sweet smell of old coolant mixed with the sour notes of his own sweat filled Finn's nose and he ran a dry tongue over his cracked lips. He hadn't had anything to eat or drink for a long time and he felt his stomach rumble incongruously.

"Although in another way I should be thanking you, for without your interference in 2002, I wouldn't now be on a path that will change the world forever. I would have happily contented myself with simple revenge, paying the West back a thousand-fold for what it took from me. And in time I would have turned my attention to the Mullahs, and made them reckon for the part they played with such eager cruelty. No, when you blew up my chemical weapons inside that mountain you forced me to start over, to reexamine my goals. To improvise."

Reza's eyes glittered and he paused to take a swig of something from a thermos before continuing.

"I guess that's another thing I should thank you for, teaching me the value of improvisation. It's a strategy I've always found untidy and unpredictable, but as an occasional tactic, utilized properly..." Reza waved his hands wide to indicate the scene in Boston. "It can give me moments like this, where I get to taunt you face-to-face just minutes before Anderson drives a fire truck into the middle of half a million people and blows them to wet pieces. It will make 9/11 look like an *amuse bouche*."

Pierce looked like he might start jumping up and down with joy.

"In fact," Moradi continued, real glee in his voice now, "though no one else will ever know, you'll have a front row seat to the whole affair, literally. After Anderson kills you, he will stow your body in the fire truck so any DNA or body parts that survive the explosion will be rather unfortunately mixed up with quite a lot of other people's." Reza shook his head in mock regret. "It will probably take them years to sort out which bits belonged to whom, and by then it won't matter — I'll have already made my final move, and you'll have simply vanished from the face of the Earth."

Reza shifted his gaze to Tony for the first time. "Mr. Russo. As evidenced by tonight's video, you were also on that raid into the Zahedan Mountains, so I'm afraid you'll be going in the fire truck with Mr. Koenen." Dismissing Tony and turning to look at Mike, he said, "Sgt. Miller. Under normal circumstances, I would have no quarrel with you. I understand you killed a fair number of Iraqis, something I generally approve of, only to be abandoned by the broken system you gave your soul to protect. I'm doing what I'm doing to help people just like you escape your cages and live better lives."

He sighed heavily. "Unfortunately, you are also the only person left alive who can connect me to the Tsarnaevs as well as to the Chechens and Anderson here. For that poor luck, you too, will shortly be an intimate part of the fireworks on the ground."

The mask of sadness dropped and Reza addressed Anderson, anticipation cracking through every word.

"Shall we begin?"

*   *   *   *   *

10:20PM

"Sully! Hey Sully!" yelled Heather over the noise of the storm during a break in the music as she spotted the officer wending his way through soaked and happy revelers.

"You know that guy?" asked Cat, hastily hiding her wine-filled water bottle behind her back.

Heather laughed. "I do, and don't worry, he won't bust us."

The officer spotted Heather's wave, returned it, and began making his way over to them. After introductions, he asked with a sheepish look towards the heavens, "Enjoying the show?"

"Actually, we are!" replied Heather brightly.

"Very much so," agreed Cat. "How about you? Can you have any fun or is it miserable trying to keep all this," she gestured around, "under control?"

Patrick gave a rueful snort. "Let's just say this is probably the first and last time I run point on one of these things."

Cat was impressed. "You're in charge?"

"Don't look so surprised," teased Heather, "Sully here is occasionally competent. Average, even." She punched him lightly on the arm, causing water droplets to spray into the air.

"And your friend Heather here," Sully poked her in the shoulder right back, "is almost as big of a pain in the ass as her brother!"

They all laughed but Cat saw that the officer's eyes never stopped roaming the crowd, presumably scanning for trouble.

"Speaking of, where is Finn?" asked Sully.

Heather pulled a face. "Fuck if I know. He'd better have a good excuse though, because he invited poor Cat here to join us in this monsoon and then never showed!"

Sully looked concerned. "That's weird."

"He's weird." She shrugged.

"And now he owes me one. A real big one," Cat chimed in, then felt the blood rush to her cheeks as she realized what she'd said. Unfortunately, so did Heather and Sully, and they each gave her pointed looks before bursting into peals of laughter.

Sully patted Heather on the shoulder and shook Cat's hand. "Well, duty calls. Nice to meet you, Cat. I can see why Finn likes you so much."

Her cheeks burned even hotter at this and she thanked the officer to cover her embarrassment. "I hope the rest of your night is easy and quiet," she called, just as a particularly large gust buffeted them, forcing each to take a step to keep from being blown over.

"Thanks. Let's hope this is as bad as it gets."

*　*　*　*　*

10:22PM

"Shall we begin?" asked Moradi, eager and venomous, from the screen.

A burst of muffled, unintelligible rage came from Finn's right as Tony struggled mightily against his chains. Pierce took a couple quick steps back even though he was several feet away next to Miller, who had dropped the pretense of a stupor and was busy testing the strength of his own bonds. Finn continued working his own wrists and felt the ropes slip ever so slightly. Another ten or fifteen minutes would have seen it done, but it looked like the fun was beginning rather sooner than that.

Anderson walked across in front of Finn to stand over near Russo, taking care to place himself just far enough away that the thrashing ball of fury couldn't reach him.

For the very first time in his life, it dawned on Finn that he might be in a situation he wouldn't get out of. Despite all the covert missions, the nighttime firefights, the frantic escapes, he'd never really considered the possibility that he might lose. He'd taken his lumps over the years, of course, and been in some pretty desperate circumstances, but never once had he doubted that he would get over the hurdle; finish the mission; win the game. He had always found a way to pull through, whether through his own actions or those of his team. Right now though, he was out of time and with Sully busy securing the Esplanade and Russo and Miller captured here with him, the cavalry wasn't likely to come riding in anytime soon.

And if anything did happen to Mike or Tony, it would be on Finn's head. He was the reason they were here. They were his responsibility. So he just would have to find a way to get them out, stop Pierce, then track down Reza and...

As if reading his mind, Moradi interrupted from wherever the hell he was, saying, "You've lost the game, Finn, and while I'm sorry I can't be there in person for the denouement, the wonders of modern technology will allow me to enjoy it well enough." He jerked his head and Anderson sidled behind Russo. "But unlike the games of chess we used to play as children, you don't get your pieces back after you lose. When I remove pieces from the board in this game, you lose them forever."

A whisper of a noise, a soft metallic clunk, and the sound of something wet splattering across the floor. Just like that, the side of Tony Russo's head was gone, blown away by the silenced pistol in Anderson's outstretched hand.

*   *   *   *   *

Finn was in shock. He had been in the heat of battle many times, but this... this cold-blooded slaughter of a brother in arms, a friend of twenty years, a man who had saved his life more than once, jarred him in a way that squeezed his jackhammering heart like a vice.

The smells of copper and acrid powder and viscera hit Finn's nose as blood continued to pump weakly out of the entry wound on the side of Russo's head to soak his shirt, where fat drops formed and fell to the floor with a sickening, irregular patter.

"I have never been much for the hand of God, or Fate, but it is moments like this that make me think I might have it wrong." On the monitor, Reza shrugged. "How else to explain everything falling into place like this?"

A dozen retorts sprang immediately to Finn's mind (*Because you're a fucking lunatic? Because sometimes the asshole wins?* And then, *Are you sure this game is over?*), but he kept them all to himself.

"But then I remember that this," Reza gestured to indicate the whole macabre scene in Boston, and Anderson's imminent attack on the Esplanade, "is more than just fate. This is what happens when one man has the vision to see what must be done and the will to shape events to that vision. This is what true leadership looks like."

"Let Sgt. Miller go," Finn broke in. "It's me you want. I'm the one who fucked up your little plans. Get your pound of flesh from me, but let him go," he pleaded as Anderson walked slowly around behind Finn to take up a position a few feet from Miller, who was tense but not panicking, eyes blazing as they tracked from Finn to Reza on the monitor and back again.

"Let him go," Finn said softly, intently, trying to pull the attention back to him and away from Miller. "You won, Reza. You won. There's no need to hurt him. He's just a poor homeless guy I said I would help out, so I gave him some odd jobs. He doesn't know shit and no one would believe him anyway. Plus, he's a heroin addict; how much longer does he really have?" Finn took Reza's silence as opportunity, so he kept talking, all the while straining his wrists against he stubborn knots binding his arms to the back of the chair.

"Honestly? Letting this poor bastard live is worse than killing him, trust me." Finn hoped that Mike knew he didn't mean what he was saying; that he was trying to buy time to get his hands free; to find that one magical thing that, when said aloud, would set them both free.

"MMmmMMmM," said Miller, voice strangled by the filthy gag in his mouth. He looked intently — but not psychotically, as Russo had — at the camera, clearly trying to communicate something.

"MmmMMm MmM MmMMMMm," he said again.

"I think that our Mr. Miller here who, based on your kind description, Finn, will welcome the sweet oblivion of death that awaits him, has something he would like to say." After a moment, Reza cocked his head and Anderson reached over and yanked the gag out of Miller's mouth.

Mike coughed and tried in vain to spit.

"Anderson. Could you please fetch Mr. Miller some water?" asked Reza, magnanimous. The blond man walked out of view and returned with a bottle of Poland Spring water. He unscrewed the cap and poured some into Miller's mouth, most of it spilling down into his matted beard or onto the floor.

Miller coughed again, spat and fixed Finn with an intense stare.

"I'm sorry, Mike," Finn said, hating his impotent helplessness. "I'm sorry I got you into this."

Unexpectedly, Mike grinned. He spat again, this time on Pierce's shoes. "Not your fault," he croaked. "You ever walk down a hostile street?" he asked, recalling their first conversation, three and a half months and a lifetime ago.

"That and worse." replied Finn.

"I can feel that little red dot on the back of my head, Finn," Miller said, neither sad nor scared, "I just hope it's clean."

"Do you have any further final words for your 'friend', Mr. Miller?" asked Reza derisively.

"Actually, yeah, I do," said Mike. "I want to say Happy Birthday."

"Happy Birthday? To whom?" asked Reza, caught off-guard.

Mike winked at Finn, put his game face on and stared straight at Moradi on the monitor.

"America," he said, and in a loud, clear voice, began reciting:

I pledge allegiance

To the flag

Of the United States of America

Pierce pistol-whipped him across the jaw. Miller spat out a bloody tooth but didn't miss a beat.

And to the Republic,

For which it stands

"Shut up!" yelled Anderson, punching Mike hard in the gut, causing him to gasp for air. After a few deep, rasping breaths, he continued, unbowed.

One nation, under God

Indivisible

With liberty and justice, for all

Miller's head snapped back as if pulled by a string. Bits of his skull and brain matter flew into the air to land somewhere behind him in the shadows with a sickening damp splattering noise. His lifeless body jerked a few times, then fell still, gently rocking slower and slower as friction robbed it of kinetic energy.

Entropy as eulogy.

CHAPTER 49

10:30PM

Several dull thumps signaling the start of the fireworks show over the Charles River eight blocks north intruded into the silence following Miller's execution.

Finn screamed in boundless rage, a throaty roar filling the room with ferocity. A red miasma began to obscure his vision.

"Hurts, doesn't it," observed Reza, "to watch your family die and be unable to prevent it."

Finn felt himself physically swelling with anger and frustration he could no longer control; that he no longer wanted to control.

"Especially when it is you yourself who killed them."

The truth of it skewered Finn: the ineluctable, irrevocable, inevitable truth: that Mike and Tony were dead because of him; that a ghost had risen from his past to meet out pain and suffering; that he had lost.

"In an ideal world," continued Reza, checking his watch, "it would have been you that pulled the trigger, but alas, Time is an unforgiving master, and we have more important matters to attend to this evening. Besides, it's checkmate. I need move but one more piece."

Reza turned his attention to Pierce, who was still standing next to Miller's gently swaying corpse. "Are you ready?"

"I am," replied the upper-middle class suburban Connecticut kid from a good family.

"Then end this and get on with your true mission."

Just then, perhaps due to the torrent of righteous fury arcing through his body like lightening, the knots constraining Finn's wrists behind the chair came loose. His vision instantly cleared, hope's unexpected return dousing the flames consuming his heart and focusing his mind as sharp as a razor.

Anderson was looking at Finn with something like delight and anticipation.

That's it, Keep your eyes on mine, thought Finn, working his hands free while Pierce stepped closer, the barrel of the silencer rising to point at his temple.

"You know *Zaza*," said Finn to cover the noise of the ropes dropping to the floor behind him, "there's one important difference between moving people and moving chess pieces."

"Oh? And what's that?" asked Moradi, half amused, half irritated.

"Chess pieces stay where you put them."

* * * * *

Koenen exploded out of his chair, smashing his head and shoulder up into Anderson's extended arm. Completely taken by surprise, Pierce heard himself yelp in pain and astonishment as they both fell heavily sideways and his gun skittered away into the shadows.

What the fuck he wondered as he hit hard and slid across the floor, *is happening? How is Koenen free?* And then, remembering that the man was quite literally a trained killer, *I just murdered his friends. He's going to make this hurt.*

Anderson's head rang from having tapped the polished concrete and he vaguely registered that Finn was reaching for him and that Reza was shouting something from the laptop. Lying here on the floor he noticed just how dusty it was, and how much it smelled like machine oil. A slight giggle escaped his lips as he watched Finn cover the distance between them, hands and forearms doing the work because his legs were still tied to the metal desk chair. He looked like a very angry merman chasing his prey onto land.

The giggles stopped abruptly once Koenen got his hands on Anderson's calf, the murderously strong grip instantly dispelling the fog of lassitude brought on by what was most likely a bad concussion. Dismay rolled over him like a wave as Finn began pulling him closer.

Snapping into action, Pierce frantically tried to scramble backwards but found his strength no match for the detective's. Panicking, he kicked and bucked wildly and in a stroke of pure, dumb luck somehow managed to crack Koenen full in the nose with his knee. It broke with an unmistakable snap and blood started pouring out all over his face, his grip momentarily relaxing.

Seizing the opportunity, Pierce tried rolling away but wasn't quite quick enough. Koenen's fingers wrapped around his right ankle preventing a clean escape. At the same time, Pierce felt something dig painfully into his left hip and he suddenly remembered his backup plan, brought just on the off chance something went wrong. He twisted in Koenen's grip to flip onto his back and pulled a sleek black cylinder out of his pants pocket. Quickly checking that the device was properly oriented, he aimed its nozzle at the detective.

Just as Anderson pressed the red button on top of the cylinder, Koenen used him for leverage, pulling hard on Anderson's leg and pivoting on his hip to snap his legs — and the metal chair they were tied to — around to smash into Anderson's face and chest. Pierce howled in pain and the pepper spray flew out of his hand in the opposite direction from where the gun had gone, a jet of noxious chemicals roping through the air well wide of its intended target. Ancillary blow-back mist, however, enveloped them both.

Pierce immediately clamped his own eyes shut and held his breath, kicking savagely at Finn with his free leg, the heel of his heavy work boot making a satisfying thud as it connected with the top of Koenen's head. The detective, now coughing violently, let go and Anderson blind crab-walked several yards backwards to escape Finn's reach and away from any chemicals that might still be hanging in the air.

He stopped, suddenly unsure of where he was in the room and afraid of hitting his head again on the metal table or one of the klieg light stands. The fear of not being able to see what was happening outweighed that of getting residual pepper spray in his eyes, so he cracked one, expecting Koenen's fist in his face at any second.

Relief flooded through him when his eye watered but did not truly burn or swell shut — he had escaped the worst of it — and then through tears he couldn't control he saw warped and multiplied images of Koenen writhing and cursing on the ground several yards away, the chair thrashing awkwardly around like some strange, heavy beaver tail. *Beaver tail?* Pierce thought somewhat abstractly. *I definitely have a concussion*, he concluded as he gingerly got to his feet.

As much as he wanted to go find the gun and finish the job he'd accepted from Reza, he knew he hadn't hit Koenen with the full blast of pepper spray and consequently didn't know how long it would be until he regained his senses. He vacillated just a moment longer then bolted out of the old machine shop as fast as he could manage and headed for the stairs.

Fuck it, he thought as he took the steps down two and three at a time, *what's more important, one guy dead or twenty thousand?*

A rectangular package duct-taped to the wall opposite the bottom of the stairs caught Anderson's attention and he skidded to a halt. He stared at it for a moment and then let his eyes follow the wires trailing out of it and along the wall to snake into and out of a second identical brick taped to the wall thirty feet away. More wires emerged out the other side and disappeared around the corner. He sprinted down the hall and across the empty expanse of the loading bay, past the neat stacks of empty barrels and over to the far side of the quiescent fire truck. He snatched a gas mask hanging on a nail and rapidly donned it, running forward to press the button to open the loading bay door leading to the back alley. He ran back and faced the wall next to the driver's side door of the truck. He checked the fit of the gas mask then reached out to the first of the thirty-one identical rectangular packages strung along the walls around the entire first floor of the building.

Anderson fluttered his fingers then reached out and crossed the stripped ends of two wires protruding from one side of the package. He cursed and flinched as sparks flashed and burned his fingers, but successfully twisted the ends together nonetheless. He had planned to don rubber gloves to set off the white phosphorus-based incendiary devices that would reduce ILS's building to a smoldering ruin but didn't really have time to observe proper OSHA procedures just now.

Instantly, the first brick began to smoke, the tape holding it to the wall warping, turning black and then falling away as a white-hot burst of flame shot out as if from a tiny angry dragon. Pierce pulled his eyes away just in time to avoid being blinded by the intensity of the glare and clambered up into the diver's seat. He reached over and grabbed the fireman's helmet on the passengers seat and jammed it awkwardly on his head, the straps of the gas mask preventing it from fitting properly. Underneath where the helmet had lain were the two items he would shortly need: a cell phone and a small metal box with an almost comically obvious single big red button set into it that he would use to ascend into *Jannah.*

Fat drops of rain spattered against the windshield, blown sideways by gusts of wind as the steel slatted garage door finished it's noisy ascent. Glancing in the side view mirror, Anderson could see the other incendiary devices along the wall starting to burn, producing thick, white, toxic smoke, the chemical's characteristic garlic smell managing somehow to get through the filters in his mask. White phosphorus reacted with the oxygen in the air and would burn so hot the entire building would be engulfed in minutes if not seconds.

He hurriedly turned the key, shifted into first and put the fire truck into motion, nosing the thousand gallons of explosives carefully out into the hurricane, a grin spreading underneath the gas mask.

I am doing what needs to be done.

The world will be cleansed.

It will be beautiful.

* * * * *

Finn shook the last of the ropes from his legs and stood up, tears continuing to well in his inflamed eyes as he shook his head in disbelief. Why hadn't Pierce grabbed the gun and finished him off while he lay blind and defenseless on the floor?

Thankfully, the bulk of the pepper spray had missed wide and his incapacitation had been short-lived. Finally able to breathe and open his eyes without pain, he found the room unexpectedly empty, Pierce clearly having opted for escape over execution. Finn quickly scanned the room but was unable to spot Anderson's discarded gun. He strode over to the laptop but Reza (*Reza!*) was gone, the connection cut sometime during the brief melee. *Shit.* His job now was to stop Anderson from doing whatever it was he was about to do. He had been wearing a fireman's uniform, which meant it would be very difficult to track him down if he made it to the Esplanade.

Fireworks continued to thump somewhere nearby and reminded Finn that any further delay could prove devastatingly fatal. Nonetheless, he couldn't help taking a long moment to regard the corpses of his two friends hanging in chains in front of him. *Would he have to call Tony's ex-wife Sandra to tell her? Did Miller even have any living relatives to contact?* And then: *I'm gonna kill that motherfucker,* meaning both Anderson and Reza, two facets of the same evil design.

The sound of a metal door rumbling into life somewhere below him cut short the silent farewell to his brothers in arms. Finn sprinted out of the old machine shop, grabbed the door frame and spun himself into the corridor outside, pelting for the stairwell just up ahead. Halfway down, however, something on the wall across from the bottom of the stairs started hissing wildly then burst into a white hot flame. Thick white smoke immediately poured out and enveloped the bottom few stairs.

Finn arrested his descent and threw himself painfully back down onto the steps, arms covering his head, expecting an explosion which never came. Instead he felt the heat of the flames growing quickly on his legs and the taste of acrid garlic in his nose.

Recognizing the smell of white phosphorus (he'd utilized it many times in the Army), he realized he wasn't getting out that way and sprinted back up the stairs, down the hall and back into the old machine shop. Knowing next to nothing about the building he had been brought to, he figured the best chance of finding a fire escape would be outside of the windows he'd guessed were hidden behind the rusty metal racks standing against the exterior wall. Tossing shelves to the side with a tremendous crash, he tore dirty brown construction paper away and quickly unlocked a rattling window. Throwing it open unleashed the full fury of the storm into the room, soaking him instantly and drowning out any indications of what might be happening downstairs. Fearing the worst, Finn shot a quick look over his shoulder and saw a bright flickering in the hall that caused crazy shadows to jump all around the macabre scene.

Time to go.

He ducked and stepped through the open window out onto the slippery metal grate of the fire escape. He was twenty feet above the alley and could see flames and thick white smoke billowing out of the empty loading bay door below and to the left. Finn snapped his head to the right and saw a Boston Fire Department truck slowly accelerating up the narrow alley towards Arlington Street several blocks ahead.

Gotcha.

*   *   *   *   *

Pierce flicked the wipers to their highest setting (totally unhelpful) and concentrated on shifting up to second gear. He had always been somewhat indifferent about vehicles in general and had only learned how to drive the fire truck from YouTube. It wasn't like he could take it out onto the streets of Boston to practice, of course, and he had lied to his Benefactor about his expertise in this area. He had driven forklifts however and concluded they were close enough he'd be able to guide the thing to the Esplanade. Besides, if he hit a few other cars or people along the way, all the better so long as he completed the mission.

Speaking of... Anderson grabbed the cell phone from the passenger seat and tried to thumb in the pass code to unlock it. The thick plastic of the gas mask made it hard to see, so he let go of the wheel and threw the mask and his helmet onto the floor of the truck cab.

Judging he had enough time before needing to turn the huge vehicle left onto Arlington, he selected the one phone number in the Contacts list, sending a signal winging at great speed up to the satellite and back down to the package he'd hidden several hours ago in the tower on the Longfellow Bridge over the Charles.

*   *   *   *   *

"What was that?" Heather asked sharply as something pulled her attention away from the fireworks display above. The bursts were partially obscured by the storm, making them eerily spectacular.

"What was what?" replied Cat, eyes still fixed skyward, hands held up in a fruitless attempt to keep rain out of them.

"That," said Heather, stomach dropping as she pointed to an expanding orange ball of flame roiling up into the chaotic sky above the Longfellow Bridge behind and to the left of the stage.

"Is that a…" asked Cat, perplexed, then, "Holy shit!"

"Time to go," Heather declared, starting to gather up their few belongings.

Cat caught Heather's blooming anxiety and quickly bent to grab her bag. "Dammit," she snapped as it slipped from her hands and spilled its contents into the standing water on the lawn.

"C'mon, leave it!" urged Heather as she saw a ripple of panic begin to run through the crowd from the direction of the explosion. She grabbed Cat by the arm and pulled her towards the rear of the great lawn, shouting to Cat over the din of the storm, rising voices and an otherwise rousing rendition of John Philip Sousa's "Stars and Stripes Forever":

"I think we know why Finn blew us off!"

*   *   *   *   *

Finn grimaced as he hit the broken pavement below the bottom of the metal ladder and rolled his ankle, though thankfully not catastrophically so. He had been forced to adopt a reckless approach to descending the fire escape when a loud crumpling whump came rolling over the rooftops from the direction of the river. It clearly hadn't been fireworks and Finn feared that Pierce's attack, Reza's attack, had begun.

He started hobbling, then finally running painfully up the alley after the fire truck as it turned the corner and disappeared from view before he could get a read on the license plate or on any other identifying marks.

Fuck!

Once the fire truck got closer to the Esplanade it would blend in seamlessly with the hundreds of other ambulances, fire trucks, police cars and other safety equipment surrounding the event, rendering it impossible to find. Finn had no phone, no radio, no way to reach Sully or to warn anyone. It was up to him to do whatever could be done. If it wasn't already too late.

Heather's there. With Cat.

Digging deep and ignoring the sharp complaints from his rolled ankle, he put on a burst of speed, shoes pounding holes in the river of water coming down the alley towards him in a dirty torrent. A gust of wind blew him two steps to the side and he fought hard to regain his line.

Finn fairly flew around the corner and, through unnumbered fat, sheeting raindrops tried to process the visual cacophony of vehicles, pedestrians and flashing blue, white, yellow and red lights between him and the Esplanade several blocks ahead. He forced his mind to focus only on the red and whites that Boston fire trucks sported. His pace faltered as he realized there were at least six, no… seven different fire trucks in view. One had been blocked by a vehicle moving up the street, another fire truck, actually, running dark, no lights flashing at all.

Jackpot.

No real fire truck would be driving without its lights on — that had to be Pierce. Finn redoubled his efforts and began to gain on the vehicle which for some reason had slowed considerably, perhaps because Anderson was having trouble mastering the huge truck? Or had it been spotted by the security cordon? Whatever the reason, this hiccup in velocity might just give Finn the window he needed.

He dropped chin to chest and urged his aching body forward, eating up the distance. He suddenly realized why Pierce had slowed down so much. Arlington dead-ended into Beacon Street and the home-grown terrorist would be forced to take a ninety degree turn left or right. Either would provide him opportunities to reach the Great Oval and its hundreds of thousands of revelers but Finn quickly decided that Pierce would go left, then right, under the Arthur Fiedler Footbridge, across Storrow Drive and into the Esplanade itself. Taking a risk, he angled left and found an extra gear when Anderson proved his choice of hypotenuse correct.

Finn reached the back of the truck as it lurched, shuddering and complaining, around the corner. Finn raced along the left side of the truck, noticing a series of tool cabinet doors built into it. He pulled the closest one open as he ran and grabbed a heavy multipurpose hammer-type thing out of some brackets, choosing to forgo the other two items inside: a large axe and a shovel, each would require two hands to wield. He would need one of his hands free to hold onto the vertical chrome bar set just behind the driver's-side door when he jumped onto the fire truck.

A couple strides later and he pulled himself up to stand on an indented metal step set into the rear of the cab for exactly this purpose. Crouching there for a brief moment to catch his breath, he realized he could see part of Pierce's face in the larger of the two side view mirrors affixed to the cab in front of the drivers' side door. His eyes had the feverish sheen Finn had seen in any number of fanatics he'd crossed paths with in Iraq, Afghanistan, Syria… and now the United States. Fortunately, Pierce was one hundred percent focused on maintaining control of the fire truck as he pulled it out of the left turn directly into a sharp right one.

The centrifugal force of the truck's hard swerve to the right caused Finn's feet to slip off the wet metal step and he found himself floating in midair, right hand desperately trying to keep its grip on the vertical bar while the left one flailed the hammer around in the air uselessly.

Before he could decide whether or not to drop the hammer and grab the metal bar with both hands instead, the side of the truck slammed into him as it straightened out again to head the wrong way up the exit ramp from Storrow Drive. Dozens of people dove out of the way as the vehicle entered the outer layers of the massive crowd. A sickening syncopated series of thumps and bumps almost dislodged Finn from his tenuous perch as the fire truck's huge tires rolled over at least two concert-goers who hadn't been lucky or quick enough to get out of the way.

Somehow, Anderson still hadn't noticed Finn's presence just behind him on the outside of the cab. Screams, shouted curses and the crump of fireworks filled his ears as the truck picked up speed, making a beeline for the concert.

Finn checked his footing and got a firm grip on the hammer.

Knock-knock, asshole.

*   *   *   *   *

Anderson's arms ached from the strain of maneuvering the fire truck around two sharp corners, one the opposite of the other. Taking them much faster than expected, he'd almost lost control and tipped the huge bomb over, which would have been a spectacular but criminally ineffective way to go out.

From here on though, he had a straight shot two blocks ahead, under the footbridge, across Storrow Drive and into the Great Oval itself where fire and glory awaited him, just seconds into his future. The truck lurched forward as he roughly forced it into a higher gear, right foot mashed down hard on the gas pedal to try and recover the velocity bled off by the consecutive turns. He glanced over at the detonator with its big red button sitting innocuously on the seat next to him — a simple device for a simple outcome.

"Your justice is coming", he whispered to the masses ahead. "I am here."

Just then the window to his left shattered, showering him with glass. Hurricane Arthur blasted into the cab with the force of a freight train and Anderson screamed in surprise and alarm, momentarily letting go of the huge steering wheel as his arms flew up to protect his face. Inexplicably, an arm reached into the truck through the broken window and pulled the steering wheel hard to the left. Pierce quickly regained his composure and grabbed the wheel himself, pulling it back to the right to straighten them out again.

"Fuck. Off!" he snarled through clenched teeth, realizing that Koenen must have somehow escaped the conflagration back at ILS and tracked him down. Anderson let go of the wheel with his left hand and tried to pry Finn's hand off the wheel but it was like rubber trying to break iron. Even worse, it quickly became apparent that Anderson needed both hands on the wheel to counter the strength of the detective's one, so he abandoned the futile efforts and refocused on controlling the steering.

Abruptly, Pierce realized that he had taken his foot off the gas and that the fire truck was slowing down again. He hammered his right foot down and glanced frantically to his right, relief flooding through him when he saw that the detonator was still on the seat, though the swerve to the left when Koenen grabbed the wheel had caused it to slide away over by the passenger-side door.

Frustration and anger at the detective's continued interference filled his heart and he put all his strength into pulling the wheel to the right, trying to jerk it out of Koenen's grasp, but failed. The two of them were locked in an awkward sort of equilibrium, and the truck continued to speed ahead, pedestrians yelling and diving out of the way. Looking up, Pierce saw that they were heading straight for a concrete abutment supporting the jam-packed Fiedler pedestrian footbridge which crossed over the road ahead. He grunted again with the effort of fighting Koenen's relentless pull on the wheel and realized with a sick feeling in his stomach that he couldn't both prevent Koenen from wrecking the truck and reach the detonator at the same time.

Everything slowed to a crawl.

He would have to choose: let go of the wheel to reach the detonator, which would guarantee explosion of the bomb, though well short of the optimal kill zone; or keep both hands on the wheel so he could hopefully thwart Koenen's apparent desire to crash them into the abutment and then deliver the 1,000 gallons of ANNM to the center of the panicked crowd, thereby maximizing the carnage for which he was sacrificing his life.

Fireworks threw half-hidden, slow motion tracers and sparks into the clouds above the footbridge abutment as it slid inexorably closer, as if it were coming for him.

Even the storm held its breath.

Time to decide.

*   *   *   *   *

Sully's spine prickled. Something was wrong. Very wrong. Well, technically speaking, something *else* was very wrong.

Not five minutes ago something had happened (exploded?) on the Longfellow Bridge over the Charles, and they still didn't know if it was some sort of electrical or gas line accident, a wayward firework, or (most worryingly) a bomb of some sort. At the time he had been perched atop the Fiedler Footbridge, having decided to head up there to enjoy a bird's-eye view of the fireworks finale from above the soaked and heaving crowds to reward himself for a job well done. Despite the growing glow of accomplishment building in his belly, the whole experience of running point with a dozen different agencies had confirmed how much he hated politics and egos. Too many assholes and not enough toilet seats. All he had wanted now was to usher people safely out of the area, go home, sit on his couch with a drink and get back to his normal job tomorrow. Thoughts of single-malt scotch in his skivvies abruptly vanished, however, when he heard the crack and thump roll over him and a cacophony of voices had begun cascading through his ear piece.

His team had responded quickly and efficiently, and officers were about to reach the site of the incident on the bridge to provide a first-hand report. The fireworks — cold, computerized logic sending them unabated skyward from their barges — continued to flash and flare, partially obscured by both the storm and residual smoke of their own making.

As he waited impatiently for the update, he spun slowly around to scan what was happening around and below him. Movement at the far end of the Storrow Drive access road caught his attention and something about the fire truck careening around the corner wasn't right. It was heading the wrong way up the exit ramp and its flashers were off, for starters. And he had ordered all safety personnel to stay in position until his S.W.A.T. team signaled all-clear, so what was this idiot doing barreling up the access road?

He thumbed the mike clipped to his shoulder lapel and barked, "All safety personnel hold position. Stay at your posts and do not approach the bridge, and whoever the fuck is driving that fire truck towards the Fiedler footbridge is ordered to stop immediately. I repeat: stop your truck!"

"All fire equipment accounted for and holding," came a voice over the radio. "We have no one approaching your position. Do you have a situation?"

Sully unsnapped the holster on his Glock 22 as the truck mowed several people down and he yelled into the mike, "Code Red! We have a Code Red at the Fiedler Footbridge! Hostile inbound in a Boston Fire Department pumper truck, lights off!"

Through the blinding rain he could see a figure clinging precariously to the outside of the truck, desperately holding onto the driver's-side door.

He shouted for people to get away and civilians began scattering in both directions on the footbridge as he stepped forward and aimed his pistol at the vehicle, which swerved erratically as it accelerated towards him.

Taking a deep breath, he aimed down the barrel of the gun and began firing.

*　　*　　*　　*　　*

Finn kept pulling hard on the steering wheel from outside the cab of the truck with his left hand, wishing he had the use of both hands but not quite willing to risk unhooking his right arm from the metal bar he was using for purchase. He briefly wondered if he would have been better off keeping the hammer to bludgeon Pierce with rather than discarding it to grab the wheel, but trusting his instincts had gotten him this far in life.

And maybe no further.

He refocused on the stalemated battle he and Pierce were locked in for control of the vehicle, neither able to overpower the other. Finn could see they were heading right for the concrete support structure ahead, and figured hitting the bridge was preferable to letting this lunatic get to the crowds on the Oval. A partial victory would be better than none, even if it cost him his own life.

Suddenly, the windshield exploded and a half second later something punched sharp and hard into the muscle behind Finn's left thigh, knocking him back and causing him to let go of the steering wheel and clutch instinctively at his leg. A half second after that, the pain blossomed angrily, radiating up into his hip, and he lost his footing on the step.

The fire truck pulled hard to the right and Finn dangled precariously for the second time in as many minutes, his right elbow hooked through the metal bar, as Anderson steered the truck away from the abutment and towards the Esplanade beyond. The toes of Finn's shoes started skipping off the wet pavement and he belatedly realized two things: that (a) he had been shot and (b) the fire truck was in the process of tipping over on top of him.

He didn't know which was worse: running full-speed into the concrete wall or getting smeared into a red paste when the truck fell on him. Either way, he just hoped it wouldn't explode, because if it did, he was going to be one pissed-off goddamn ghost.

*   *   *   *   *

Anderson decided.

He prepared to relinquish the wheel and dive for the detonator when the air was suddenly filled with shards of glass followed by even more howling wind and blinding rain.

What the fuck?!

A half second later the wheel jerked violently to the right as Koenen's counter-force disappeared. The truck leapt and Pierce somehow managed to reestablish his grip with both hands. He didn't know what the fuck was going on and didn't really care. Right now his entire being was focused on guiding the truck under the footbridge and safely past the concrete abutment. It seemed Allah was giving him one last chance to complete his mission and he could still make it to the Esplanade to fill it with fire and blood.

He felt a funny sensation in his stomach and realized he wasn't going to make it.

The sudden swerve to the right was causing the truck to start tilting over to the left, but if he steered into it he would plow straight into the abutment. Screaming inchoately and refusing to quit — he was so very close — he did the opposite and pulled the steering wheel hard to the right again.

The front of the truck slowly came round to point past the concrete wall and towards the crowds on the Esplanade, but before he could celebrate, Anderson felt the massive vehicle groan as it tipped up onto its left wheels, moments from flipping over.

A nasty shock ran through the truck as Anderson registered the unmistakable sound of metal hitting concrete. The top right corner of the cab, angled into the air by the tipping truck, had clipped the underside of the footbridge, sending chunks of concrete spraying out in front of him as the truck's light-bar went pinwheeling into a group of revelers. The collision also caused the right wheels of the fire truck to slam back down to the pavement, leaving him heading more-or-less in the correct direction.

Pierce giggled and bounced up and down in the seat as the truck turned more infidels into speed bumps. He just needed to cross a short stretch of Storrow Drive and he'd be on the great lawn with its half a million soaking wet, inebriated, decadent revelers.

A particularly strong gust of wind carried the cannon blasts of the 1812 Overture, the fireworks finale's traditional accompaniment, which would make a fitting soundtrack for the carnage he was about to unleash.

Grinning at his good fortune and supremely confident at having overcome all manner of unexpected difficulties, he leaned over to his right and stretched out his arm towards the detonator.

*   *   *   *   *

Clinging precariously to the outside of the fire truck, right arm still hooked around the metal bar, Finn tied to shake concrete dust out of his eyes, but the rain instantly turned it into a gritty paste, so he let go of his injured thigh and used his bloody left hand to wipe his face. More blood stained his rain-soaked jeans as it pumped unabated out of the wound and he could tell the leg was useless. On the plus side, clipping the footbridge had righted the truck and given him the opportunity to stay alive and in the game.

Unfortunately, Pierce was now headed right for the Esplanade and its hundreds of thousands of people, including Cat and Heather. He had a bad leg, no weapons, no plan, and one, maybe two seconds to prevent the worst terrorist attack in American history.

*   *   *   *   *

Anderson strained but the detonator was just out of reach on the far side of the passenger seat next to him. He didn't want to take his eyes from the chaotic scene in front of him that was his destiny, and he felt his fingertips just graze the side of the smooth metal rectangle before maddeningly pushing it further away.

Without thinking — the time for thinking was done — Pierce let go of the steering wheel so he could dive to his right to grab the detonator. At the same time, Koenen came hurtling through the window, head-butting and knocking Anderson off target. The detonator slipped out of his grasp and clattered to the floor on the far side of the truck.

Head ringing, time went all swimmy for Anderson and he momentarily forgot what he was doing, soaking wet, falling through space and time, under attack. He vaguely recalled that he had been about to do something, something real and important, but for some reason it wasn't happening. He could hear someone yelling, it was the person half lying on top of him, and that seemed kind of weird.

With an almost audible crack, reality snapped back into place with a vengeance. He was lying sideways across the cab of the fire truck, Koenen's elbow digging into his back as he steered half-in, half-out of the window. Rock salt-sized pieces of broken windshield glass pressed into his cheek while his left hand scrabbled unseen around the floor of the passenger seat for the detonator, which he could hear rattling around somewhere with the gas mask and fireman's helmet he had discarded earlier. If he could only reach the detonator he could still complete the mission and ascend to his heavenly rewards.

Anderson suddenly realized that the truck was riding smoothly forward. It wasn't bumping over bodies or grass. They must still be on the road. Which meant Koenen had directed them away from the Esplanade!

He was failing. He had never failed at anything, ever in his life. He would not fail now.

Then Allah intervened again. The heavy elbow digging into his spine disappeared. Pierce turned his head to see Koenen falling away backwards out of the window, leaving him alone in the cab of the fire truck.

He slid his cheek along the glass and debris until he could see the detonator lying unceremoniously in the floor well and grabbed it, somehow holding onto it despite the truck taking a sudden tremendous lurch.

He wasn't sure where he was exactly, though he was pretty sure it wasn't the Esplanade anymore. It wouldn't be the body count he'd hoped for, but...

"Every little bit counts," he whispered, just a millisecond before his mother did, as he pressed the big red button.

EPILOGUE

Only the dead have seen the end of war.
— George Santayana

CHAPTER 50

The blackness was absolute.

And then it wasn't.

Almost imperceptibly, the universe became one microscopic shade of gray lighter, and then another, and another, until all in a rush it became a white so intense it hurt.

Finn tried to blink, to move his head but found himself unable to do either. A confusion of muffled, incomprehensible sounds thudded into his consciousness. Had they be there before? He had no way of knowing. He was untethered from time, floating uneasily between physical sensation and conscious awareness.

* * * * *

And then it was later.

He couldn't have explained why or how he knew it was later, but he just did. The painful white came to him much faster this time, with none of the sly tiptoeing from before. The sounds he heard almost resembled words, but fell short of meaning.

Not quite yet, he intuited before relinquishing his hold on the edge of consciousness and slipping once again into the deep, still waters of not-being.

* * * * *

Finn coughed himself awake and was surprised to find that he was finally actually, fully conscious, though his eyes stayed shut against the brightness beyond.

"Easy there, partner," came a man's voice from his right as a hand patted his forearm. Confused by not being dead, Finn thought for a fleeting second that Tony Russo was addressing him.

A machine in the room stirred and started beeping, amplifying Finn's sudden, formless anxiety. In response the beeping increased in both frequency and urgency.

"Hey, it's okay Finn. You're okay."

"Where am I?" he managed to croak painfully in a voice that sounded like wind over hot coals.

"You're in the hospital, Mass General. You're okay,' the voice added hastily, "though it was touch and go there for a little while. I knew you were a tough little bastard so I took the Over and made out pretty well in the squad room pool."

Finn wasn't quite sure what to make of this, but thought he at least knew who he was talking to now. He cracked his eyes and began the process of acclimatizing them to daylight again.

"You know," continued Sully, sitting in the visitor's chair to the right of Finn's hospital bed, "a few guys were kind of rooting you wouldn't make it, so I actually made a shit-ton of money. So, thanks for not dying yet — I owe you one."

Finn chanced moving his head and took a look around. He was lying under crisp white sheets in a standard hospital room with two semi-comfortable wooden armchairs (one containing Sully), a small TV mounted high on the far wall, and a small table with a vase of wildflowers over by a window that allowed muffled city street noise into the room. Finn saw he was connected to several tubes and sensors and he resisted the urge to yank them all out.

He felt sore all over and weak, but not crippled. The back of his left thigh burned something fierce, he had a low-grade headache and his throat was exceptionally parched, but all-in-all he was surprised at how good not being dead felt.

"Thirsty?" asked Sully, worry creasing his brow. At Finn's nod he poured water from a plastic pitcher into a small Dixie cup that had a surprisingly pretty floral pattern on it. Finn nodded his thanks and carefully gathered the cup in his shaking hands. Bringing it to his lips, he sipped, letting the small splash of water revive his dry, cracked lips and mouth. It was heaven.

"Don't gulp it," admonished Sully, reaching out to tip the cup back from Finn's mouth. "The nurses have been busting my balls non-stop about not letting you chug that when you woke up." He softened his tone. "You've been out for almost a week, buddy. IV's been keeping you fed and watered, so if you drink too fast you could throw it right back up."

Finn nodded again and raised his eyebrows to indicate he understood and would comply. Sully let go of Finn's hands and he raised the cup for a smaller sip this time. Satisfied that he wasn't going to disobey, Sully sat back down in his chair and filled Finn in on what he'd missed while he slowly started the process of coming back to the world.

*   *   *   *   *

"You shot me?" asked Finn incredulous.

Sully looked hurt, "Not on purpose. I mean, I shot *at* you on purpose, but I didn't know I was shooting at *you*. How could I?" he asked, understandably getting a little defensive. "All I saw was a rogue fire truck mowing people down on the Storrow exit ramp!"

Finn raised his hands in a placating gesture. "It's fine. I get it. I'd have done the same thing."

Sully gave him a grateful nod and continued his narrative, "Anyway, after I tried to take out the driver, you guys drove underneath me, clipped the underside of the footbridge and headed straight for the Esplanade." The cop dropped his eyes and he paused. "I froze," he said, looking at the floor. "I wanted to stop the fire truck but didn't dare shoot into the crowd and risk hitting civilians. Even though I knew — I knew — that something much worse was going to happen if I didn't try to stop that firetruck, I still couldn't risk shooting any civilians."

He stared at Finn, eyes practically begging for absolution. Finn gave it to him.

"You did good Officer O'Sullivan," he said in a low, raspy voice. "Plus, I'm glad you shot me, because I plan on milking this for a lot, and I mean a lot, of free drinks."

Sully smiled, bittersweet at first then morphing into relief as he realized Finn understood, and approved how Sully had handled the crucible he'd been in. "I don't know exactly what happened next, because the fire truck was driving away from me and, well, it was in the middle of a goddamn hurricane, but something definitely happened because instead of plowing into the middle of the crowd, the fire truck angled right and headed off the wrong way down Storrow."

"I remember that," said Finn, his throat and voice starting to improve.

Sully shot him a look. "What else do you remember?"

Finn thought for a moment, trying to take himself back. He pushed almost physically past the broken shards of his disjointed recollections until, quite abruptly, the memory slammed into him.

"After you shot me in the leg," he began slowly, "I knew I didn't have much time, so I just dove through the window and head-butted Pierce. He fell over sideways and I steered the fire truck away from the crowds and on down Storrow Drive. He had his foot on the accelerator and I was hanging half out of the truck so I couldn't slow down, only steer, but I guess that was enough?" He trailed off, making it a question, even though his continued existence answered it.

"And he was reaching for something, and I was holding him down so he couldn't get whatever it was, and then I could feel myself passing out, maybe from blood loss or whatever, but the last thing I remember was my legs getting really heavy, and losing my grip on the steering wheel, and falling backwards into a deep, dark hole."

They sat in silence for a full minute before Sully filled in the gaps.

"You also did good, Sergeant First Class Koenen," Sully said gravely, raising his own Dixie cup in salute. "You managed to steer the truck away from the masses and down along Storrow. You also managed to fall off the fire truck just moments before it went straight into the Charles River and exploded." He shook his head in disbelief the held up his hand, index finger and thumb virtually touching. "It was *this* close," he said, admiringly. "This close."

"How so?" Finn asked, a chill running through him.

"That pumper truck was filled with explosives. ANNM, like they used in Oklahoma City."

Finn nodded his understanding.

"But more. A lot more." Sully seemed to have trouble finding the words and he directed his gaze up at the ceiling tiles. "If that truck had exploded in the middle of the crowd, well," he shook his head again before meeting Finn's eyes. "It would have been bad."

They both contemplated that for a few moments.

"As it turns out, you fell off at just the right time. Any closer, and they'd be putting your name on a wall somewhere."

"That's a little disconcerting."

"Is it? Well, the doctors say you've paid for it. You were close enough to the blast, which vaporized part of the Longfellow bridge and left a huge crater on the edge of the river, to have sustained some real damage. The fall from the truck and the blast itself combined to sear the inside of your lungs, give you a vicious concussion, and generally fuck your shit right up. By the time the EMTs found you, your brain had swelled up so much that the doctors had to put you into a medically-induced coma. They started taking you out of it yesterday, and here we are now."

"How many people died?" Finn asked quietly.

Sully paused before responding, giving him a sad, concerned look. "About twenty thousand fewer than if you hadn't gotten involved, buddy."

For the next five minutes the only sounds were Finn's awkward sips of water, Sully shifting in his chair, and the soft hum and beeps of medical equipment. Then Sully drained the contents of his cup and produced his flask out of thin air to refill it with what must have been his trademark Dewar's.

"Do I get some of that, Officer?" Finn asked, getting a weak smile and shake of the head from Sully. "Where do you keep that thing, anyway?" His words started to slur as consciousness began fading again, the exertion of speaking taking its toll. He began to slip away even though he had a thousand other questions, important questions, he wanted to ask. He also wanted very badly to tell Sully all about what had happened to Tony Russo and Mike Miller in that machine shop, but something stopped him. He was soul-sick about the entire episode but also knew this was neither the time nor the place for a proper debrief, nor did he have the energy or mental acuity for that yet.

But that wasn't what gave him pause as he fell asleep, it was something else.

Or more precisely, someone else.

CHAPTER 51

10:02PM IRDT MONDAY, JULY 14TH 2014
TEHRAN, IRAN

Reza hung up and slowly reclined in his desk chair, eyes focused inward. Pale blue light from the open laptop gave his face and tented hands a cold, eerie pallor as he sat motionless, sifting through the evening's many calls.

On balance they had all gone well, better than expected, actually, though not quite so well as to raise suspicion. Given the mixed success of his recent Boston ventures, overly positive conversations would have set his alarm bells ringing. No... there had been sincere concerns raised and real reluctance to commit but in the end, they had. All of them.

Since Reza had never shared the details of his plans for Boston — only committing to two separate incidents during two major and heavily secured public events — he could claim credit for the chaos rather than explain why he'd failed to truly complete said plans. So even though he hadn't achieved the desired five-figure body count across both the Fenway and Esplanade attacks, he had managed to spark a hyperbolic firestorm of fear, confusion, and even racism, as unprovoked attacks on Muslims (or even those who looked like they *might* be Muslim) had spiked dramatically across the country in the ten days since the Esplanade. As such, the 'partners' he needed for the Three Wise Men attacks next year would never know that he hadn't done exactly what he planned to do, though the rather untidy way things had played out (in particular the Chechen episode) understandably spooked them.

Yet their greed for chaos and profits along with a manic desire to kick America in the teeth ensured that each and every one still promised him their support and pledged their fealty to his designs. As he had known they would.

His thin smile faded though, as his relentless mind turned back to the problem of Finn Koenen. It had taken Reza a very long time to get his apoplexy under control, much longer than it ever had before. Distressingly, there had been several moments in the days directly after the botched Esplanade attack when he thought he might actually lose control of himself, something that had never happened. Even more alarming than this realization had been the almost irresistible allure it held for him. To let go, to let everything go and finally let his true self out to play became more attractive the closer he got to actually doing it.

However, he knew this to be a mirage. His unyielding thirst for setting the world onto a new path — his path — would not be slaked if he went there. So he scratched and clawed back into control of himself and got to work salvaging what he could from this latest debacle. And then he would remember the common factor in each of his failures, both recent and past, and thoughts of Finn would untether his fury and he would have to struggle to contain it again. But contain it he did, until he was able to focus his attention on how best to address this new and complicating factor from his remote past.

Despite priding himself on always planning for every possible eventuality, Reza could not fault himself for failing to anticipate Koenen's involvement. He hadn't seen the man since they were eleven, and only the most tortuous of routes would have put them back together. Yet here Finn was, fucking up his carefully laid plans. Normally, Moradi would have arranged for Koenen to meet some particularly nasty end, but at the moment, he was seriously and annoyingly constrained, as he couldn't risk exposing his one remaining asset in the US. No, his man at the CIA was absolutely crucial to the successful execution of The Three Wise Men plan.

Among the multitude of branching pathways that led from today to tomorrow, Reza could not find one that neutralized Koenen without unnecessarily endangering his man in Langley. Plus, Reza couldn't ignore the nagging feeling that Koenen somehow knew more than he should about Reza's ultimate aims, which suggested the existence of a loose end somewhere that Reza hadn't accounted for. He itched to interrogate Finn personally but knew this was flat-out impossible.

He sighed and stood, shutting down the laptop, plunging the office into darkness. Unfortunately, whatever Finn did or did not know lay beyond his reach for the time being. Reza had secured the necessary commitments from his 'partners' and could now turn his attention to ensuring that the next steps in the plan went more smoothly than the last few. For now, it was Finn's move and Reza would just have to wait and see what it was.

He smiled, teeth bared in the shadows, contemplating what he would do with Finn - and to him - when the time was right.

CHAPTER 52

Finn was dreaming. He and Tony Russo were trying to capture the wayward teenager Brian Stevens, but then all of a sudden, Brian turned into Anderson Pierce and started stalking Finn, Tony and Mike Miller. Finn wanted to stand and fight, but he knew he had to get the other two to safety, so they all ran. Finn led them all over Charlestown, through back alleys, up onto rooftops, behind the monolithic Bunker Hill Monument, but they could never quite get away. Finally, Finn brought them all to Zoe Kraft's living room, where she bustled in and proceeded to serve steaming hot mugs of tea. Finn motioned with his hands for the others to be silent, but he still heard a faint conversation, like a radio was playing in another room of the house. The conversation got louder. Two women were discussing what a failure he was, that he would never atone for his sins, that he should have died. He turned to ask Zoe Kraft who was speaking when she lunged at him with a knife, a feral snarl on her patrician face.

Finn awoke with a start, gasping in surprise and expecting pain. As he gathered his bearings, he saw his sister and Cat Rollins sitting next to his bed in the two chairs, looking at him in mild surprise.

They all stared at each other for a moment until Heather said, "To Finn. Welcome back, brother." The two women tapped Dixie cups and knocked back whatever was in them in a manner that suggested they'd learned a trick or two from Sully.

"Hey," he said to Heather, then, "Hi Cat."

Cat smiled sadly at him. "Hi Finn."

"I guess you think this absolves you from ditching us at the fireworks display last week?" Heather asked, deadpan.

"What are you drinking?" he asked, ignoring the question.

"Some of this," said Heather mischievously, pulling a bottle of Macallan 25 from behind her chair.

He was pretty sure she had pilfered this from his apartment but given that she had presented it to him for his 40th birthday, he couldn't really complain. He almost never, ever doled any out, given how rare and insanely delicious it was, but fuck it. What was he saving it for if not for moments like this, for celebrating them all still being alive?

After pouring him a cup of his own, they toasted to each other's health. Finn lost himself for a moment as the smooth, rich peat burned across his tongue and down his throat. He closed his eyes and took a second sip, savoring the complex, smoky liquid.

"Thanks," he said to Heather. "I needed that."

"Oh no," she replied, sharing a look with Cat, "the pleasure is all ours. It is your bottle after all."

The three of them sat in companionable silence, content to be in the moment.

Finn could feel the liquor starting to soften up his consciousness and realized he hadn't eaten anything in a long time. His eyes fluttered and he could feel someone taking the cup from his hand.

"I'm sorry I dragged you into this," he managed to get out.

"Stop it," said Heather, but kindly. "Though I have to say, you're not very good at this whole dating thing."

Finn chuckled sleepily, eyes fully closed now.

"Remember when we promised to always tell each other the truth about assholes?" came Cat's voice, close to his ear.

Finn smiled. "Of course I do," he mumbled, sleep overtaking him as he felt the warm pressure of her hand on his arm.

"Well," she continued, as he drifted back into the darkness, "the truth is I really like this asshole."

* * * * *

"Mr. Koenen."

"Wake up."

"Finn," said the man, insistent.

"What?" Finn griped irritably as he struggled to pull himself back to consciousness. Something about the man's voice required him to try. He cracked first one eye, then another, finding the room dark except for a bright rectangle of light around the pulled shade in the window.

Heather and Cat were gone from their chairs, though the bottle of Macallan still sat behind one of them. In the gloom Finn could make out a tall, gaunt man standing at the foot of the bed. He had a high forehead, a hook nose, prominent cheekbones, and full lips. He wore a long dark-blue overcoat and a black tie over a white button down shirt. His dark hair was slicked back away from his face. Finn would have been hard-pressed to dress someone more like a Government Agent than this guy was.

"Who are you?" he muttered, still trying to get his wits about him.

"A friend of a friend," replied the stranger. "A friend of a friend of your father's, to be more precise."

Finn wasn't sure he'd heard him correctly. "Who are you?" he tried again.

"I'm on your team," answered the man, rather unhelpfully. "And I'm here to deliver a message. Two messages, actually."

Finn realized there must be some sort of drugs in his IV drip, because for the life of him he could not clear his head enough to fully process what the man was talking about.

"What messages?" he finally got out.

"1986."

"What?" Finn wasn't sure he heard the man correctly.

"Message number one is the year 1986," the man repeated, firmly. "Amsterdam. Jan and Elise. Your parents. 1986. That's your way in."

"Into what? What the hell are you talking about?"

The man continued as if Finn hadn't spoken. "Message number two: you really managed to kick the wasp's nest earlier this week, Mr. Koenen. And I have been instructed to ask you to kick it again."

"What wasp nest?" asked Finn, feeling like he was two steps behind everything this stranger was saying. "What are you talking about?"

"People who kick at wasp's nests get stung." The man waved an arm to indicate Finn's current situation. "And I assure you, you will be stung again before this is all over." He headed for the door but kept his oddly intense eyes on Finn's.

"Watch your back, and trust no one."

"Trust no one? Fine. How can I trust you then?"

"You can't," said the man, and left.

*   *   *   *   *

The Mystery Man at the foot of his bed was gone, replaced by his sister, quietly reading her Kindle in the chair next to his bed.

"Where'd he go?" asked Finn, the drugs slurring his words.

"Where'd who go?" asked Heather, absently.

"The Mystery Man," said Finn, struggling to come fully conscious. "The guy with the dark trench coat."

Heather looked concerned. "I think it's time we start dialing back your meds," she finally said.

"No, no," countered Finn, pushing the button that raised the mattress so that he could sit up straight, the fog starting to clear. "He was just here, like five seconds ago."

"Finn, sweetie, other than nurses, no one's been here for hours, except me and Cat, and I just walked her out like twenty minutes ago. We chatted for a bit, you drank a small amount of scotch then passed out." She poked him gently in the shoulder. "You're kind of a lightweight when you're in the hospital, you know that?" she said, laughing to herself. "Anyway, you must have been dreaming."

"No," he said, getting frustrated, " I wasn't."

"Okay, Finn," she said, in her most condescending older sister tone. "Whatever you say."

They sat in silence for a few minutes while Finn's mind, finally running at something close to full speed. started formulating a plan. She wasn't going to like it.

"Hey Heather," he asked, "Would you do me a favor?"

"Sure Finn, anything. What do you need?"

"Can you get me a ticket on the next plane to Amsterdam?"

Apparently Heather found this request amusing, as she barked out a laugh. "Amsterdam? You're not going anywhere for a least another day or two," she informed him. "I mean, you just got out of a medically-induced coma. That's kind of a big deal, you know."

Finn tried hard to tamp down his growing annoyance. She was just worried about him and frankly, she wasn't wrong to be so. He could barely stay awake for any meaningful length of time and he certainly didn't have the strength to get up and walk out of here yet. He hated when she was right in that way that only younger brothers can.

"Okay," he said, accepting his fate, "it can wait a couple more days."

"What can wait?" she asked, puzzled.

"The past," he said, closing his eyes and enjoying being obtuse about it. "It's not going anywhere."

This is the end of *Questions of Iron and Blood*.
The story continues in *Swatting at Wasps with a Crowbar*,
And comes to its thrilling conclusion in *This World of Dust and Matter*.

Thank you for reading this book - I hope you enjoyed it. If you are so inclined, please leave a review on Amazon - all feedback is greatly appreciated.

You can stay up to date on Finn's continuing adventures as well as my other upcoming writing projects here:

https://www.facebook.com/RCBrewerAuthor

@RCBrewerAuthor

Acknowledgements

Questions of Iron & Blood is the direct result of an incredible amount of support from a wide range of most excellent individuals, all of whom freely offered up their time, ideas, suggestions and enthusiasm, for which I am eternally grateful.

In particular, I would like to thank some people who went above and beyond over the course of this adventure. Dave Johnson and Tony Wion both read multiple drafts, each time providing indispensable feedback, ideas and edits - all of which strengthened the book and made me a better writer. Megan McConagha also provided uncompromising line edits for two of the drafts and in addition designed the excellent cover of this book.

Invaluable insights from reading later versions came from my parents Curt & Nancy; my in-laws Bob & Linda; my sister Laura; cousins Chris & Kim, Gretchen & Phil, Sandy, Stephanie; and my brother-in-law Scott. I greatly appreciate Trish Grinnell's and Lizzie Campbell's thoughtful, incisive commentary. Dave & Cynthia Brown's early and enthusiastic support were a huge boost, both literally and figuratively.

Jonathan Gardner's incredibly detailed and on-point review of what I thought was the final version of my manuscript guided me past my own blinders and significantly improved the end result. Tom Mendicino and Melissa Kim each freely shared their deep knowledge of publishing and writing, and Julie Kingsley and Jessica Sinsheimer of The Manuscript Academy also provided invaluable support and advice for this first-time writer.

Colonel Rush Filson, USMC provided critically valuable details and insights into all matters military. Any mistakes, misrepresentations or errors on these items are entirely on me. The sharp end of the stick is a dangerous place to make a living, so I would also like to thank Rush - and everyone like him (including my father, father-in-law and my cousin's husband) - who put themselves in harm's way to keep the rest of us safe day in and day out. Your sacrifices are greatly appreciated.

Fellow Bowdoin Rugby Alumni, especially Tad Renvyle, Matt Torrington and Mike Appaneal offered kind support and assistance. My

Pizza Villa Pylons and Sebago Brewing hockey teammates endured endless conversations about Finn over the past five years and kept coming back for more.

The staff at the Bird Dog Roadhouse and Elsmere BBQ listened, discussed, encouraged and, of course, provided much-needed sustenance (both solid and liquid) along the way.

Finally, and most importantly, I want to thank my wife Biz. Her faith in me never wavered, even (and especially) when mine did. Her patience is the stuff of legend. Her sharp eye spotted all of the errors - both large and small - that I couldn't. Most importantly though, she saw what this book could be and then set about doing whatever she could to bring it to fruition. Like all that is wonderful in my life, it would not have happened without her. Thank you for everything - I love you.

Endnotes

[1] Huntington, Samuel P. *The Clash of Civilizations and the Remaking of the World Order.* Touchstone, 1996. P. 21

[2] Kasparov, Gary. *How Life Imitates Chess: Making the Right Moves from the Board to the Boardroom.* Bloomsbury USA, 2010

[3] Boot, Max. *War Made New: Weapons, Warriors, and the Making of the Modern World.* Penguin Group (USA) LLC, 2006

[4] Friedman, Thomas. *From Beirut to Jerusalem.* Anchor Books, 1995.

Printed in Great Britain
by Amazon